ANGIE HAD TOLD THE ARRESTING OFFICERS NOT TO HANDCUFF DANNY.

He couldn't stand to be restrained. And he was so strong. He used a shoulder to slam one officer against the wall and his head to knock the other one off his feet. One of them had actually reached for his handgun when her father's voice suddenly resounded through the entry hall. "Get out of here . . . both of you. I'll take my son to jail myself."

"I'm sorry, Judge Tarrington, but you know we can't do that," the older detective explained.

"The hell you can't," he said, pointing to the door. "I will call the mayor, the police commissioner, the governor, the president, and God himself if you don't take off those damned handcuffs and get out of here!"

But Danny would have to go through it all again Monday morning when they handcuffed him and dragged him into a courtroom, where he'd be asked how he pled—guilty or not guilty of killing Beth Williams.

Angie tried to think—did Danny even know what the word "guilty" meant?

"Oh, God," she said out loud.

Also by Judith Henry Wall

MOTHER LOVE

Judith Henry Wall

DEATH ELIGIBLE

BANTAM BOOKS
NEW YORK • TORONTO • LONDON • SYDNEY • AUCKLAND

DEATH ELIGIBLE

A Bantam Book / January 1996

ISBN 0-553-56788-8

Published simultaneously in the United States and Canada

Bantam Books are published by Bantam Books, a division of Bantam
Doubleday Dell Publishing Group, Inc. Its trademark, consisting of the
words "Bantam Books" and the portrayal of a rooster, is Registered in U.S.
Patent and Trademark Office and in other countries. Marca Registrada.
Bantam Books, 1540 Broadway, New York, New York 10036.

PRINTED IN THE UNITED STATES OF AMERICA

OPM   0 9 8 7 6 5 4 3 2 1

This book was written with my son Douglas S. Wall. The idea for the book came out of a research paper he wrote during his last year in law school documenting the great inequities in this country in determining death eligibility for the mentally deficient, for the insane, and for minors accused of a capital crime. The story developed during many hours of brainstorming as we created Danny Tarrington and his family.

Douglas and his brother, Richard, practice law in Norman, Oklahoma, and the issues raised in this book continue to perplex them both.

We are indebted to University of Oklahoma law professor Randall Coyne and his attorney wife, Lyn Entzeroth, for lending their expertise to this project and to Joan Atterbury for her assistance.

Many thanks to my editor Wendy McCurdy of Bantam Books for her encouragement and wisdom.

And as always, I am grateful to my agent Philippa Brophy of Sterling Lord Literistic for her support, guidance, and friendship.

Prologue

Angie sat alone in the dark breakfast room, watching out the bay window as first light crept into the yard. The upper branches of the two stately magnolia trees glowed with the radiance of a Bierstadt painting, but the rose garden and the terrace were still submerged in shadow.

She took another soda cracker from the package on the table, hoping that some food in her stomach—along with three aspirin—would ease the ache in her head. She hadn't eaten since lunch yesterday—a carton of yogurt and an apple at her desk. Maura, the family housekeeper for as long as Angie could remember, had cooked a birthday dinner for her last night even though Angie asked her not to.

Danny was the reason they had continued to make a fuss over birthdays, with balloons and a candle for every year. This year, there were no balloons, and Danny hardly noticed the cake.

The police had come just as they were sitting down to dinner—to arrest him for murder. Hours later, Maura had cleared away the uneaten meal, stopping every few minutes to wipe her eyes with her apron.

Angie took a sip of water to help the cracker go down and took another from the package.

Had the rest of the household been able to sleep, she wondered, or had they like her, in spite of bourbon and sleeping pills, replayed the horrible scenario of Danny's being arrested, over and over? And the ten-o'clock news with Danny being dragged into the city jail.

She could make out up some of the paler rose blossoms now—the Pascalis, Icebergs, and Mount Shastas. Yesterday, she had watched Manuel select the most spectacular blossoms for a birthday bouquet from the more than one hundred bushes, many of them hybridized by Manuel himself.

The roses were in full bloom, every bush laden with blossoms ranging from purest white to deepest maroon, from delicate yellow to vibrant orange, from palest pink to brilliant red. And coral. The corals were Angie's favorite. Tropicanas and Montezumas. When she was a little girl she'd told Manuel she wanted hundreds of coral roses at her wedding, and he'd promised that he would provide them. He'd planted some Vogues and Fashions to round out the range of corals so he'd be prepared when Miss Angie got married.

Manuel didn't mention her someday wedding anymore. She knew that in his Latin mind, a thirty-two-year-old woman was an old maid, destined to live always in the house of her parents.

Angie had been certain that she would marry her college sweetheart, but she gave him back his ring on graduation day rather than agree to a wedding date. She'd moved back home the week before her twenty-first birthday, thinking she would live here in the stately old house of her childhood only until she finished law school.

She'd been sitting here at this same table on the morning of her twenty-first birthday, when her parents asked if they could name her Danny's guardian in their wills—darling Danny, who was even then taller than Angie but would remain forever a child.

Angie was surprised that her parents felt the need to ask. She'd always assumed that eventually she would be the family member to assume responsibility for Danny. But assumptions weren't enough for her parents. They needed a formal commitment from her. They wanted her to look them in the eye and say yes, she would be Danny's guardian after they were gone.

Angie had come around the table to kneel between

her parents, to put her arms around them and say, of course, she would look after Danny. Always.

She accepted responsibility for him even though being his guardian would limit her options and complicate her life. But she loved him too much not to. Her love for him was unconditional. Maternal even.

Angie pushed the package of crackers away and took another sip of water. All about her, the house was heavy with silence.

She'd told the arresting officers not to handcuff Danny. He couldn't stand to be restrained. And he was so strong. He used a shoulder to slam one officer against the wall and his head to knock the other one off his feet. One of them had actually reached for his handgun when her father's voice suddenly resounded through the entry hall. "Get out of here . . . both of you. I'll take my son to jail myself."

"I'm sorry, Judge Tarrington, but you know we can't do that," the older detective explained.

"The hell you can't," he said, pointing to the door. "I will call the mayor, the police commissioner, the governor, the president, and God himself if you don't take off those damned handcuffs and get out of here!"

But Danny would have to go through it all again Monday morning when they handcuffed him and dragged him into a courtroom, where he'd be asked how he pled—guilty or not guilty of killing Beth Williams.

Angie tried to think—did Danny even know what the word "guilty" meant?

"Oh, God," she said out loud.

At first, after he didn't die of the encephalitis that left him mentally impaired, he'd been a happy little soul, unless he thought someone was mad at him. Then he would cry. Even when he was a pest, they were seldom mean to him. Except Matt. Matt had little patience with his retarded twin.

But, after the kidnapping, Danny came home a changed boy. He screamed if startled. His feelings were easily hurt. He had nightmares. He got hysterical if re-

strained. A momm cat got upset with his handling of
her babies and scratched his hand. Danny stomped on
the cat and killed it. And he beat up Manuel's son, after
he jumped out from a behind a bush and said "boo"—
really beaten him, breaking his nose and collar bone.

Beth came to live in the room next to Danny's after
the kidnapping—after it was decided to keep Danny at
home, where he would be safe, where no strange
woman would walk onto the school playground and
take him away.

When Beth first came to them, she was twenty years
old, a special-education major at University of Texas–
Arlington. Frank had been eighteen, Angie fifteen, Julia
twelve, Danny and Matt almost eight. Their parents had
called everyone into the living room to meet her. Beth,
wearing a crisp white blouse and a navy skirt, was standing in front of the high, arched window, her mass of
hair a halo of golden red in the sunlight.

Beth had knelt in front of Danny, her smooth tan
face very close to his. "I've always wanted a friend
named Danny," she said. "It's the sweetest name in the
world."

Danny reached out and touched her hair. "You're
pretty," he said in awe.

"And you are handsome. All of you are so handsome," Beth said looking around the room at parents
and children. "You are quite the most handsome family
I've ever seen."

After Beth came, Danny did better, even started
singing again. Beth taught Danny to count and write his
name. She taught him to swim and when it was all right
to laugh and sing and when he was supposed to be a
very quiet boy. She encouraged him to run sprints, timing him, training him, teaching him technique. When
he was the first runner across the finish line in the one-
hundred-yard dash finals of the 1980 Special Olympics,
the whole family cheered and wept with the joy of it. It
was a miracle. And they had Beth to thank for it.

But Danny never completely lost the dark side that
he brought home from the kidnapping. His nightmares

became occasional, but when he had them, they were terrible. And what had previously manifested itself as frustration when he couldn't work a puzzle or color inside the lines would sometimes cause him to dissolve into bouts of uncontrollable crying. The whole family learned to intercede when tears threatened, to redirect his attention to some other activity. It hurt too much to see Danny cry. Sometimes, all that was required was to hug him, even after he was no longer a little boy, even when physically he was the largest member of the family, larger even than his twin brother. Danny needed lots of hugs. Because of him, they were a family of huggers.

Looking back, Angie often wondered if the kidnappers hadn't meant to take Matt, the normal twin. Those outside the family always seemed to regard Danny as some sort of a stepchild or charity case and not a true Tarrington.

But Danny made them special and defined them as a family. He taught them tolerance and patience. He shared his wonder of the world with them—and his innocence, even after he was grown, with whiskers on his chin and a disturbing fascination for anything female.

Beth didn't have a family. Angie couldn't imagine such a thing. With three brothers and a sister, she had always been surrounded by family. Her Tarrington grandparents lived behind them, just the other side of the back gate. And her family visited frequently with her mother's parents, who had retired in Austin.

Angie and her little sister, Julia, decided right away that Beth was to be part of the their family. Their big sister. And it did seem that way sometimes. But they were born Tarringtons, and Beth only worked for their family. She wanted it though—to be a Tarrington. None of them realized how much.

BOOK ONE

Chapter One

*A*ngie was seven when Matt and Daniel were born. The family had known twins were on the way for several weeks, and a pair of white wicker bassinets with starched lace skirts awaited the babies in the freshly painted nursery. Frank's former bedroom had been made ready for the practical nurse who would help take care of the new arrivals.

Ten-year-old Frank had been moved to the third floor, which in a previous era had been the domain of live-in servants. Norma Tarrington had two of the small bedrooms combined into one large corner room with four dormer windows that offered a view of the mirrored towers of downtown Dallas in the distance. She had a wall of shelves built along one wall for her son's books and collections—model airplanes, rocks, stamps, coins, insects.

Frank's bedroom was now bigger and nicer than her own, but Angie felt sorry for her brother being up there on the third floor all by himself. Maura, their longtime Irish housekeeper, insisted the third floor was haunted, that the ghost of a long-ago pregnant housemaid who hanged herself in the third-floor hallway wandered around up there at night searching for her baby. Angie's parents said there was no such thing as ghosts, but even if there were, the thought of a dead girl looking for her baby didn't scare Angie so much as make her sad. And even though Frank was older than she was and claimed he didn't believe in anything supernatural, Angie couldn't sleep at night for thinking about him up there all alone, listening to the old house creak.

When Norma discovered that Angie was sneaking

upstairs to crawl into bed with Frank, she sent Manuel to the animal shelter to find a well-behaved adult dog in need of a boy. Manuel returned with a lanky yellow animal who appeared to be part Lab and part something else and who seemed to understand from the first that his duties included sleeping with his young master and following him everywhere. Frank named his dog Buddy. Norma claimed that Buddy was a gentleman and a saint. He was even allowed in the dining room at meal time as long as he didn't beg.

With Frank situated and the arrangements for the twins complete, Norma followed her doctor's orders and took to her bed to await the birth of her babies.

Whenever she could, Angie liked to eavesdrop on grown-ups, lurking in the shadows on the landing of the front staircase next to the grandfather clock, and on two occasions, she heard guests gossip about Norma's pregnancy, about how they hoped one of the babies was a boy, how Norma wanted a son that was hers *and* Perry's. If the twins were girls, they wondered, would Norma try again? The consensus seemed to be that, yes, she probably would. But so many children. No one had that many children nowadays, not even Catholic families.

Angie knew that Frank was their father's son by his first marriage to a woman named Lucy. Twice a year, Frank went to Lubbock to visit Lucy's mother, his grandmother Claire, who had given him a little white leather album filled with pictures of Lucy—Lucy as a baby, Lucy wearing a Girl Scout uniform, a high-school drill-team uniform, a cap and gown, a swimsuit with a banner across it that said Maid of Cotton. Lucy had been beautiful. Really beautiful. With long white-blond hair, incredibly large eyes, a pouty mouth, a figure like Marilyn Monroe's.

Frank said that Grandma Claire had a stack of magazines with Lucy's picture on the cover. Angie kept asking if he would borrow them sometime so she could see them, but he never did. She loved to look at the white album and speculate about the mysterious Lucy. Frank never looked at it. He said it made him sad. He said their father looked at it sometimes—in the night, when he thought Frank was asleep. He'd take the album out of Frank's desk drawer, carry it to the window, and stare at in the moonlight. Angie wished that Frank had never told her that. She didn't want to think of their father looking at pictures of Lucy.

Angie couldn't decide if her mother was as beautiful as Lucy had been. Norma had dark hair and eyes and smooth skin the color of honey. People were always telling Angie that her mother was beautiful. But now that she was pregnant and tired all the time and her hair was dull and limp, she didn't look very beautiful.

Angie worried that her father still loved his first wife. Would he still be married to her if she hadn't died? If Lucy wasn't dead, Angie wondered who her mother would be? Would she even have been born? Maybe she should be glad that Lucy was dead.

Frank wouldn't talk about Lucy or what might have been. Angie suspected that he wished his own mother were still alive, even though he surely realized that Norma loved him very much. In fact, sometimes Angie was jealous of him when it seemed that Norma loved him more than she did her two daughters. But if Norma loved Frank so much, why was it so important that she have another son?

"Why do people want sons more than daughters?" Angie asked her mother. Norma was propped up in bed, listening to Angie read stories from her second-grade reader. Julia had already fallen asleep on the other side of the bed.

"People want both," Norma answered, smoothing Angie's hair from her forehead. "But for families like ours, where a son often follows in his father's footsteps, it's nice to have a boy."

"Frank says he doesn't want to be a lawyer," Angie mused. "He wants to be a minister when he grows up, like Father Lawrence. Sometimes he puts a white shirt on backwards and plays like he's preaching."

"Well, maybe one of these new babies will be a boy and let Frank off the hook."

Angie wasn't sure what "off the hook" meant. But obviously it was important to her mother that one of her twin babies be a boy.

When she put her hand against her mother's hard belly, she could feel them moving around inside. Big as her belly was, it was hard to believe there were two babies scrunched inside.

"Will the babies have pretty hair?" Angie asked.

Norma laughed. "I hope so. Don't worry about my awful hair, sweetie. It will get back to normal eventually. And the rest of me, too. I won't be fat forever."

Angie looked over at her favorite photograph of her mother that hung among the display of three generations of family pictures covering one wall of her parents' bedroom. Norma's waist was tiny in a white and gold dress, her shoulders bare, her shining black hair swept up on top of her head. She looked like a princess. Lucy looked more like a movie star than a princess in her pictures.

"Is that your wedding picture?" Angie asked, pointing at the photograph.

"No, that was taken at a party your Grandpa Paul and Grandma Edna held to announce that your father and I were engaged to be married."

"Where is yours and Daddy's wedding picture?" Angie asked.

"Your father and I had a very small wedding."

"Didn't anyone take pictures?"

"I don't remember." With her hands on her belly, Norma put her head back on the pillow and closed her eyes. "I'm very tired, dear. Go ask your father to carry Julia to her bed."

Aware that she had somehow displeased her mother, Angie crawled down from the high bed and went to fetch her daddy. She watched as he picked up her sleeping sister and carried her out of the room, then she tiptoed over to the bed and planted a kiss on her mother's cheek. Norma opened her eyes and smiled. "You're my sweet big girl," she said. "I don't know what I'd do without you."

A few weeks later, early in the morning, an ambulance came to take Norma to the hospital. She was very pale. Even her lips. Her eyes were closed. "It's time for the babies to be born," she said without opening them. "Come kiss me good-bye, children."

Frank cried all day long. "What if she dies like my other mother?" he kept asking.

"Shhh. Julia will hear you," Angie admonished. The three of them watched television and played cards all day. The house was very quiet. Maura tiptoed around as if she was afraid of waking someone. Whenever the phone rang, she crossed herself before she answered it. Perry called at dinner time. It was going to be a while. He needed for Maura to sleep over. The practical nurse couldn't come until tomorrow.

Julia fell asleep on the sofa in the family room, and Maura carried her upstairs. Angie and Frank waited up until well past midnight, playing cards and watching a movie about a wagon train on its way to California. One of the women had a baby in the wagon while the Indians shot flaming arrows at it.

It was after midnight when their father finally came home to tell them they had a matching set of baby brothers. Identical twins, who were robust and healthy in spite of being born almost a month too soon. Their names were Matthew and Daniel.

Perry poured himself a glass of Scotch. "Five children," he said in awe. "Incredible." Then he sat on the sofa and held out his arms to Angie and Frank. He hugged them close for a long time, pressing his lips to first one forehead and then the other. "You're going to have to be patient with your mother and me. Two babies take a lot of time. But you must remember that even if we don't have as much time for you, we still love you just as much as before. Remember that, okay? And to help with Julia. She's going to need you two more than ever."

Angie and Frank nodded solemnly.

"But isn't it wonderful?" Perry said, tears in his

eyes. "Two little babies like two peas in a pod. I think we have the best family in the world, don't you?"

Once again, they nodded.

"Hey, this is too serious. We need to have a celebration. Let's wake up Maura and Julia and have a party!"

And they did just that. They popped corn and made Coke floats and did the conga around the kitchen. Even Maura, with her fat bottom giggling up and down under her flannel robe.

Chapter Two

*P*oor Julia was no longer the baby. She started sucking her thumb and wetting the bed.

Angie and Frank tried to pay more attention to
Julia. But she asked too many dumb questions—like did
dogs get married and were there houses in heaven. And
she wanted them to play stupid card games like old
maid and war and pouted when she wasn't allowed to
win.

Angie liked it better when it was just her and Frank.
He knew about things that even their parents didn't
know—like the names of the stars and all the Greek
gods and goddesses. He knew about scientific discover-
ies and the voyages of all the famous explorers. He
could recite great long passages from the Bible and had
memorized "The Charge of the Light Brigade" and
"Paul Revere's Ride."

But their Grandfather Clifford thought she and
Frank spent too much time together. "Why can't you
play with your school friends?" Clifford demanded of
Angie.

"She does," Perry told his father. "They both do.
But Angie and Frank are very good friends, too. Their
mother and I think it's nice that they get along so well."

"Boys his age shouldn't play with girls," Clifford
warned. "He's already a sissy."

"Frank is a fine boy," Perry said. "I'm sorry you
can't see that."

Grandfather Clifford had played center for the
University of Texas Longhorns and spent two years with
the Providence Steamrollers, which Angie knew no
longer existed but once had been league champions. A

picture of the team hung on the wall of her grandfather's study. Clifford had weighed thirteen pounds at birth and, according to the newspaper clippings in the big album on the table under the Providence Steamrollers' picture, tipped the scales at around three hundred during his playing days. No one knew how much he weighed now, but Frank said if he weighed three hundred pounds when that picture was taken, he must weigh at least four hundred now—which made him four times bigger than his tiny wife.

Clifford and Belle lived directly behind them in one of the largest houses in an old Dallas neighborhood, where all the houses were old and grand, with spacious grounds maintained by gardeners who were either Mexican or black. Clifford's father, Aaron Perry "Preacher" Tarrington, had started an oil company and been elected governor. His picture hung over the mantel in Clifford's study.

Angie had heard the story about how, at the party celebrating her father's christening, Grandfather Clifford had toasted his own father and his new son, predicting that Perry would follow in Preacher's footsteps and someday be elected governor of the great state of Texas. When Angie asked her father if he thought Grandfather Clifford's prediction would ever come true, Perry had sighed and looked a little bit sad. "I'm not sure, honey. Sometimes I daydream about being elected governor and standing on a stage in front of a roomful of cheering people, with my family at my side and a band playing 'Texas, Our Texas.' That would probably be the proudest day in your Grandfather Clifford's life, but your mother and I aren't sure what would happen to us after the celebration."

"Grandfather will be mad if you don't try, won't he?" Angie asked.

"Maybe so, honey. But your mother and I are the ones who have to decide what's best for our family."

Even so, Angie couldn't decide if Granny Belle was afraid of him or not. Clifford and Belle never said much to each other, never touched like Angie's parents or like her other grandparents did, who touched and hugged all the time.

As for his grandchildren, Clifford mostly ignored Frank but sometimes held Angie and Julia on his lap and told them stories about his mother and father, about living in the governor's mansion in Austin. Other times he shooed them all away as if they were Mexican children on the street.

Clifford and Belle wept when they looked through the nursery window at their twin grandsons. Angie couldn't get over it. Her Grandfather Clifford *crying*.

Clifford and Perry were both partners in the law firm founded by Clifford's father after he didn't get elected to a second term as governor.

Clifford still grumbled because Perry had come to work there after he finished law school instead of being the kind of attorney who puts people in jail. That kind of attorney got written about in newspapers and could run for governor. But Perry said he was more interested in helping people than putting them in jail. Angie decided that if she were a lawyer, that's what she would do —help people.

The twins became a constant source of curiosity for Angie. How could two human beings be so much alike? She would study them carefully—every inch of their perfect little plump bodies, trying to find differences. For weeks, they wore tiny beaded bracelets with their names on them, or else Angie never would be able to know which baby was which. But gradually she was able to tell without looking at the bracelets. Danny was a tiny bit rounder. Matt fidgeted more. Danny laughed louder when she blew into his stomach. Matt made slurping noises when he nursed.

Angie decided that she was glad she didn't have a twin sister. Twins were special, but she wouldn't like being half of a pair. She'd rather be just herself.

Clifford and Belle stopped by several evenings a week before dinner—to have a drink with Perry and

Norma, quiz the three older children about their activities, hold the babies for a few minutes. Clifford would examine Matt and Danny carefully, ask if they were on schedule with their growth, then tickle them under the chin before returning them to the nurse or one of their parents. Belle often stopped by in the afternoon to spend hours rocking and singing to the twins. When she sat in the big rocking chair with a baby on her shoulder, singing hymns and nursery songs, she would close her eyes, put her head against the high back, and look younger and happier than she usually did. She said that being with babies was better than taking medicine. "After your father wasn't a baby anymore, I wanted another baby more than anything," she told Angie. "Babies are the best part."

Grandfather Clifford had already decided that Matt and Danny should be sent to separate schools when they were older. "Twins can be too dependent on each other, you know. You want each boy to grow up to be his own man."

"I want them to grow up brothers," Norma informed her father-in-law.

Clifford frowned at her.

Norma often said things that made Clifford frown. Angie didn't think that her mother liked Clifford very much.

Norma's parents came from Austin once a month, usually on a Sunday afternoon. In the summer, Grandpa Paul and Grandma Edna would bring flowers and vegetables from their garden or sometimes a pie made with blackberries they had picked along the creek that ran across their five acres. The pie would make Maura mad. She could make a better pie than the Edmondson's cook any day of the week.

Paul and Edna usually took the three older children on an excursion, to the zoo, a museum, the botanical gardens, or a matinee performance at the State Fair Music Hall. Only after they'd spent what they called "quality time" with Frank, Angie, and Julia would they focus on the twins, marveling at them, indulging in baby talk to make them laugh. Often they'd eat dinner, each holding a baby.

Grandpa Paul had been president of Dallas's largest bank, but he and Edna turned over their Highland Park home to Norma and Perry and retired to smaller, prettier Austin to live in the wonderful old Victorian house that Edna had inherited from her parents. They went to UT football games, tended a huge garden in the summer, and spent their winters traveling and deep-sea fishing. Their Austin house was full of trophy fish. Even the entry hall. They had names for them. The sailfish in the entry hall was Captain Cook.

Every day the twins were funnier and cuter than the day before. Suddenly they were crawling around like little puppy dogs. It made Angie laugh to watch them. They were silly and plump and perfect with green eyes and wavy brown hair like their daddy. Angie loved it when company came and fussed over them. She didn't like people who didn't say how darling Matt and Danny were.

Julia started crawling around too. Poor Julia. Crawling wasn't cute when you're almost five. Neither was thumb sucking.

Norma started setting aside some time every afternoon just for Julia. She would hold her on her lap and read to her or play tea party with her. Sometimes they would take walks in the park or up and down the sedate, tree-lined streets of their neighborhood.

Even at age seven, Angie knew that she was privileged to live in such a beautiful, wooded neighborhood with big, important-looking houses. Their own Tudor mansion, at the top of a long sloping yard, looked like the king's hunting lodge in a fairy tale.

Angie had seen parts of Dallas where poor people lived in horrible little houses, usually with no grass or trees. "Why don't they paint their houses?" she asked Frank.

"They don't have any money for paint, dummy," he told her.

She'd asked her father if he would give the poor people some money to paint their houses.

"That's a sweet idea," he said, "but don't you think they need other things more—like food and clothes? Your mother and I give money for that."

"But I think they'd be happier if their houses had paint. Being happy is important, too."

The following evening, her father showed Angie a letter he had written, stating that one thousand gallons of paint were being sent to the Salvation Army to be distributed free of charge to families willing to paint their house. The gift was being made in the name of Angela Marie Tarrington. Angie crawled onto her daddy's lap and kissed him. "I'm glad we're not poor, but it makes me feel kind of funny that we're not and some people are."

"Me, too," Perry agreed.

With the discovery in 1901 of the Spindletop oil field near Beaumont, a new era began for the state of Texas. Between 1900 and 1920, the number of cities and towns in the state doubled. The sparse road system was vastly expanded. Irrigation brought farming to land previously fit only for livestock. Farmers still were being exploited by the railroads and struggled mightily to make the land pay, especially in the hill country where the soil was thin and the weather unpredictable. And Pancho Villa was making life very difficult for citizens in the Texas border towns along the Rio Grande. But great fortunes were being made in oil and railroading.

Clifford's father, Aaron Perry Tarrington, grew rich by accident when oil gushed from under the ranch outside Burkurnett he had inherited from his uncle. But it was shrewdness that parlayed his riches into a fortune. Rather than lease the mineral rights to an oil company, Aaron borrowed against the now valuable land and began his own refinery, APT Petroleum, which —before his death—he sold to Texaco for enough money to endow his descendants for generations to come.

The power that comes with wealth and impressive physical stature enabled him to enter the state's political arena successfully. He moved his family from rural Wichita County to bustling, growing, and politically corrupt Dallas, where he established a power base, bought his way into the state House of Representatives in Austin, then into the state Senate. At age forty-four Aaron won a hard-fought campaign for governor, during which he carried a Bible, began every speech with a prayer, and preached with the fervor of a zealot about the great future awaiting the state of Texas if the right men were elected to high office. The *Dallas Times Herald* dubbed him "Preacher" Tarrington and the name stuck. The *Herald* also pointed out that candidate Tarrington kept, between the pages of his Bible, hundreds of crisp dollar bills that he passed out to those who attended his ralleys.

Preacher Tarrington's favorite theme was a better life for all Texans. He recalled the dawn-to-dusk toil that made hardworking, God-fearing people tired and old before their time—people like his widowed mother. Rural folks needed electricity, telephones, better roads. City people needed jobs and decent schools for their children.

Preacher liked to talk about his mother. Faith Tarrington had been a schoolteacher back in Kentucky, and after the family moved to Texas, she taught her own children and those from adjoining farms in her kitchen until the county built her a schoolhouse. And she insisted that her own children continue their studies at the university in Austin. The greatest regret of Preacher's life was that his mother didn't live to see him elected governor of Texas. He owed everything to his mother, who taught him the importance of thinking before he spoke and to treat all God's children with respect, even "niggras" and Mexicans—as long as they kept their place.

Well over six feet tall, Preacher was a barrel-chested

man with broad shoulders and massive forearms and thighs. Unlike his son, Clifford, however, Preacher ate and drank in moderation and remained lean and physically active throughout his lifetime. Legend had it that Preacher rode in a Klan raid that burned the house of a black schoolteacher the evening before he was found dead of a heart attack in the extra long bed he'd had made back during his years in the governor's mansion.

Clifford's mother, however, went from being a willowy bride with a hand-span waist to an old woman so large her funeral was delayed to give the carpenter a chance to finish an oversize casket.

Preacher loved his older son, Aaron Junior, who had tuberculosis and spent most of his short life in bed. And Preacher doted on his daughter, Alma Jane. When Alma Jane married, he wept openly, then after the ceremony he took his new son-in-law aside and said that if he ever laid a hand on Preacher Tarrington's little girl or treated her with other than profound respect, he was a dead man.

But as much as he loved Aaron and Alma Jane, bright, inquisitive, athletic Clifford was Preacher's pride and joy. Clifford went with his daddy to the statehouse in Austin from the time he was just a boy, shaking hands, listening. He loved politics as much as he loved football, and he grew up assuming that he would someday enter public life as his father had. His reputation as a lineman, first in high school, then for two years at Texas University, and finally with the Providence Steamrollers, gave him a leg up on his future political career.

The two years Clifford left Texas to play professional ball greatly enhanced his reputation within the state, establishing him as something other than the son of a former governor who'd been rejected by voters in his bid for a second term.

During his third year in office, Clifford's father had pardoned ten Klan members convicted of hanging a black boy who'd been caught peeking through a knothole in the back of a public outhouse while a white woman was using the facility. State historians in later years viewed the hanging of nine-year-old Clem Washington as the beginning of the end of the Klan's stranglehold on rural Texas.

Throughout the years, Clifford publicly defended his father's action, explaining that ten families, including wives, aging relatives, and thirty-seven children, would have been without breadwinners if the men had gone to prison. But in private, Clifford admitted his father had been unwise, negating in one foolhardy act the accomplishments of an extraordinary life. The Tarrington name would forever be associated with the Clem Washington hanging. Preacher Tarrington was judged as harshly as the men who did the hanging.

In Clifford's mind, the only way to neutralize that negative connotation was to put another Tarrington in the governor's mansion. But he was beginning to doubt that he himself was destined to be that individual.

Clifford always gained thirty or forty pounds offseason but lost most of it by midseason. When he stopped playing football, he gained weight year-round and never lost any of it. By the time he'd reached his mid-twenties and was back in Austin finishing his legal education, Clifford already was a fleshy mountain of a man whose insatiable appetite for food seemed to exceed even his desire to return a Tarrington to the governor's mansion where he'd spent four years of his childhood. He understood that Texans wanted their politicians lean—the sort of men who were at home in a Stetson and boots and could sit a horse as well as they could walk. The citizens of the Lone Star State would no more vote for an obese man than they would for a Mexican or a colored.

But the dream of a second Governor Tarrington had embedded itself in Clifford's psyche. He had promised his father on his deathbed. But he was beginning to understand that any hope of fulfilling that dream would fall on the shoulders of the next generation.

Clifford began a serious search for a woman to marry. This woman had to be intelligent, from a good family, and, most important, small in stature to compensate for his girth in their offspring.

Belle Marshall was the youngest, tiniest, and least attractive of the three daughters of a Houston railroad baron who was himself barely over five feet in height. Belle's sisters had married by the time they were eighteen. At age twenty-two, Belle had never had a serious suitor and had already resigned herself to a spinster's life. She gratefully accepted Clifford's offer and moved into the two-story house Clifford's father had purchased for them near the campus in Austin.

Perry was conceived almost at once, but subsequent pregnancies ended in miscarriages. Finally, Clifford could no longer bear the disgust in his wife's eyes when he pulled his erect member from underneath the fatty apron that by that time hung below his testicles, and he stopped his infrequent visits to her room altogether. With enormous relief, Belle took to locking the door of her bedroom—just to make sure.

After they moved to Dallas, Clifford began buying the services of the city's limited supply of oversize whores, eventually establishing as his favorite a madam with her own comfortable establishment outside the city on the road to Grapevine. Clifford kept his own bedroom at Mae's whorehouse and slept more frequently there than he did at home.

Belle never tolerated unkind words about prostitutes. "They are victims of circumstances," she insisted. "No woman ever entered such a life willingly, and they are to be greatly pitied." Her favorite charity was the Haskell Street Rescue Mission, which catered to down-and-out prostitutes and helped support them when they were too old for the streets.

Chapter Three

Norma had grown up with Perry living in the house just over the back fence and always assumed she would marry him. Her life had proceeded seamlessly from childhood summers on Padre Island, where their families had adjoining cottages, through the years as college sweethearts at the University of Texas, toward the day when she would become his wife surrounded by the Gothic splendor of Highland Park Episcopal Church. She bought her first *Brides* magazine at age twelve. She had file folders full of pictures of wedding dresses; china, crystal, and sterling patterns; perfect honeymoon locales. She thought of him the last thing before she went to sleep at night and the first thing when she woke up in the morning. She had never kissed another boy, never allowed herself to think seriously about going to bed with another boy. She thought about it with Perry all the time but never did. They did everything but. She'd even taken her clothes off for him, allowing him to see as well as fondle her naked body. He wanted more, of course, which she loved. Making him crazy with wanting her was one of her greatest pleasures in life. He begged and pleaded but never tried to violate the limits that she set. He understood that she wanted their wedding night to be the first time—and even though he was desperate to have sex with her, Perry was proud to have chosen a girl who was saving herself for marriage. Such girls were to be prized.

But after years of dreaming about the perfect wedding and wedding night, what Norma got was far from perfection.

Even after ten years of marriage, remembering was

still painful for her. They had been at Aunt Ruth's three-story Victorian on Galveston Island, having what was to be Norma's last vacation with her family before her marriage. The wedding invitations were ready to mail. Her wedding dress was hanging in her closet back in Dallas.

Her parents came together that morning to wake her, to sit on the side of the bed and tell her that Perry had married someone else. The white lace curtains billowed with the breeze from the ocean. Sunlight filled the room. The air smelled salty and clean. In the distance, gulls squawked at one another.

If Norma was going to chart her life, that day would be the lowest point. The bottom. No place further down to go. She had wanted to die—to climb over the sea wall and walk out into the ocean until the water took her and made the pain go away.

Perry had flown off to Reno to marry Norma's sorority sister Lucy Ledbetter, when he'd sworn he was over her, sworn that Lucy was just a fling, that he would never hurt Norma again. Norma had wanted so desperately to believe him. But she could tell, when he looked at her, he now found her lacking. Her hair was not the color of summer sunshine. Her eyes were not breathtakingly blue. Her skin was not lily white. Her breasts were less full, her legs shorter, her fanny less provocative, her laughter less spontaneous. But she clung to the word "fling" like a talisman. A fling had a beginning and an end. A fling was not an enduring relationship, not "till death us do part."

Lucy had majored in drama at UT. She wanted to be an actress but launched a modeling career to help open doors. Her picture had been on the May cover of *Glamour*—a wonderful sweet-sexy picture of her looking at the camera over her smooth, white shoulder, whose two tiny freckles bore witness to the fact that the photograph had not been retouched and the cover creature truly was that smooth and poreless. Norma had recreated Lucy's pose in front of her dresser mirror while holding up the magazine cover to compare. What she saw was a pretty, dark-haired girl and a gleaming blond goddess.

But Perry had promised. Of course, he still wanted to marry Norma. Norma had class and the sort of innate elegance he greatly admired. They came from the same world. They understood each other. He couldn't imagine a life without her. He allowed her to plan their wedding for the week after he graduated from law school and buy the wedding dress of her dreams.

Hate became the balm that soothed Norma's pain. She actually thought, if Perry ever came back to her, if he knelt at her feet, throwing his arms around her legs, begging her forgiveness, swearing his marriage to Lucy had been the most terrible mistake of his entire life, that she would turn her back on him. Norma fantasized about how Perry would weep, his face twisted in anguish.

When Perry did come courting, he was carrying a baby in his arms instead of flowers. Lucy's baby.

They walked out in the yard for privacy from her parents, who didn't know whether to welcome Perry as a suitor or take a horsewhip to him for humiliating their daughter. Norma and Perry sat facing each other under the arbor of her parents' Dallas home, dappled sunlight on their faces, surrounded by the heavy perfume of wisteria blossoms, the baby sitting on Perry's lap, his great dark blue eyes watching first one adult face and then the other.

"How dare you," Norma said. Her voice was calm, but her heart was racing, her skin clammy. She wanted to hurt Perry, to scratch his beautiful face.

But when she looked in his eyes, there were tears. "I'm so sorry," he said, rubbing his hand up and down the baby's tiny back. "I think about you all the time."

"Do you think about her, too?"

Perry paused, considering.

Would he tell her truth or lies, Norma wondered. Maybe lies would be better.

"Yes, I think about Lucy a great deal," Perry admitted, his face and voice solemn. "I suppose we never should have gotten married. She wanted to be a star, not a wife. We were happy and unhappy. There were good times and bad. I took the New York bar, but I didn't want to practice there. I missed working with my dad. Missed my family and Dallas and having people know who I was. And driving up and down Texas highways, hearing Texas voices, eating Texas food. I wanted the marriage to end, and I wanted to come home. But yes, I will always think about her. Always miss her. Always wonder what would have happened to us. Even if it wouldn't have worked, I wish we could have played the marriage out to its natural conclusion. I wish I'd understood better about depression and gotten help for her. I wish I didn't have to feel so sad. I'm sorry Frank will never know her, never have a memory of her."

Norma could see her parents anxiously watching from the breakfast room window, not even trying to stay out of sight. These last two years had been hard on them, too. Norma's brother had died years ago, and she was all they had. She was the focus of their love, their only hope for grandchildren.

"Are you sure he's not still in love with her?" her mother asked when Norma announced her plans to marry Perry.

Norma shook her head. No, she wasn't sure. She wasn't even sure why she had agreed to become his wife —his second wife.

After Perry married Lucy, Norma had entered graduate school and was finishing up a master's degree in English at SMU. Now it was time for her to do something else. She could earn a Ph.D., dedicate her life to Jesus, get serious about tennis, or get married. And if it was marriage she wanted, she would have to look for a husband. She would have to date and flirt and pretend. But suddenly Perry had reentered her life, offering her instant marriage.

Instead of a church wedding in a white satin gown with a cathedral train, she would get married in her beige Chanel suit in her parents' living room. There would be no wedding showers, no prenuptial parties.

People would always know that she was Perry's second choice. She would have to be stepmother to the son of the woman who had stolen Perry away from her. She hated Lucy, and she hated Perry for succumbing to her charms. But she would marry him anyway. She didn't know what else to do after spending most of her life planning to become his wife.

Two days before her wedding, over Cokes at the SMU student union, Norma asked one of the teaching assistants from the English department if he would have sex with her. He had a boyish face, red hair. His name was Russell. Norma wasn't sure if that was his first name or last name. "I thought you said that you were getting married," he said, glancing at her hand, verifying the presence of an engagement ring.

"I am," Norma said. "But I need to settle a score first."

They rented a room at a motel on the Waco highway. Norma paid.

An old fashioned evaporating-type air conditioner hummed noisily from the window and spit out a fine mist into the room. The room smelled damp, closed in. "I've never been with a girl," Russell confessed as she closed the door behind them.

"I've never been with a boy, so we're even. I don't want to take my clothes off."

Russell nodded and turned away to step out of his trousers and undershorts while Norma reached under her skirt and slipped off her panties, garter belt, and stockings.

Wearing only his shirt, Russell sat down beside her on the bed. "I need to kiss you or touch you or something to make . . . you know, to be ready."

Norma laid back on top of the worn chenille bedspread and opened her arms. He kissed her for a long time, and Norma surprised herself by responding. "Do you want to now?" he whispered in her ear.

"No. Kiss me some more."

He obliged—for another long time. Norma felt drunk and dizzy. It was lovely.

"Have you ever touched a man's penis?" he asked, still whispering.

"Yes."

"I'd like for you to touch me there."

He was very hard. Ready. He wanted her. Or more correctly, he wanted to have a woman. But it was sort of sweet to think it was the first time for both of them.

She didn't stop him when he reached between her legs to touch her. "You're wet," he said.

Yes. Wet. And open.

"Maybe I'd better get a towel from the bathroom— you know, to protect the bed," she said.

"I'll get it."

He helped her position the folded towel under her hips. "Okay?" he asked.

"I think we should take off all our clothes."

Sitting on opposite sides of the bed, they removed the rest of their clothing.

The feel of flesh on flesh took Norma's breath away. He told her she was beautiful. He was too skinny to be beautiful, but she said he was anyway.

He came too quickly for her to feel very much. So they waited, kissing, touching, talking. He told her he'd been accepted in a doctoral program at Berkeley. His mother was an English professor at the women's college in Denton.

Norma told him about Perry. "I love him and I hate him. I want to have children by him, and I hope he dies tomorrow. Is that not too sick for words?"

The second time he lasted long enough for the warmth to begin in her thighs and spread upward into her belly. A feeling like no other. Different from when she made it happen to herself. Better. Infinitely better.

He fell away from her, his breathing ragged. Reaching over to touch his face, she realized that she was smiling. "Hey, Russell, we did okay."

"Yeah. I don't suppose you want me to fall in love with you."

"Absolutely not. But don't you dare ever forget me."

Two nights later, she was with Perry in the bridal suite at the stately old Melrose Hotel. She should have insisted on another hotel, she realized, where she wouldn't have been reminded of wedding night fantasies that would never come true.

She went into the bathroom to put on her silk nightgown, blue instead of bridal white. When she came out, Perry was in his robe, opening the bottle of champagne.

"Let's have a good life," he said, lifting his glass to her. "Let's make it work. I do love you, Norma. I've always loved you."

Yes, Norma thought, but not enough.

They drank the entire bottle, as they talked about finding a house in Dallas, buying a car, catching the plane in the morning for Honolulu.

Norma looked at the empty bottle regretfully. It was time.

"Remember how we used to get ourselves hot talking about how it would be on our wedding night?" he asked.

"It's not the same now," she reminded him.

"I know I don't have the right to ask, but have you been with a man?"

Norma thought of Russell and smiled. "Yes," she said. "Yes, I have."

"Well, then, shall we go to bed?"

She put a hand on his arm. "I do want us to have a good life together. But I don't have the high hopes that I once had for bliss and eternal joy. Probably that was unrealistic anyway. But if you ever hurt me again, I'll hurt back."

He nodded.

Norma didn't try to have an orgasm. That would come later. Her wedding night was something to get over with.

But she damned sure expected more on her honeymoon.

*　　*　　*

Throughout their three-week second engagement, Norma had harbored hopes that Perry's parents would offer to take Frank to raise. Belle was crazy about the baby, but Clifford seemed distant, as if he couldn't make up his mind whether he loved the baby or not. Or if Clifford and Belle wouldn't take him, maybe Lucy's mother would. On their honeymoon, she planned to bring it up. To ask Perry to think about it, to ask the baby's grandparents if he hadn't already. It'd be so nice for just the two of them to start out married life.

Perry called his mother everyday from Honolulu to check on the baby. He talked about Frank too much. He was anxious for Frank to have brothers and sisters, to grow up in a normal home environment. Never once did Perry say he was anxious to have children with Norma—just for Frank. Norma felt cheated. By a baby.

But she resigned herself to taking in Frank—at least for the present.

From the first, she hated taking care of a baby. Frank was crawling by then, getting into the things, tipping over lamps, hurting himself. He had to be watched every minute.

And Frank threw up a lot. Nothing to worry about, the doctor said. He'd outgrow it. But their house smelled like vomit and sour milk and dirty diapers. Norma gagged when she changed his messy diapers. She couldn't believe she was rinsing out the shit-filled diapers of Lucy Ledbetter's baby in the toilet. She hated Lucy's baby. Lucy's baby was ruining her life.

Frank would look at her with big questioning eyes. He knew she didn't love him, Norma would think with a stab of pity. And she would pick him up, kiss him. "It's not your fault," she'd say.

Maybe, if Frank had been a fat cuddly baby with downy hair, he would have been easier to love. But Frank was long and thin. His hair was already that of a little boy with a part and a barber-shop cut. And his face was too old and serious for a baby—except when Perry arrived home in the evening, Frank's face would light up, and he would squeal with delight. Perry would nuzzle his neck and throw him in the air. *They love each other more than they love me*, Norma would think. But was that so surprising? She was still angry at Perry and didn't love his baby at all. Perry deserved her anger, but the baby was different. He hadn't done anything to her except be born. She felt like the wicked stepmother from childhood fairy tales and hated herself for not being able to feel even a modicum of love for baby Frank. She would be kind to him. She would care for him to the best of her ability. But she wished he would be stolen away in the night by some heartbroken young woman whose baby had died and who would love Frank like her own.

One night, Frank wouldn't eat and felt a little feverish. His fever had crept up to one hundred by bedtime, but he took a bottle of apple juice and went to sleep. In the night, he woke burning with fever. They rushed him to the emergency room at Parkland. By the time a doctor examined him, Frank was listless and barely able to whimper.

Clifford and Belle arrived. Lucy's mother came from Lubbock. Throughout the night and morning they wailed, watching the clock, holding their collective breath every time someone in white approached.

By the following afternoon, Frank's fever had broken, and he was sleeping peacefully. "Babies often get well as quickly as they get sick," the pediatrician explained. "But sometimes they die. If he gets that feverish again, don't wait so long to get him to a doctor."

Norma looked down at Frank in the metal hospital crib. Such a helpless little person. She reached down and ran a finger along his pale smooth cheek. His eyes fluttered open.

Such big eyes, too big for his face. She smiled down at him. "Hi, little man. Feeling better?" And she was surprised to realize she had tears in her eyes.

Frank lifted his arms to be picked up. Norma obliged, and he curled his little body against her, his head resting on her shoulder. She kissed the top of his head. Her tears were flowing freely now, down her cheeks, rolling off her chin onto the baby in her arms. He could have died. If he had died, it wouldn't have been from the fever, it would have been because he didn't have a mother to love him and do a proper job watching over him.

Norma thought of her own mother, the greatest constant in her life. How sad not to have a mother who loved you. It was the saddest thing Norma could imagine.

She was sobbing now, rocking Frank back and forth in her arms. He reached up and touched her wet face. She grabbed his little hand and kissed it, tasting the salt of her own tears. She bent her face to kiss his mouth, his chin, his eyes. She covered his face with kisses, wetting him with her tears.

"It'll be okay, baby Frank. I promise. It'll be okay."

Loving Frank was one of the great surprises of Norma's life. She always felt grateful to him for teaching her how to be a mother. Mother love was the sweetest love, she discovered, the purest—not complicated like her love for Perry. But love in any form made one vulnerable and afraid. And wicked things were done in the name of love.

Chapter Four

"Still up?" Perry asked. Loosening his tie, he crossed the room to give Norma a peck on the cheek. "Sorry I missed Angie's ball game. I'll make it up to her?"

Pulling off his suit jacket, Perry headed toward his bathroom.

"And just how will you make it up to her?" she challenged.

His back stiffened. "Don't, Norma. I'm tired."

"She kept looking around to see if you'd come. She drove in the winning run."

Norma could hear the shower door opening, the water starting.

She put her reading glasses on the bedside table and turned out the light. God, she was tired. Every muscle ached with fatigue. A day of tennis had never made her feel as tired as a day of mothering children. But if Perry had shown up at Angie's game, if he had been there beside her in the lawn chair she'd brought along for him and then gone with her and the children for hamburgers at McDonald's, if they had replayed the evening over a glass or two of wine, she would be able to shake off the tiredness, maybe even be in the mood for sex.

It had been weeks since they'd had sex. Not that she was feeling all that lusty these days, but no sex worried her. After a time, no sex took on ominous overtones.

Maybe she should have put her arms around Perry's neck when he leaned over to kiss her. She could have acted sincerely sorry that he'd had to miss Angie's game. She could have told him that she knew how disappointed he was, told him what a good game their daughter had played, offered to get him a brandy or a beer, asked him about his day.

He had two jobs these days—practicing law and organizing his upcoming race for the state legislature. Already he was making speeches for anyone who would listen to him. Clifford was overjoyed, even though Perry's politics were far too liberal to suit him. He assumed his son would become more realistic with experience.

Norma had been the dutiful wife at a couple of Perry's campaign appearances. Smiling. Shaking hands. Perry was a good speaker. A sincere man. But she wasn't sure he was really the political animal that his father wanted him to be. And she couldn't envision herself as the perpetually smiling politician's wife. Not with five children and a house to run. She felt as if she was being sucked into Clifford's sick dream of restoring honor to the Tarrington name.

A pity Clifford hadn't entered the political fray himself years ago. But people probably wouldn't vote for a man of his girth—or for attorneys who'd made a career out of successfully defending high-profile clients who were very rich and often quite guilty.

Of late, Norma found herself wondering if Perry attended almost nightly meetings to avoid the chaos of his home life. Dinners with colleagues, clients, and party officials were more peaceful than dinners with their lively, talkative brood, with Frank discussing the evolution of cockroaches, Angie asking why they couldn't invite poor children to dinner, Julia whining about not being allowed to get her ears pierced like Manuel's daughters, the twins spilling their milk and sneaking food to Buddy under the table—if, indeed, clients and colleagues were who Perry was having dinner with.

Perry probably was too honorable ever to leave her, but he might not be above having an affair with a woman who made him feel young and virile. Men his age often did. And there wasn't much happening on the home front to make him feel that way. Not that she'd excuse an indiscretion. Ever. They were just at a time in their marriage when children came first. They'd get back to each other later. Just as her parents had done. There had been a time when her father didn't come home much. After her brother died.

Tomorrow, Norma vowed, she'd look into hiring a woman to come in three or four evenings a week, after Maura went home, to corral the twins and get them ready for bed. She had tried the plan twice before, but the twins had managed to get the best of the middle-aged women she'd hired. Maybe a teenager would be better—someone who would get down on the floor and play games with them or take them outside to run and ride their trikes and work off some steam.

At age three, the twins were a handful. They were noisy, messy, unrelentingly energetic, mischievous.

But Matt and Danny still seemed an absolute miracle to Norma. Her carbon-copy boys. Of course, they really weren't exactly alike. Matt was more aggressive. Danny cried more. Matt wouldn't eat anything green. Danny ate everything with gusto and grew plumper than his twin. But they were duplicates in so many ways —the curve of their chins, the tilt of their noses, the green of their eyes, their teeth, fingernails, toes, lashes, brow lines, dimples, cupid's bows, cowlicks, widow's peaks, voices. Even Norma could not recognize which boy was which by his voice alone.

Like most twins, Matt and Danny got along amazingly well—too well actually—with two little minds creating more havoc than one alone. Both boys fought more with eight-year-old Julia than each other. Julia announced daily that she hated them, that Matt and Danny had been put on earth to make her life awful, that she wished she could go to live with another family where there were no twin brothers to get into her room and break her toys.

Norma still tried to spend time with just Julia. With Angie and Frank, too. Take one child at a time shopping, to play tennis, or to lunch. But it was hard to find the time. Sometimes she fell into bed at night realizing she'd neglected her three older children—especially Frank and Angie. Julia demanded attention. Frank and Angie waited patiently for it and as a result got short-changed.

Angie was just enough older to be more gracious about their twin brothers than her sister. And she no longer possessed toys that would lure them into her room.

Frank adored the twins and played games of chase with them, running wildly through the house, Buddy following, barking incessantly. But Frank didn't want his brothers so much as to set foot inside his private domain, which now looked like a museum with all his carefully arranged and labeled collections and specimens. Matt and Danny weren't allowed up on the third floor, but they would sneak up there anyway. Norma had finally decided that Frank was old enough and responsible enough to be given a key to his door, which brought howls of "that's not fair" from Julia in spite of the fact that she lost some item—a schoolbook, a shoe, her lunch money, a hair ribbon—almost daily and would most certainly lose a key to her room.

Julia was jealous of the attention the twins garnered whenever the family went out. Frank was indulgent. And from the first, Angie wanted to be the one pushing the double stroller down the sidewalk. The twins were like a magnet. People smiled and pointed. Old ladies came to fondle their fat little legs and touch their silky heads, to marvel at their beauty, their sameness.

The miracle of the twin's sameness came to an end the month before their fourth birthday.

Matt had a cold and sore throat first, then Danny. But Matt got better and Danny didn't. Mostly, he slept a lot. And ran a fever. Not high. Not like Frank's had been the time when he scared them so.

When Danny said his head hurt, Norma called the

pediatrician, just to make sure. Should she bring him into the office?

The doctor offered to stop by on her way home.

Norma apologized as she led Dr. Mary Sullivan upstairs to the twins' bedroom. Danny hadn't really seemed that sick, she explained. Just sleepy. It did seem strange for him to sleep so much.

"I wake him up every little bit and take him to the bathroom, make him drink some juice or milk, but he crawls right back into bed and falls asleep—when usually, it's such a battle to get him to go to bed. Neither boy takes naps anymore. And they'd stay up half the night if we let them."

Norma watched from the door as the diminutive physician attempted to wake Danny. She talked soothingly as she felt his throat, his stomach, pulled back his eyelids and shone the light in his eyes. Then she shook him more vigorously. "Come on, Danny, let's wake up now."

Norma's nagging worry changed to stark fear so abruptly that she had to gasp. Dr. Mary couldn't wake her son. Danny was no longer just a sleepy little boy. He was an unconscious little boy.

Norma felt Perry come up behind her and reached blindly for him, grabbing his arm, holding her breath.

"You have a very sick boy," Dr. Mary said, rising. "Where's the telephone? I need to make arrangements at the hospital."

Perry took her to a telephone. Norma collapsed beside Danny's bed and buried her face against his sturdy little body. And started making bargains with God. Take her money, her home, her health, her own life, anyone else's life, but not one of her children.

The diagnosis was encephalitis. The grandparents gathered with Norma and Perry at the hospital. Maura and her daughter came to the house to sleep over and look after the other children.

Norma and Perry never left the hospital. Edna and Belle brought them clothes and helped Maura with the children.

"Can you die of a coma?" Angie asked Grandma Edna, following her around as she gathered up a change of clothes and some toiletries for Norma.

"A coma means Danny is unconscious." Edna explained. "He can't wake up right now because something made him very sick."

"But all he had was a cold," Angie persisted.

"But the cold turned into something worse," Edna said, wondering how truthful to be with the child.

Dearest Angie, their little worrier. Just the other day she'd been fretting about all the people in China and Africa who had never heard of Jesus Christ and therefore couldn't possibly have accepted him as their Savior. Surely God wouldn't send them all to burn in hell for something they couldn't help.

Edna wanted to tell Angie not to worry, that Danny was going to be all right. But that probably wasn't so. Danny was at death's door. The doctor had warned them to expect the worst.

But Danny surprised them. He didn't die.

After two weeks in a coma, he opened his eyes and asked for a drink of water.

That evening, at home to bathe and finally see their other children before they went back to Danny's side, Norma and Perry told the story over and over, their faces glowing with joy and relief. "Just like that, he asked for a drink of water."

Maura led them all into the dining room where she had a celebratory buffet ready. All afternoon, ever since they got the news, Maura had been bustling around the kitchen, stopping every few minutes to cross herself and say, "Praise the Lord."

Angie was amazed by the appearance of her normally well-groomed parents. Their clothes were mussed, their hair unkempt, her mother's face devoid of makeup. Her father hadn't shaved today, maybe not yesterday either. But even so, they looked rather beautiful as they kept smiling at each other. Touching. Touching them all. So much hugging and kissing all around.

Matt wanted to know why they couldn't bring his Danny home right that minute. Julia bounded out of the room and up the stairs to fetch her teddy bear with the radio in its tummy for them to take to Danny at the hospital.

Angie didn't want to eat. She stood behind her mother's chair, not quite knowing what to do with herself. She knew she should be dancing around the room with Julia and Matt. Or praising the Lord like Maura. But she felt so strange. Danny didn't die, but he could have. She wanted to believe that all their wishing and praying had somehow saved him, but she couldn't. They were just lucky. This time. She looked at Frank. He was sitting by their father, his face serious like her own must be.

Chapter Five

*B*elle was out of town, attending a distant cousin's funeral in Waco. Over Norma's objections, Perry had invited Clifford to dinner. "I won't have him discussing Danny," she warned.

But other than Danny insisting on sitting on her lap, dinner went well. Nothing was spilled. Julia didn't get in an argument with Frank or Angie. Matt was absolutely charming for his grandfather. And precocious. He wanted to know if Clifford had a twin brother. Or a nontwin brother. Or sisters. "You mean they both died?" he asked. "That's even worse than being 'tarded. Do you miss them?"

Clifford seemed taken aback, then acknowledged, that yes, sometimes he missed his brother and sister. Especially Alma Jane, his older sister. They had spent a lot of time together growing up. Their parents were often preoccupied with their younger brother, who was sick in bed all the time.

Matt got out of his chair and hugged Clifford's neck. "Don't be sad," he said.

Clifford hugged him back. And was uncharacteristically quiet for the rest of the meal.

The adults took their coffee out to the terrace, the French doors open behind them so Norma could keep an ear out for the children inside. But the household was oddly peaceful. Frank was upstairs with Angie, helping her write a theme for school. Julia was spending the night with a school friend.

And the new evening girl had managed to get Matt upstairs with promises of a game of Chutes and Ladders, and Danny had followed along.

Mostly, that was what Danny did—followed people around. But sometimes, he wandered off. If a door was unlatched, he wandered outside. Norma was constantly checking to make sure doors and the gate to the pool were securely locked and, in spite of the inconvenience, insisted the front gate across the driveway now be kept closed and locked at all times. Yesterday, she'd lost Danny for more than an hour, finally finding him asleep on the floor of her closet. When she opened the closet door and saw him there, his thumb in his mouth, using her bathrobe as a security blanket, she sat down beside him and cried. For a long time. She had to do that every so often. Then she would dry her eyes and assume her disguise—Norma the calm and brave. But she wasn't either. Her insides churned constantly with . . .

With what?

Anger? Disappointment? Guilt? Helplessness? Fear? Whatever, it kept her stomach raw and robbed her of sleep. Clifford didn't help. For months he had been telling them Danny would be better off in a special home for children "like him," insisting that she and Perry were shortchanging the rest of the children. Danny would hold them all back. With a retarded brother, they themselves would always seem different. Especially Matt. Norma simply must think of Matt. Matt was such a bright child and showed tremendous potential. And he was still a little boy, too. He needed his mother's constant attention, and his damaged brother was getting it all. Sacrificing normal children for abnormal ones was wrong.

Last month, Clifford even made an appointment for them at a home in Fort Worth. They hadn't gone, of course. Norma had been furious and refused to have the usual dinner party for Clifford's birthday. The man had no social consciousness. Sometimes he actually seemed proud that his father had ridden with the Ku Klux Klan. To his way of thinking, different was not to be tolerated, especially not in his own family.

Clifford's constant pressure for them to "do something" about Danny made her apprehensive. Her father-in-law was wrong. Dead wrong. But sometimes Perry seemed to agree with him, as did her own parents, who seemed more concerned about her than they did about Danny. Norma hadn't helped matters when she screamed at them a couple of months back. And Clifford. She'd really lost control, probably for the first time in her adult life. Only Belle hadn't seemed horrified. She told the rest of them to leave Norma alone. Norma was Danny's mother. How dare they try to force her to do something that went against her mother's heart.

Paul and Edna had gone back to Austin and hadn't called for weeks. Then one day, they were there with gifts for everyone. And they resumed their monthly visits. Taking the other children on excursions. Avoiding Danny. When Norma accused them of not loving Danny anymore, they both cried. "We don't know how to make him smile," her mother said.

"Play the kissy game like you used to. Tickle him. Or just hold him on your lap. He's still Danny, Mom." And then Norma had cried herself, of course.

Belle's relationship with Danny actually improved. She had been more comfortable with the children when they were babies. The older they got, the more they seemed to intimidate her with their boisterous behavior and active minds. But Danny was quieter now. Easier. She liked to take him for walks and show him the bugs and birds. And he would sit quietly while she sang songs from her childhood or read story books. He was too big for her to rock to sleep, but she would sit beside him on his bed and rub his back until his eyes closed and his body relaxed.

Tonight, when Danny saw Clifford sitting at the table, he'd looked around for Belle. And had seemed puzzled when he couldn't find her. Belle often came without Clifford, but Clifford never came without Belle.

"Did you know Belle's cousin—the one who died?" Norma asked Clifford.

"I'd met him a time or two. Belle hadn't seen him in years. She just likes to go to funerals."

"No," Norma disagreed. "She likes to see her relatives and get away for a day or two. Everyone does."

"When was the last time you 'got away'?" Clifford asked pointedly.

"Don't start in on that again," Norma warned, looking away. The man himself was disgusting enough with his huge belly resting on top of enormous thighs, his round face sitting atop layers of chins. Even his eyelids were fat, his earlobes, his fingers. But to have to listen to him was even worse than looking at him. For years, she had been trying to convince herself that Clifford was overbearing but well intentioned. Now, she regarded him as the enemy.

"You don't even play tennis anymore," he was saying. "Or golf. I'd be willing to wager that you haven't had a lunch out with friends in six months. You wear a juvenile-looking ponytail instead of getting your hair fixed. Your husband fulfills the social aspects of his legislative office without his wife at his side, which causes rumors and whispers. You're living like a recluse. And for what? For a child who will never be the same again. For a child who is ruining the entire family. You're not even doing what's best for Danny himself. He'd be better off in a home equipped to take care of children like him, where he'd be around others in his same condition."

Norma threw Perry a look. Did his silence indicate that he sided with his father or was afraid to speak up?

"Excuse my skepticism, Clifford," Norma said, her tone deliberately icy, "but somehow I don't think what's best for Danny has anything to do with what you're suggesting. Danny is obviously better off with his family."

"He needs special teachers," Clifford said.

"The public schools have special-education classes," Norma said. "He'll be sent to the same school as Matt."

"But he's never going to get better," Clifford said.

"Well then, if that's the case, why would he need special teachers and a special school? Come on, Clifford, what really concerns you is Perry's political career."

The two men exchanged glances. Norma wanted to throw something at them.

"I've been looking into this, Norma," Clifford went on, his tone overly reasonable. Condescending. "The larger Danny gets, the more of a management problem he'll become. You know how difficult these last months have been. Perry says that you're exhausted all the time."

Norma laughed. "We have five children. I was exhausted long before Danny got sick. But, yes, it's been hard—emotionally. I've had a difficult time accepting that Danny isn't a normal little boy anymore, but this family is managing just fine. Right now, what Danny needs most is a lot of love and understanding."

Norma fixed her gaze on her husband. "Why are you just sitting there letting your father do all the dirty work? Obviously the two of you have discussed this. Do you really think our son would be better off living away from us among strangers?"

"I don't know what's best, Norma," Perry admitted. "I suppose, if we're ever going to place him in a home, it would be better to do it now while he's little and can adjust more easily."

"You need to think of the other children," Clifford injected. "Matt especially. Danny gets more than his share of your time and attention."

"And if we send Danny away, what's the message for the other children?" Norma challenged. "That they're a part of this family only as long as they keep up—that they'd better not get sick or they might get sent away, too? And we're not talking about a child who is indifferent to his environment and the people around him. We're talking about a little boy who still loves us all, who still smiles at us and puts his arms around our necks, who still calls us Mommie and Daddy, who likes us to sing 'Old MacDonald' with him. Could you really do that, Perry? Could you really send him away just to get your father off your back?"

"Maybe not," Perry said, staring out at the shadowed rose garden, not looking at Clifford.

Norma studied the two men. Father and son. With Clifford's great bulk, piercing eyes, heavy brows, and commanding presence, if he had been an actor, he would have been cast in the role of Mafia godfather or ruthless despot. Once Norma had thought her husband handsome enough to be a leading man, another Gregory Peck or William Holden. And Perry was still a handsome man. But either the beholder had changed or the man himself, because he no longer seemed leading-man material, not the sort of person who would lead the charge or make a daring rescue. Perry was almost forty and still couldn't stand up to his father. Had she realized the hold his father had over him back when she loved him completely and was building her future around him, when she was making him the center of her existence? Sometimes she wished Clifford would die so that her husband could at last become his own man. She found herself taking comfort in newspaper articles about the health hazards of obesity. Clifford was never ill, but surely he wouldn't live to a ripe old age. And when he died, she would not cry. She doubted if Belle would either.

"What's really bugging you, Clifford?" she asked. "Do you think that Danny will be a problem if you talk Perry into running for the state senate instead of a second term in the house? Or that I can't possibly be a good candidate's wife when I have to spend all my time looking after Danny. And if we don't hide Danny away when we parade the family out in public, he might sit up there on the platform picking his nose or scratching his bottom?"

"Norma, that's not fair," Perry said harshly. "You know Dad has always wanted what's best for us and our children. Forget about the election. Look what Danny is doing to us."

"Danny is not doing anything to us," Norma said evenly.

She rose from the chair and looked from father to

son with what she hoped was an expression of cool disdain, even though the heat of anger was making her heart race and her skin moist. "You both can just go to hell," Norma said. "I will raise my own children, normal or otherwise."

She left them and sat alone in the dark living room for a time, her eyes closed, willing her heart to stop pounding. At that moment, she hated her husband and his father.

The two men left behind on the terrace were silent, listening to the night sounds. An owl was softly hooting. And a cicada chorus was tuning up in the shrubs and trees. The futuristic mirrored towers and frantic traffic of downtown Dallas were only minutes away, yet this fine old neighborhood provided an island of peace and nature for those wealthy enough to own a home along its wooded parkways. Here, they were protected from ugliness and poverty.

Even so, Norma's parents had moved away, leaving this house for their daughter and her family, in search of a simpler life on their acreage outside of Austin. They no longer attended galas and openings. Paul didn't even golf. The two of them fished, gardened, attended an occasional concert or football game, read, traveled. And still made love Perry suspected, judging by the small intimacies that passed between them when they thought no one was looking.

He wondered what life would be like for him and Norma when they were that old. Would they find the sort of peace and contentment that Edna and Paul seemed to have found? Or would their lives still revolve around Danny?

Probably revolve around Danny, he acknowledged, if Norma had her way. And when it came to her children, Norma was a force to be reckoned with.

Perry could feel his face break into a smile. Then he started laughing. "Rather magnificent, wasn't she?" he asked his father. "The lioness protecting her young.

How long has it been since anyone told you off like that, Dad?''

"What are you going to do about her?" Clifford asked, ignoring Perry's taunts.

"Nothing. I'm just glad my wife has enough back-bone for both of us."

"You're going to let her make the decisions for your family?"

"It's our family, Dad, Norma's and mine. Drop it, Dad. You've lost this battle."

Perry tried to count the times he'd stood up to his father. Not more than half a dozen, at most. When he refused to look at his grandfather's body in the casket. When he went out for track in high school instead of football. When he married Lucy and moved to New York. When he insisted on raising Frank when Lucy's mother would have given anything to take him. When he asserted that even the people his father referred to as "the dregs of humanity" had a right to equal protection under the law and that, when the situation warranted it, he would put the full force of their prestigious law firm behind the defense of such individuals.

And now, Perry would not be declaring himself a candidate for the state senate. He probably could retain his legislative seat without a full-blown campaign. But the state senate race could turn into a real ball game. And he couldn't do that to Norma. Not now.

He should probably go ahead and tell his father. But he wouldn't. He'd put it off for a time, drop a hint or two first to pave the way.

Perry wasn't sure if he actually loved his father, but whatever emotional ties he had to the man were strong ones. He needed Clifford's respect and approval, and found it very difficult to set a course that would anger or disappoint him.

Tonight, however, it was Norma who had won Clifford's begrudging respect. Norma would have been a better lawyer than he was, Perry decided, and realized that the thought pleased him, made him feel proud for having such a woman as his wife.

So, how did he feel about tonight, he asked himself as he locked the door behind his father.

Not good, exactly, he decided, heading for the brandy decanter. Just relieved to have gotten his father off their backs about Danny. Clifford knew better than to bring it up again. Surely.

Maybe the boy deserved to stay with his family, as Norma wanted. But her concern for him had become obsessive, as disruptive to their marriage as Danny himself was. Norma seemed fearful that if she didn't keep a constant vigil and continually remind Danny who and where he was, he would slip into himself and be lost to them. When they first brought him home from the hospital, he would be Danny one minute and out of touch the next. It was almost as though, by sheer force of will, Norma would reach inside of him and pull him back. He was Danny. She was his mother. This was his family. In the night, she was constantly slipping out of bed to check on him. She couldn't bear to be away from him. The few occasions since his illness that they had gone out for the evening, she called home with annoying frequency. Perry felt as though he never had her complete attention, even on the occasions when they actually made love.

But her constancy seemed to be paying off. Danny was more aware of them all, more alert. Not that he would ever be normal. All the physicians they had consulted had agreed.

He wondered if Norma would like a brandy after she finished with the children's bedtime rituals. Even Frank and Angie still wanted their mother to sit on the side of their bed and help them decide what sort of day it had been and plan for tomorrow—and tell them how special they were and how much she loved them. Sometimes Perry joined her. Other times, he hadn't the patience for all the stalling and drinks of water and rambling prayers with the relentless string of "God blesses" while they put off the moment of separation. Norma's endless patience seemed almost abnormal.

Strange to think that Frank was better off because

Lucy was dead. Lucy wouldn't have been any better a mother than she had been a wife.

But then, Perry didn't want to think of Lucy. Thoughts of Lucy made him feel old and sad.

When Norma finished her bath, Perry was leaning against the headboard, pillows piled up behind him, a brandy glass in his hand. Another glass waited on her bedside table. "I'm sorry," he said, surprising her. "I never should have allowed Dad to bring up that business about Danny. You're right—what happens to Danny is between you and me."

"Obviously, the two of you had discussed things and come to a decision," Norma reminded him, not ready to accept his apology. She sat on her side of the bed and reached for the glass. "I wasn't being asked, I was being told what was best for my son, when you both know very well what's best for Danny is for him to grow up here in this house with his brothers and sisters."

"Maybe so, but Dad worries about Matt. Did you hear what he said to Matt at dinner about his brother? I think that he remembers his own parents ignoring him and his sister to care for their sick brother and sees history repeating itself. He thinks that it will be hard for Matt to grow up with a brain-damaged brother, that he won't get the love and attention he deserves."

"That's another thing," Norma said, turning to face him. "Why is your father so preoccupied with Matt? He does have other grandchildren, you know."

"He sees himself in Matt."

"My God, the boy is only four years old."

"But you know how Matt is. He wants to run the fastest, jump the highest, yell the loudest. And how many times have you heard him say, 'I'll do it myself.' He doesn't want help putting on his coat, brushing his teeth, buttering his toast. At preschool, he's the leader of the pack. I wasn't like that, and Dad was always disappointed in me."

Yes, Norma acknowledged, Clifford had already

anointed Matt as the crown prince. Not Frank. Frank was scholarly, not tough, not worthy of his grandfather's consideration. Even before Danny fell ill, Clifford had favored Matt.

At first, after Danny did not die, Norma had refused to listen to the doctor's ominous warnings about possible brain damage and arrested development. Danny seemed fine. Quieter maybe. Confused sometimes. But after all, he'd been very ill. In a coma, for God's sake!

But he wasn't fine. A part of Danny never completely woke up from that coma—the part of him that could learn and reason.

He and Matt still had the same features, but while bright, inquisitive Matt was dancing around asking questions about everything under the sun, Danny would hunker down and stare at a ladybug, unaware of anything else, not listening to his brother's questions or the answers to them. Matt was a sponge absorbing knowledge and insights at every turn. Danny was a tea strainer, retaining little of what was poured through him.

Norma and Perry took him to specialists in Houston, Kansas City, Chicago. They watched with growing realization while Danny fell further and further behind his twin brother. They hugged their children more but hugged each other less.

The new Danny was more docile, sweeter. Only Matt fought with Julia now. Danny seemed happy enough just to be in the room with family members. Sometimes he'd sit and hum to himself, rocking back and forth, but he usually would look up when one of them left the room. He seemed happiest when they were all around the dinner table at night. He loved to watch them and loved to eat. He was noticeably heavier now than his brother.

No one got the Tarrington twins confused anymore. The plump, slow one was Danny. The dynamo with a million questions was Matt.

Watching the gap widen between her twins, Norma felt a great sadness that she knew would never go away. The person that Danny would have become was lost to her. What remained was a boy who would grow in body and stature but would never be able to read Dickens or Mark Twain, never have any understanding of science or history or geography, never be able to make his own way in the world, never marry, never have children, never know the full range of the human condition. But even though her expectations for Danny were enormously diminished, Norma loved the child himself more. Fiercely she loved him. Damaged as he was, he was still her child, still her darling Danny.

Chapter Six

$\mathcal{N}$orma knew that people meant well when they said what a blessing it was that she and Perry had four normal children, as if four normal children made up for some sort of deficit caused by Danny's presence in their life.

But life was full of such incredible ironies. The tragedy of Danny's damaged brain did rob her and Perry and their two older children of their innocence. Perhaps even Julia. They now understood that wealth, burglar alarms, seat belts, healthy living, looking both ways before crossing the street did not necessarily insulate one from harm and that fairness was a fickle commodity at best. Yet, they were blessed by Danny's presence in their lives. They learned to look at the world through his eyes. Caterpillars were marvels worthy of close scrutiny. Passing trains were a wonder. Clowns a joy. Elephants thrilling. Christmas lights enchanting.

Norma was surprised that, with time, Danny was even able to share his world of wonder with Clifford. Danny would sit on his grandfather's lap and listen to the tick-tock and delicate magical chiming of Clifford's beautiful pocket watch. And Clifford could carve whistles from balsa wood, a talent left over from boyhood and resumed for the sake of a retarded little grandson who marveled at small things.

Danny also taught the members of his family the blessing of their own normalcy as they watched his frustration, tears, and anger at not being able to do even simple tasks. He could not do the things his brother Matt could do. He could not tie his shoes, read books, tell time, play even the simplest of card games or build high towers with blocks. Matt could draw pictures of houses, trees, boats, ducks, all manner of things, but no matter how hard Danny tried, how much Norma tried to help him, his crayons made only scribbles.

When Frank won the state interscholastic math competition, his picture and an article about him appeared in the Sunday newspaper. Frank was quoted as saying that he wasn't the smartest kid in his high-school class but he probably worked the hardest. "I watch my little brother Danny struggle to learn such simple things," Frank explained. "Whenever I start thinking about sloughing off, I think how lucky I am to be able to learn geometry and history and all those things that Danny will miss out on." Norma wept when she read Frank's words. Frank was a better person because of Danny. They all were. Except Matt, perhaps.

Matt resented the attention Danny received. He protested when Danny received more praise for setting the table than he himself got for a star on an arithmetic paper. And Danny didn't even put things in the right places. Everyone bragged when Danny put together a baby puzzle with five pieces, when Matt could work puzzles with a hundred pieces.

Yes, Matt was a worry. But he was young and would learn humility with time. He would come to understand that, but for a quirk of fate, he was normal, and Danny was not.

And Norma worried about Perry, who sometimes had a haunted look in his eyes, and she knew that he was feeling trapped by five children and the responsibility of Danny, by passing years and unfulfilled dreams—as she herself was. But it was different with men. They were more fragile, less able to adapt.

When Danny started school, Norma went with him every day and sat in the back of the special-education classroom. She ate with him in the school lunchroom. It was weeks before Danny left her side and explored the housekeeping corner and took some of the toys from the shelf. One day, the teacher got out the rhythm-band instruments and offered Danny a tambourine to play.

And he joined the lively march around the room, each child keeping time with his or her assigned instrument while the teacher played "The Stars and Stripes Forever" on the piano. The next day, Danny joined in a game of drop the handkerchief.

Every day, Norma asked him if it would be all right for her to leave for a while if she promised to wait for him outside the door at the end of the schoolday. Finally, Danny agreed. He was a big boy now. Like Matt.

Over the next year, Norma and Perry began to relax a bit and allow themselves to enjoy life more. Danny had adjusted to school. Their other children were doing well. Frank and Angie were in high school, Julia in sixth grade, Matt in the second. Matt and Julia played on ball teams. Angie volunteered at the children's convalescent hospital. But tranquility came to an end suddenly when, once again, Norma and Perry found themselves facing the very real prospect of losing Danny.

Danny was in his second year of the grade school's special-education program, which accommodated twelve children, from ages six to ten, classified as educable or trainable. Some of the children were learning to count and read about Spot, Jane, and Dick. Mostly he played with blocks and looked at picture books. He did learn, however laboriously, to write his first name and numbers from one to ten. He had no concept of numbers above ten. Eleven, to him, was two ones. Danny also learned to walk in line, to put the toys back on the shelf, and he knew he must not call out, across the lunchroom when he saw Matt or Julia, but waving was okay.

What Danny liked best about school was singing. He would ask his teacher constantly if it was time yet to sing. Danny couldn't remember the words to a simple poem or even his teacher's name, but he was able to remember the words to songs. When his parents came to visit the class, Danny showed them where to sit, he brought them juice and a cookie, and he sang "I'm a Little Teapot" louder than anyone else.

The grade school had recently been honored as one of the ten best in the state, so nothing seemed amiss when a woman presented herself on a Monday morning to the principal, Mrs. Vera Benson, offering a business card that identified her as Melinda Blain, an education reporter with the *Dallas Morning News*. A feature on the school was planned for the following Sunday. Photographs would be taken later in the week.

Journalist Blain asked Mrs. Benson what made the school so special, what new programs the principal had introduced during her tenure there, what outdated practices she had discarded, what was the place of new math in the curriculum. She'd even asked why a school that served the affluent Turtle Creek–Highland Park area had a lower teacher-student ratio, was better maintained, and had more landscaping and more playground and audiovisual equipment than schools in other areas of the city—the sort of pointed questions a real journalist would ask. Mrs. Benson credited the school's active and generous PTA with much of its equipment and landscaping. She gave Miss Blain a tour of the building and granted her request to look around on her own, observe in some classrooms, and visit with the children in the lunchroom and on the playground. Mrs. Benson even sent a memo to her teachers alerting them to the presence of a newspaper reporter in the building.

The woman was Caucasian, of average height, in her twenties, with dark hair styled in a Jackie Kennedy pageboy. She was wearing a loose-fitting navy suit, glasses with tortoise-shell rims, little makeup, no jewelry that anyone could remember. Except maybe a watch. Maybe a wedding band. But certainly nothing important. Throughout her visit, she had taken notes in a narrow reporter's tablet.

Miss Tollifero, the special-education teacher, seldom left her twelve charges, but even special-education teachers have to go the bathroom, she tearfully told the police. She was inside the building for less than five minutes.

She had asked Mrs. Moore, the second-grade teacher who was on playground duty during the lunch recess, to keep an eye out for the special-ed students. Mrs. Moore said that the newspaper reporter, holding the hand of little Danny Tarrington, had followed Miss Tollifero into the building. "I thought the three of them were going inside for some reason," she said, "maybe to look at the special-education room."

Miss Tollifero had made an immediate right into the teacher's restroom. Apparently the kidnapper and Danny had continued down the deserted hallway to the front door. No one had seen them leave the building.

When the bell rang at one o'clock, the special-education children lined up outside and quietly filed into their classroom. Miss Tollifero realized at once that Danny was not among them and immediately summoned Mrs. Benson. A frantic search of the building and playground was undertaken. The police were called.

Mrs. Benson made the phone call to the Tarrington home. "We can't find Danny," she said, her voice trembling.

"What do you mean, you can't find Danny?" Norma demanded.

"We've looked everywhere," Mrs. Benson said, sobbing now. "I'm so sorry. I think someone has taken him."

Norma got through the next few hours by practicing denial. Danny had just wandered off. He still did that sometimes. Or he'd fallen asleep in a cloakroom. He would be found.

But as the hours wore on, reality settled in. Someone had taken her child. How frightened he must be. Was he crying? Hungry? Surely, they would feed him. But would they be kind to him? *Oh, please, help them be kind to my little boy. We'll pay whatever they want.*

Perry was in Austin for the day, not due home until late evening. Belle put in a call to his legislative office, asking his secretary to track him down and tell him to come home at once. She called Norma's parents in Austin. The minister from the church. She started calling close friends when Norma told her to stop. "We're not getting ready for a funeral, Belle. Danny will come home. I don't care how much it costs, we'll get him back."

Maura made coffee for the policemen, her eyes swollen and red from crying. Her daughter came to help out in the kitchen. When Perry arrived home a little after six, children, parents and grandparents gathered around the table for dinner, but no one ate much. A physician friend stopped by with sleeping pills. He and Perry talked Norma into taking two of them, and Angie took her mother upstairs to bed.

The pasted-together ransom note arrived on Wednesday with a Polaroid of Danny. He was sleeping, drugged or dead, his arm around a brown teddy bear. The teddy bear reassured Norma. Surely a person who'd bought a teddy bear to comfort a child wouldn't harm that child.

"It's worse than when he was sick," Norma told Perry in the hours after the kidnapping. "When he was sick, I knew where he was. Even if he had died, I'd be able to go to the cemetery and know he was buried there in that place. But now I don't know where he is. All I know is that he's afraid. And it's eating me alive."

Angie seldom left her mother's side. Perry would perch beside them from time to time, but he needed to be in motion, to pace back and forth in the dining room, where the FBI had installed extra telephones. He helped Maura serve sandwiches and drinks. And he began making preliminary calls to his banker and investment broker to alert them that he might be needing a large amount of cash.

Frank took charge of Matt and Julia, helping them work a thousand-piece puzzle of the Grand Canyon and playing Monopoly with them through numerous bankruptcies.

"You need to get some sleep," Norma told Angie the second day.

"It's worse when I close my eyes," Angie said.

Norma nodded. She understood.

"I can't bear to think of him alone," Angie said. "He's never been alone."

That was true, Norma thought. The one thing Danny needed most was to be with someone he knew. Or Buddy. The old yellow dog had started sleeping with Danny not long after he came home from the hospital. Buddy seemed to understood which child needed him the most in the night.

The ransom note gave them forty-eight hours to gather $300,000 in cash. They would receive a phone call at 4 p.m. Friday afternoon giving directions for delivering the money. Norma was to take the call.

The call came at exactly four. Norma nodded at the FBI agent sitting by an extension in the dining room, and they picked up their respective receivers at the same instant.

A man's raspy voice told Norma that her husband was to come alone, in the black Mercedes. He was to park the car outside Gate 8 at Arlington Stadium, walk to the center of Section 8-B and leave the sack of money by the light pole. If anyone came with him or attempted to follow the person who picked up the money, the boy would be set on fire.

"You get that, lady?" the voice asked. "I'll pour gasoline on your kid and burn him to a crisp."

And Norma's tightly held control shattered as if a crystal wineglass dropped on a marble floor. From a distance, she heard herself screaming and screaming and screaming, felt someone prying the telephone receiver from her hand. Heard Perry's voice trying to soothe, Angie sobbing hysterically, felt herself being led to the sofa. But still she couldn't stop screaming.

At last, a white-clad someone was kneeling beside her, sticking a needle in her arm, and a soft cloud of oblivion fell over her like a blessing.

The money was left as instructed. Policemen posted in the stadium press box watched through binoculars as a black Dodge truck sped across the lot and a man leaned out to pick up the sack of money. At Representative Tarrington's request, the vehicle was not followed, but they were able to ascertain the license plate number.

The truck was found the next day in a shopping center parking lot in Grand Prairie. It had been stolen from a farm outside Gainesville.

Then there was nothing but waiting.

The next day went by with no word. And the next. And the next.

Norma kept thinking about the teddy bear in the Polaroid. The woman would have given Danny that teddy bear—not the man on the phone. If she'd given him a teddy bear, she wouldn't let anything bad happen to him.

When the police discovered that Clifford's former chauffeur had once done time for stealing a car and quit only a few weeks before, they looked through his apartment over the garage and the possessions he'd left with Beatrice, the senior Tarringtons' cook. He was going to send for his things when he relocated, she told the police. He was heading for Montana; he'd been talking about going for years. A man could find himself in a place like that. The police had sent out an all-points more to cover all bases then because they had any reason to suspect the man.

At the end of the first week, Norma slapped her husband when he tried to start the process of preparing her for the worst. She looked at the faces of her parents, of Clifford and Belle, and knew that they had lost hope. In their hearts, they had allowed Danny to die. She wanted to slap them, too. How could they!

Norma shut herself in her room, seeing no one but Maura, who for three days and nights tiptoed in and out of the darkened room with tea and toast.

The fourth evening, Angie carried in the tray. "Mom, tomorrow is Matt's birthday."

"And Danny's," Norma said. She covered her eyes as Angie switched on the bedside lamp.

"We've lost Danny," Angie said bluntly. "I know you loved him. We all did. But don't you love the rest of us, too?"

"Don't make me cry," Norma said wearily, her arm still shading her eyes. "I'm so tired of crying. I wish I didn't ever have to cry again."

Angie put down the tray and sat on the side of the bed and took her mother in her arms as though she were the child and Angie were the mother. "Come on, Mom. You smell bad. You need to take a bath and wash your hair. And eat something. Jesus Christ, you're nothing but skin and bones."

"Don't take the name of the Lord in vain," Norma said automatically.

"Yes, ma'am," Angie said, helping her mother to a sitting position. "Just think how nice it will feel to be clean."

"Do you think he's dead?"

"Probably. It's almost easier to think of him dead than alone and scared and mistreated. He's never known anything but love. Not in his whole life."

Norma nodded and took a deep breath. "A bath would be nice," she said, allowing Angie to help her to her feet. "I don't have any presents for Matt."

"He doesn't want any. And he doesn't want a cake or for anyone to sing 'Happy Birthday' because it would just make everyone cry. All he wants is for you to come downstairs."

Norma squeezed her daughter's hand. "I've always been able to count on you. You've always been my big girl."

Paul and Edna were with Norma when the call came. The three of them were having lunch in the kitchen with Maura. Danny had been missing for two months to the day. The minister had asked about a memorial service.

The call was from Perry.

"Are you sitting down?" he asked his wife.

"Yes. Why?"

"Agent Fulton just called. Danny's alive!" Perry sobbed. "They've found our boy, Norma. He's alive."

Norma closed her eyes. Maybe there was a God after all. She felt as though heaven had opened up and encased her in a beam of white, warm light. She put her arms around herself imagining Danny in her arms. Her baby. He would always be her baby. How she had missed him. *Thank you,* she whispered over and over. *Thank you.*

An elderly bum had been found in the Denver rail yard. When the police came to investigate, they found a filthy, emaciated little boy sitting by the body. The boy would not speak and had no identification.

He was taken to the juvenile services, where a kindly social worker scrubbed off months of grime from the boy's body and shaved the matted, lice-infested hair from his head. She tried to get the boy to speak, to write his name, to draw a picture of his house. But he was unresponsive.

In going through the dead man's clothing in search of some form of identification, an orderly at the morgue found a dirty, crumpled piece of paper wadded in the bottom of a jacket pocket. Written on the paper were the barely discernible words "My name is Danny Tarrington. Call the Dallas police."

Norma and Perry chartered a flight to Denver. At first, Danny didn't recognize them. "It's Mommy and Daddy, honey," Norma said, kneeling in front of him.

He looked from one face to the other. And nodded. Very solemnly. Yes, they were his mother and father.

"May we hug you?" Norma asked.

Again he nodded. Perry picked him up, and they held their bald little boy between them. Crying. "Oh, baby, we missed you so," Norma said. Perry was crying too hard to say anything.

Later, Perry asked Danny where he had been. "In a dark place" was all he said. That was all he ever said about that time away from them.

The money was never recovered.

Chapter Seven

*E*ver since he saw Beth standing in his father's study, bathed in a pool of sunlight, her burnished red hair like a halo around her head, Frank had been smitten.

Radiant Beth. Lovely Beth. Shapely Beth. Who was going to come live with his family at the end of her college term.

Her simple skirt and blouse revealed her slim waist, the roundness of her breasts. When she smiled, she looked like an angel.

Frank had thought about her incessantly over the past weeks. His mother kept asking him if he was sick and feeling his forehead. And he did feel strange. Altered. Strung out. His nerves on edge.

Last night, after his mother asked him to move Beth from her campus dorm to Highland Park, he hadn't slept at all. He wasn't sure he could bear it—just him and Beth in his Bronco. Alone. Without the buffering presence of his family. And he needed that, at least at first, until he got comfortable with the idea of her, with having her be a part of his daily life. Frank drove his Bronco west on the turnpike toward the UT-Arlington campus, his hands clammy as they gripped the steering wheel, his mouth dry, his head throbbing from lack of sleep. He had to force himself to concentrate on the traffic, lots of traffic, heading for Six Flags, he supposed. Or maybe the Rangers had an afternoon game. He was probably the only person in central Texas who didn't know if the Rangers had a game today.

Maybe she wouldn't be at the dorm. Her boyfriend could have helped her move.

Of course, she could be between boyfriends. Or

maybe she'd never had one. Lots of guys must have asked her out, but maybe she never found anyone she really liked. Maybe she was a virgin—a thought that made him suck in his breath.

He glanced over at the empty passenger seat. They would be sitting there. What would he say to her? How should he act?

If he played the radio kind of loud, they could just listen to music and wouldn't have to talk. But what kind of music? Would she like country, classical, rock 'n' roll? Other than Olivia Newton-John, the only performers he recognized when he heard them were the Beatles and Elvis Presley. When Elvis died, kids cried at school as if they'd known him. Most of them could rattle off the names of rock stars just as he could recite national and world chess champions. God, he was square!

He'd actually bought a tape of Olivia Newton-John that he played over and over—the only tape he owned. "I Honestly Love You" was the most beautiful song he'd ever heard. He was in love with Olivia Newton-John, too.

Except for the red hair, Beth looked like Olivia. She had the same sweet smile.

Beth didn't seem stuck up like the girls at school, who either disregarded him altogether or wanted him to help them with their math homework or chemistry experiments. A couple of the girls were really nice to him, but he knew they considered him just a school friend—not someone they would ever date or kiss or anything like that.

He was eighteen years old and had never kissed a girl. Never even held a girl's hand—except his sisters, of course, when they were little. And his mother's. Even now, his mother would reach over and take his hand for a minute or two, caressing it more than really holding it, while they were sitting on the sofa watching television or riding in a car. His mother was like a goddess or a queen. He loved her more than any other person in the world and was sure that he always would and worried that he was abnormal to feel that way.

He still thought about his other mother, occasionally imagining scenarios with her not being dead after all—his favorite portrayed her as a CIA agent whose cover had been blown. She would have had plastic surgery, been given a new name, new assignments. But she had grown weary after a lifetime of intrigue and wanted out. She wanted to get to know her only child, to make up for all the years she'd missed.

Every year, when Frank went with his Grandmother Claire to the cemetery in Lubbock on the anniversary of Lucy's death, he didn't know how to act. He was sorry Lucy was dead, but if she had lived, he wouldn't have the same family. He might have brothers and sisters but they wouldn't be Angie, Julia, Matt, and Danny. Norma wouldn't be his mother. The only one who would be the same would be his dad.

Claire said that Lucy had loved him very much and still loved him from up in heaven.

But she had killed herself, and that was a hell of a way to show a kid that you loved him. She'd been so beautiful, though. It was hard to have bad feelings about a person who was so beautiful.

His father no longer came in the night to look at Lucy's pictures—not for years. He wouldn't have found them anyway. Frank had hidden them in a shoe box on the highest shelf of his closet. He had formulated of policy of thinking about her only when he was in Lubbock. In Dallas, he had only one mother. And his father had only one wife.

Although he'd never admit it to anyone, his best friend was his sister, Angie, who scratched his back and let him ramble on and on about black holes and quarks and the human genome. His other friends were computer hackers, chess freaks, and members of the Dungeons and Dragons Club. And those guys weren't the sort of friends you'd talk to about girls or sex or religion or politics or anything real. Except Oscar Clark, the dragon master. They'd kind of started talking about real stuff—like if there was a God and how much jacking off was normal.

Frank wondered if he was going to be one of those men who never got married, maybe never even left home, like Lucy's older brother, Luke, who lived with Claire in Lubbock. Luke grew cotton on two sections of irrigated West Texas land and read books about wars. The Civil War was his favorite, and every fall, after the cotton was harvested, he traded in his last-year's Cadillac for a new one and visited Civil War battlefields. Frank was more like Luke than he was any of the Tarringtons, which made him wonder if he had inherited a predisposition to bachelorhood and weirdness.

Actually, Frank didn't mind the idea of someday being the caretaker of aging parents. He wanted to lead a socially useful life and thought it would be nice to feel needed. He still thought about becoming a minister. But it seemed stupid for an agnostic to study theology. Except that it might help him make up his mind one way or the other.

Of course, he was four years away from graduate school, and who knew what he'd be like in four years? Maybe he'd be less weird. Maybe his face would stop breaking out, and he'd grow a few more inches, put on a few pounds, get some hair on his chest, stop blushing whenever a girl spoke to him, achieve coolness. Lots of guys didn't get their act together until they were in their twenties. He might become a famous science fiction writer or a NASA scientist. Someday a girl might look at him with the same sort of eager admiration that he saw in the eyes of the girls at school when they looked at a first-string jock. Maybe when the right girl came along, he would overcome his shyness and get on with things. Fall in love. Get married. Have kids.

Yeah, maybe. But Frank doubted it. Those things were no more likely to happen than Lucy showing up alive.

Frank had the ability to lose himself in his studies and projects and probably wouldn't spend much time at all thinking about things that weren't going to happen except for his penis perpetually demanding gratification like a greedy parasite with no respect for its host.

And while Frank was performing the required gratification ritual, images would come in his head of female
bodies and faces—sometimes the face of a girl at school
who had smiled at him. Or Maura's daughter, Rosie,
who was almost forty but whose cleavage he had viewed
on numerous occasions when she bent over in the execution of some household chore. Or Olivia. Now there
were images of Beth with her mass of red hair, which
seemed both innocent and pagan and he wanted to
bury his face in it. And his penis. His soul. But after he
came in the wadded-up towel, he would feel his incom-
pleteness in a burst of overwhelming sadness.

When Norma was trying to decide about how to
rearrange their household to accommodate Beth, Frank
had suggested that he move into the unused apartment
over the garage. He was starting college in the fall—at
academically prestigious Rice in Houston—and would
be away during much of the school year anyway. He
hoped that he would feel more of a man living under a
separate roof from his parents. A bachelor pad. He'd
undertaken redecorating the apartment on his own,
tearing out the old carpet, varnishing the wooden
floors, painting the walls and ceilings—all of which was
much harder than he thought it would be but surprisingly satisfying.

Matt had moved into Frank's old bedroom, and the
remaining space on the third floor was being gutted
and turned into a guest suite with two bedrooms and a
sitting area in between. Beth would move into the former guest room on the second floor—next to Danny's
room.

He wondered if he'd ever have occasion to show his
apartment to Beth. Would they just be friends or something else? He thought about them eating together at
the table by the window that looked out into the
branches of a huge native mesquite tree. He'd even prepared a simple meal last night to practice—just maca-
roni and cheese from a box, applesauce, broccoli. He
sat at the table eating and thinking what it would be like
if she were there. But she wasn't. And he felt silly sitting

there alone eating such a mundane meal when his family was gathered around the big table in the dining room eating one of Maura's delicious dinners.

Beth was sitting on the low wall in front of the dormitory, waiting for him, a pile of cardboard boxes stacked in front of her. Her hair looked like fire in the sunshine.

Frank busied himself loading the boxes in his vehicle, then made himself look at her. "Where's the rest of your stuff?" he asked.

"That's it," she said. "Poor girls travel light."

"I'm sorry," he stammered. "I didn't mean to sound . . ." Then he stopped, unable to think of a word for how he didn't mean to sound.

"Insensitive?" she suggested.

"Something as if that, I guess," he said and knew he was blushing.

Other than her clothes, Beth had a lamp, books, a clock radio, some trophies, a pot of ivy, and not much else. He thought of his sisters, who both had closets full of clothes. A couple of times a year, their mother asked the family to cull out the clothing they didn't wear anymore and box it for the Salvation Army. Julia and Angie would each give away more than Beth had. But then they were all spoiled rich kids—except for Danny, who was in a special category. And Beth had always been poor. Somehow, Frank found that ennobling.

She had run the 880 in high school, she explained when he asked about the trophies. But she hadn't been good enough to get a college scholarship.

"Where did you go to high school?" he asked as he pulled away from the curb. Beth didn't even bother with a backward glance at her home of the past year.

"In Mineral Wells. I lived there with my aunt since I was ten. My brother and I. He was low mental, like Danny. Down's syndrome. She got money from welfare for keeping us. But my brother died, and I turned eighteen."

"Mom and Dad said you showed them a picture of your brother. That really impressed them. Other women applied for the job, but I think they trusted you more because of your brother—even though you're still in college."

"Your parents are nice. Real class. You know that just by looking at them."

"Who's been paying for your college expenses?" he asked, driving with extreme caution, as though she might decide whether or not she liked him on the basis of his driving.

She laughed at his question. "Ever heard of working? I waited tables three nights a week and worked as the night clerk at a motel on weekends. Last summer, I worked in a gift shop at Six Flags—in the Mexican section. But now I have a new job and a new home. I like your family. And Danny. He and I are going to get along just fine."

Julia and Danny hovered about while Beth arranged her few possessions in her new bedroom, including a picture of her brother, which she put on the dresser. Her only picture.

"What was his name?" Julia asked.

"Wilburn. But I called him Willy."

"Why?"

"It suited him better than Wilburn," Beth said, putting her underwear in the bureau. White cotton, Julia noted, and not much of it. She must do laundry a lot.

"Where are your mother and father?" Julia asked.

"They were both killed in a car wreck—a long time ago."

"Aren't you sad to have everybody dead?" Julia persisted.

"Yes, but now I have you and Danny and your wonderful family," Beth said smiling. "And I'm going to live in this beautiful house and have a bedroom fit for a princess. I don't have to be sad anymore, do I?" she asked, directing her question to Danny as she put an arm around his shoulders. "Let's make a deal, okay? No sadness. Got that, Danny? No sadness. No sadness."

Danny smiled and said it over and over with her. "No sadness." Julia joined in. And Beth put her other arm around Julia. They stood like that for a time, linked.

When Frank brought up the last box from the Bronco, they were marching around Beth's new room chanting the words.

Beth flashed Frank a smile. "Join the parade," she said.

He fell in behind her, putting his hands on her waist. She was slender but not fragile. She felt firm and healthy and full of life.

After a few more turns around the room, she clapped her hands, calling the parade to a stop. "Seems to me we have time to swim before dinner. I can't believe that you have such a big pool in your yard. It's actually big enough to swim laps."

"Frank would like that, wouldn't you, Frank?" Julia taunted. "I'll bet he's dying to see you in a bathing suit."

"I'd like to see you in a straightjacket," Frank shot back and felt his neck growing very hot.

Clifford and Belle came to dinner in honor of Beth's first night. Actually, Clifford had been the one who referred her to Perry and Norma. She'd come by the law office soliciting contributions for Special Olympics. She was vivacious, a special-education major, coached retarded kids. He'd picked up the phone and called Norma.

"Beth got Danny to put his face in the water," Julia reported as she attacked her salad.

Danny nodded. "I did," he said proudly. "I held my nose and put my face in the water."

"Why, Danny, that's wonderful!" Norma said, obviously pleased.

"Beth has a bikini," Julia went on. "You should have seen Frank's face when she took off her shorts and shirt! I think Frank's in love with her."

From her place next to Danny, Beth looked at Frank, who was staring at his plate, his neck very red. "Well, that's nice," she said. "I'm in love with Frank, too. I'm in love with all of you. I think you are a very lovable family."

Clifford raised his glass to her with an approving smile. "Well done, young lady. Welcome aboard."

He intentionally had not said "welcome to the family." Clifford was very careful about who was family and who was not. Perry and Norma were sloppy about that. They allowed their housekeeper and her daughter to call them by their first names, and sometimes they ate in the kitchen with them. And the Mexican gardener.

But Beth, he realized, would never be just another domestic. She was the sort of young woman who made him wish he wasn't old and fat.

Chapter Eight

Beth had been with them only a week when Norma was called to Austin. Her mother had passed out and been taken to the hospital in an ambulance. The by-pass surgery that Edna had been putting off for more than a year would now have to be performed on an emergency basis. Norma's father was barely coping.

"You're sure you don't want me to go with you?" Perry asked as he carried his wife's suitcases out to the car. It was just dawn, the broad front lawn silvery with dew, the birds in the dozens of trees greeting the morning.

Norma shook her head no, a hand on the door handle.

Perry knew that she was anxious to leave before Danny woke up. Departures were upsetting for the boy.

She glanced back at the door, as though expecting to see Danny padding out in his pajamas. Her frown lines were deeper than they used to be, but when she wasn't frowning she was still lovely—not the unblemished, fresh loveliness Perry had once admired, but then he'd aged, too. When she looked at him, she probably had similar thoughts. His hair was still thick and full, but the flesh of his face was no longer smooth and taut, and he'd thickened some about the middle.

But the fact that he and his wife were aging bothered less than the people they had become. They were incredibly blessed with health and wealth and children they adored, but they were not joyful and had not committed an impetuous act in years. He and Norma had gone from youth directly into responsible middle age with nothing in between—not that he would trade places with anyone. He seldom even wondered anymore what his life would have been like if Lucy had lived, if he had moved out from under his father's shadow, if Danny were normal, if he had been brilliant enough to be a law professor instead of a law partner, if he were courageous enough to leave law and politics altogether and become a cattle rancher or grow cotton, like Lucy's brother Luke. But even before the kidnapping, anticipation had gone from his life and responsibility had taken its place. He sighed a lot more than he used to.

He almost wished Norma would tell him to hurry and pack a bag, that yes, she wanted him to come with her, that she was afraid and needed him close while she waited to find out if her mother had survived the surgery. He really didn't have the time to spare, but he wanted her to want him to go. She was shaking her head no, though.

"I'd worry too much about Danny if one of us wasn't here with him—at least at night," she said. "He's not used to Beth yet."

He kissed her good-bye and hugged her close, savoring the feel of her, the scent of her hair. "Call me as soon as you know anything. Tell Edna I love her. I really do, Norma. Your parents are an inspiration."

His words brought tears to her eyes. She nodded, her chin quivering a bit.

He watched her pull away. Alone. She was right, of course. Danny seemed fine with Beth as long as a family member was with him. But he wasn't ready yet to be alone with her. And he would want his mother when he hurt himself or in the night, when the nightmares came. But if his daddy was the one doing the comforting, that was okay, too. Or Angie.

Since the kidnapping, nights had been hard for Danny—even with a light on and Buddy curled beside him. Norma only half slept and was out of bed at the first whimper, trying to get to Danny before he started screaming.

In the morning, Danny wouldn't remember being awake, wouldn't remember crying or being afraid. But at bedtime, he fought sleep, as though he knew that bad things were waiting in his dreams. Dr. Mary said that he'd get better, that all Norma and Perry could do was comfort him, help him believe that he would never be without them again.

"If only he would talk about what happened to him," Norma said.

"I suspect that he's erased a lot of it from his conscious mind," Dr. Mary said.

"It must have been terrible for him," Norma said.

"Yes, dear. I'm sure it was. Maybe he'll always have nightmares, but they'll become less frequent. You'll see. You and Perry are doing all the right things."

That night, with Norma away in Austin, Perry didn't hear Danny right away. Beth was already with him by the time Perry had pulled on his robe and raced into his son's bedroom. They both sat on the bed with Danny, soothing him. Beth sang little songs. At Danny's request, Perry recited "The Night Before Christmas" in its entirety.

"Wow, I'm impressed," Beth whispered when Perry finished.

"Yeah, I'm probably the only person in the world who knows the whole thing by heart. I learned it for a Christmas program in the fourth grade and for some unfathomable reason never forgot a word. And now, I have the opportunity to say it at least once a week, no matter what the season. Danny thinks it's my most noteworthy talent, don't you, son?"

Danny leaned into the curve of his father's arm and put his thumb to his mouth. His body was relaxing. He'd be asleep soon.

Beth was wearing a white cotton nightshirt with lace on the collar. Not immodest. But Perry was aware of her braless breasts under the thin fabric. Wonderfully full breasts for such a slender girl. Fuller than Norma's.

For the first time, Perry wondered how the presence of this young woman was going to change the dynamics of life in this big house—for him, for his family.

*   *   *

Beth's request had seemed like a reasonable one. Since the carpenters and painters were working in the house anyway, creating the guest suite on the third floor, would it be possible for them to cut a door between her room and Danny's? Then she could see to him more readily when he woke in the night, and he'd learn to depend on her instead of always disrupting his mother's sleep.

It never occurred to Perry that he should clear Beth's request with Norma during their nightly phone call. But he should have. The house was her domain, actually her house, deeded to her by her parents.

Her mother's surgery had gone well, but Edna had developed pneumonia. She was out of danger, but Norma felt as though she should stay a while longer. "Why don't you bring Danny down here Sunday," she'd suggested. "Now that the surgery is over, I can manage with him."

"Danny's fine," Perry assured her. "Really he is. Beth is quite good with him. She's been working with him on his numbers. At dinner tonight, she asked him how many ears of corn were left on the platter, and he counted five."

Then Perry related how Beth had taught Danny to skip. And draw an almost recognizable house.

"I thought that was pretty remarkable," Perry had told his wife. "All he's ever done before is scribble. Beth says he is capable of learning lots of things."

Now, with Norma standing in Danny's room, staring at the new door, Perry wondered if he'd bragged about Beth too much.

"I wish you hadn't," she said. "I need help with Danny, but I'm still his mother."

Before dinner, Perry took Beth aside. "You need to make sure your relationship with Danny is that of teacher and companion."

"I take it the door was a bad idea," she said. "I'm very sorry."

Her eyes were very brown, a wonderfully arresting combination with all that red hair. She had it pulled

back from her face with a tortoiseshell headband, re-
vealing a flawless expanse of forehead, with not a line—
not even a hint of a line. But then she wasn't much
older than Frank. Why would she have lines?

Probably they should have hired an older woman,
Perry realized. Someone matronly and invisible. This
young woman would be a presence. It was unavoidable.
Even his father was aware of her. Clifford watched her
whenever he was in the room with her and actually con-
versed with her, when he never more than grunted at
Maura or other people he considered underlings.

But Beth was good for Danny. As the days and
weeks went by, Perry became more certain of that. Instead of always rushing to help him, Beth insisted he do
things himself. He could button his own shirt. Cut up
his own food. Run his own bathwater. Brush his own
teeth. She wouldn't just read his storybooks but point to
the pictures and make him say the names of things. And
she was careful to pay attention to Matt and Julia. She
was their friend, too. She organized games of hide and
seek and treasure hunts. Angie, she treated like a contemporary, sharing fashion magazines and going to
late-night movies together. With Frank, Beth walked a
tightrope. He obviously had a tremendous crush on
her, but somehow she managed to keep him at arm's
length without pushing him away.

Beth won Norma over by being a bit in awe of her,
by seeking her advice on how to proceed with Danny,
what books she should read, what classes she should
take next semester, what music she should listen to, how
she could improve herself and not seem like such a
small-town girl. Would Norma help her select a dress to
wear to the symphony? Would Norma help her shop for
a rug to put by her bed? Did Norma think she should
cut her hair?

"She's quite a girl, our Beth," Norma told Perry
one evening as they sat by the pool watching Beth orga-
nize a game of Marco Polo with Matt, Julia, Frank, Angie, and two of their neighborhood friends. Danny sat
with his feet in the water, laughing and clapping as he

watched their antics. "She'll have Danny playing with them by next summer and Lord knows what else. I heard him singing this morning. The Bingo song. It made me cry."

"You're okay about her now?" Perry asked.

Norma laughed. "You mean, do I still feel threatened? Of course, I do. I should have my head examined for allowing a young, sexy, clever young woman into my home. What did you and she do—get together and plan a PR campaign to help me feel more comfortable about her? Lord, the next thing I know, she'll be wanting my advice on selecting a brand of toothpaste. But she made Danny sing again. And if she can do that, I can deal with the green-eyed monster lurking in my soul."

When they finished in the pool, Beth lit a fire in the barbecue pit and gave everyone a stick to roast their marshmallows for their 'smores. "I feel like I'm at Girl Scout camp," Norma whispered to Perry.

He reached over and stroked her bottom. "You won't later," he promised.

As they walked up the hill to the house, Angie slipped her arm around her mother's waist. "I used to think I'd scream if I heard him sing that Bingo song one more time, but I'll never say a word, even if he sings it a hundred times in a row."

"Me neither," Norma said, brushing a kiss to her daughter's forehead.

"Why has she been able to do that for him when we couldn't?" Angie asked.

"Maybe because she's not his sister or mother. She's his teacher. We'd grown so accustomed to tiptoeing around him, being careful not to make him cry, not to get him upset, that we never really asked anything of him."

"She's a miracle worker, like Anne Sullivan was for Helen Keller."

"Yes," Norma agreed. "She's a little like that— maybe a lot."

At Clifford and Belle's forty-fifth anniversary party, Norma took Beth around and introduced her to everyone. "This is Beth," she would say "Our miracle worker. She made Danny sing again."

When the hotel waiters rolled out the tiered anniversary cake, Perry lifted first Matt, then Danny, up on the bandstand. With the orchestra playing softly behind them, the brothers stood in front of the microphone and sang "Happy Anniversary to You," for their grandparents.

Chapter Nine

$\mathcal{F}$rank had been home for Thanksgiving only a month before, but it seemed like much longer. Of course, the month had been a long one as he tried to prepare for finals and arrive at some sort of decision about next semester—and the rest of his life. He couldn't sleep at night and fell asleep in class when he tried to study.

The back of his Bronco dragged on the pavement as he pulled into the driveway. Books weigh a lot, he thought. He'd taken a ridiculous number of books with him to Houston, stacks and stacks, envisioning himself as entering a scholar's life. Now, he was bringing them all home.

The front porch of the house was handsomely draped in evergreen garlands, and a huge holly wreath hung on the front door.

Danny came bursting out of the house before Frank's truck was halfway up the drive. He would have been watching from the window seat on the landing of the front staircase.

As the truck rolled to a stop, Danny and Buddy were waiting at the bottom of the front steps. Buddy's tail was thumping furiously. Danny was jumping up and down. Frank had to smile. Those two didn't care whether he was coming home the conquering hero or the vanquished warrior. They were just glad to see him.

Danny was wearing a Cub Scout uniform, with a blue shirt, yellow scarf, brass buckle, silly little billed cap. Vaguely, he recalled his mother saying something about a special Cub Scout den during her telephone litany of news from home. Frank wondered if they left out the mentally alert part of the Scout oath for kids like Danny.

As he got out of Bronco, Danny threw himself into Frank's arms with such force that he knocked him into the side of the vehicle. "Hey, Danny boy, you're getting too big to be a human bullet."

"I'm a Cub Scout of America, and we got a Christmas tree!" Danny said in a rush. "Momma said we had to wait for you to put it up. Will you hold me up so I can put the angel on top?"

"I think it's Matt's turn for the angel this year," Frank said. "But I need you to help put Joseph and Mary and the baby Jesus in the barn with all the animals and Wise Men."

Danny considered this. "Maybe Matt doesn't want to put the angel on top," he said hopefully.

"If he knows that you want to, he'll insist on it," Frank said.

Frank could almost see the gears moving around in Danny's head as he contemplated his older brother's words for a few seconds before abandoning the effort. "Momma said we can turn off the lights 'cept the Christmas tree and sing 'Rudolph' and 'Jingle Bells' and 'You Better Watch Out.' "

"Hey, man, that'll be cool."

"Yeah, cool man," Danny said grinning, reaching up to muss Frank's hair.

"And you look pretty cool in that uniform," Frank said.

Danny stood up straight and tall to do his uniform justice. "Beth is a Cub Scouts of America mother so I can have a uniform like Matt. We're going to have a Cub Scouts of America party today. Beth says everyone has to help."

"Speaking of everyone, where are they?" Frank asked.

"Daddy's at work. Mom and Angie and Julia and Matt are buying Christmas presents. Beth already took me to buy presents. I got presents for everyone, but don't ask what I got you because I'm not going to tell."

"Oh, yes, you will. Just when you're least expecting it, I'm going to pounce on you and tickle it out of you."

"Not if you can't catch me," Danny said, shaking his head, grinning again. "I can run fast now. Beth's teaching me ready, set, go."

At that instant, Frank realized that Beth was coming down the front steps. Beth. He felt as though an electrical field had passed over him, making the hair on his arms stand up, his heart fibrillate, his flesh tingle. He couldn't look at her. Couldn't say hello.

"I got your letter," she said softly.

Frank turned back to his vehicle, fumbling with the lock, opening the back to reveal a clutter of books, clothes, shoes. He grabbed an armload of books.

"Why don't you drive the Bronco around back, and Danny and I will help carry your things up to your apartment."

Yes, he should drive the truck around back before he unloaded it. He threw the books inside and slammed the tailgate closed.

Fortunately, the honk of a horn announced that his mother's station wagon, with Angie at the wheel, had turned into the driveway. Gratefully, he waved at them, relieved to be spared from committing further acts of idiocy in Beth's presence.

Norma waited for the girls and Matt to have their hugs before she slipped her arms around Frank and kissed him softly on the lips. "Are you all right, darling?" she asked, her voice full of concern.

"Yeah. Fine."

"But you're so thin. And you never seem to be there when we call. I've been worried."

"I just need some of Maura's cooking to fatten me up. It's good to be home, Mom."

"Yes, we're going to have a lovely Christmas. I'm glad you're here, son. For three whole weeks. I've missed you so. We all have."

Frank felt his heart turn over. For so long he'd loved his mother the most. Now, that wasn't so.

With Frank's homecoming taken care of, Beth began issuing orders. Her Cub Scouts would arrive shortly for a Christmas party. They needed to wrap the favors, set out the refreshments, turn Manuel into Santa Claus.

Danny's seven den mates also were retarded—with Down's syndrome, PKU, and other genetic disorders. Only Danny had been normal at birth. But the end result was the same. They were such simple little souls, quick to laugh over any sort of silliness and quick to cry over hurt feelings and dropped ice cream cones.

Perry arrived home early for the occasion, followed by a truck with a horse trailer. The Cub Scouts stared in open-mouthed wonder as an enormous black man unloaded a black-and-white Shetland pony from the trailer. And shortly, a photographer arrived to record each boy's turn on the pony. Belle brought a bag of shining silver dollars to use for game prizes. Matt had on his uniform, too, and even acted halfway decent, not insisting on a turn at the various games, which he would, of course, have won. He cheered and whistled and offered high-fives to the winners of the three-legged and sack races, the jumping contest, drop the clothespins in the milk bottle, pin the tail on the donkey. Beth managed to manipulate outcomes so that each boy went home with a pocketful of silver dollars.

Throughout the party, Frank had a hard time taking his eyes off Beth. She was everywhere, encouraging, hugging, being Santa's helper. The boys adored her. Frank adored her. Worshiped her. Idolized her. And wanted to touch her everywhere. Make love to her. All night. For the rest of his life.

He talked to his parents after dinner—in the study with the door closed. He wasn't sure what his grades would be for first semester, he admitted, but they weren't going to be good. "I don't think I failed anything, but I may have come close in my English composition class."

"I'm stunned," Perry admitted. "You're a brilliant student, Frank. How could you just go down there and waste a whole semester?"

"I've been lonely," Frank answered. "I'm not the

type of person who makes friends easily, and I missed you guys a lot. At dinner in the cafeteria, I'd think of my family having dinner together without me, and I couldn't eat. So, I'd go home and sleep. I slept when I should have been studying and writing papers, when I should have been in class. I even slept through a couple of tests. I want to live at home. I'd like to withdraw from Rice and enroll at SMU.''

His mother was looking at his father, her expression soft. The boy was lonely. His father looked unsure. Frank knew that his dad was worrying about Grandfather Clifford's reaction. Clifford would tell him to kick the boy's butt and make a man of him.

"I don't know, son . . .'' Perry said.

"Just let me try one semester at SMU,'' Frank interrupted. "I really do want to take some theology classes. I could be the first person ever to have a double major in math and theology. They'd write me up in the alumni journal. Maybe I'll prove the existence of God with a mathematical equation.''

"This is not a joking matter,'' Perry said in a stern voice.

"Yes, sir,'' Frank said.

The conversation ended with Perry saying he'd think about it. He never said yes during the first round. But if he didn't say no, everything was all right. Frank knew his mother would see to that. He breathed a sigh of relief. Come January, he'd start classes at SMU.

Frank had been guilty of avoiding the truth in the past, but he'd never out and out lied to his parents— until tonight. He'd already withdrawn from Rice and applied for admission to SMU. And he hadn't done well at Rice because he couldn't study, couldn't sleep, couldn't do anything except think about Beth. He wanted to move back home to be with her. The family that had sustained and loved him all these years now existed only in the outermost periphery of his mind. He'd avoided their phone calls, hadn't missed them at all, hardly even thought about them. Or current events, chess, the latest Tolkien book, developing the numerical model to predict emotional responses to art that he'd been planning to work on for years, as soon as his math was sophisticated enough.

His roommate had asked to be changed to another room because Frank groaned all the time. It was true. *Groaned.* He'd think about Beth and how much he loved her, how much he wanted to make love to her, how much he wanted to marry her. And he would groan with the excruciating pain of wanting so desperately that self was obliterated and only need remained. He didn't even care if she loved him in return. That's what he'd written in the letter. If all she wanted was financial security, he could accept that. He explained how much land he'd inherit when his Grandmother Claire died. Even more when his Uncle Luke died. He was their only heir. When he was twenty-five, he would come into his share of a trust fund established by his mother's maiden aunt. And eventually, there would be other money from the Tarrington side of his family.

If she didn't want to be married to a minister or a mathematician, he'd become a physician, a lawyer, a college professor—whatever she wanted. He'd live wherever she wanted. He'd never touch her unless she wanted him to. He just needed to be with her. More than anything in the world. And to know she wasn't with someone else. She was the center of his universe.

Just thinking about the letter made him groan. He'd gotten drunk out of his mind and actually mailed it! Then prayed to God or Satan or whomever that it would get lost, that she'd never receive the damned thing.

But it had arrived, and she'd read it.

He still hadn't unpacked his truck. He could just get in and drive. To Lubbock. To Canada. To a distant monastery where he could live a reclusive life and cleanse his mind of demons.

He'd even written in that letter that he'd die for her. He wasn't sure, when it came right down to it, if he really meant that, but he wasn't sure he could go on living if Beth shut him out of her life. It was all so sick.

Insane. Love was supposed to make people happy, life worth living, sunlight everywhere. But maybe it wasn't love he was feeling. He could almost believe in sorcerers and spells. Everything seemed so abnormal. He had departed from the world of reality and mathematical equations and been plunked down in a realm for which there were no physical laws, no frame of reference. He'd never been more miserable, more unstable. He hated the way he was. Hated Beth for her hold over him.

He kissed his parents good night and protested that he was too tired to start a game of Clue with Matt and Julia, too tired to go out with Angie and a girl she wanted him to meet.

Under the pretext of telling Danny good night, he went upstairs to find Beth. They were in his parents' room, building with Lego tiles and watching Mary Tyler Moore on television. He joined them until Norma came upstairs to claim her time with Danny.

Beth went with him to unload the Bronco. It took a dozen or more trips to get everything upstairs. She discovered a bottle of bourbon in one of his boxes and regarded him with lifted eyebrows.

She came back a little before midnight, her hair down, wearing a fleecy green robe and white leather slippers. "You haven't put anything away," she said, looking around at the disarray. The television wasn't on. Only the light in the tiny kitchen. He was still wearing the same jeans and plaid shirt.

"I fell asleep on the sofa," he lied.

She poured a finger of bourbon into each of two glasses and filled them halfway with water. Handing him a glass, she said, "Sit down. We need to talk."

"I'm sorry about the letter," he said.

"Why?"

"I'm not sure. Probably because you haven't given me two thoughts in the past three months. I was an idiot to write it." He downed the bourbon quickly. Beth handed him her glass.

"Oh, but I have thought about you," she said. Her

voice was low. It made him shiver. "But you seemed like one of those boys who hadn't made up his mind yet about sex."

"What do you mean?"

"I decided that you probably aren't gay because of the way you noticed me. But I didn't think you'd ever have the guts to come on to a girl. Then I got that letter. My goodness, Frank, that was quite a letter! A simple 'I'd like to take you out to dinner' would have been enough for starters. But you got way ahead of the game. Your parents would hate me if we got married now, unless I came up pregnant, in which case, they'd have to forgive me. But I don't want that. I want a big society wedding when the time is right. I want a wedding gown with a cathedral train. The works. I want to hold my head up and know I've earned a place in this family. And that can't happen until you're older, until your parents are ready for it. So, you and me, if there's to be a 'you and me,' has got to be a secret. And before we agree to anything, I need to know some things. Is the land you'll inherit in West Texas worth a lot?"

"I don't know," he said. "I guess so," he added.

"You mean you've never found out?" she said, her tone incredulous.

He shook his head no. He had never found out. It had never mattered before. It didn't matter now, except that she cared enough to sit here and talk to him about it. She smelled like talcum powder. He wanted to bury his face in her lap. In her hair. Between her breasts.

"And the trust fund from your mother's aunt," she went on, two little frown lines appearing between her eyes. "Is that Norma's aunt or your birth mother's aunt?"

"My Mom's—Norma's. She lives in a nursing home and doesn't know anyone."

"How much will your share be? And are you sure you will share in the estate since Norma is not really your mother?"

Frank had to admit he didn't know the answer to either question. Beth didn't have a nightgown on under her robe. He could see the curve of one breast where her robe gaped open. He wondered about panties. Did she come here to let him do it? What if he was too nervous and couldn't? He was sweating now. A lot. Under his arms. His crotch. His palms. He resisted the urge to lift an arm and check if he had body odor.

Beth went to the kitchen, the robe hugging the contours of her bottom. He wanted to kiss her bottom. And everyplace else. She came back with the bottle. "Well, is the trust fund a lot of money? Or just a few thousand?"

"I've heard my mother talking about it, but I don't know how much it is."

"Did Norma legally adopt you?" Beth asked. She pushed a hand through her hair. The movement revealed a centimeter more of her left breast.

"I don't know. Is that necessary?"

"When it comes to an inheritance, it can be. What about your father? I assume he legally adopted you or your name wouldn't be Tarrington. Or did they use his name on your birth certificate?"

Frank ran what she had just said back through his brain to make sure he hadn't misunderstood. "What are you talking about? My dad wouldn't need to adopt me. I'm already his son."

Beth stared at him, her mouth ajar, silence between them. "Well, of course, you are," she said finally. And stood, pulling the belt on her robe tight. "I'd better go."

"No," he said, grabbing her arm. "Why did you ask if my father had adopted me?"

"You're hurting my arm," she said.

"Why?" he demanded, squeezing harder.

"I assumed you knew."

Frank stared at her, his insides shriveling with fear, his heart flopping around in a great empty cavity. "Why are you saying such things? Who told you that my dad isn't really my dad?"

"I must have misunderstood," she said in a small voice.

"Misunderstood from who?" He was yelling at her. "Who, damn it?" He took her shoulders and shook her, shaking her robe open in front. And there were the breasts he'd dreamed about for months and wanted to fondle and suck and put his penis between. Large high breasts with big rosy nipples. A dream come true. Only now he didn't care. He had a newer, more urgent need than Beth's naked body.

"Come on, Frank, you're really hurting me," she protested, trying to push his hands away.

"Who?" he yelled, squeezing hard, digging his fingers into her shoulders.

"Your grandfather," she said. "Clifford. He told me."

Frank let go and backed away. "I don't believe you."

But like the water of a broken dam, knowledge was thundering down on him, threatening to overtake and engulf him.

"Look, I didn't know it was a secret," she said, pulling her robe closed. "I figured if he was telling me, then everyone already knew. Actually, I thought it was kind of symbolic, with you and me both being orphans. That either means we're meant for each other or should run in the opposite direction. I'm just trying to figure out which. I mean, orphans have to make their own way in the world. They can't afford to be sentimental or weak. But let's just forget the whole thing. I'm sorry I ever brought it up. It's just that if we're going to come to an agreement, I needed to make sure about things."

He heard the door close behind her. His knees were going soft, and he had to grab the back of a chair for support. Had he always known? In the deep recesses of his mind, had the truth always been lurking there, waiting for an opening, waiting to assault him and rob him and leave him helpless along the side of the road?

He stumbled into the bathroom and locked the door. His bowels and his stomach let go of their contents at precisely the same moment.

Chapter Ten

$\mathcal{N}$orma wasn't quite asleep when the bedroom door crashed opened and the overhead light was suddenly turned on. She started to scream, then caught herself when she realized the intruder was Frank. A wild-eyed Frank. His chest heaving. Fists clenched.

She struggled to a sitting position. "Frank, what is it?"

"What the hell?" Perry was saying, swinging his feet to the floor.

"Are you my father?" Frank demanded from across the room. And Norma could actually feel her heart sinking in her chest. *Dear God, no.*

Perry was a second too slow in answering. "Of course, I'm your father. What are you talking about?"

"Grandfather told Beth that you weren't." Frank's breath was ragged, his chest heaving with each gasp.

Angie, wearing a flannel granny gown, appeared in the doorway behind him, eyes wide, her hand clutched prayerfully in front of her mouth.

Norma grabbed her robe and hurried to Frank, putting her arms around him. "Calm down, Frank. Of course, you're our son."

His arms hung limply at his sides, not returning her embrace. "Is he my father?"

"Yes, he's your father, and I'm your mother. And I'll do battle with anyone who says otherwise."

"I mean really. Not my stepfather. My *real* father."

Perry was beside Frank now, taking his arm, leading him to the love seat. Norma sat beside him, and Perry sat across from them on the side of the bed. Angie came timidly forward and fell to her knees on the floor beside her brother.

"Well, are you?" Frank demanded again.

Norma took his hand. Her poor baby. Her poor dear baby. She wanted to scream, to weep. How could this be happening?

"Your birth mother—Lucy—had a hard time coming to terms with reality," Perry said, wearily, rubbing his forehead, the overhead light making harsh shadows on his face. "All her life everyone told her how beautiful she was and how she was going to be famous. She expected too much."

"I don't want to hear about her," Frank interrupted. "I want to know about you. Are you my father?"

Perry fell silent. Norma held her breath and waited, aching for them both. Father and son. But there was also anger, rage, hatred in her heart. For Beth and Clifford. And for Perry himself. Perry should have dealt with his father years ago. His cowardice had caused this.

"Well, are you?" Frank demanded again, already guessing the answer but apparently needing to play this hideous scene to its conclusion.

Perry sighed. "I was never sure. But it didn't matter to me. I'd done everything else all wrong. I wanted to do right by you. With Lucy, I'd been so concerned with what *I* wanted and what *I* needed. She did get a couple of roles that first year, but the plays closed after a few weeks. They ran just long enough to prove that she really wasn't a very good actress, and I was glad. I thought we could move back to Dallas and have a normal life. But she kept on. Audition after audition. We argued all the time. She said I didn't care about her dreams. She still got some photographic assignments, but not many. She'd lost something by then. She started drinking and having trouble with depression. She'd disappear sometimes for a day or two and come home sick and scared. I didn't deal with things very well. When she needed my help and encouragement the most, I turned my back on her. I wasn't even at the hospital when you were born."

Norma watched Frank's face, not sure he was really listening to Perry. His mind was still hearing that one sentence. *I was never sure.*

"Lucy walked out of the hospital when you were only a few hours old and checked into a hotel," Perry continued, his shoulders slumping, his hands hanging between his legs, his eyes begging Frank to hear him. "The maid found her the next morning, hanging over the side of the bathtub, her wrists slashed. From the very first, I knew I wanted you. I wanted to make it up to Lucy by raising her son. But that was only part of it. The first time I picked you up and held you in my arms, I knew that we needed each other."

Perry fell to his knees in front of his son, his hands on Frank's shoulders. He was sobbing now, having a hard time forming his words. Angie reached out and put a comforting hand on her father's shoulder as he struggled to go on. "I vowed to do everything I could to give you a good life. You were mine to love and raise. The biology part didn't matter to me. Just to my father, damn him. Damn him to hell! He made up his mind a long time ago that you weren't really a Tarrington, whatever that's supposed to mean. Hell, Frank, he doesn't think I'm a true Tarrington either because I don't have enough ambition to suit him. I was supposed to have been governor by now. I've never been able to please him, never been able to make him proud." Perry wiped the tears from his face, his voice stronger now. "And now I'd like to kill him. Forget about him, Frank, and think of your mother and me. Think of your life in this family, of your sisters and brothers. Don't you know that you're loved, son? Don't you know that you're one of us?"

But Frank wasn't listening. Not really. Perry sank back on his haunches, and Frank started to get up, but Norma pulled him back. "Talk to us, Frank. We have to work through this thing. I don't want you to walk out of this room until I know you understand that in our hearts we are your parents."

"Yeah, I know," Frank said, his voice wooden.

"You're good people. Both of you. But I'm not who I thought I was."

Norma continued to cling to his arm, but very gently, he pried her fingers away. "I'm okay, Mom," he said, standing, backing toward the door. "I just need some time. I've always been confused about you and Lucy. I've had to go see her grave every year and act like I was sad. And I was. But she didn't care enough about me to stick around. I was glad I had you and loved you a lot. Maybe more even than Dad. But I never was confused about Dad. It never crossed my mind that I might not be his son. Maybe I should have figured it out, though. I'm the misfit."

Then he turned and ran out the door, his footsteps thundering down the back steps. Angie scrambled to her feet and followed him. They heard him yelling at her in the kitchen, indistinguishable angry words, the back door opening and closing. Angie came back upstairs to stand once again in the doorway, her face full of despair.

When his car started, Norma began to weep. Then suddenly Beth appeared beside Angie, sobbing hysterically. She hadn't realized that it was a secret about Frank. She'd assumed that he knew. She was so sorry. So very sorry. "I'll pack my bags and leave right now," she said.

Norma allowed Angie and Perry to do the soothing, not quite believing Beth, wanting her out of the house but needing to be fair.

"What were you doing with Frank at this hour of the night?" she asked.

"We needed to talk," she said, wiping away her tears with the back of her hand. "He'd written a letter asking me to marry him."

"Marry you? What did you tell him?" Norma asked.

"That we were both too young," she said, sniffling, accepting a wad of tissues from Angie. "But maybe someday, I told him. Maybe two orphans like us kind of belonged together. But he didn't know. I'm so sorry. I'd heard him talk about his birth mom. I never would've said a word if I'd realized that he didn't know about Mr. Tarrington, too."

Finally, after Beth had calmed down and Angie invited her to come sleep with her, Perry and Norma had to deal with each other.

"You knew all along?" Perry asked.

"I guessed. Not at first, but later on. He looked different—not like you, not really like Lucy either. His long nose, his thin face, his heavy hair."

"And you didn't care?"

"No more than you did. I found it quite admirable that you would accept him as your own. Most men wouldn't, you know. I don't want to lose him, Perry. He's our child, every bit as much as the others. How can we make him know that?"

"I think in his heart, he knows. Maybe what we have to have now is patience."

"And what about Beth's role in this? And your father's? Why in the world would he say such a thing to Beth, even if he believed it? And when did he say it? He and Beth don't *talk* about things. He interrogates her sometimes like he tries to do with me, but they don't talk. Maybe it's time for Beth to go."

"I don't know, Norma. What about Danny?"

Perry called Claire Ledbetter in Lubbock and asked her to let them know if she heard from Frank. "We had some problems here tonight. I think he's probably headed your way."

Claire called back at dawn. Frank had arrived. And gone straight to bed. He said for her to tell them he'd call sometime. He didn't know when.

"He said that he's not really your son," Claire went on. "Is that right, Perry?"

"I never knew for sure."

"Come on, Perry," Claire demanded in her flat, West Texas drawl, "be straight with me."

"I put down an ultimatum a month or so before

Frank was born. Our child was going to be raised in Texas, not in New York. She said she'd die before she came back here. She didn't want to be a cowgirl or a Junior Leaguer. And in Texas those were her only options. Then I said that the baby and I would go back without her. That's when she told me the baby might not be mine. I really didn't believe her, but I never would have risked finding out for sure. My father took care of that. When Frank was in the hospital with that high fever, Dad inquired about his blood type. It seems there's no way I could have been his father."

"Why in the hell didn't you give me the boy like I wanted? He's my flesh and blood. My daughter's only child."

"I wanted him, too," Perry said. "Knowing that his mother killed herself was enough of a burden. I didn't want him thinking his father abandoned him as well. I owed Lucy's baby that much."

"He says he's going to call himself Frank Ledbetter from now on."

"He can call himself whatever he wants, but his home is here with us. He's hurting, Claire. Take good care of him and tell him that his mother and I love him."

Chapter Eleven

*A*ngie had never sneaked out at night before. She'd heard girls talk at school about sneaking out to meet their boyfriends. But Angie had never had a real boyfriend. She couldn't bring herself to flirt and was regarded as stuck-up by most boys. And the Tarrington name did set her apart. Her great-grandfather had been governor. Her retarded brother had been kidnapped. Her family was beyond rich.

Eddie Rankin was the closest she came to having a boyfriend. He lived the next street over and studied with her sometimes. They'd both represented their school at the state high school United Nations in Austin. And they'd agreed to go to the prom together in the spring. But they'd never even held hands. Julia was only thirteen and had already kissed several boys. *Tongue kissed* even. Julia looked like Tuesday Weld. Angie didn't look like anyone.

Angie had found it wonderfully exciting to creep down the back stairs to the dark kitchen, where she telephoned for a cab to take her to the downtown bus station. She met the cab at the entrance to the driveway as per her instructions. The cabby thought she was running away from home and said he didn't think he should drive her. But Angie offered him an extra twenty dollars.

The round trip ticket to Lubbock cost $77.72. She had time for a glass of orange juice and a sweet roll in the station coffee shop before the bus to Abilene, Lubbock, Hobbs, Carlsbad, and El Paso was announced.

Her seat companion was a retired schoolteacher from Grapevine, who was on her way to Levelland to spend Christmas with twin cousins. "None of us Carry girls ever married," the woman said with a sigh. She was old and wrinkled but surprisingly handsome, with close-cropped snow-white hair and a tilt to her chin.

"We were old-maid schoolteachers," she chattered on. "I never minded so much until I retired. Now I miss having young people in my life. Some old people are all right, but most of us are rather tiresome. I go every day to the senior citizen center to play cards and take water-color lessons. And every other weekend I go to Levelland. It's on past Lubbock. In the middle of no place. I grew up there. Terrible place to grow up. Blizzards in the winter. Hotter than Hades in the summer. And very Baptist. I couldn't believe it when Emily and Edith went back there to teach after we graduated from Stephen F. Austin. I go there to visit, because it's cheaper for me to go to them than for the two of them to come to me. They pay half my ticket. We don't get along all that well, but we're all we have left. I won't go to church with them, though. You're not a Baptist, are you?"

"No, ma'am," Angie said.

"You're not pregnant, are you?" Miss Carry asked.

"No, ma'am!" Angie said, shocked at such a question.

"No offense, dear. I've heard that there's a doctor in Lubbock who does abortions. Southwest of town— out toward Posey. Has for years. A regular cottage industry. Girls from all over go there. You look troubled. I just wondered."

"I'm going to Lubbock to try to talk my brother into coming home for Christmas," Angie explained. "We've always been together for Christmas."

"He had a fight with your father, I imagine. Tell him that no matter who he's trying to punish, he's the one who will suffer the most. Family is who we are. Past and present."

Angie's great-grandmother had come from Amarillo, and her Grandpa Paul had spent childhood summers on his uncle's cattle ranch, which encompassed fourteen sections of arid West Texas land. Grandpa Paul claimed that, by the time God made West Texas, he'd run out of rivers, lakes, trees, mountains, and even bushes, so he made people who liked it that way.

Angie thought of her grandfather's version of the creation legend as she looked out the bus window at the flat, featureless, winter-brown landscape, with only fences, utility poles, widely spaced farmhouses, and lack-luster little towns straddling the highway to break the monotony of her ride. Why would anyone choose to live out here, she wondered.

But then, she supposed that West Texans probably wondered why anyone would live in Dallas with all the people, traffic, and crime.

Her parents would have found her note hours ago —and telephoned Claire in Lubbock. She wondered how upset they were with her and what punishment she would face on her return tomorrow. Probably they wouldn't let her go to Gracie Winchester's New Year's Eve slumber party. Maybe they wouldn't let her go to New York with them in January. Except, with Beth gone, the trip probably would be called off anyway. Who would take care of Danny? But if she could get Frank to come home, missing a slumber party or a trip—even to New York—would be worth it. Maybe if she brought Frank back, they'd forget to punish her.

The bus stopped at each highway town to let a pas-senger or two on or off. The passengers were of assorted races and ages, including several fussing babies, an el-derly Mexican couple who held hands, and two middle-aged nuns who seemed oblivious to their fellow passen-gers and whispered away the miles. Angie wondered what was so engrossing. Convent gossip? Interpretation of a passage of Scripture? Church politics? Or maybe one of them was trying to talk the other out of renounc-ing her vows and marrying her childhood sweetheart. She asked her seat companion from Grapevine what she thought.

"Oh, honey, they're probably discussing remedies for constipation."

Frank and his uncle Luke, both wearing cowboy

boots, jeans, and sheepskin coats, were waiting for her
at the bus station. Frank was bareheaded, but Luke was
wearing a sweat-stained Stetson. Luke's weathered face
and hands were tanned to a dark brown. His teeth were
stained brown from a lifetime of dipping snuff.

Frank avoided her hug.

"For God's sake, Frank. It's me—Angie."

He shrugged and opened the door to a blast of icy
air, Angie realized her lightweight coat was scant protection against the West Texas wind.

Luke's boots and jeans were old and worn, but his
car was a new Cadillac. "Did you bring your uncle along
so I'd be polite and not say anything?" Angie asked,
turning to look over the seat at Frank. "I'm sorry, Mr.
Ledbetter," she said, glancing Luke's way, "but I'm
really upset with my brother. He has turned his back on
the family that's loved him his entire life."

"Yes, ma'am," Luke said, his eyes on the arrow-
straight road in front of him.

"You don't know how it feels," Frank said defiantly
from the back seat.

"No, I don't know how you feel. But I know how I
feel. I feel really bad."

They drove the rest of the way in silence. Angie
knew from Frank's description that the barren fields on
either side of the blacktop highway would be green with
cotton come summer. The Ledbetters used to be cattle
ranchers, like her great-grandmother's family, back in
the days before irrigation.

The Ledbetter home sat atop a rise, with outbuild-
ings spread behind it. Mature cedar trees lined both
sides of the long drive to the house, and a row of small
barren trees stood at the base of the rise, but the large
stone house itself had no softening trees or shrubs. It
did have, however, a wonderful, broad veranda that
wrapped around the entire house. Angie knew from
Frank's Lubbock stories that in the summertime his
Grandma Claire had her morning coffee on the east
veranda and her evening whiskey on the west one. She
shucked corn and plucked chickens on the back ve-

randa by the kitchen and waited for folks on the front
one. That's where she was now, in spite of the cold,
rising from a rocking chair, waiting at the top of the
steps attended by three large mongrel dogs.

Claire was a tall woman—taller than Frank, taller
than Luke. She was dressed in boots, jeans, and a sheepskin coat exactly like the ones her son and grandson
were wearing.

"Welcome to our home," Claire said, extending a
gloved hand.

From the veranda, Angie could see all the way to
the horizon. Two farmhouses were visible in the distance with their brave rows of planted trees and beyond
that, miles and miles of emptiness. And above it all, the
vast winter sky was the purest cobalt blue.

"If you live out here long enough, you see beauty,"
Claire said.

Her gray hair was pulled back in a no-nonsense
bun on the nape of her neck, and on first perusal, Angie had dismissed Claire as plain. But she wasn't. She
was an older, unmade-up version of the stunning Lucy
of the white photo album. Perfect cheekbones. Perfect
teeth. Vividly blue eyes.

"Dinner's in an hour," Claire said. "Call your parents first, Angie. Then you and Frank go sit by the fire
and have your talk."

Julia answered the phone.

"Tell Mom and Dad I'm fine and will be home
tomorrow."

"Have you seen Frank?"

"Yes, I'm here with him now."

"That took guts, Angie."

"Are they mad?"

"Probably more shocked than mad. You're their
nice, predictable Angie who's never given them a minute of trouble. Is Frank coming home?"

"I just got here. We haven't talked yet."

"Tell him that he promised to take me to Africa
someday to see giraffes in the wild. I don't want to see
giraffes with anyone but him."

"I'll tell him."

"Did you hear Danny in the night?"

"Yeah. Before I left. It made me cry—and gave me courage to come here. Danny needs his family to be okay."

"I'm scared, Angie."

"I know. I love you, Julia. I never tell you that, but I do."

"I love you, too. You're a good sister. And I love Frank, too. You can even tell him I said so."

The living room was a large room with tall windows, polished wood floors, a haphazard clutter of overstuffed furniture, and ornate dark tables overflowing with piles of books.

"I thought she'd have a picture of Lucy over the fireplace," Angie said.

"She has lots of them upstairs. Claire doesn't think that people should inflict their own grief on other people."

Without his coat, Frank looked beyond thin. He was wearing suspenders to hold up jeans that might have fit a few months ago but were now inches too big.

The fire felt wonderful. Angie settled into a plump chair and pulled an afghan around her knees. Frank sat on a footstool by the fireplace, elbows on his knees.

"It's like a funeral parlor at home," she told Frank. "No Christmas music. The Christmas tree is still standing in a bucket in the garage. Dad smells like bourbon half the time. Julia and Matt spend most of the time next door with the Edwards kids. Maura goes to mass twice a day. Mom told Beth to pack her bags and leave. She and Danny just sit most of the day. She holds him on her lap like he was a baby—big old overgrown thing —and they rock."

"Mom sent Beth away?" Frank asked, sitting up straight.

"Yes. Poor Danny asks a hundred times a day when Frank and Beth are coming home. He's worried about Christmas and getting the angel on top of the tree. And having you open your present from him. He bought you a calendar with a funny picture for every day so you can laugh every morning. He had a bad nightmare last night. I heard Mom with him. I'm worried about him, Frank. I'm worried about us all.''

"There was no need for her to send Beth away. That's part of why I had to leave—so Beth could stay. She's good for Danny. And she has as much right there as I did.''

"Christ, Frank. Don't pull that noble stuff with me. You're a member of the family. And Mom blames Beth for your leaving. And Grandfather Clifford. She told him that he was no longer welcome in her home. Belle can come anytime, but he can't. Then Dad got mad at her for firing Beth and alienating his father without talking things over with him first. Unless you come home, I think Mom is going to send Julia and Matt to Austin to have Christmas with Grandma Edna and Grandpa Paul. At least they'll have a tree up. Tell me you'll come home, Frank. We need you.''

"Where did Beth go?" he asked, staring into the fire.

"She moved into a dorm at the college. They keep one open over the Christmas holidays for students who don't have anyplace to go. Mom and Dad are going to pay for her to finish college. I went to see her yesterday. She's pretty upset. She says that she should have done more to discourage you, but she wasn't sure that she wanted to. She wasn't in love with you, but she liked you and the idea of becoming a member of the family. She said if she were a Tarrington, she'd never have to worry about money again, that she'd spent most of her life on welfare. Money gives people dignity. She wanted to have dignity. And she would have agreed to marry you when you both were out of school if she knew that you really stood to benefit from family money. Apparently, she'd told Grandfather about your letter and asked what she should do—which seems weird. He's about as approachable as a bull elephant and has never struck me as the Ann Landers type.''

"How did he know about me?" Frank asked. "Did Dad tell him?"

"No. He figured it out on his own. According to Beth, years ago, he saw your blood type on some medical records and realized that you and Daddy couldn't be related. And you know how Grandfather is with all that blood-is-thicker-than-water crap. He thinks that bloodlines are sacred. He's not going to leave you anything in his will because he doesn't consider you a *real* Tarrington. Danny gets a token trust fund like Julia and me 'cause he's retarded. He plans to bypass Dad and leave the bulk of his estate to Matt, the one Tarrington who not only will carry on his seed and family name but is a go-getter, not retarded, not female, and therefore—according to the chauvinistic, elitist reasoning of our esteemed grandfather—deserving of vast wealth."

"How do you know all this?" Frank asked.

"From Beth. While Grandfather was explaining to her the story of your tainted birth, he told her the terms of his will. Maybe now she'll just wait around and marry Matt when he's old enough in ten or twelve years. But I'm being hateful. I've never been poor and have no idea what I'd do if I were Beth. Do you still love her?"

"No, I suppose not," he said with a tremor in his voice. "But I don't feel right about anything. I don't think I'll ever feel right about things again."

"What things?"

"Family. Who I am. What I'm supposed to do with my life. Money. Falling in love. Getting married."

"What about Danny? How do you feel about him?"

"Danny's different. It's safe to love him."

"And it's not safe to love me?"

"I don't know, Angie."

"And the rest of us? Have any of us ever done anything to deserve your turning your back on us? I know you're confused and hurt. But so are we. Can't we help each other feel better? Can't we have Christmas? Can't we get our family back?"

"I'm never going to use the Tarrington name again."

"That's your choice. All we want is to have you be a part of our lives. We've always been a family. You can't just run off because you find out your birth mom screwed around. Hell, maybe Grandmother Belle screwed around, and Dad is the gardener's kid."

She was crying now, fumbling around in her pocket for a tissue. "I love you, Frank. You're my big brother. What will I do without a big brother? And who the hell is going to scratch your back and listen to you go on and on about mutant genes and black holes?"

After dinner, Frank told Angie that he was going to school in Massachusetts. "I went to the Unitarian Church in Houston. It was the only good thing that happened the whole time I was there. I was so distracted I couldn't really appreciate it, but I know that Unitarianism is right for me, Angie. I want to study for the ministry."

"Do you have a calling, or whatever it is you're supposed to have to be a minister?"

"No, that's not a prerequisite of Unitarianism. I just want to lead a quiet, contemplative life and not cause any problems for anyone."

"Will you come home for Christmas?"

"It's easier to stay away," he said.

"But it's not right. If nothing else, you owe it to Danny."

He was silent for a long time. "Only if Mom lets Beth come back after Christmas," he said finally.

"You'll have to take that up with Mom," Angie said, closing her eyes and offering thanks. She'd won.

And so, her family was together at Christmas. The carols sung around the tree had never been sweeter, nor had the faces of her family. Angie loved them all so much. But all the love in the world could not keep this family from change. From children who grow up and away. From grandparents and parents who grow old and die.

She didn't love Danny and Frank more than the other members of her family, but her love for them was different—more poignant, more tender. Her damaged brothers. How alike they were. Both not capable of dealing with the real world. Danny would be protected from that world by family and kindly folks who care for people like him. And protected by the vestments of clergy, Frank could retreat into an ecclesiastic life.

Chapter Twelve

She had passed through the period of initial resistance, when her body insisted that the water was too cold and it really didn't want to swim laps today, and she had crossed over into euphoria where aches and weakness miraculously disappeared and there was nothing but her and the water and the feeling that she could swim on and on. As long as she wanted. Mind over body. Trophies on the shelf. Julia the swimmer. Julia the Olympian. Julia the Wonder Woman.

As her head broke the surface after turning into her fifteenth lap, she heard Beth calling. At first, her mind discarded the intrusion and told her to swim on.

But her concentration had been broken. She heard her again. "Julia, help me!" And she wondered how long Beth had been calling to her.

She stopped midstroke, planted her feet on the bottom of the pool and looked around.

"Julia, for God's sake, get him away from me!"

Beth's voice was coming from the far corner of the pool, but all Julia could see was the back of Danny's head and tan, broad shoulders—only twelve years old but already he had the physique of a man.

Holding on to the side of the pool, Danny was facing a corner in the deep end of pool. It took Julia a minute to realize that he had Beth pinned in the corner. The top to Beth's chartreuse bathing suit had been tossed just out of reach on the pool decking.

"Danny," Julia yelled and raced toward him, pulling herself through the water with long, hard strokes, her feet kicking furiously, form forgotten in her haste.

Julia grabbed Danny's shoulder. And realized his

pelvis was moving back and forth under the water, humping against Beth.

"Get him away from me," Beth said, her jaw clenched, fear in her voice.

"Beth wants to swim, Danny." Julia was breathing hard, but still she tried to emulate the soothing tone of voice they all knew to use with Danny when he was out of control. "You need to let her out of the corner so she can swim."

His eyes were glazed. He was pushing hard against Beth, the humping movements getting faster and stronger. His legs were wrapped around Beth's torso. Her head was being pulled underwater with each thrust of Danny's hips.

"Danny," Julia said in his ear, more demanding now. "You're hurting Beth. Let her go! Right this minute. Let her go."

But he was oblivious to his sister, his expression animallike. A dog mindlessly humping his master's extended foot.

Julia pounded on him with her fists, then tugged on his arm in a futile attempt to pull him away.

She scrambled out of the pool and, waving her arms frantically, ran across the lawn toward Manuel on the riding lawn mower.

Without waiting for an explanation, Manuel turned off the mower and raced after her.

Beth was completely underwater now, Danny clutching her head against his chest with one arm, clinging to the side of the pool with the other. His eyes were closed, his face screwed up like that of a person in intense pain.

Julia and Manuel both jumped in the pool. Julia ducked underwater and worked to separate Beth's head from Danny's hold while Manuel tugged at him on the surface. Beth's hair was floating around her head. Feebly, she raised her arms and tried to help Julia release the vise of Danny's grip.

So strong, Julia thought. *How could a twelve-year-old*

boy be so strong? Beth was still conscious, but for how long? In desperation, Julia bit down hard on Danny's upper arm. And scratched at him, then plunged deeper and sank her teeth into his side. With no reaction. No reaction at all.

Julia lifted her head above the surface and took a big gulp of air. "Pull, Manuel. Hit him. Choke him. He's going to drown her." And she plunged again under the water and tried to pry Danny's arm away from Beth's neck.

But suddenly, his body went limp, and Beth floated free. Julia pulled her to the surface. Manuel crawled out of the pool and pulled Beth's choking, gasping form to the deck.

Julia scrambled out of the pool and knelt beside her. "Are you all right? Tell me you're all right."

Vaguely, she was aware of Manuel talking to Danny, telling him he needed to get out of the pool now, to go find his mother or Angie.

Weakly, Beth reached out to Julia, and Julia gathered Beth's topless body against her chest. *He could have drowned her. My God, he could have drowned her.*

Beth was gasping and sobbing at the same time, her body shaking almost to the point of convulsions. And through her fear, Julia found herself thinking how odd it was for Beth to be out of control. A first.

Beth could even control passion.

Julia could feel the goose bumps of Beth's bare breasts pressed against the exposed flesh of her own midriff. And imagined Danny's hands grabbing those breasts. Poor baby boy. How puzzling it all must be for him to be inhabited suddenly by a demon. Beth said he was jerking off all day long. Making himself raw. All she could do was make him go in the bathroom to do it privately. Julia knew her parents were having discussions with Danny almost daily. He must control his urges. Matt had them, too, but Matt didn't tackle poor Beth. Matt didn't put his hands on her.

Perry tried to explain further—that sex was what

married people did to make babies in the mommy's
tummy, that people like Danny couldn't get married
and have children. They couldn't take care of children
because they needed people to help them take care of
themselves.

And Norma had conversations with Dr. Mary and a
child psychiatrist recommended by the pediatrician.
There was talk of giving Danny tranquilizers.

How sad, Julia thought, that he couldn't find some
willing playmate to experiment with—like she herself
had done. Or rather, the playmate had found her. The
experimenting had been done in the safe, warm darkness of her own bed.

But what Julia had discovered about herself, she
didn't want to know. The future she had planned for
herself was now at risk. She wanted to be normal. To
date and have fun. To be in a sorority at UT like Angie.
To meet the right man, fall in love, get married, have
babies. But even if she did walk down the aisle someday
on her daddy's arm, the love of her life waiting for her
at the altar, now she would be afraid that she was walking into a lie.

Even as she held Beth's shaking body, her heart
still pounding at the horror of what almost happened,
Julia almost wished that Beth had drowned.

If she had waited until later to swim her laps, Beth
would now be floating facedown in the pool. Even so,
maybe Danny had done her a great favor. Either Danny
would be sent away now, in which case Beth would have
no further function with this family. Or Beth would be
sent away, and some big burly male keeper would be
brought in for Danny. Either way, Julia wouldn't have to
live in the same house with her. She would be able to
put Beth behind her. Start over.

Manuel handed Julia a towel. She covered Beth's
bare breasts and continued to hold her. Maybe it would
be the last time. Yes, the last time. It was for the best.

Finally, it was over. She pressed her lips against
Beth's wet forehead. And began to cry.

*   *   *

It had come as no great surprise when Matt became a hairy, sweaty, overgrown, horny adolescent with girlie magazines hidden under his mattress. Twelve seemed a little young, but some boys mature early.

But it had come as a shock for Danny, forever the child, to erupt with whiskers and pimples and hormones. Suddenly, he wanted to hug Beth all the time, to kiss her, put his hands inside her blouse, tell her that he wanted to marry her. With Beth's training regimen and his love of Maura's cooking, Danny was heavier and stronger than Matt. He could push Beth to the ground, crawl on top of her.

These incidents were mostly dismissed as harmless. Just a phase he was going through. The psychiatrist said that he would learn control, just as he had learned as a young child not to bite or throw food. Children like Danny could learn to follow social norms. The need to be accepted and to conform would eventually outweigh his primitive urges.

Rescuing Beth from Danny's bear hugs and tackles became an almost daily occurrence. He would be chastised and made to promise that he would never push Beth down again, never try to get on top of her. But then everyone would go on with what they had been doing, acting as though the incident was no more extraordinary than a glass of spilled milk. Patience was the key, Norma insisted. They had overcome so much with Danny. They must work together to help him get over this new hurdle.

Julia found it interesting that Danny seemed instinctively to honor the incest taboo, putting the female members of his family and Beth into different categories. On only a few occasions had he tried to touch Julia's breasts, and he went through a period when he stole her underwear—Angie's, too, but never their mother's. Julia went in one morning to wake him, and he was still sound asleep, wearing a pair of her panties over his face. Julia didn't know whether to laugh or cry. But any lewdness directed toward his sisters was more tentative. He never tried to put his hands inside their clothing, never tried to rub against them.

With the incident in the pool, Julia wondered if her parents would finally give in to Grandfather Clifford's long- held contention that Danny belonged in a special home. All evening, Clifford kept reminding them that if Julia hadn't been swimming in the pool, Danny could very well have drowned Beth. They could be facing a family tragedy, a horrible scandal.

Julia wondered if a scandal would have kept her father from being appointed a judge on the federal district court—something she knew he wanted very much, something that would allow him to deal with law at the purer, more abstract constitutional level as he judged how effectively trial lawyers and lower court judges did their job. He would be freed from his father's law firm and billable hours, from his father's ambition. The federal appointment would be for life, ending the speculation about Perry's political career. He would never be governor of the state of Texas. Her grandfather's dream of a Tarrington return to the governor's mansion would be passed to the next generation. To Matt.

Angie was spending the afternoon at the country club with several of her sorority sisters who were in town for the summer rush tour. Last night, they had entertained a bevy of new high-school graduates from the city's best families. Angie had offered her house for the party, but Cindy Bartlett, the chapter rush chairman, had opted for the even grander home of Mrs. J. Robinson Bechtold, a Dallas alumna whose husband was president and chairman of the board of Bechtold Oil and Gas.

Over lunch, and now during sun-bathing by the country club pool, the young women were assessing the rushees who had attended last night's party. Who did and who did not have the makings of a Pi Phi?

This was Angie's first go-round with the other side of rush. Last year, she herself had been a rushee. She didn't like it from either side. Sorority, like most things in life, was turning out to be a dichotomy. She loved the instant friendships and the sense of belonging. And for the most part, her sorority sisters were admirable young women. Only the few planning to go on to professional or graduate school were as serious about their studies as Angie was, but Pi Phis had a reputation for making good grades and being a cut above the rest in decorum and dress.

Most of the time, Angie could forget the elitist nature of the entire Greek system and enjoy the camaraderie and fun. But rush disturbed her. She didn't like judging people—deciding if family position, wealth, talent, good grades, and personality compensated for broad hips, chewed fingernails, Coke-bottle glasses, overdone makeup, overpermed hair. Deciding if beauty outweighed poverty. If brains were more important than a bad complexion.

"What do you think about Debbie Clarkson, Angie?" Cindy asked. Cindy, a Fort Worth senior, was on the UT cheerleading squad and engaged to the SAE president. Her father owned a bank.

"Which one was she?" Angie asked.

"The homecoming queen from Richardson High," Cindy said, in a tone that indicated she couldn't believe Angie had forgotten such a noteworthy personage. "Her dad died, and she and her mom are poor as church mice. I swear that dress she was wearing last night just screamed homemade. She has scholarship money, but she'll have to work to pay her house bill. On the other hand, she finished in the top ten of her class, and she's a three-way Pi Phi legacy. Seven different alumnae wrote recs on her. And she'll probably be a yearbook beauty queen. God, did you ever see such skin! I'd die to have skin like that."

"Work doing what?" chimed in Sarajo Hornbill from Odessa. Sarajo's family made their money in oil. Sarajo seemed to think that an extensive designer wardrobe made up for her short, dumpy body. She actually got upset when the house wouldn't put her up for Sweetheart of Sigma Chi.

"It says in one rec that she was a part-time secretary in an attorney's office and did some modeling," Cindy said. "That would be all right, don't you think?"

"Of course, it's all right," Angie said. "How could it not be all right? Or does it say in the Pi Phi charter that only the overprivileged need apply?"

"If it was up to Angie, we'd give a bid to every girl who went through rush," Billie Thompson said, reaching over to give Angie an affectionate pat on the arm.

"What if Debbie can't find a job in an attorney's office in Austin?" Sarajo asked. "We don't need another waitress like Judy Kay Fitch. God, that was embarrassing."

Angie sat upright on her chaise and, shading her eyes against the glare from the pool, looked across Billie's prone body to where Sarajo was stretched out. "God, Sarajo, I can't believe you said that. Her family lost all their money! Judy Kay moved out of the Pi Phi house and worked god-knows-how-many hours a week just to stay in school. What did you expect her to do, give back her pin and stop coming to chapter meetings because she was suddenly poor and had to wait tables? As I recall, she still made better grades than you did—and was accepted to medical school. And you're saying she was an *embarrassment*!"

"Look, Angie," Sarajo said, "I know it sounds coldhearted. But if we pledge girls who have to work, then the girls who have money won't want to join. There are other really good houses who cater to that sort of girl. That's the way it's always been, and I think you know that. And if you're so goddamned liberal, Angie, why didn't you pledge one of those other houses instead of Pi Phi?"

"My daddy doesn't approve of girls going to medical school," chimed in Ruthie Blanchard, whose daddy was a plastic surgeon in Houston. "He says they're just taking the place of some young man and will end up either dropping out to get married and have babies or graduate and only see a few patients a week working out of a home office.''

"I don't think Debbie Clarkson wants to go to medical school," Cindy said, looking down at her clipboard. "Right now, she thinks she wants to major in physical education. Which would be nice, I guess. She could be intramurals chairman. Except, she'll probably change her mind when she gets on campus. Most of the PE majors are jocks."

Enough, Angie thought, getting up abruptly and diving into the pool. They all reminded her of Matt. Ungrateful. Not humbled by their good fortune.

She swam around for a while, knowing that she herself was now the topic under discussion. How could a Tarrington be so idealistic? She came from generations of money on both sides. Maybe having a retarded brother had screwed up her mind a bit, too. Her older brother was also strange—the son of a rich man studying to be a Unitarian minister! *Nobody* was Unitarian except eggheads and college professors.

Billie would be sticking up for her. They should all try to be a little more like Angie, she would tell them. They should listen to themselves sometimes. God, they were all such snobs.

She and Billie had been roommates their freshman year. A good match. They challenged each other and in the process were forced either to shore up their beliefs or alter them to fit into broadening horizons. The first thing they tackled was sorority rush—which Angie found disturbing. She herself arrived on campus a third generation legacy from a wealthy family. She was pretty enough, had been salutatorian of the best high school in Dallas, and her grandmother was a close personal friend of the national Pi Phi president. "And I didn't chew gum or bleach my hair," Angie told Billie. "So, Pi Phi almost had to give me a bid. But when girls started getting dropped midway through rush and had to pack up and go home, that really bothered me. Sorority is fine for those of us on the inside, but it sure sucks for the girls who get shut out."

"So, it's not fair," Billie said with an exaggerated shrug. "What in life is? Is it fair your little brother is retarded? Is it fair that my darling forty-year-old aunt Amy is dying of cancer? Is it fair that we have money and other people don't? I haven't seen you out on the sidewalk giving away your allowance and cashmere sweaters to less fortunate students."

Pragmatic Billie insisted that class served a purpose. If everyone was equal, who would clean houses and collect garbage? If people were smart enough, they rose to the top. But people with eighth-grade educations can't be bank presidents. Blind people can't be surgeons. Short people can't be basketball stars. Dumb people can't be math professors.

Class made people more comfortable, Billie insisted. Angie could be comfortable with family servants, and they with her, only when they all kept to their established roles. If Angie were to go to their home, no one would be comfortable. On a weekend home, Angie had tested Billie's theory and invited herself to Maura's home. She'd given Maura rides home before but never been inside the tiny house in Oak Cliff with a vegetable garden in the postage-stamp front yard. The inside of the house was immaculate, of course, and Angie recognized most of the furniture as Tarrington family castoffs. Maura was so nervous, Angie had been afraid she might a heart attack.

"But it's not fair that our families have everything and people like Maura have to live in a part of town where people get raped, robbed, and murdered," Angie insisted after telling Billie about her visit.

"So, you're back to 'fair' again," Billie said, rolling her eyes heavenward. "God, for a smart girl, you're really dumb. Rich people get raped, robbed, and murdered, too."

"White men are never executed for killing black men, but black men almost always are given the death sentence for killing a white person," Angie countered.

"When you're a lawyer, I suppose you'll do all pro

bono work," Billie said. "You'll spend your life working for the dregs of society."

"And what would you have me do? Handle society divorces?"

"Why can't you just sit back and enjoy what you have?" Billie challenged. "Don't you get tired of feeling bad about being fortunate?"

"Don't you think that, because people like us have so much, we have a greater obligation to give back?"

"Damn you, Angie," Billie had said in exasperation, "it would just kill my parents if I changed my major to social work."

Angie would almost have preferred living in the dorms next fall rather than moving in the Pi Phi house. But if she didn't play by the rules, they might not pledge Julia a year from now. And she couldn't do that to her sister. Julia wanted to be a Pi Phi like her sister. Like their mother had before them. And her mother before her. But when Julia was safely initiated, Angie planned to move out.

On bid day last year, Norma, and Grandma Edna, leaning heavily on a cane, had been waiting for her on the front lawn of the Pi Phi house, laden with corsages and gold Pi Phi jewelry for the new pledge. Both women had burst into tears when they saw Angie coming down the sidewalk. And they had all hugged and cried. Three generations of Pi Phis. Angie was thrilled to have made them so happy. The photographer had taken their picture. A day to remember always. And when Angie was initiated, they both had come again. Norma had pinned the gold Pi Phi arrow over her daughter's heart just as her own mother had done for her with the same pin almost twenty-five years before.

And even before Angie had traveled to Austin for rush week, getting ready for it had been a special time for her and her mother. They had spent weeks shopping for appropriate outfits for each day's parties, and Norma had gotten nostalgic about her own time as a college student.

"I was so in love with your father," she told Angie

over lunch in the restaurant at the North Park Neiman Marcus. "It was a lovely time with all the dances, parties, picnics, serenades. Even walking to class together and studying together at the library was delightful. But I made myself stop thinking about all that after he married Lucy. Our years together in Austin seemed tainted, and I tried to erase them. When he came back to me, I started the clock ticking anew. But now, with you on your way to Austin, I want to remember. I want to hear about everything you do and think. I want the next four years to be as wonderful for you as my time at UT was for me. It should be the most special time in your life. I want to live it all again through you, and through Julia when she goes there. I never had a sister to share it with. I'm so glad you girls have each other."

Angie remembered how her mother's eyes had shone, actually gotten misty, while she talked. It was the first time Angie had ever heard her mention Lucy by name. Her own going off to college somehow had helped her mother come to terms with what seemed to Angie as very old business. She wondered if there shouldn't be a statute of limitations on crimes of the heart.

Angie swam back across the pool to her Pi Phi sisters. "So, how's it going?" she asked, toweling herself off. "I was thinking about the girl from Plano. What was her name? Rachel something. She played first-chair flute in the state youth orchestra. Just think how neat it would be at our Christmas reception for the faculty to have a flute accompanist for the caroling?"

Billie smiled at her and winked.

Chapter Thirteen

*I*t was after six when Angie arrived home from the
country club. She was surprised to see that the table
wasn't set for dinner. Maura didn't come in on Wednes-
days, but her mother usually fixed something with pasta
or made a pot of soup. Sunday evenings, she made waf-
fles or omelets, and they ate in the kitchen.

"Welcome to Crisis City," Julia said, coming down
the stairs, her long brown legs bare in cutoff jeans.

"What's going on?" Angie asked.

"Well, the good news is that Danny didn't drown
Beth. The bad news is that Danny needs a keeper who's
bigger and stronger than he is. Beth's in the study with
Mom and Dad now. I imagine they are terminating her
services with a very large check."

The two sisters walked arm in arm to the terrace
and sat on the glider, while Julia explained the events of
the day.

Julia smelled faintly of chlorine, like always. Eau de
Julia, Matt called it. She was their fish. She had almost
as many trophies from swimming as Matt did for track.

With Frank in seminary in Massachusetts and Angie in college in Austin, the life of the Tarrington family
revolved, in great part, around the athletic activities of
Matt and Julia. Norma and Perry laughed about their
lack of social life. While others of their friends went to
parties and concerts, they went to track and swimming
meets. Almost every weekend. But Angie knew they
loved it. Danny usually went, too. And Beth. Then twice
a year, when the Special Olympians convened, the focus
was on Danny.

"Maybe Beth doesn't realize what a close call it was.

She's a whole lot more upset over the prospect of leaving than she is about what happened in the pool," Julia said.

"You must have been scared to death," Angie said, when Julia finished relating the events of the afternoon.

Julia nodded, her chin quivering. "I thought he was going to kill her. I was afraid for her and him both. Would they have sent Danny to jail?"

"Not jail. But probably someplace where he'd be kept locked up. Even for assault, Beth could have called the police and really made trouble."

"Yeah. Like I said, I imagine her severance pay will be more than generous."

"And so, the Beth period in our life is finally over. How do you feel about that?" Angie asked, using one foot to push the glider back and forth.

"Maybe Frank will come home more. It's not right that he comes only when she's away."

"It's for the best that she leave, you know."

"Yeah," Julia said, looking away. "I know."

"I often wondered why she stayed on after the business with Frank. She's earned her degree. What does she get from staying on with a family who no longer adores her?"

"Danny and money, I guess. Mom and Dad paid her more than she could get teaching school. Since her desanctification, I think Mom has actually been more comfortable with her around. Maybe Beth was more comfortable that way, too. And until Danny's hormones hit, she was wonderful with him. She really loves him, you know. You can see it in her face when she's with him. Maybe she's enjoyed doing for Danny what she never had the chance to do for her brother."

"Yes, she's been good for Danny," Angie admitted. "But I can't help think that she stayed on here because it suited her purposes, whatever they were. I don't think she ever planned to leave."

Angie leaned her head against the back of the glider. How beautiful it was here, with the rose garden, the magnolia trees, the willows, the lilacs and crepe myrtle. Manuel had installed a fountain this summer, and the gentle sound of water splashing added a sense of peacefulness and beauty. Angie closed her eyes and concentrated on the scent of the roses—Manuel's wonderful roses. The Tropicanas were in full bloom. The ones Manuel had planted for her wedding. One of these days, she'd have to start looking for a groom.

"Strange how all this conspicuous consumption can be so satisfying," she said. "That's what Thorstein Veblen called it. I studied one of his essays in honors English."

Julia made no response, and Angie realized that her sister's shoulders were shaking with silent sobs. She put an arm around her and pulled her close. "She's not worth your tears, honey. Really she's not."

"For a while I wondered if I was in love with her."

"I think we all did, one way or the other. She knew how to sparkle. How to make everything fun."

"I don't want to be a lesbian."

Angie didn't say anything for a time as realization sank in. *A lesbian?*

Should she have known that Beth seduced her sister?

"You're not a lesbian," Angie said, taking Julia's hand. "Everyone experiments. Rosemary Moore and I kissed each other in the seventh grade. Down in her basement."

"Beth and I did more than kiss. For several years."

Angie wanted to cry. To run in the house and find Beth. Hurt her. "She shouldn't have done that," she said. "You're just a kid."

"But I wanted her to come to my bed at night. I waited for her. Sometimes I cried when she didn't come."

"Look, Julia, I've seen you flick that cute little fanny of yours around guys. You like them to notice you. Beth was a phase you were going through—like when you were nuts over horses or wanted to be a nun."

"But what if she converted me? Everyone will hate me. Mom and Dad. Everyone."

"Honey, if you have 'converted,' I can safely promise that no one is going to hate you. Do you for one minute think that Mom and Dad are even capable of hating one of their children?"

"Why did she ever start with me in the first place? She didn't love me."

"For sex. And power. Because you wanted her to."

They didn't say anything for a time. A cricket was chirping in the rose garden. The glider needed oil.

"Did you know?" Julia asked.

"No. If I had, she would have been sent away a long time ago. Just like any guy who did that to you. Mom and Dad trusted her to do right by their children."

"I wouldn't have wanted Mom and Dad to know. Parenthood's been hard enough for them. You don't think she'll tell them, do you?"

Angie sighed. "I don't know. She might. But I promise you, they won't freak—at least not over you."

Beth had left for the evening by the time Angie and Julia went in. The sisters helped their parents put together a hasty meal in the kitchen. Danny set the table then went to summon Matt. "Does he know that Beth's leaving?" Angie asked.

"Your mother and I decided that we'll all go down to Padre this weekend," Perry explained. "When we get back, she'll be gone, and we can avoid tearful farewells. We told her to wait for a month or two before she came back to visit—long enough for Danny to have adjusted to the change."

Angie waited for Beth and met her at the back door when she came in. "I'm sure, knowing my parents, that they told you in their gracious way that you'd always be welcome in our home. But you've hurt my family, and I don't want you ever to come back here," she said, digging her fingernails into Beth's arm. "Not ever."

"I never meant to hurt anyone. I loved you all. Danny especially. No one could be sweeter than Danny."

"Yes, and he'll be heartbroken when he finds out

you've gone. But quite frankly, you don't deserve him, not after the way you screwed up Frank and Julia.''

Which was true. And there was another name she could have said but didn't. That name hung in the air between them. Beth knew who it was.

Chapter Fourteen

$\mathcal{D}$anny walked back and forth across the entrance to the driveway, from brick pillar to brick pillar, five giant steps over, ten regular ones back, constantly looking up the street to see if the big blue van was coming. The old van broke down, and some days it didn't come. He would wait and wait, till finally his mother came down the driveway in her car and drove him to work, and he would be late, but other people would be late, too, because of the broken van. Just the people who lived across the street from the factory in the big white house would be there on time.

His daddy had bought the new van for Jimbo to drive. A big blue one with ten seats. The old van had been blue, too, but it only had eight seats, and it wasn't shiny. And it didn't have words on the side. The new van had words that said Jobs for Friends. In white letters. Danny couldn't read the words, but his daddy told him what they said. Danny was a man now. Grown up. That's why he went to work. It was very, very important to go to work. And get paid money. Some people were too retarded to do work.

He used some money to buy videos. He liked to watch them over and over. And he used some money to buy presents for people. Maybe he'd buy another dog. Buddy was dead and buried behind the swimming pool.

Even with the new van, he still worried that it wouldn't come, and it made him feel happy when it turned the corner and he could see Jimbo in the driver's seat. Jimbo was nice. He could whistle better than anyone, and he could wiggle his ears. Jimbo was retarded, too, but only a little. He could read and tell time. He had a little plastic card with his picture on it that said he could drive.

Danny's mother got him a plastic card with his picture on it, but it wasn't for driving. It was for his telephone number and address in case he got sick—so the police would know how to call his mother. But he lost the card. So his mom had his name and phone number engraved on the back of the gold Special Olympics medal that he always wore around his neck to show that he was a champion.

He stomped up and down a few times to make his feet feel not so cold. He liked to blow out air and see it be white like smoke, but he didn't like cold.

His mother'd said it was time for him to go wait for the van. And she said don't forget his lunch box, like she always did—and to button his coat because it was cold this morning. But it seemed like he had been waiting at the gate a long time. The wind was making him colder and colder. He reached in his coat pocket and pulled out his gloves. They were new and hard to get on. Maybe by the time he got them on, the van would come around the corner.

Very carefully, he put on the gloves without once looking up to see if the van was coming. After he got the gloves on, he even counted to ten very slowly before he looked up the street, and sure enough, there was the van coming around the corner. Danny hopped up and down a couple of times. The van was coming! He was going to work!

When he got in the van, everyone said, "Hi, Danny." And Jimbo asked if he had taken any wooden nickels. He always asked him that. Danny had never seen a wooden nickel.

It was warm in the van. It would be warm at the factory. And everyone would talk about what they did on Saturday and Sunday and about the Cowboy game on television. And at lunch, he had a piece of Maura's chocolate cake for Mary Ann. Danny patted his lunch box. It was black. It was a man's lunch box, not one with

'toons. He liked 'toons—but not on his lunch box because he was a man.

And he was strong. He stacked up the boxes and
then loaded them on the truck when it came. When he
wasn't lifting boxes, he sanded the wooden handles until they felt very smooth. Like a baby's bottom, Mr. Leroy said, that's how smooth they were supposed to be.
Danny had never felt a baby's bottom, but he thought it
must be very smooth for Mr. Leroy to say that.

The other workers at the broom factory were all
retarded like him. Mary Ann Singleton was his best
friend. She was one of the Down's people and looked
funny. But she had big tits. He knew the names of almost everyone. He was the strongest so everyone knew
his name. They'd say look at Danny lift that big box. He
sure is strong. Beth taught him about being strong.
He still remembered Beth. His mother had said that he
would stop remembering Beth. But he still did. Beth
taught him about warming up and running and doing
pushups and going up and down the steps at the SMU
stadium and chinning himself on the bar in the basement and drinking lots of milk.

Beth went away. Like Frank did. But Frank came
back. He was a church man now and lived in the apartment over the garage. When his church had enough
money to buy an old white house by the church, he'd
move there. And Danny could spend the night sometimes. Help Frank work in the yard. Danny was a good
worker in the yard. He helped Manuel all the time. He
could rake leaves and put 'em in bags and hose 'round
the swimming pool.

The evenings when Frank was home, Danny would
go out to his apartment and tell him good night. Frank
would give him a glass of milk or juice and read him a
book. Danny liked that. The best book in the whole
world was about Bartholemew Chubbins and his five
hundred hats, and Frank read it better than anyone. He
had a different voice for all the people.

Beth never came back. College boys from her
school came to stay in her room and be his friend. He

used to love Beth. Boy-girl love. He knew it was boy-girl love because that is when you think about a girl lots. And you want to be with her more than anyone, even your mom and dad. Then one night, Beth wasn't at dinner, and her stuff was gone from her room, and he never saw her anymore. It made him cry and cry. And he didn't want to eat. Matt said it was his own fault for feeling Beth's tits. You can only do that when a girl wants you to, and no girl would ever want him to 'cause he was retarded.

But Beth loved him. She said so all the time. If Beth had told him she was gonna go away if he didn't stop feeling her tits, he would have sat on his hands all the time. His mom said that he would feel better soon and stop thinking about girls all the time. And he mustn't feel bad about Beth. It had been time for her to go be a teacher in a school for retarded kids like him.

His mom was right. He didn't think about girls all the time. Just sometimes. Like when he'd been close to a girl. And she smelled nice. And he wanted to touch her. Jimbo said that just because they were retarded didn't mean they didn't think about girls. Danny wondered if other retarded guys thought about girls in their bed at night and did it in a towel. Maybe sometime he'd ask Jimbo. But Jimbo was only a little retarded. He could drive and tell time.

After Beth went away, first Larry came and then Jerry and then Big Bob. One of the Three Stooges was named Larry. Larry hadn't stayed very long, and Danny couldn't remember his face—just that he was very big and made the basement into a gym with a punching bag, weights and a bicycle that didn't move. And they would go down there in the evening and make themselves strong. Matt and Dad and Julia came sometimes. And Frank. Julia was stronger than Frank.

After Larry left and Jerry came, they still went down to the gym but Jerry liked to run, and he and Danny would run on the track at SMU every evening and sometimes along Turtle Creek. Jerry could play the harmonica. "She'll Be Comin' Round the Mountain

When She Comes" and "Mister Moon" and "Froggy
Went a Courtin'." Lots of songs. Danny liked to sing the
words while Jerry played the music. He was sorry when
Jerry went away to work on a big boat and see someplace 'sides Dallas, Texas.

Big Bob came next. He taught Danny how to stand
in front of the basket and hold the ball with both hands
and whoosh it through the hoop. Danny couldn't drib-
ble the ball, but he could get it in the basket almost
every time. Big Bob said Danny was a deadeye. Big Bob
didn't sleep anymore in Beth's old room, but he'd
come over to run and swim with Danny. And shoot baskets. Big Bob was saving his money to buy a restaurant,
and when he did, he said that Danny could be his official dishwasher.

Except Danny liked the broom factory. He had
friends there. He hoped Big Bob wouldn't be mad at
him. But he had to lift the boxes. He was strong.

Sometimes Danny wished he could tell Beth about
his job. He wanted her to know that he was grown up.
When he said that, his mother would frown and say that
she was surprised he still remembered Beth, that it had
been a long time since Beth had been with them. But
he did. He remembered her a lot. He had a picture of
her in the bottom of the cigar box where he kept pictures of his friends from school. She was sitting on the
diving board with Buddy. Buddy was dead and Beth was
gone. Sometimes he looked at Beth's picture and felt
sad. Other times, he wanted to tear it into little tiny
pieces and flush them down the toilet. But he didn't
because if he did, the picture would be gone and he
might want to look at it again sometime. And it
wouldn't be okay to tear up a picture of Buddy. Buddy
had been a good dog.

He didn't love Beth anymore. She had promised
they would always be friends. Forever and ever, she said.
She wanted him to be strong and healthy and know how
to take care of himself so he wouldn't die like her
brother who had not looked both ways and gotten run
over. Danny remembered how Beth had kissed his eyes

and nose and mouth. And rubbed his muscles when they got sore. And tickled his ribs to make him laugh. And held his hand when they went for a walk. And sang songs with him. And hugged him when he did good or cried. And let him brush her hair and put suntan oil on her back and shoulders and legs. And watch her put on makeup and paint her toenails. And dance with her to music. But she had lied. Sometimes when he remembered being happy with Beth, he would smile. But then he remembered that she went away without ever saying good-bye. And she never called him on the phone or sent him a birthday card or postcards like Frank did when he went away. Frank sent postcards all the time. With a different picture on every one.

Chapter Fifteen

"Those guys are never going to let me get a Ph.D.," Nathan insisted from the other side of the foldout shelf that served as his kitchen table.

"How come, other than the fact you'll probably never get around to writing a dissertation?" Julia asked, holding her wineglass out for a refill of the really incredible merlot. Nathan refused to take money from his parents, but he did raid their wine cellar on his trips home to Houston. A real wine cellar apparently, with a vaulted roof and rack after rack of vintage wines from the world's best wineries. She knew without asking that his parents lived in River Oaks, which made Dallas's Highland Park look quaint. Houston was the old-money capital of Texas.

"Hey, I already have a topic—the establishment in Texas politics," Nathan said indignantly. "I could write a damned fine dissertation, but it wouldn't make any difference. They'll let me hang around and teach American history to the freshmen for another year or two. But the master's is a terminal degree for guys like me. The esteemed faculty of the history department only grant Ph.D.s to serious scholars—not to the lost boys who hang out in graduate school as long as they can to put off whatever comes after—like wearing suits, civic responsibility, joining the country club."

"So, why are you still here?" she asked, helping herself to the last of the salad and another slice of French bread. She'd finished her omelet. Nathan was great with omelets—and soup, stews, gumbo. She tried to think if she'd ever cooked for him in all the years she'd known him—other than grilled cheese sand-

wiches. She'd have to do that sometime. He could bring
the wine.

"I am still here because it's been easier to delude
myself than face reality."

"So what are you going to do?"

"Ah, what *does* one do when forced to disembark
from the fine old ship of academia and enter that alien
land called adulthood? This is my eighth year at UT—
and your seventh, I believe. And all that time, I have
been practicing disdain for the world from whence I
came. I've always known that I'll never have a secretary,
do business lunches, attend board meetings. I will never
give up my ponytail. The gold earring is a part of my
very soul. Right? Tell me that I'm right."

"But you love good wine and fine cuisine," Julia
reminded him as he cleared away dirty dishes from the
shelf. She scooted her wooden stool against the wall so
he could open the door of the ancient refrigerator and
get out a wedge of cheese.

"And you're tired of shut-off notices from the utility companies," Julia continued. "You're really sick of
cockroaches and rusty hot-water heaters that only heat
enough water for half a shower. And remember ironed
sheets? Swimming laps before breakfast in the backyard
pool? Dressing up? Eating great meals in really snobby
restaurants? I miss fluffy white towels and manicures.
I'm tired of having my parents love me in spite of what
I've become."

"And what have you become?"

"A pseudobohemian—which translates into not
much of anything. You're right about graduate school.
I'm here to avoid making any decision about the future.
I think graduate-level courses in educational theory and
educational philosophy are a crock. I don't need those
courses to teach retarded kids—provided I really have
the courage to do that. Every semester, I think about
quitting. But I'm scared shitless of leaving Never-Never
Land. I love my brother Danny, but maybe I'm not noble enough to spend my life working with the 'mentally
challenged,' as we refer to them in the College of Ed.

But can I go back to the world from whence I came? I'm not lady material. I hate propriety. I like having my life measured out by semesters with the opportunity for a fresh start always just around the corner."

"I wish we could have just kept on swimming," Nathan said wistfully.

Julia nodded in agreement. Those were the good years. Training. Being on a team. Striving, always striving to be the best she could be. Feeling the elation of getting better and of the occasional victory. Having an identity that set her apart and excused her from the mundane. Her Pi Phi sisters didn't expect her to serve on committees or show up on time. She was an *athlete*. She had a higher calling. She sometimes wondered if anything would ever be so perfect again. If friendships would ever be so sweet. If hopes and dreams would ever be so clear-cut. She already knew her body would never achieve the same level of fitness. Her muscles had lost definition. All those laps that she swam every day at the university pool weren't the same. They were exercise—not training.

She would have kept on swimming competitively forever if she could, but a swimmer had to be world class to compete past college. Like Nathan, she had placed a few times in conference meets. Never qualified for the NCAA. Was not Olympics-bound. Her undergraduate degree was in psychology, Nathan's in history—fields that required graduate degrees or teacher's certificates before gainful employment became a possibility.

"Do you ever think it's inevitable?" Nathan asked, carefully placing a wedge of apple between two slices of cheese.

"Depends on what you mean by 'it.' "

"That we become our parents."

Julia allowed herself a sigh and another sip of wine. "A year ago I would have said no way, but now I'm not so sure. Thing is, I admire my parents. They've done a damned good job of being who they are. Of course, it wasn't like they've had to grovel around for money. Dig-

nity was never hard to maintain. But they put us kids
first. My mother always did. My dad had his father and
societal expectations to deal with first, but he came
around. I never understood what a gift they gave us kids
until I stepped back from that world so I could criticize
it and them, and I realized I didn't want to. And now, I
think about having kids and putting them first, but I'm
not sure I have the courage."

"But maybe kids are the consolation prize."

"What do you mean?" she asked.

"First prize is finding someone to be passionately
in love with for a lifetime."

"You can't have both?" Julia asked, knowing that
she, at least, never could—she, of the screwed-up sexu-
ality. When she was with a man, she wanted him to be a
woman. And the times when she'd fallen off the wagon
and found herself in bed with a woman, she longed for
a man. Orgasms were overly powerful, drug-induced
trips that were as dishonest as steroid-induced muscles
and plagiarized words—not really hers, not really part
of the normal human experience and left her feeling
isolated and alone, like an abandoned space traveler
floating around in the great black void. As a rule, she
preferred alcohol as her crutch. Sex was best when
she'd had just the right amount of booze—before she
crossed the line into total drunkenness but was freed of
inhibitions enough to value the intimacy more than the
gender of the person.

No, she was hardly a candidate for being "passionately in love with someone for a lifetime." But then,
neither was Nathan. He had lived too long as an ob-
server of the human condition ever to be a successful
participant.

"No, people like us can't have both," he was explaining. "All the pot, booze, screwing around, and late-
night philosophizing have left us jaded. There's no wonder left."

"Except through the eyes of a child," Julia said.

Nathan leaned against the sink, folded his arms
across his chest. "But what if we've gotten too intro-

verted, with all the mind trips and journeys through our inner soul, to be good parents?''

During his swimming days, Nathan had looked the part. Close-cropped bleached-out hair. Total leaness. He'd even tried shaving his head, chest, and limbs to diminish water drag.

Now he looked like a scuzzy graduate student. Hairy. Unkempt. Library pallor. He never used the word physique anymore. But even with unironed shirts, ponytail, and earring, Julia knew her mother would actually approve of Nathan Pearson. Not that she'd ever expressed disapproval for any of Julia's ''men friends'' in the past. ''Jesus, Mom!'' Julia once blurted out. ''Don't you know you're supposed to freak over your daughter hanging out with worthless drug-head musicians who have no ambition or future, who shack up with me because it's better than sleeping in their van?''

Her mother's approval of Nathan would have nothing to do with his pedigree—even though a park in Houston was named for his grandfather.

During her undergraduate days, while she was still playing the part of sorority girl, Julia had been engaged to a man she thought would please any girl's mother. Abner Chesbro stood to inherit millions, was top in his class at the law school, and had an eye on a political career. Grandfather Clifford had been totally impressed with him. Julia's father indifferent. Her mother cool. When pressed to explain why, Norma said simply that Abner seemed ''a bit self-centered.''

Her mother was right, of course. Julia now realized that the only reason she'd allowed herself to become engaged to Abner was because he had no capacity for love, and she therefore would not feel any great responsibility for making him happy.

Their engagement first began to unravel over movies. Abner seemed to think that it was some sort of male prerogative to select the movies they watched. Abner became irritated when she balked at his choices. Which made her find other things to irritate him. Inevitably, he asked for the ring back.

The next time Julia went home, Norma reached for
Julia's left hand, took note of its ringless state, and gave
her daughter a hug.

"You were worried, weren't you?" Julia asked

"Not really," her mother answered. "I didn't think
you'd really marry him, and if you did, I knew it would
never last."

But Julia knew that her mother would approve of
Nathan because, were she ever to meet him, she would
see at once that he was kind and decent. Norma had
unerring radar when it came to kindness and decency.

Not that it mattered what her mother thought.
Julia and Nathan had been friends since their under-
graduates days, since they lived next door on Greek row
and saw each other daily at the pool. They'd never
dated, just hung out some. That's what they did now.
Hung out. Sometimes, they had low-key sex after a bottle of wine and free-flowing conversation. She didn't
even try to have an orgasm with him. That made it easy
to curl up with him afterward and fall into a gentle
sleep.

They'd never even discussed living together. She
believed, and maybe he did, too, that moving in together would be the kiss of death. Instead of friends
who occasionally screwed, they'd be in a *relationship*.
And it would end—badly. With yelling and pain. She'd
never see him again. That was the pattern.

Julia always scrubbed her apartment from top to
bottom after parting company with a man. And for a
few weeks she would feel strong and secure. She didn't
need some guy to clutter up her apartment and her life.
But she'd always take up with someone else. Not someone she'd marry. Just some male person to occupy
space in her bed for a time. She liked the smell of a
young, healthy man clean from the shower or sweaty
after sex. But after a time, she'd start being a bitch so
he'd want to leave and she'd be spared the nastiness of
locking him out. She'd done that once, and the guy had
kicked in the door, beat her up and trashed the place

pretty bad. No one had ever hit her before. She sobbed all night, more from the indignity than the pain.

She'd had to camouflage the bruises with makeup the next time her mother came to check on her Grandpa Paul. He lived in a nursing home now, refusing to move to Dallas and live with his family. He needed to put fresh flowers on Grandma Edna's grave every week. If his daughter or granddaughter didn't show up to take him to the cemetery, he'd call a cab. Except of late, he sometimes forgot that Edna was dead and demanded to be taken home. Or couldn't remember in which cemetery she was buried.

The last time Julia went with her mother to the nursing home, Grandpa Paul hadn't recognized her.

"This is Julia," Norma explained. "My younger daughter. The one who swam in all those races. She takes you to the cemetery sometimes."

"I didn't know you had children," he said.

"You sure that you want to do this—the white dress and respectability?" Angie asked when Julia brought Nathan home to meet the family. Maura's arthritis was acting up. They'd sent her home and were cleaning up after dinner.

"The white dress is for Mom. I don't know about respectability. Maybe that's for her, too. Maybe not." Julia covered the leftover asparagus and put it in the refrigerator.

"Why is it so important for you all of a sudden to get married and start teaching?" Angie asked as she rinsed off plates. "You certainly haven't seemed in any rush before."

"True. But suddenly, I needed to move on. Nathan, too. We simultaneously arrived at a point where we needed to graduate from limbo—even if it means living on family money. I think Mom's going to let us live in Grandma Edna and Grandpa Paul's house. Maybe his folks would pay for a pool. We'd like one big enough for laps. And we could raise animals and tomatoes. Kids, too, maybe. Someday. I think we have to prove to ourselves that we're worthy first.''

"You seem okay about this. Do you love him?''

"We get along. I've never been able to say that I loved anyone except my family. But I kind of feel related to Nathan. I told him about Beth. He told me about his nasty uncle.''

"I like him,'' Angie said.

"Grandfather Clifford doesn't,'' Julia said.

"What greater testimonial could you hope for?''

Chapter Sixteen

"*H*e's your brother," Norma said softly, fingering her wineglass, not allowing herself to be angry. Not yet. "I'd think you'd want to include him in your wedding party."

They were having lunch out, just her and Matt, something they hadn't done for years, not since she'd carefully planned her days and weeks to make sure she spent sufficient time with each of the other children. That's how she often thought of Frank, Angie, Julia, and Matt—"the other children." Danny's needs were always so immediate that it took a concerted effort to parcel herself out to the rest.

Life was easier now. Danny had his wonderful job, and Norma herself had a new cause—Jobs for Friends, what a godsend that organization had turned out to be! Matt was getting married and starting law school in the fall. Angie was living at home for now, working long days and some nights with legal aid and organizing fund-raisers for Jobs for Friends, trying as always to assuage her guilt over having been born rich.

Norma had given Julia and Nathan her parents' house in Austin, grateful not to have to sell it. They swam a lot. Gardened with a passion. Took in stray animals. Volunteered at the homeless shelter, women's shelter, animal shelter. And had endless discussions about what to do with their lives.

Frank had moved into the church parsonage, but she lunched with him every Wednesday, and he came to dinner most Sundays. After church. She still hadn't joined his Unitarian church. But she was weakening.

Religion wasn't so important anymore. Family was more of a religion with her than Episcopalianism.

She and Matt had been shopping for his fiancée's wedding gift—for lovely Gretchen, whom Norma was already starting to love. They had narrowed the choices to a string of opera-length pearls with a diamond-and-ruby clasp or an unusual gold bracelet set with diamonds and turquoise and were having lunch at the Mansion while they decided. Norma was high with the sheer pleasure of sharing this beautiful son of hers with no one, of lunching with him in this fine old establishment—until he told her Danny wasn't going to be his best man. And she felt the pleasure of the day dissolving all around her, the soft focus fading.

"Everyone would be waiting to see if he picks the flowers or blows out the candles," Matt was explaining. "Gretchen and I have talked about it. Danny can ask people to sign the guest book. He can usher you and Granny Belle down the aisle. You can list him as a groomsman in the newspaper. But he can't stand with us during the ceremony. He has to sit with you so you can make sure he keeps his pants zipped."

"Matt, that's cruel! You know that hasn't been a problem for years."

"Yeah, I know. I'm sorry. Danny's very well behaved for a retarded person, but that's not good enough for our wedding."

Norma looked away, out the window at the courtyard, not wanting to see the face that her son was now wearing—the face of the other Matt, the one she almost didn't like. The petulant child. The boy who resented his brother's special needs. And she felt guilt pushing her down. She hadn't done a good job with Matt. His faults were of her making. She had shortchanged him by trying too hard with Danny.

Propriety was not Danny's long suit. He didn't do anything outrageous, but his voice got too loud when he was excited. He stared at people he found strange or pretty. She had to remind him constantly not to talk with his mouth full, not to put his finger in his nose, to control belches and farts—and not giggle when one accidentally escaped. But he could rise to the occasion and wear his best behavior like a suit for church. She would coach him. They would practice over and over what he was supposed to do. And he would be so proud. So dear.

Norma took a sip of wine. And another. "He's your twin, Matt. And he'll never have a wedding of his own. Don't you think he deserves to be at your side when you get married?"

"Come on, Mom, even if he behaves exactly right, people will be watching him, not us, and holding their breath. And can you really promise that he won't say something or start humming a tune? Or tug on his underwear or turn around and wave at you? Frank's officiating. I'm going to ask Dad to be best man. Julia and Angie will both be bridesmaids. The family hardly will be underrepresented in the wedding party. Look, Mom, I'd like nothing better than to have Danny at my side when I get married. He's my brother, and I love him. And admire him. Who ever thought he'd be able to go to work every day? He's got real character. In fact, Gretchen and I plan to name our first son Daniel. Danny will never have children, so we thought that's the least that we could do. And no boy could have a better uncle than Danny."

"You mean that?" Norma said, touched to the point of tears. And Matt's face was beautiful again. He did love his brother. "That's a lovely gesture, Matt. Really lovely."

"I know that I've been a real jerk about Danny at times," Matt said, putting his hand over his mother's. "He was dumb and still got more attention than I did. It was hard to figure sometimes. But even after I was old enough to understand, I still got jealous. And mean. I'd hide his toys, booby-trap his closet, hang his teddy bear from the chandelier and tell him it was dead. I'd tell him that too much ice cream would make his lips freeze and fall off and that huge, man-eating spiders were marching across Texas on their way to Dallas. Some of those nightmares he had were probably my fault. It amazes me, sometimes, that he loves me anyway. He's always so glad to see me that he makes me feel bad that I don't do more with him."

"He had a wonderful time on his birthday with you and Gretchen. He has the picture of the three of you with the sheriff and outlaws tacked on his bulletin board."

"Six Flags was Gretchen's idea. I would have just bought him a video game and a card. She's really great with him, and we had a ball. A real ball. We rode every ride out there. And watched the gunfight and the puppet show. Danny gets so excited. Being with him is like being a kid again. I didn't even care that people stared at us, trying to figure out how Danny and I could be so alike and so different. But I just can't risk having him screw up the wedding. It wouldn't be fair to Gretchen. You know how girls are. Gretchen's been planning her wedding since she was three."

Yes, Norma thought, remembering all her own daydreams and plans for the wedding she never had. Would she have been willing to risk a less-than-perfect wedding to include the groom's retarded brother in the ceremony?

"It's just that I've had this notion in my head for so long," she said. "Danny can't get married. I'm beginning to doubt if Frank ever will. You may be the only one of my sons to have a wedding, and I wanted it to be special for the three of you. But then that doesn't really make sense, does it? Gretchen is marrying you, not your brothers."

Gretchen Schneider looked like Lucy Ledbetter— with masses of white-blond hair, vividly blue eyes, skin like satin, long legs, voluptuous. A Viking princess.

Norma met her first—Matt had brought her by one Saturday afternoon. Proudly. Showing her off to his mother, even though they'd only gone out twice. Norma knew he was serious about this girl.

She had not forewarned Perry about Gretchen. The first time he met her, he actually stammered. He managed to tell her that he knew her father and was sorry to hear about his illness, sorry he wasn't well enough to join them tonight before excusing himself to pour a fresh drink. And then another in quick succession.

Of course, Gretchen and Lucy really didn't look alike so much as they were the same type. Lucy had had higher cheekbones and a narrower face. Her eyes had been lapis blue. Gretchen's eyes were more turquoise. Gretchen had a fuller face, a warmer smile, and dimples that made her seem less intimidating than elegant. But women like Gretchen and Lucy—the bold, statuesque, born blonds, with full mouths and breasts, slim hips, perfect teeth and features, with the assurance that comes from being as beautiful as youth and nature permit—were so rare that people tended to elevate and revere them.

Perry had held his anger in check all evening, but after the good-byes, he exploded. "Why in hell didn't you tell me?" he demanded, pulling off his shoes and throwing first one and then the other hard in the direction of his closet. "Did you enjoy watching me see a ghost?"

"I guess I wanted to see how you would react," Norma said, stepping out of her shoes, pulling off her earrings. "You still think about her, don't you?"

"Only when I see someone like Gretchen. And your not warning me about that young woman's appearance makes me think that you've never forgiven me."

"Perhaps at some level," Norma admitted, perched on a corner of the bed, toying with her earrings. "I guess the old hurt is still buried in there someplace, but I only think about Lucy when you get remote, when I wonder if you regret our life."

"Come on, Norma," he was saying, "have I really been such a rotten husband that I'm still on probation after thirty-three years?"

"Of course not. You're a wonderful man. A fine

husband and father. But, foolishly perhaps, we women want to be loved more than anything. I guess it hardly ever works out that way, though, and when it did for Lucy, she up and killed herself."

Warning signals were going off in Norma's head. She'd had too much to drink. She'd been nervous about meeting Gretchen's stepmother and uncle. No, that wasn't what made her nervous. It was knowing that she'd set Perry up for a shock when he saw Gretchen. All through dinner, she had avoided her husband's gaze and reached for her wineglass. And she had several brandies after dinner. And now her tongue was loose. She should go take her bath right this minute and not say another word.

Perry allowed himself a long sigh. "The way I felt about Lucy wasn't healthy. Like Frank was about Beth Williams. It was bound to end badly. But I told you all this years ago. I can't believe I'm having to talk about it again."

Norma could see herself in the mirror over the dresser. And sat up a little straighter. She had a tendency to slump even after a lifetime of her mother's reminding her to stand tall, to sit like a lady. But still, she was a stylish woman. Slim. Athletic. Tan. "Lovely" was the word most often used to describe her. But lovely was a cool word. She wasn't a cool person. "I've often wondered if you told Lucy that you loved her only when you were making love—like you do with me," she said, still studying her reflection. "Or if sometimes you would feel the need to tell her over dinner or during a television commercial."

As soon as she said the words, Norma wanted to take them back. Her mother had always said to leave well enough alone. That's what she and Perry had. Well enough. Not more or less. Well enough to continue as man and wife, to share their family and life.

She could not bear the stunned look on her husband's face and escaped to her bathroom. And soaked for a long time, her mind in a fog. A fog surrounding the ghostly form of Lucy Ledbetter. Which was so stupid. Lucy had killed herself long, long ago, leaving Norma in possession of her husband and son. Ancient history. Think about tomorrow. About the Special Olympics board meeting. Tennis at the club. A fund-raising dinner for the governor's reelection campaign.

When she emerged, Perry was still sitting on the love seat, fully clothed but for his shoes, his necktie loose around his neck. He looked tired. And old. Older than Norma had ever seen him look.

"I do love you, Norma," he said in an old, tired voice. "I'm sorry I haven't been very good about letting you know it."

Yes, she thought. He did love her. A safe, respectful sort of love. And what was the matter with that? Not the sort of love that seared souls, but the sort of love that endured.

She was almost fifty-five years old. She had been a silly young girl when she convinced herself that Perry was the love of a lifetime. The grand passion. Two souls who touched. Even after all these years, she still felt cheated. Still wondered if they could have had that sort of love if it hadn't been for Lucy. Or maybe she had chosen unwisely. Maybe she should have looked further for a man with fire in his eyes and hunger in his kiss. For a man who knew his mind well enough to break away from a tyrant father before middle age set in. And maybe if she had found such a man, he would have broken her heart. Certainly, he would not have given her the same set of children, whom she loved more fiercely than she loved Perry. But her need for her husband was greater than her need for her children. She needed Perry for a lifetime. She would not leave him even if the man with fire in his eyes came at last to adore her.

She went over and knelt in front of Perry, took him in her arms. And began to tell him about the day she realized that she was truly in love with him after all those years of just assuming they'd grow up and get married. He was playing volleyball on the beach at Padre and looked over his shoulder at her. Smiled at her.

Just her. The most beautiful boy on the beach. After the
game they walked for hours. Just the two of them and
the ocean. Really talking for the first time. By the time
the sun touched the horizon, she had taken out her
heart and written his name on it. And his name was still
there. Would always be there.

Chapter Seventeen

$\mathcal{D}$anny was absolutely smitten with the image of himself in a tuxedo. He insisted on getting dressed hours before it was time to leave for the church, promising he would stay out of the kitchen and not spill anything on himself. "I look like a prince in a storybook," he announced, standing in front of the full-length mirror in his mother's dressing room.

"Indeed you do," Norma agreed and came to stand beside him in her shimmery emerald green gown. Not bad for a mother of the groom, she thought, assessing her own image.

"And you look like a queen," Danny said, regarding the two of them in the mirror. "The most beautiful queen in the whole wide world. You need a crown for your head."

"Why thank you, Prince Danny," Norma said, tossing a kiss to his mirrored image. "You know something? I'm very, very, very glad that you're my son."

"Me, too," he said, throwing a kiss back.

"And now, my prince, I'd like the first dance of the evening with you," Norma said, taking his hand and executing a formal curtsy.

Danny adjusted the radio dial to his favorite country and western station and sedately they twirled around the bedroom to the strains of Kenny Rogers bemoaning the errant Lucille.

After a minute, a tuxedo-clad Perry emerged from his dressing room and joined them. The three of them together. Twirling until they were dizzy and ended their dance with a three-way embrace.

With one arm around her husband of so many

years and the other around the larger man who was their little boy, Norma closed her eyes. Remember this sweet moment always, she commanded herself.

Danny took his job as guest-book attendant seriously, making absolutely sure that no one slipped by without writing his or her name in the white book. Even his parents and grandparents were instructed to sign in. At one point, it occurred to him that he also should sign the book. Laboriously he printed Danny Tarrington in big block letters. He still made the *g* backward. Even Beth the miracle worker had not been able to teach him to make a front-facing *g*. Norma no longer corrected him. That's who he was—Danny Tarrington with the *g* backward.

She wondered if Danny felt slighted by being left out of the wedding party. Probably not, especially since he would be sitting with her. He knew that no one would slight his mother.

When the moment came, she took Danny's arm, walked down the aisle with him, and sat down beside Clifford and Belle. Norma felt a moment of deep, overwhelming sadness that her parents weren't here with them and drew in her breath, fighting for control. Belle reached over and took her hand. "They're with us, dear," she said.

Gretchen was a breathtaking bride, radiant on the arm of her retired-colonel father in his military uniform. Joseph Schneider, after years of fighting cancer, was joyous that he had lived to see this day.

Norma watched Matt's face as he watched his bride come down the aisle. Did he really love Gretchen or did he love the idea of marrying such a glorious woman, she wondered. And did Gretchen really love Matt or was she in love with love and the idea of becoming a wife before her father died and providing a grandchild for him to hold in his arms?

During the ceremony, Clifford pulled out his handkerchief and wept openly at the wedding of his favorite grandchild. His favorite person. He'd always been foolish over Matt. Matt was the only one of her children Clifford deemed worthy of his very conditional love. Her other children recognized Matt's special status and had come to accept it over the years. Their other three grandparents scrupulously avoided favoritism. Clifford announced it to the world.

Although less enormous than before, Clifford was still a mountain of a man. He had already lived longer than could reasonably be expected for an obese man. Clifford didn't smoke anymore, except for his afterdinner cigar, but he drank and ate to excess with seemingly little fear of dying—his favorite afterdinner toast was "May we live forever." Perry had disappointed him, but Matt was going to make up for that. Matt would carry the Tarrington seed into the next generation. Matt would be governor if he played his cards right. But surely Clifford realized he could never live long enough to see that happen. Surely.

Norma, too, had come prepared with a handkerchief, knowing she would cry seeing Matt get married. But she hadn't expected to be so moved by the words of the service. Frank's words. About how the road through marriage and family was not always an easy one. How there would be times of sickness and tragedy and incredible fear. But there would also be times of accomplishment and hope and incredible joy. "I think that ultimately what separates good marriages from not-so-good marriages is teamwork. Pulling together. Facing both the downhill and uphill stretches with the sure knowledge that each will carry a fair share of the burden and do so gladly with love and concern and respect."

From his place at Matt's side, Perry looked over his shoulder at Norma and mouthed the words "I love you." For all to see. They had endured. He had tears in his eyes, too.

And for the second time that day, Beth Williams pushed her way into Norma's thoughts. Their family had endured, in part, because of Beth. It almost seemed like she should be here. Almost.

Years later, after Beth was long dead, Angie would find herself staring at the picture of Danny that she kept on the back of her rolltop desk and find herself replaying the Beth years, searching for clues that she had failed to notice at the time, clues that would help her understand. Beth had almost destroyed them, but Angie had never been able to decide if that was by happenstance or intent. Had she targeted their family or stumbled on them? Was she simply an opportunist or were there deeper motives?

Outwardly, photographs seemed absolutely truthful, a moment in time faithfully recorded down to the minutest detail—but usually they represent a posed moment with people aware of the camera, posturing themselves, putting on their picture smiles, often not giving a hint of what was in their hearts.

Even Danny would wear his say-cheese smile whenever a camera was pointed in his direction. But not in this picture—the picture that had come to signify for Angie the paradox of Beth.

At the instant the picture was snapped, Danny had been totally unaware of the camera and photographer. The gold medal for his Special Olympics victory had just been placed around his neck. His hands were clutching the medal to his heart, his eyes closed, his head thrown back, his lips parted in ecstasy, the expression on his face so sweet, so joyful, so grateful. He was a winner! The whole family was there watching—Frank, too, home for the summer after his first year in seminary. All were crying, cheering, hugging each other, hugging Beth, thanking her again and again. She'd done that for Danny. She'd run with him every day, taught him about warming up, starting blocks, waiting for the gun, concentration, wanting something enough to work for it and even to endure pain in pursuit of it. For years, Danny had watched from the sidelines while his wondrous brother Matt won races and matches and games, and his talented sister Julia won trophies for swimming. And now, Beth had made him a champion, too.

Beth had cared about Danny. Angie had to believe that. She'd never seen any evidence otherwise. Beth's affection, and even love, for Danny was sincere. Beth once told Angie she would do for Danny what she never had the chance to do for her own brother. Beth wasn't a sentimental sort of person. She seldom ever spoke of her brother unless asked. But she had cared about him, too. Perhaps, like Frank, Beth thought that loving someone like Danny or her brother was the only safe love. But Beth's brother died, and Danny's parents fired her. There was no such thing as safe.

The evening after that meet, Perry had made a little speech after dinner about how Beth had given them a family memory they would treasure for the rest of their lives. Then he said, "Danny and I went shopping. We have a little surprise for you, Beth."

Danny was so excited that he forgot the words he had rehearsed. "A car," he blurted out, thrusting the keys in Beth's hands. "We got you a car." Then he jumped up and pulled her from her chair, and they went racing out to the garage to show her the new red VW convertible. Beth cried. "I love you all so much," she'd said. "You are my family. My only family."

After the success of Danny's first meet, the Tarrington family became involved in Special Olympics events as judges, timekeepers, huggers. It became a part of their lives and, along with Danny himself, their shared cause. The Tarrington name became synonymous in Dallas with Special Olympics.

Even when Danny was too old to compete, the family continued its involvement in Special Olympics. The year before Beth's death, Norma served as state chairman.

Beth had changed their lives, Angie acknowledged. But who was she, and why had she singled out their family? And why in the hell had she come back to their house to get herself murdered?

BOOK
TWO

Chapter Eighteen

*C*lifford leaned toward Norma and whispered, "Well if they're getting along 'just fine,' why isn't she pregnant yet?"

"Why do you keep asking me that?" Norma whispered back. "I'm not in charge of their family planning." She looked at her watch. Why were funerals always late in starting?

"I ask because I want to know," he snapped.

Norma glanced to her left to see if Perry was aware that his father was interrogating her. Again. But Perry was having his own whispered conversation with Nathan. And on the other side of Clifford, Belle was huddled with Angie.

"I don't know," Norma said, and pointedly directed her attention to the printed program.

Clifford placed both hands on top of his cane and sagged back against his seat. In his late eighties, he was still oversized but shrinking inside of baggy skin as he approached the end of his life. It was a marvel that he lived on. And still went to the office almost every day, still was the moving force behind the law firm his father had founded. "Is something the matter with her?" he demanded. "Has she been to see a doctor?" He was forgetting to whisper.

Norma put a finger to her lips and lowered her own voice to an even more discreet tone. "Look, Clifford, with a dying father, Gretchen's had about all she could handle."

"They haven't talked to you about it?"

"No. They have not." She wanted to say it was none of her business—or his. But Clifford was into succession. His whole outlook on family and the future, on how he would dispense his fortune, rested on the status of Gretchen's uterus.

"A pity Joe died before he saw his first grand-child," Clifford said, looking toward the flag-draped casket in the front of the funeral home chapel.

"He lived long enough to see his daughter happily married," Norma reminded him.

"A pity," Clifford repeated. "Of course, it's not like he'd had a son. His line wasn't going to continue."

" 'Lines' come and go, and the world keeps turn-ing," Norma whispered.

Clifford decided to stare at Joseph's casket rather than respond to her comment. Norma leaned close. "I'm curious, Clifford. What will happen to your estate if Matt and Gretchen don't produce an heir?"

His eyes still on the casket, Clifford's chin sagged against his chest and he sighed. "Establish a founda-tion, I suppose—to keep the fortune intact. I don't want some judge dividing it up and neutralizing it."

The man actually saw himself as a tragic figure, Norma realized. His "line" might die out. His estate wouldn't have a suitable home. She didn't know if she should hate or pity her father-in-law. Family was not about money and power and pride. Family was about love.

What would Matt do with all that money if he did inherit it? He and Gretchen could live well if he never got a dime of Clifford's money. But Matt wanted it. And had come to think of it as his due. He was the anointed one. The heir apparent. Sometimes Norma was sur-prised that Angie, Julia, and Frank weren't disgusted by him. Or jealous. But they had long since divorced them-selves from their grandfather's fortune.

Norma didn't care so much about the money itself, but she chafed at Clifford's unfairness. And stupidity. Her other children should share in what was afterall their birthright. Danny's share should go to the Friends organization.

She realized that Joseph's family was finally filing in

the cloistered area behind a louvered screen. There would be just five of them. Gretchen and Matt. Her considerably older brother, an Air Force colonel stationed at Pearl Harbor. Gretchen's stepmother. And Joseph's older brother who lived in Phoenix.

Joseph Schneider had lived longer than anyone expected, but Gretchen was having a difficult time dealing with her father's death. Norma realized that her daughter-in-law's almost hysterical grief was due in part to the fact that she had not been able to place a grandchild in her father's arms. She had adored her father and been adored by him. Gretchen's stepmother had always seemed like an outsider. Nellie Schneider had apparently grown impatient with her husband's endless dying and left him to his daughter's determined care while she traveled about the state attending tennis clinics and playing in seniors' tournaments. Gretchen had barely been civil to her at the prefuneral brunch Maura had prepared.

Norma could come closer to speaking with Gretchen about her behavior toward her stepmother than about her childless state. But she wouldn't do that either.

Gretchen had had a difficult three years caring for a dying father and all but putting her status as newlywed on hold. Now that her father was dead, maybe she and Matt wanted some time to enjoy each other a few years before they began a family.

But Norma doubted it. On more than one occasion, Norma had seen Gretchen look at a baby with such hunger. She was four years older than Matt and entering into that period in a young woman's life when maternal longing hits like a disease. Gretchen wanted a baby more than anything. Every pore in her body was waiting and yearning. Her empty uterus felt like a great gaping hole in the middle of her being.

Frank entered from the left and took his seat in the large thronelike chair behind the pulpit of the nondenominational funeral chapel. He was wearing a coat and tie at Gretchen's request. Her father hadn't held with organized religion and wouldn't have wanted ecclesiastical vestments—or prayers, Scripture, hymns, liturgy. Frank had no problem with following her wishes. Unitarians didn't have rules, an approach Norma found rather admirable. If a family outside Frank's congregation asked him to conduct a nonsectarian service for a loved one, he never said no. He'd buried a convicted murderer following his execution at Huntsville and several gay men for whom their pastors had refused to hold funeral services.

The special music began. A hidden cellist and piano player offered a poignant rendition of "Bridge over Troubled Waters" that was so sad and beautiful Norma's eyes filled with tears. She reached for the comfort of her husband's hand.

Frank read the lengthy chronicle of Joseph's life that Gretchen had written—about his parents, education, combat service, medals, affiliations, second career as a professor of military history at Texas A&M.

After a medley of military marches, Frank told of Joseph's bravery during his last great battle. And the comfort he received from his daughter.

"Joseph's last words were for Gretchen," Frank said. "He told her not to cry, that he was very tired and it was time for him to go. He asked for her to hold his hand and sing their favorite song from Gretchen's childhood. And she did. I'd like for us all to sing or hum that song now—for Gretchen and Joseph."

The piano and cello began playing softly. It took Norma a minute to recognize the sweet familiar melody. "Puff, the Magic Dragon," which at first seemed an unseemly selection for a funeral. But then not. It was a song of death and hope. She thought of Gretchen singing it as her father took his last breath. Gretchen the constant daughter to the end. What bravery that must have taken to sing when she wanted to beat her breast in anguish.

Norma didn't remember all the words—but some of them came forth, recalled from the times she had sung it with her own children. Dear Joseph. He had earned his place in the land called Honah-Lee.

And she thought of her own father's death. Of holding his hand at the end. Life and death. Poor Clifford. He didn't understand any of it.

When the nurse called out "Matthew Morris," it took Matt a few seconds to realize she was referring to him. He had felt foolish not using his right name when he called for an appointment, even more foolish writing the name on the medical-history form he filled out. But people in Houston knew people in Dallas. The reason for his appointment was private.

The nurse showed him to Dr. Rinselier's starkly simple office and said that the doctor would be with him shortly.

The office had the usual framed diplomas and certificates covering one wall, but the furniture and decor were functional, not the tastefully furnished, paneled retreat Matt associated with a physician's private office. Maybe physicians who taught in medical schools and practiced at university hospitals couldn't be bothered with decor.

Dr. Jean-Claude Rinselier had been quoted in an article on male infertility in the *Dallas Morning News*. A "foremost expert," the article had called the Baylor Medical Center urologist. Matt had made an appointment with him two months ago but canceled, not yet able to deal with the issue.

But his and Gretchen's fourth anniversary was next week. And now that Joseph was dead, Matt knew everyone was wondering when they planned to start a family. Clifford especially. "What are you waiting for, boy?" he'd asked Matt on several occasions.

He and Gretchen had never practiced any sort of birth control. But law school had placed tremendous demands on Matt's time and energy during the first three years of their marriage, and her father had been dying since before their wedding day. Their childless

state had not been a great concern—to him at least.
Passing the bar had greater urgency. But Gretchen became depressed and withdrawn every month when her
period came.

Although he would never have admitted it, Matt
had found it difficult not to be jealous of his terminally
ill father-in-law. Gretchen was obsessive in her care for
him, all but driving away her stepmother of more than
twenty years who did not share Gretchen's desire to
do whatever was necessary to prolong Joseph's life.
Gretchen absolutely refused to let her father die, taking
him to yet another specialist, insisting he have another
operation or endure another round of chemotherapy
or radiation when he was ready to call it quits. The last
two years of his life, she had spent more nights taking
care of her father than she had with her husband. The
consensus among family and friends seemed to be that
it was a blessing Gretchen and Matt hadn't yet started a
family. Gretchen had her hands full.

But Gretchen's fondest wish had been to have a
child before her father died, to have the satisfaction of
seeing her child in his arms. She had consulted doctors
about her childlessness and wanted both her and Matt
to submit to a fertility workup. But Matt was unwilling. It
was too soon. She was overreacting. He was preparing
for exams or moot court competition, writing an article
for *Law Review*, studying for the bar. Getting established
in his practice. And then there would be a another crisis
with her father.

Matt wondered how much of Gretchen's profound
grief over her father's death had to do with that unfulfilled dream. Otherwise, shouldn't there have been
some sense of relief that it was finally over? That her
father was no longer suffering? That she had her own
life back? Matt grew weary with all her grieving. Her red
eyes and tears annoyed him.

She was starting to come around, though. They had
a trip planned to New Orleans for their anniversary.
She thought it be would be lovely if they started a baby
there. They could give it a French name—Maurice or

Nanette. As Maura would say, it was time to fish or cut bait. It was time to make his wife pregnant.

If he could.

She was talking about a fertility workup again. They needed to know if there was a problem or if they just needed to keep trying. Lots of problems were fixable. And there were other options.

Other options. Like using donor sperm. Or adoption. But surely she understood that his status as heir to his grandfather's estate would be in jeopardy if he didn't father his own children. His own son. For Gretchen, having children was more important than being rich. Maybe she was right. But Matt wanted both.

Too bad Clifford hadn't been the one to kick off— before the old man realized the possibly ominous significance of Matt and Gretchen's childless state.

As his grandfather's heir, Matt knew that Clifford expected two things of him—that he pursue a political career and that he carry on the Tarrington name and line. He knew that Clifford's fondest dream was that someday a Tarrington would once again be governor of the state of Texas. The old man had never gotten over the humiliation of his father's disastrous defeat when he ran for a second term. And Matt had schemed and planned with Clifford, allowed his grandfather to think that he shared the dream. Of course, Clifford would be long dead before Matt was old enough and powerful enough to be thinking about running for governor. In the meantime, however, Matt planned to file for his dad's former seat in the state legislature. Clifford expected it of him. The incumbent was getting senile. The timing was good, Matt supposed. And if he won, Clifford would be ready to carve his last will and testament in stone—provided there was a child on the horizon. A boy child.

Matt could almost wish that Clifford didn't have all that money. It had colored everything about his life since boyhood. Matt wasn't sure he even liked the overbearing old man. Yet, he had always played the role of devoted grandson to the hilt. Sometimes he'd feel Angie watching him with Clifford and sense her disappointment in him.

If all that money hadn't been waiting for him, Matt wouldn't be launching a political career. He could think of lots of other things he'd rather do—like practice sports law, own a professional ball club, run the U.S. Track and Field Federation, serve on the U.S. Olympics Committee, get back into training, run marathons. He believed more in athletics than politics.

And being Clifford's heir meant that he couldn't be objective about adoption. Did the fortune Clifford was dangling in front of his nose have something to do with the repulsion he felt to calling some other man's offspring his own? His parents had done that with Frank, and Matt had no doubt that they loved his older brother as much they did their natural children. Matt admired them for that. But was it fair to the children who were true Tarringtons to give an outsider equal status? Clifford said no. Angie claimed that Clifford was a Nazi. Matt wouldn't go that far, but he did wonder if his grandfather would have been a nicer man if he weren't so rich.

Matt was in Houston for a three-day meeting of the state bar association's young lawyers committee. This time, he had kept the appointment with Dr. Rinsalier, submitting to a complete workup, providing blood and semen specimens. He wanted to learn the truth on his own—in private. Then he'd decide what, if anything, needed to be done.

There had actually been a stack of girlie magazines in the windowless room where he'd been taken to jack off. He sat there for a long time, staring at the empty specimen bottle in his left hand. Not wanting to do this. Not knowing was better.

Reluctantly he picked up a *Penthouse* and opened it to the centerfold, who was a rather tough-looking brunette with pouting lips and a tiny rose tattooed on the inside of her right breast. He tried to imagine himself coming in her mouth. But decided to look further.

In the fourth magazine, the centerfold had fiery

red hair. Like Beth Williams's. Beth had been less voluptuous. Her eyes brown instead of blue. But this
woman reminded him of Beth. And it wasn't just the
hair. She looked both angelic and determined. Beth
had been like that. Like a woman in a religious painting. Holy and strong. Beth had never been laid back.
Never let things just happen. But she'd lost control of
Danny there at the end.

Matt remembered the shock of her departure.
He'd thought Beth would be with them always. And
then shock turned to anger. At Danny. He'd marched
into Danny's room and pummeled his brother on the
bed. With both fists. It was Danny's fault Beth had been
sent away. Stupid Danny who couldn't keep his hands
off of her. Matt had wanted to touch her, too. But he
didn't. He'd lusted after her, too. While he showered.
In his bed at night. Sometimes he'd be sitting at the
dinner table watching her smile and talk and eat—and
feel himself getting hard. Beth Williams had been the
image in his mind the first time he ever jacked off. And
even into adulthood, he'd suddenly realized it was her
face, her body, he was imagining when maybe he hadn't
even thought of her for months or even years.

He put down the magazine and allowed the image
in his mind to bring him to erection. He allowed himself to be twelve years old again and desperately in love
with Beth. Beth wet from the pool, her nipples erect
against the material of her suit. Beth asleep on the sofa.
Beth running with him at the track, her breasts bouncing with each step, her firm bottom rubbing against her
nylon running shorts. Beth naked in front of her mirror, not knowing that he was hiding under her bed,
watching her, fondling himself. Had any moment in his
life ever been more erotic?

His task completed and feeling strangely melancholy, Matt stared at the come in the jar. Where had she
gone, he wondered. She must have been devastated
when his parents sent her away. "If I had a fairy godmother, I'd asked her to turn me into a Tarrington,"

she'd told him once. "Then you'd be my little brother. I'd like that. I'd like that a lot."

Matt zipped up and left his specimen on the shelf as instructed. That had been two days ago. Now, he was back for the results, waiting in the ascetic little office with a window that overlooked a parking lot.

He wiped his palms on his pant legs. God, he was nervous. You'd think he was waiting to hear if he had cancer.

Dr. Rinsalier, who managed to look debonair in his crisp white coat with a stethoscope dangling from his neck, apologized for keeping Matt waiting and got straight to the point. Matt had a very low sperm count, he said. Mathematically, the odds of him getting a woman pregnant were too great for hope. Rinsalier could find no organic cause for the problem. "Perhaps it was the result of mumps or some other childhood disease. Even a sustained high fever can screw up the testes' ability to produce sufficient numbers of viable sperm. Or an athletic injury. Environmental contaminants. We're seeing a much higher incidence of male sterility now than even ten years ago."

Matt thanked the doctor, paid his bill with cash at the front desk and took a cab back to his hotel. He bought a newspaper and a Chap Stick in the hotel gift shop before taking the elevator to the twentieth floor. He'd have time for a nap before tonight's dinner. The state attorney general was the speaker.

But with the door to his room safely closed behind him, he sank to the floor and began to sob.

No one must ever know. Ever. Not even Gretchen. Most of all, not Gretchen.

He managed to get to the bed and kick off his shoes. Then he buried his face in a pillow. How could such a thing happen to him? He'd always been so lucky. He'd never had a wreck, never failed an exam, never been jilted, never been sick even. It was his brother who'd had encephalitis and ended up retarded, not him. His brother who'd been kidnapped, not him.

Would he ever feel like a whole man again? Jesus, he was shooting blanks! He was *sterile*!

If only it had been Gretchen's fault rather than his. Then he could have divorced her and found another woman to produce the son that would ensure his inheritance and preserve his pride.

He'd never hold his newborn son in his arms. Never have a daughter. Never.

If he couldn't have his own children, he didn't want to have any.

But that wouldn't be fair to Gretchen.

What if she left him for a man who could give her children?

He never should have had that affair with Suanne Belmont. Maybe that was why this happened; was being punished for being unfaithful.

Suanne, a law clerk in the federal magistrate's office, had thought she might be pregnant. He had toyed with the idea of divorcing Gretchen and marrying Suanne just to get the baby issue settled. But she hadn't been pregnant after all. And Matt was relieved. He wouldn't have to face such a difficult decision. He hadn't strayed since then. And never would again, he realized. Gretchen was his safe warm place in the world, and he'd probably be lost without her—just as his father would be lost without his mother.

And through the tears and a bottle of bourbon from room service, Matt figured out three things. He wanted a family even if the children were not his own. He wanted to have this family with Gretchen. And he wanted Clifford's money. He just had to figure out a way to manage all three.

Adopted children would never work. Their name might be Tarrington, but they wouldn't be Tarringtons as far as Clifford was concerned. They would be no more entitled to a birthright than any children Frank might father.

After Frank found out that Perry wasn't his birth father, he'd used the name Tarrington-Ledbetter for a time but found it cumbersome and dropped the Tarrington altogether when he was at the seminary. The family had ganged up on him when he returned to Dallas and insisted he return to the name he'd been raised with. The Ledbetters were dead by then—Lucy's mother and uncle—and Frank agreed. Even cried about it. His family. He began calling himself Frank Ledbetter Tarrington—no hyphen.

Clifford had been opposed to Frank's changing his name back to Tarrington and fought with Norma and Perry about it. Belle stepped in and told Clifford that it was time for him to be gracious in defeat, that the issue was out of his hands. "Not as far as my will is concerned," Clifford had said. "Frank has the Ledbetter estate. He'll not get a penny from me."

Then there was artificial insemination. Another man's sperm. A baby that was Gretchen's but not Matt's. Which would be a noble and generous thing for him to suggest. And allow. Saintly even. But Matt's insides shriveled at the very thought. He was as small-minded as his Grandfather Clifford.

He drank himself to sleep and woke up hung over. He was supposed to preside over a panel at ten in the morning, but he called Southwest Airlines instead and booked the next flight to Love Field. Then he called his mother and invited her to lunch.

"We had lunch here the day we shopped for Gretchen's wedding present," Norma recalled.

Matt nodded. "Yeah. The day I told you Danny couldn't be in the wedding. You were pretty upset with me."

"Yes, until you told me that you and Gretchen planned to name your first son for Danny."

They were both quiet for a time. Norma sipped her sherry. Matt finished his coffee. The discreet voices of other diners hummed softly around them.

Matt found himself admiring his mother. Even the signs of aging hadn't diminished her. She was more than just beautiful. She had a calm, quiet dignity that made people like and trust her. More and more, he realized that she was the power and the heart that drove them all. Not his father. Not Clifford.

This morning, waking up hung over and devastated, just knowing that he would see his mother in a few hours, that she would share his burden, had calmed him. His relationship with his mother was probably the most steadfast in his life. Nothing would change it.

"You have to tell her," Norma said.

"I can't. Not yet. Maybe never."

"Why? Do you think she'll love you less?"

"I think she'll be terribly disappointed. And feel sorry for me. I think that I'll feel diminished in her eyes, which—for all intents and purposes—is the same as being diminished, isn't it?"

"Do you feel diminished in my eyes?"

"You're my mother. That's different."

Norma closed her eyes and offered a prayer of sorts. For strength. And wisdom.

When she first began to suspect an infertility problem in her son's marriage, she'd realized there might be a solution. But she'd wondered if Matt's failure to produce an heir was some sort of cosmic judgment on Clifford. And she'd actually taken satisfaction in the prospect of his dream being thwarted once again—for the last time. And all her children would either share in Clifford's fortune or all be passed over.

But Gretchen deserved a child, and if she could bear her own baby, she should have the opportunity. And for an entirely different set of reasons, Norma wanted this child every bit as much as Clifford. Her very soul ached for a grandchild. For a very special grandchild. The baby of her twins—of Matt and Danny.

Even if Matt didn't yet know it himself, there was a very good reason why he had turned to her in his hour of need rather than to his wife.

"Have you thought of Danny?" she asked softly.

"In what way?" he asked, his eyes narrowing.

"He's your identical twin. A child of Danny's would be as genetically close to you as your own would be. Of course, there's the possibility that the cause of your sterility is genetic, which would rule Danny out as a donor. But that would be easy enough to find out."

Matt was shaking his head. "God, Mom, that seems positively incestuous."

"Nonsense. Artificial insemination is a clinical procedure. Sisters and mothers have helped out as surrogate mothers. I don't see how this would be any different."

Matt was staring over his shoulder as though visualizing the scenario she was suggesting. "No, I couldn't deal with my wife having my brother's kid. I don't think Gretchen could either."

"Not just your brother, Matt. Danny's your identical twin. A baby of his would be your baby, too."

Matt pushed his chair back an inch or two, announcing an end to the conversation. "I'd rather just forget about kids all together," he said.

Norma understood. He felt emasculated. And was raw and hurting from this new knowledge about himself. Until he came to terms, his greatest fear would be that others would know his secret—most of all his wife.

"The decision is for you *and* Gretchen, not for you alone," Norma said softly. "In the meantime, I'll find out about Danny."

Chapter Nineteen

Frank stepped up into the pulpit, which was too high for his liking. He didn't feel right looking down on his congregation from such a lofty position. But he loved the rest of the stately, simple church, with its only adornment the rich woodwork and proud display of organ pipes. Tall windows let in the sunlight and, on this bright spring morning, were open to admit a soft breeze that rustled the pages of his sermon.

As always, he took a contemplative minute to look out at the members of the congregation with their uplifted, reasonable faces. His was a congregation of ethical, learned people who had accepted his right to stand in this pulpit, who allowed him to marry and bury their own, who listened to his sermons with interest, who sometimes questioned his logic and often were correct in their challenges.

If he allowed himself, Frank could work up a bit of guilt that he was here among people who long ago had worked out the issues in their lives concerning religion and faith and belonged to the Channing congregation primarily for reaffirmation of their beliefs and the fellowship it provided with others like themselves. If he were a more worthy person, he would do more for his fellow man than provide food for thought to already thoughtful people and instead be working among the poor in some big city or third-world country. Not converting them—Unitarians didn't do that—but teaching and touching lives in a more meaningful way than he accomplished here among his sane little flock. But for now, he was content with contentment. He was back among his family and had a church of his own when

he'd thought that he was the sort of lackluster clergy-
man who would be forever delegated to assistant pas-
torhood.

"Life is good," he said, echoing his feelings, the
space under the vaulted roof giving a rich resonance to
his otherwise ordinary voice. "And we have a responsibility to celebrate the life we have been given, to enjoy
it, to use it well no matter what adversity or tragedy
might come our way. From time to time, we hear that
something 'ruined' a person's life. Perhaps at some
point you have thought that about your own life—that it
was ruined—which implies that from that time forward
there could be no celebration or joy. Only pain and
sorrow. That you could no longer enjoy nature, litera-
ture, music, family, friends, pets, a good movie, a delicious meal, a glass of fine wine. Nothing. I want to tell
you this morning about a young policeman who never
said that his life had been ruined in spite of—"

At that instant he saw her. The woman in the
fourth row with masses of golden red hair that the sunlight was turning to fire. Hair like Beth's.

But she couldn't be Beth. She was just a woman
who looked like Beth.

Frank closed his eyes and opened them again. But
already realization was thundering through his body.

She nodded her head ever so slightly, acknowledg-
ing his gaze. He grabbed the sides of the pulpit for
support.

He had no breath, no words for his waiting congregation. He could only stare. *Beth.* Seated in his church.
But why? After all these years?

She was wearing white, like the first day, when their
parents had called them into the living room to meet
her. She looked no older. Frozen in time. Beth, who
had altered the course of his life.

Restless sounds were beginning to erupt throughout the sanctuary. Shuffling feet. Cleared throats. People straining to see who in the fourth pew had so
captured their pastor's attention.

Frank cleared his own throat. And tried to remember what he had been saying. *Lives must not be ruined.* He looked at his notes. Thank goodness for his notes. Usually he never looked at them, their presence merely a comfort.

But despite the notes, he repeatedly lost his train of thought. Left out anecdotal material. Backtracked. Stammered. Members of the congregation exchanged glances. *What's going on with Dr. Tarrington?*

At the end of the service, Beth stayed in her seat, waiting while Frank shook everyone's hand. Finally, the sanctuary was empty but for the two of them—and Ramona, the young widow who'd invited Frank to her home for Sunday dinner. With her son. Her parents. Except he'd forgotten even to look her way throughout the sermon. Forgotten she existed.

Ramona was waiting by the last pew. Her parents would have already left with little Billy. She was going to ride with him to show him the way.

Beth rose from the fourth pew and came down the center aisle. The white of her dress took on a luminous quality in the light-filled sanctuary—like the princess bride's dress in a fairy tale. Ramona was watching as Beth held out her hand to Frank, as Frank took it. A cool hand. His was hot and sweating.

She spoke softly, but her words seemed to echo from the high ceiling.

"I've decided to marry you after all," she said.

Norma had just finished changing from her church attire into slacks and a silk shirt when the doorbell rang. *Who,* she wondered.

She went to stand at the top of the stairs. Maura was rushing down the hall.

As soon as Maura opened the door, a woman in white rushed in and threw her arms around the housekeeper's neck. "Maura, darling Maura," she was saying.

Norma couldn't see her face. But she knew the voice. And that hair . . .

The skin on Norma's face tightened. No, surely not. Not after so long a time.

She began descending the stairs. Slowly. Dear God in heaven. *Beth Williams.* What could she possibly want?

For this could hardly be a social call. No one in the family had seen her, talked to her, heard a word about her in how many years? Thirteen maybe? Fourteen? Not since the day Danny almost drowned her in the pool, and they had that horrible session with her in the study, when they told her that they thought it best that she leave—quietly with no good-byes to upset Danny. Beth had cried and begged to stay. She wouldn't let anything like that happen again. What had happened in the pool was her fault. She should have been paying more attention to him. She knew how to handle him better than anyone. She loved them. They were her family. Her life. Danny needed her. What would happen to him without her? She loved Danny more than anyone in the whole world.

Norma had wept with her, for her. Or maybe with relief. She hadn't wanted Beth under her roof for a long time but kept her on because of Danny. Perry had given Beth a check for a year's salary and told her to stay in touch. Apparently Angie, however, had told her otherwise. She'd never come back. Called. Written.

Maybe Beth wanted more money. Could she press charges against Danny after all this time? Or maybe she was soliciting for a charity. Needed a reference. Or something else.

Frank.

Norma stopped midstairway. Beth was looking up at her, smiling shyly.

At this moment, Frank would be at the home of one of his parishioners, having dinner with her and her family. Norma had been so thrilled, so hopeful when he told her. The woman's name was Ramona. She had a little boy named Billy. For days, Norma had thought of little else. She'd fallen in love with a woman and little boy she had never met. *Please let them be perfect for her Frank.* Please. Ramona was the first woman Frank had allowed himself to admire since Beth almost destroyed him all those years ago.

She had to get Beth out of here. Send her away. Frank couldn't see her, couldn't know she was here.

Perry emerged from the study, and Beth threw her arms around his neck. Perry stepped back, a stunned look on his face. Beth giggled shyly. "I know you all must think I'm terrible not to have stayed in touch. I kept thinking I needed to call or drive over. I've missed you so. Every day I think about you, wonder what you are doing. Wonder how my darling Danny is getting along. He's a man now, isn't he? All grown. My heart is just pounding away in my chest at the thought of seeing him."

Norma came down the last few steps and managed to rebuff Beth's embrace, firmly offering her hand instead. "Beth, what a surprise. What can we do for you?"

"Just let me stay for a while. See everyone. I've already visited with Frank at his church. I just couldn't stay away another day."

"We're getting ready to sit down to dinner," Perry said. "Would you care to join us?"

"I'm sure that Beth has plans," Norma said quickly, throwing Perry a look.

But Beth was already in the dining room, reminiscing about meals around this table. Maura's cooking. Centerpieces of Manuel's beautiful roses. The good times.

Still chattering, Beth went to the silverware drawer in the buffet and took out a place setting of sterling, which she added to the four places already laid on the carefully set table with its bouquet of cheerful yellow roses.

Norma heard the kitchen door open, voices in the kitchen talking to Maura. "Beth Williams!" Angie's voice rang out.

The door from the kitchen swung open. "Beth, what the hell are you doing here?" Angie demanded. Danny was following close behind her, peering over his sister's shoulder.

Beth ignored Angie and rushed to Danny. "What a handsome man you've grown up to be," she exclaimed. "Big and strong just like I always said you'd be if you used your muscles and ate your vegetables. Come on Danny Boy, give your Beth a hug."

The young, blue-jean clad director hurried from behind his cluttered desk to greet Norma. "Mrs. Tarrington, how nice to see you. What can I do for you?"

"I understand you've hired Beth Williams," Norma said, refusing to take an offered chair.

"Oh, yes," Mr. Bittle said. "That's all been taken care of. She's already taken over as resident counselor at Friends House."

"I would think that, as a board member, I would have had the opportunity to vote on a new staff member before she was hired."

"Well, of course, her employment is contingent on the board's approval," Bittle explained. "If you'll remember, we talked about Jacob Harden joining the army and the need to hire a replacement for him at the last meeting."

"What about references?" Norma demanded. "Since the woman had once worked for our family, I would think that you at least owed Mr. Tarrington and me the courtesy of a call."

A puzzled frown creased Mr. Bittle's smooth forehead. "But your father-in-law told us about the miracles she worked with Danny and offered a generous donation to help underwrite her salary. And her former principal called from Fort Worth and assured us that Miss Williams was the best special education teacher she'd ever had. We're quite impressed with her, Mrs. Tarrington. Last night she had even the most withdrawn residents square dancing. But if there's some problem we should know about . . ."

Norma hesitated. Yes, Beth would probably be the perfect resident counselor. The last counselor did little more than allocate chores and see that they were carried out. Beth would perform her miracles. She would get the residents dancing, exercising, hiking. There would be wiener roasts and excursions. They would adore her. And after all, Danny didn't live there. The resident counselor at Friends House had no responsibility at the factory.

And what could she tell Mr. Bittle? That she was afraid of Beth? That Beth had almost caused them to lose Frank?

"Why would a qualified special education teacher settle for the counselor's job?" Norma challenged. "The position doesn't require a degree."

"Beth said that she wanted to have the freedom to do some grant writing to fund some special community programs—like a day-care facility for severely retarded adults who are being maintained in their home. She really does have some wonderful ideas . . ."

Mr. Bittle's voice trailed off. Norma realized he was puzzled by her displeasure and not sure just how he had erred. Such an earnest young man—willing to work for a poverty-level salary in order to do good work in the world. Like Angie. Maybe Beth was that way, too. Apparently, she really had become a special education teacher, which pleased Norma. After all she and Perry had paid for her education, encouraged her to finish her degree.

"Mrs. Tarrington, if you would prefer that Beth not work for us, just say the word. Frankly, the organization can't afford to lose the support of you and your husband."

"No. I'm sure she'll work out nicely," Norma said.

And Beth did indeed "work out nicely." Friends House had never been a busier place. She convinced an athletic equipment company to install a basketball goal by the driveway and scuffle board equipment for the court she'd painted on the concrete. She had morning exercise sessions before residents went off to work at the broom factory or were delivered to various other jobs in the Friends van. During the day she worked with two residents preparing the evening meal. In the evening, there were games and square dances. Residents began working on their own puppet theater, making the puppets themselves and learning lines for simple enactments they could perform for special education classes in public schools. She began a program that would train Friends people to be teachers' helpers. She was full of ideas, and the residents followed her around like the Pied Piper. The Friends board was enchanted with her.

"So why are you sitting around waiting for the ax to fall?" Perry asked Norma. They were curled up in bed, a movie waiting in the VCR, a bottle of wine on the bedside table. Saturday night in the fast lane, they joked. More and more often they chose to spend Saturday nights in their own company.

"Because I don't trust her. Because she's joined Frank's church and is there every Sunday. Because he's nervous and lost weight and isn't himself."

"But they haven't gone out, have they?"

"Not that I know of. But he's never taken that woman from the church out either. Ramona. I tried to get him to invite her here for dinner with her little boy. But he said it probably wouldn't be a good idea now. I'm so disappointed. She sounded like a lovely person. And a five-year-old boy. God, how I wanted that—a five-year-old running around the house again. I'd even thought about getting another old yellow dog to chase after him."

Chapter Twenty

"*L*adybug, ladybug, fly away home. Your house is on fire and your children will burn."

It tickled when the ladybug crawled across his hand. Little tiny feet. Pretty little bug.

Danny pushed the bug off his hand onto the ground and sang the song again as she went off in the grass. To her babies maybe. Not to her house. Bugs didn't really have houses.

He reached in his lunch box for the last of Maura's peanut butter cookies. Maura made good cookies. In the lunchroom, people wanted to give him a brownie or a cupcake for one of Maura's cookies.

Some days other people came to eat outside. But not today 'cause of the wind. He didn't like being the only one outside. But he didn't want to eat in the lunchroom 'cause everybody looked to see if Mary Ann was sitting by him or not. Everybody knew she was real mad at him because Beth Williams came to see him at the factory all the time and brought apples and candy and said hello how's it going. Mary Ann said that Beth Williams wanted to be his girlfriend. Mary Ann was a dumb bunny. Everyone knew that retarded guys gotta have retarded girlfriends. Like Mary Ann. Mary Ann was his girlfriend. Everybody knew that.

The last thing in the lunch box was a red apple. A big one. It went *crunch* when he took a bite.

After he finished the apple, he closed his lunch box and just sat there. Nobody was going back to work yet. Everybody was still in the lunchroom. He liked to eat in the lunchroom with all the people, but he didn't like them to giggle when Mary Ann didn't sit by him.

And he didn't like them to ask him if he was in love with Beth Williams.

He lifted his face to the sun and closed his eyes. When he got home he'd eat more cookies and watch his new video again. Free Willy. Angie bought it for him. She watched it with him the first time. But she didn't like to watch videos over and over and over again.

"There's my Danny Boy," a voice said behind him. Beth's voice. "I've been looking for you."

She was wearing blue jeans and a white shirt, and her hair was blowing all around in the wind. She was pretty like a movie star. Down's people weren't pretty. Except Mary Ann was a little bit pretty at the Christmas party when she had on lipstick and a red dress that made noise when she walked and her mom had taken her to the beauty shop for curly hair.

Beth sat on the bench beside him. "Why are you sitting out here all by yourself?"

"Just 'cause," Danny answered, scooting away from her.

"Hey, don't you like me anymore, Danny Tarrington? You used to like me a lot. You used to love me and want to kiss me all the time."

"I was little and you left and never wrote a postcard or called up to say happy birthday or how's it going and that was mean."

"Oh, but I thought about you every single day and wanted to be with you. You'll always be my Danny Boy. Don't you know that? Once you really love someone, that love never goes away. It's always there in your heart." She put her hand on Danny's chest. "In there you still love me the best of all. Don't you feel that love in there under my hand?"

He looked down at her hand on his shirt.

"It's like a warm ball," Beth said, her face very close. She was looking into his eyes. "Right under my hand. Do you feel it?"

He nodded. Yes, he felt it. A warm ball. Under her hand. She was so close that he could see the little baby freckles on her nose.

"Good," she said, pushing on his chest a little harder. "I want you to feel the love. And next time I sit beside you, I don't want you scooting away, you hear?" She planted a soft kiss on his cheek, then jogged across the grass to Friends House.

Danny put his hand where hers had been. *A warm ball.* Did it really mean that he loved her most of all?

His family all thought that he couldn't remember Beth Williams from when he was a little kid 'cause he was retarded. But he did. Not everything. But some stuff. Like brushing her hair. And singin' the song about up in the air junior birdmen. And now that he could see her again, he remembered more things. He remembered that she could swim and run really fast. She and Julia used to swim races in the pool. And Beth would run races with Matt. And him, too. Round and round the track. Then he ran in real races with people watching.

Danny touched the gold champion medal that hung around his neck. Him and his dad bought Beth a car for helpin' him be a champion.

Beth came to see him everyday. Every time the little bell on the door went jingle jingle, he looked to see if it was Beth Williams. Sometimes she followed him out to the loading dock and watched him put boxes in the truck. He liked her to see how strong he was. Sometimes when she was watching, he'd pick up two boxes at the same time.

She asked him stuff about his family. Lots of stuff. Who came to see them? If they got sick. If Matt and Gretchen kissed and held hands. If Frank came to dinner. If Julia and Nathan lived in a big house.

Beth asked him once if he remembered the picture of her brother who was dead. But he didn't.

Danny couldn't decide if Beth loved him like family or like boy-girl stuff. She said that she was almost family and that one of these days she wanted to be family. Like Gretchen got to be family. And Julia's husband Nathan got to be family. But Julia wasn't named Tarrington anymore. And Nathan wasn't named Tarrington.

There had to be a wedding to make people family.

Weddings were nice. The lady got to look like Princess Di. Mary Ann loved Princess Di and saved pictures of her in shoe boxes. Lots of pictures. Mary Ann wanted a white bride's dress and a wedding more 'n anything in the whole wide world.

He thought about Beth more than he thought about Mary Ann. And he used to think about Mary Ann a lot. He was always trying to remember things to tell her like how Matt acted silly and made him laugh or how he helped Manuel dig out a big tree stump or when Frank took him along to visit the building where a bunch of old people lived. He and Mary Ann would talk some at work but mostly they'd talk at night on the telephone. She could dial his number all by herself, but he had to have his mom or dad or Angie dial hers. Last night Mary Ann wouldn't talk to him because Beth Williams had talked to him a long time that day and made her mad.

Him and Mary Ann wanted to have a wedding. Clyde and Sara had a wedding, and all the Friends people got to watch and eat tall cake. Danny's mom and dad were there, too. Clyde and Sara were Down's people like Mary Ann. They lived in Friends House now and worked at McDonald's making french fries and cleaning up stuff on the tables.

Mary Ann said that if Clyde and Sara could get married, maybe they could, too. And live at Friends House and have sex in bed and not in the storage shed where there were bugs and dirt. Mary Ann liked sex but hated dirt and bugs. Danny liked sex, too. A lot.

Mary Ann's parents and his parents said him and Mary Ann couldn't have a wedding cause retarded people weren't supposed to. But that was before Clyde and Sara.

Retarded people weren't supposed to have babies, so Mary Ann's parents got her an operation. Gretchen didn't have a baby, and she hadn't had an operation like Mary Ann. Her daddy was dead now. He'd been real sick for a long long time.

Beth was always asking him about Gretchen's daddy and if she was going to have a baby. Beth said she needed to know about the people she loved. And she loved Gretchen because her name was Tarrington.

Danny followed Beth up the stairs. "I want you to move the furniture in my room so I can have my bed by the window and feel the breeze at night," she said over her shoulder. "Do you still sleep with all the windows closed? You used to say that open windows made you afraid."

"No, I didn't. I'm not afraid," Danny said. But sometimes he was. He'd wake up and be afraid. His mom'd come and say he'd had a bad dream and rub his back.

"Well, you were afraid when you were a little boy. You wanted the windows and closet door closed, the hall door and the door to my room open, and Buddy in bed with you."

Beth's room was the first one on the second floor. There were more rooms on the third floor—where Clyde and Sara lived. They had a microwave and a little tiny refrigerator and a great big television.

"Buddy's dead," Danny said.

"I'm sorry. He was a good dog."

While Beth watched, he pushed her bed to one side to make room for a big cabinet with doors that was next to the window. Then he started pushing it over where the bed had been.

"You want me to help?" Beth asked.

"Nah. I'm a strong man."

He pushed the cabinet across the floor and then pushed the bed next to the window. Beth was nodding her head. "Yes, I'm going to like this much better."

She pulled a green rug over by the bed. Then she straightened the cover and sat down in the middle of the bed, crossing her legs like an Indian.

"Come sit down and talk to me," she said, patting the side of the bed.

"Mr. Leroy said not to hang 'round and bother you."

"Well, you're not bothering me, and I still need for you to pull up that old carpet in the living room before you go back. But first you need to rest a minute." She pointed at the side of the bed again.

The bed squeaked when he sat down.

"Remember my bedroom at your house?" Beth asked. "It was so pretty. I loved the window seat and big high bed and the dressing table with the round mirror. This room isn't pretty."

Danny looked around. It was a little room with just the bed and the big cabinet he'd just moved and a little chair pushed up to a table with a mirror and bottles and stuff. There was a picture of yellow flowers on the wall.

Beth was wearing shorts. The skin on her legs was smooth and tan. Mary Ann's legs were white and had lots of hair.

Mary Ann stuck out her tongue at him when Mr. Leroy told him to go help Beth Williams. When he got back to the factory, Mary Ann'd probably turn her back and not look at him. Or maybe she'd stomp over and hit him on the back.

"I came to see you yesterday at the workroom," Beth said. "But Mr. Leroy said your mother took you to the doctor. Were you sick?"

"Nah. I'm big and strong."

"Then why did you go to a doctor?" Beth asked.

" 'Cause my mom wants me to help Gretchen and Matt."

"Did the doctor look at your throat?" Beth said, touching his throat.

Danny shook his head no.

"Did he listen to your heart with a stethoscope?" she asked, touching his chest.

Danny shook his head again.

"Did someone stick your finger and get blood?" she asked picking up his hand and touching a finger.

"Nah. And they didn't want me to pee in a jar."

"Well then, what did they want?"

"I can't tell because it's a very big important secret. It's the biggest most important secret ever and I can't tell anybody not ever ever ever."

Beth nodded. "Secrets are important. At the doctor's office, did you go into a room by yourself and look at magazines?"

Danny grinned. "Yeah. I was supposed to find a picture of a really pretty lady."

"And the lady that you found—what was she wearing?"

"Nothin'," he said. He covered his mouth to muffle a giggle.

Beth pulled his hand away. "And what was pretty about her?"

"Her titties 'n' her butt 'n' she had smooth skin like you."

"Have you ever seen a naked lady for real?"

"Not all naked. Just some naked."

"Have you seen some of Mary Ann naked?"

"Yeah."

"Does Mary Ann like you to see her naked?"

"Nah. But she likes me to touch her."

"Do you like to touch her?"

Danny nodded.

"Did you unzip your pants while you looked at the picture of the pretty naked lady?"

He nodded again. Beth was leaning forward while she talked to him. He could see the top part of her tits.

"You used to want to touch me all the time. Do you remember that?"

"No."

"Well, you did. And you'd push me down and try to get on top of me. It made your mom and dad mad, and they sent me away. But I knew you did it because you loved me. Do you love Mary Ann?"

"Yeah, her and me, we wanna get married like Sara and Clyde."

"Do you love her more than me?"

"I don't know."

Beth took his hand and kissed it inside. For a long

time. She kissed and kissed and then rubbed it over her check and neck. "Yes, you do too know, Danny Tarrington. You love me best of all."

When he got back to the factory, Mary Ann came over and put her mouth next to his ear. "You kissed Beth Wilson, didn't you? And fucked with her."

Danny shook his head. "Nah, I didn't."

"I don't love you anymore," Mary Ann said and hit him on the back real hard. And everybody laughed at him.

It was the first time Belle had ridden in Clifford's new limousine. She felt as though she were going to a funeral instead of a birthday party. But Clifford claimed it was more comfortable than a sedan.

For years, the current chauffeur had driven Clifford in a Lincoln Town Car—a new one every year. The only vehicle Clifford ever drove himself was a golf cart he kept in the garage to take him across the bridge and up the hill to Norma and Perry's house. Then he started having the chauffeur drive him around to their front door.

Belle still came through the back gate. She seldom rode anywhere with her husband, preferring to drive herself in her vintage white Mercedes—still, although she hadn't driven at night for several years.

The chauffeur drove them around the block to pick up Norma, Perry, Danny, and Angie. Frank no longer lived in the garage apartment, having moved into a house by his church only last month. Belle had given him an oak tree for his barren backyard—the largest oak tree the nursery could transplant.

Danny had been waiting for them by the front gate. He could hardly contain his excitement—a birthday party and a ride in Grandfather Clifford's giant car all in the same evening. And he had a new sport coat and a necktie with pictures of dogs and cats all over it.

"My, how handsome you look," Belle said. "Doesn't he look handsome, Clifford?"

Clifford grunted.

Danny checked out the refrigerator and television and tried out the jump seats before sitting down by his grandmother and taking her hand. Like always. Her tiny hand in his very large one. So satisfying, Belle thought.

The occasion was Matt and Danny's twenty-seventh birthday party. Gretchen was having it this year. Lovely Gretchen. How lucky they were to have her. Belle had worried at first that Gretchen loved Matt more than Matt loved her. Matt loved Gretchen's beautiful face and glorious body. He loved the image of himself with such a stunning creature on his arm. But he had been too young and selfish to love Gretchen herself. That seemed to be changing, though. The look in his eyes when he watched his wife across the room was different now. Sometimes, he'd interrupt a conversation just to cross the room and kiss his wife's cheek, touch the small of her back.

But Clifford continued to be a major influence in Matt's life. He had vetoed Gretchen and Matt's first choice for a house because it wasn't in a politically advantageous legislative district. Matt courted the people his grandfather told him to court, talked over every client's case with him. Matt's race for the state legislature had been managed by Clifford. And financed. Clifford had wept on election night. Matt was on his way. Belle was quite certain that if a crazed gunman gave Clifford the choice of killing Matt or mowing down the rest of the family—herself included—Clifford would elect to save Matt.

Now that Gretchen's father was dead, she'd had the time to redecorate her home. "Eclectic" was what Gretchen called the decor, a mixture of antique and contemporary, Oriental and European, which in Belle's mind seemed like hodgepodge, but she had to admit the results were pleasing. The house was elegant yet still felt homey. And it made Belle actually consider doing something about the old mausoleum that she and Clifford lived in. At least her own bedroom and sitting room.

Maura and Gretchen had spent the past two days preparing for the party. Maura went to Gretchen and Matt's house one day a week now, but for the birthday party, Norma had sent her over for an extra day.

Julia and Nathan had already arrived from Austin. So alike they were—like brother and sister with their prematurely graying hair, tan skin, corduroy clothes, and walking shoes. Julia never wore makeup anymore. Never permed her hair. Nathan had a beard. Belle found them totally eccentric and absolutely beautiful, like poster people for wholesome living. Except sometimes she wondered if they worked too hard at it—if it was a way of escaping from other things. They were off-and-on foster parents for teenage children nobody else wanted, but they still had no children of their own—adopted or otherwise.

Perry stood up and lifted his wineglass. Belle smiled as Danny reached for his own wineglass. He didn't like wine but he loved "touching glasses." Gretchen called Maura in from the kitchen and stood with an arm around Maura's wide middle. Perry gave a little speech about how proud he was of his twin sons who each in his own way was a successful man. Then Matt stood.

Matt raised his glass and looked around the table at everyone, then over at his wife. Belle knew before the words were out of his mouth what he was going to say.

"I'd like to propose a toast to my wife, who has just made me the happiest man on earth." Angie let out a little squeal. Norma reached for Perry's hand and blew a kiss across the table to Danny. Clifford drew in his breath—closed his eyes, leaned his head against the back of his chair. Julia put her head on her husband's shoulder. Frank gave his brother a thumb's up sign. Maura crossed herself. And Gretchen hurried across the room to embrace her husband. Belle thought her heart was going to burst. The two most beautiful people in the world. So happy. So much to live for.

Danny still had his glass in the air, waiting, a puzzled look on his face. "Matt and Gretchen are going to

have a baby," Norma explained across the table.
"You're going to be an uncle."

Danny nodded his head up and down—and
grinned at his mother. Then he pushed back his chair
and stood. "We need to touch glasses and say 'God bless
the baby.' "

Belle got to her feet. The rest followed. Perry
helped his father up. Across the table, very solemnly
they all touched glasses. And said in unison, "God bless
the baby."

Danny didn't understand everything about
Gretchen's baby and the secret he shared with his
mother. But he knew he had helped. His mother had
told him it was kind of like giving blood. And he knew
about giving blood. He'd done that before—for
Gretchen's father, when Joe's body had stopped making
good blood.

After his and Matt's birthday party, his mom came
to sit on the side of the bed and reminded him again
about the secret. "You haven't talked to anyone about
going to see the doctor, have you?" she asked.

"Beth wanted to know. But I told her it was a big,
big secret."

His mom sighed, and she sat there for a long time,
staring at the picture of him and Matt when they were
little kids. Then she listened to his prayer and kissed
him good night.

The next day, Danny told everyone at Friends that
he was going to be an uncle. An uncle was the next best
thing to being a daddy.

He thought about the baby a lot. His mom said he
could hold it and rock it to sleep. She said the baby
would love him a whole lot forever and ever.

But before Gretchen's tummy even got big, she got
sick and went to the hospital and then she wasn't going
to have a baby.

Danny's mom said that the little tiny baby came out

too soon before it could be alive. And no, she didn't know if it was a boy or girl. It was too soon to know.

"Can we bury the baby by Buddy?" Danny asked.

"No, son. But we can be sad like when Buddy died and hope that Gretchen has another baby that stays inside her long enough to get born."

Chapter Twenty-one

Angie's runner was number three. Her name was Naila. A tiny little thing—much smaller than the other runners in the one-hundred-yard dash for eight-to-ten-year-old girls.

When the gun went off, Angie stared at the stopwatch in her hand. She was aware of a commotion at the official's table—people hurrying over, spectators in the stands watching whatever was going on there rather than the action on the track. But Angie focused on number three, pushing the stopwatch at the exact instant Naila crossed the finish line even though she was far behind the leaders and her time would not be good enough to advance her to the next round.

Angie hurried over to hug Naila. "You did a good job. You ran fast and stayed in your lane the whole time! And because you did such a good job, you're going to get a certificate."

Frown lines creased the girl's shallow forehead.

"A certificate—that's a beautiful piece of paper that has your name on it and says that you ran in a Special Olympics race. You can hang it on your wall."

Naila nodded and smiled. "I ran good."

"Yes, you did," Angie said, looking around for Naila's sari-clad mother—and realized that someone was lying on the ground by the official's table.

Beth and Julia were kneeling beside the person. A woman in white sweats. With very blond hair.

Gretchen.

Angie waved for one of the other timekeepers to take charge of Naila, and then ran across the infield, the stopwatch still in her hand.

Gretchen's sweatpants were soaked in blood. A lot of blood. Her hands were covering her face, her head slowly moving back and forth—a gesture of denial. Not again. Not her baby.

A circle of horrified people watched. Others were trying to keep the children at a distance.

Julia looked up at Angie, her face streaked with tears. "Nathan's calling an ambulance. Where's Matt?"

Angie took off again across the infield to find her brother. Running and sobbing. Poor Gretchen. Poor Matt. Miscarriage number three. But the first two had been early. She'd gone four and half months this time. They were all so sure this one would take. The doctor had all but promised. He'd told Gretchen she was "out of the woods."

And now, *all that blood.* God, she could bleed to death! And suddenly the prospect of losing Gretchen loomed far more ominous than another miscarriage.

Matt was by the broad-jump pit. He looked up and saw Angie racing toward him, her arms waving wildly. "It's Gretchen," she shouted, pointing toward the officials' table.

He took off like a wild man. Angie didn't even try to keep up.

Please let Gretchen be okay, she implored as she headed back across the infield, holding her side, hurrying as best she could.

Beth gave Matt her place at Gretchen's side and stood behind him, a comforting hand on his shoulder. Matt gathered his wife in his arms and pressed his lips to her forehead.

Already, a siren announced the approaching ambulance. Beth kneeled on the ground again, at Gretchen's feet, watching Matt try to comfort his wife. The look on Beth's face was odd. Not upset. Not even concerned. Just watching.

Why did Beth come back, Angie wondered as she had so many times over the last year. She fought off the irrational feeling that Gretchen's miscarriage was somehow Beth's fault. No one had caused the miscarriage, but having Beth hovering about on the periphery of her family's life made Angie apprehensive. She didn't feel safe with Beth around.

"I'll bet you still go swimming at night like we used to," Beth said. "You liked the way the pool lit up at night."

Danny downed a glass of iced tea with one gulp before turning his gaze in her direction. "You don't know what I do," he said, helping himself to a cookie from the plate she'd set between them on the back step of Friends House.

Beth had asked Leroy to send Danny over again, this time to dig a garden. She wanted each resident of Friends House to have a small plot to grow something— a lesson in responsibility. If they didn't water and weed, they wouldn't have vegetables or flowers to pick. Some of the residents—especially the newer ones who were away from home for the first time—didn't understand about responsibility. Always before clean sheets and tidy bedrooms had happened automatically. They had never cleaned toilets. One nineteen-year-old woman had never washed her own hair or cut up her own meat. Lana. She was a special challenge for Beth. Lana's hovering, overprotective mother had died suddenly, leaving her daughter with no independent living skills. Norma hadn't been that overprotective with Danny before Beth arrived. But almost. Even before Beth took the courses and read the books, she'd understood that low-mental children must be made to do tasks again and again until they could manage on their own and not be robbed of the chance to take care of themselves and develop a sense of self-worth, a unique personality—not just be some mother's justification for sainthood.

Danny had come a long way from the helpless little boy who had never drawn his own bathwater, dressed himself, or made a sandwich. He was such a hard worker and took responsibility quite seriously. He had turned sod steadily for almost two hours, his bare torso

covered with sweat and dirt, until Beth had called a halt
and said he could finish tomorrow.

It still surprised her that Danny was not the totally
trusting, wildly affectionate child she had loved like a
brother. This grown-up Danny had a wariness about
him she found upsetting. He never returned her smile,
and although he didn't pull away when she touched
him, he never tried to touch her in return. He wasn't
like her brother Willy anymore.

"I taught you to swim," she reminded him. "When
I first came to live with you, you were afraid of water.
You'd just sit on the side of the pool with your feet in
the water and watch everyone else swim. Sometimes
you'd cry when Matt splashed you."

"No way," he said, taking two more cookies.

"My very first day at your house, I got you to put
your face in the water. Then I taught you how to dog
paddle and float and finally how to swim—almost as
good as Julia. You weren't afraid anymore. We'd hold
hands and run down the hill to the pool. Then as soon
as I got the gate unlocked, you'd run in and do a can-
nonball and splash water on me. Sometimes, when your
parents were gone, I'd wake you up in the middle of the
night to go down to the pool with me. You were my
special boy. My Danny Boy. We loved each other the
most. Don't you remember? Please tell me that you remember."

His forehead wrinkled like an old man's as he concentrated. "I remember you and Julia racing in the
pool."

"You used to float on your back and look at the
stars. Do you ever do that now?"

Danny nodded. "I can float good. Like a rubber
ball."

"I haven't seen your swimming pool in a long time.
I bet the trees are bigger now. What if I came to see the
pool tonight and had a surprise for you?"

"The pool's covered up."

"I know. It's not swimming time yet. But I just want
to see it and share a secret surprise with you—after your

mom and dad get all dressed up and go to the big party. A nice surprise, by the swimming pool."

"A surprise? Like a present?"

"Yes, a present just for you. A secret present. Now don't forget to come down to the swimming pool after your mom and dad leave. I'll be there waiting for you. If you don't come, you can't have the secret present."

The brass key on Beth's old key ring still opened the back gate. She'd used the key when she took Danny back and forth to see his grandmother. And she still had a key to the pool enclosure, a house key, and a key to the car they'd given her after Danny won his Special Olympics medal. She didn't have the car anymore, just the key. She'd traded the Volkswagen after they fired her because she didn't want to have to think about them every time she got in her car.

But every time she got into the Chevy, she'd think of the Volkswagen convertible she traded for it. She'd never stopped thinking about the Tarringtons. Everyday, she'd buy a Dallas newspaper and scan every page for mention of a Tarrington. She knew about their weddings, the deaths of Norma's parents, Matt's election, Norma's charitable works. Angie had been honored by the ACLU. The family made a major gift to the University of Texas for a professorship in special education. Several times, their home had been on the annual garden tour, with special mention of the rose garden created by Manuel Rodriguez.

Beth looked up at the imposing house on its hilltop. The downstairs was dark except for a light in the central hallway, with its wonderful curving staircase that made Beth feel like a princess whenever she came down it, her hand trailing lightly on the banister, her head high, proud to be living in such a house, descending such a staircase. A light was on in Norma and Perry's room, but they weren't there. It was opening night for this year's symphony season. Norma was president of the symphony guild. The whole family would be going.

The Tarringtons were big on the symphony. Sometimes Maura or her daughter had stayed with Danny so Beth could go with them. Magical nights. The music filled her up.

The light was on in Danny's room. He must be alone. If Belle had come to keep him company, they would still be downstairs.

Her room had been next to Danny's. Her beautiful room. She'd felt regal in her room, too. Sleeping alone in the big carved bed, her own bathroom with the bathtub on clawed feet.

Beth had never forgotten the first time she saw the house when she came to be interviewed. It had taken her breath away. The cab driver had to remind her to pay. All those years in the trailer park, when she felt like white trash, she'd dreamed about living in such a wonderful house.

Her mother used to say that people who lived in grand houses were no happier than people who lived in trailers. Perhaps that was so. But people who lived in grand houses certainly had grander lives than trailer-park folks. And that's what Beth wanted. A grand life. Not the shabby, noisy, low-class life in a trailer park alongside a highway, with cars and trucks whizzing by that could kill the person you loved most in the whole world. She never told the Tarringtons that she'd lived in a trailer. Never told them lots of things. Sometimes, when she took Danny to visit Belle, she'd look up at the apartment over the senior Tarringtons' garage and think of all the things the family didn't know about her.

The pool enclosure wasn't locked. But maybe that was no longer the cardinal sin it had been when Danny was a boy. The only time Beth remembered Norma losing her cool was once when the pool was left open. Danny wouldn't always answer when he was called. If he disappeared for an instant, Norma became anxious. "Is the pool locked?" she'd say and send someone down to make sure.

It was a beautiful April evening, the moon bright, the temperature almost warm enough for swimming had the pool been up and running. The silent pool was partially drained and, a cover sagged across it, partly filled with rainwater and rotting leaves—not a pretty sight in the wintertime, but it was hidden from the house by a row of mature cedar trees.

The last time she was here, Danny had almost drowned her. She remembered thinking that her lungs were going to burst, that she'd never breathe again. By the time Julia reached them, she had passed through fear and was waiting for oblivion. This was her payment for letting Willy die. The boy she had loved in her brother's stead was going to kill her.

Having to leave this house and the Tarrington family had seemed worse than death. How could she live someplace else? How could she go back to being poor and ordinary? How could she leave Danny? It had been like Willy dying all over again.

Beth pulled a lawn chair into the shadows by the pool house and waited for a long time. She couldn't see her watch in the darkness, but it seemed like an hour or more. Maybe Danny wasn't coming to claim his surprise, she thought with a wave of irritation. Maybe his mother had a rule against him going outside at night alone—the same mother who had never taught him to shake hands or tie his shoes. To zip up his own jacket, make his bed, hang up his clothes, butter his own bread. Beth had to teach him everything. Norma thought he wasn't capable of anything, that he was going to stay a little boy forever. Maybe that was what she'd wanted.

Finally, Beth heard the back door open—the one that led from Maura's kitchen—not the French doors off the entry hall or from the study. She went and stood by the gate, watching him come down the hill. Alone. Wearing his pajamas and a bathrobe.

Beth knew that what she was about to do was wrong. People like Willy and Danny needed careful lives with routine and rules, with lines that were never crossed. She would never have done this to Willy. And even though Danny wasn't really her brother, she had allowed him to be Willy's surrogate for those years when she lived in this house.

But his parents had thrown her out like she didn't matter. They gave her a check and dismissed her like household help after treating her like one of the family. She'd thought they loved her and had allowed herself to love them in return, to worship them, to dream about being one of them. She still dreamed about having their name and living in their house. But she didn't love them anymore—including this hulking person who used to be her Danny Boy. She had tried with all of them again. One by one. Frank and Danny were confused by her. The rest afraid—as well they should be.

Without saying a word, Beth stepped forward, took Danny's hand, and led him into the pool house. There was no door on the structure, and moonlight streamed inside.

She closed her eyes to make her own darkness and put her arms around his neck. Such a big person he was. Big enough to hurt her if he wanted to. But he wouldn't do that. The gentleness was still there. And maybe the love, too, down deep inside. He just couldn't remember.

She kissed his mouth, but he didn't respond. She wondered if kissing was outside the realm of retarded lovemaking.

Then she remembered what he had wanted so all those years ago when he kept pawing at her, and she stepped back to remove her jacket, T-shirt, and bra. Then she took his hands and put them on her breasts.

For a beat or two, his hands just stayed there, but then he began to roll them around. Round and round in perfect cadence like two robot hands. But his breathing became ragged and heavy. Not mechanical.

She stepped out of her sweatpants and panties. Pulled down his pajama bottoms. And pulled him to the wooden floor. It took him only nine or ten strokes to have a hard, grunting orgasm.

The next day at work, she talked to him for a long time—out by the big tree. She hadn't really been at the swimming pool last night. He'd just had a dream. He shouldn't talk about it to anyone because it didn't really happen. Danny had just listened. He didn't say a word.

Beth had timed their copulation carefully, wanting to do it only once. Three weeks later, the drug store pregnancy test was positive. All she had to do now was marry Frank to give the child its rightful name.

And pray that it was a boy.

Her original plan had been to marry Frank. But she couldn't stop thinking about all the money Matt was going to inherit. One of the largest fortunes in the state of Texas.

Matt was seducible, but he would never marry her. Matt loved his wife. And Beth was thirteen years his senior. Even if Matt would marry her, the family would hate her for stealing him away from the saintly Gretchen.

But now she could have the name and control of the fortune. And the family would have to accept her.

Chapter Twenty-two

Belle took her afternoon sherry and a book out to the veranda to enjoy the lingering warmth of the late afternoon sun. She put on her reading glasses and opened the book but didn't focus on the words. Her mind was still with Gretchen. Belle had taken her granddaughter-in-law a loaf of banana bread that she'd made herself—her great-aunt Jane's recipe, made with walnuts and brown sugar. And she'd planned to ask Gretchen's advice about redecorating the house, thinking that the poor girl needed a project of some sort to take her mind off the tragedy.

It had been six weeks since Gretchen lost the baby. Such a horror. She'd almost bled to death by the time the ambulance arrived at the hospital. The doctor had removed her uterus to save her life.

Clifford had been beside himself. He actually came to Belle's bedroom, something he hadn't done in years, to have an audience for his ranting. Matt had to divorce Gretchen. Find a woman who could bear children.

"You leave those two children alone," Belle told him. "You've meddled quite enough in their lives as it is."

"If he wants my money, Matt will damned well do what I say."

"Listen here, old man, if you say a word to him about divorcing that lovely girl, I might just have to take a gun and shoot you between the eyes. Then he'll get your money anyway because you wouldn't have a chance to change your damned will."

She hadn't meant it, of course. She didn't have a gun. And probably didn't have the courage. But as she thought about her words, they did seem like a good idea.

Or maybe she'd burn down the house with him in it and build a new house. Here on the same lot, close to the people she loved.

So many times, she'd thought about leaving this ostentatious old mansion and buying herself a smaller, more pleasant house to live out her years. But more than having her own house, she wanted to continue to live across the back fence from her family. The back-fence arrangement with the wooden bridge across the creek had bred a day-to-day intimacy that had been Belle's salvation. If she lived someplace else, her grand-children wouldn't have grown up popping over, even if it was only for a few minutes to show off a school paper or play a hand or two of rummy. She herself wouldn't have felt comfortable just dropping in at Perry and Norma's to chat with whoever was there, even if the only person home was Maura. And she wouldn't have formed the wonderfully close attachment with Danny, who had blessed her life.

If she was going to live out the rest of her years here, she might as well fix the old place up, tear out some walls, liven it up, upset Clifford. Gretchen had done such a nice job with the vintage house she and Matt bought over by the university.

But Belle hadn't even mentioned redecorating to Gretchen. Gretchen was overflowing with talk of her own project—adoption. A shared project with Julia. Gretchen couldn't have children. Julia and her husband had decided they wouldn't bring more children into the world when there were already so many around who needed parents. After several years of being foster par-ents, it was time to get a child of their own. The sisters-in-law were exploring all their options, visiting agencies and orphanages, contacting international adoption or-ganizations, reading books and articles, keeping a file. Maybe they'd write a book of their own with what they'd learned, Gretchen explained, eyes sparkling, her voice full of excitement for the future. Angie would be their legal adviser, she said. They didn't want a heartbreak like Baby Jessica or Baby Richard.

"Has Matt said anything about his grandfather's will?" Belle asked. "I'm sure you both realize that Clifford Tarrington is probably the most inflexible person on the face of the earth."

"No, we haven't talked about Clifford's will," Gretchen had said. "Some things are more important."

But Belle wondered what was really going on in Matt's mind. She loved the boy but sometimes feared he might indeed be cut from the same cloth as his grandfather. He wanted a family for its own sake. But he also wanted to remain Clifford's heir.

Belle took the last sip of sherry. And considered a second glass. But she really should go inside and let Beatrice know that she was home—and see if she could help with dinner. Yes, in a minute, she would do that.

But it was so pleasant out here. No wind. She could smell the wisteria blossoms. Another spring had come. Her life was ticking by.

It still seemed strange having dinner with Clifford after so many years with him eating most of his evening meals away—with Mae Masters. But Miss Mae had been dead for almost ten years. Belle assumed the establishment that Clifford built for Mae and her girls had long since closed. He was too old for whoring around anyway. So more evenings than not, the two of them sat down at the table for their an evening meal prepared by Beatrice. Weekends Belle cooked something. Clifford refused to eat in the kitchen, so they ate alone in the dining room at a table that could accommodate twelve. He read the newspaper. Belle propped up a book beside her plate.

She turned her attention to the open book in her lap. An old Mary Stewart novel. She was doing a lot of that lately—taking an old book from the shelf rather than buying a new one. She'd reread Helen MacInnes, Pearl Buck, Taylor Caldwell, Phyllis Whitney. Daphne Du Maurier was still her favorite.

But after only a few paragraphs, Belle closed her

eyes and let her head rest against the back of the chaise.
Maybe she'd walk over to see Danny before dinner. See
if he was feeling any better. He'd been so unhappy. No
one knew why.

Voices woke her. The sliding door to Clifford's
study was open. Someone was in there with him. A
woman. Not Beatrice.

It took Belle a minute to realize the woman's voice
belonged to Beth Williams. But what in the world was
she doing here? Belle wondered if she should go inside
and greet her.

But if Beth had come to see Belle, she wouldn't be
in Clifford's study. Beatrice would have shown her into
the living room and looked around to see if Belle had
returned home yet.

The word "baby" caught Belle's attention. She
closed her book and moved to a chair near the open
door. "If it's not a boy, I'll terminate the pregnancy and
start over," Beth was saying. "But I know it's a boy."

"How do you know?" Clifford asked.

"I just do. It's the boy that Gretchen and Matt will
never have. Matt is sterile—you didn't know that, did
you? Gretchen was artificially inseminated with Danny's
sperm. But now she can't have a baby at all."

Silence descended over the room. Belle held her
breath and waited. And was beginning to wonder if
Beth had left when Clifford cleared his throat and
asked, "Just what are you trying to tell me?"

"Frank and I are going to get married. But Frank is
not the father of this child. Danny is. I'm carrying your
great-grandchild, Clifford, your *true* great-grandchild. A
true Tarrington. I'm going to give you the child that
Matt never can, a child that you deserve."

Then suddenly Beth's voice was right by the open
door. Belle jumped and almost dropped her book. She
slipped out of the chair and tiptoed across the veranda.

Beth had used Danny for stud—which was most
certainly wrong. Wicked even.

But Angie was showing no signs of getting married,

and Matt and Gretchen couldn't have children of their own. Julia and Nathan refused to.

And the thought of rocking a baby of Danny's in her arms warmed Belle's old heart.

She loved Danny more than any other human being in the entire world. Danny was the purest, the sweetest, the easiest to love. Even now, with him towering over her, he loved for them to go upstairs to her sitting room and sit on the sofa while she told him stories. And while they sat there, he would hold her hand and she would stroke his arm and touch his face. Danny was the only human being with whom she had any sustained physical contact.

But something was amiss with Danny. He hadn't come over in weeks. He didn't want to go to work, when his job was so important to him and made him feel like a man. He wanted to stay in his room all day and have his meals on a tray. Was Beth the reason why?

Belle's first inclination was to call Norma. But first, she needed to think about things. Secrets sometimes had a way of destroying families if they were let out of closets.

Chapter Twenty-three

The Singletons lived on Montford, between Monticello and McCommas, in an older Dallas area known as M Streets. The Singletons lived in a quaint two-story, pitched-roof stone-and-brick house that looked like a small church.

Martha Singleton was a plump, pretty woman in her mid-fifties. Her husband, Ted, was tall and rangy and appeared to be at least ten years older than his wife.

A family portrait that had been taken when Mary Ann was ten years old hung in the entry hall. Of their four daughters, Mary Ann was the youngest, Martha explained. The other three were all married now—and taught school like their parents. No grandbabies yet. "I think they're afraid," Martha said.

Norma stared at the then ten-year-old Down's syndrome girl in the picture. She was sitting between her parents, linking arms with her mother, holding hands with her father and saying cheese for the camera. Her sisters were standing behind; the one who looked to be the oldest had her hand on Mary Ann's shoulder. It was a portrait of a family who loved and protected its mentally deficient member, whose needs often dictated family life—as Danny's had. Norma understood why Mary Ann's sisters were afraid. As much as they loved their sister, they didn't want to have a child like her.

"Gladys came to take Mary Ann for a ride while you folks were here," Martha said, pointing to one of Mary Ann's sisters in the picture.

Norma caught a glimpse of a spacious, light-filled family room built across the back of the house, but

Martha directed them to a small formal living room with brocade-covered furniture and windows.

Norma and Perry declined Martha's offer of coffee and seated themselves on the love seat. Ted and Martha sat across from them in a pair of handsome Queen Anne arm chairs.

"Ted and I wanted to visit with you about Mary Ann and Danny," Martha explained. "We should have met before now, I suppose. But then, you probably were like Ted and me and never took their friendship that seriously."

"How's Mary Ann?" Norma asked. "I understand she took quite a fall."

"Actually, she jumped," Ted Singleton said. "Out of an attic window. Fortunately, she hit the roof of the family room and rolled off into some bushes. She cracked a couple of bones in her right foot and was scratched up pretty bad, but we're lucky she didn't kill herself—which she says is what she wanted to do."

"Kill herself!" Norma said. "But why?"

"She says that she wants 'to be dead' because your son doesn't love her anymore," Martha explained.

Norma pressed her hands tightly together. She'd come here expecting Mary Ann's parents to say that their daughter was pregnant. By Danny. And for the past two days, she and Perry had agonized over what would be the best course of action—alternating between abortion and offering to raise the child themselves. But suddenly that problem was gone and another just as serious had taken its place.

Norma remembered the time of rejection in her own life. Such pain. Had there been an attic window, she might have jumped out it. Of course, there had been the ocean. She had thought of that—walking out into the ocean to put an end to the pain.

"Danny's not been himself," Perry said, his voice full of sadness. "He's withdrawn. Even hostile at times. Norma and I have been at wit's end."

"I understand you know the woman who was hired as residence hall counselor," Ted said.

Perry frowned. "Yes. She worked for us a number of years ago. She looked after Danny."

"Then maybe you have a better idea of what's going on than we do," Martha said.

Norma and Perry exchanged glances. What did Beth have to do with Mary Ann and Danny?

"Mary Ann says that Danny stopped talking to her because he loves Beth Williams and wants to have sex with her and marry her," Martha said. "Ted and I used to think that people like Mary Ann and Danny didn't have the capacity for romantic love anymore than two five-year-old children would have. Sex is one thing, but real love is quite another—not that we condone the sex, but we came to realize that it's going to happen in an environment like Jobs for Friends where you have retarded men and women working together day in and day out. We considered talking her out of the sheltered work program, but she's been so much happier since she started there. So, we had her tubes tied and looked the other way—which was hard for two devout Catholics. Very hard."

Ted nodded, confirming his wife's words.

"But we wonder now," Martha continued, "if we weren't wrong about the depth of our daughter's feeling for your son. Maybe, in her sweet, simple way, she really is in love with him—in the truest sense of the word—and can't deal with losing him. Mary Ann is seriously depressed. She says she won't go back to work and that she'll jump out the attic window again if we make her return. She doesn't want to eat or watch television. She just drinks Cokes and stares out her bedroom window."

Martha sighed. Tears glistened in her eyes. "We thought maybe you could ask Beth Williams to talk to Danny. Maybe she can make him understand that there's no reason for him to be in love with her. Nothing can come of it. I'm sure she's a very nice person and is kind to all the Friends people. Your son probably just misunderstood her kindness. Maybe she can make him understand that he needs to fall in love with someone like himself, someone who can love him back.''

Ted reached for his wife's hand. "And we want to let you know that if we can get things back to normal between Danny and Mary Ann, it's okay with Martha and me for them to get married."

"Yes," Martha said, "a real wedding in a church with all their friends and her sisters as bridesmaids. We always told Mary Ann she couldn't do that, and now I'm sorry. I'd always thought of her as our happy little girl. But now, she hurts so. And it breaks our hearts."

Ted nodded. Then he looked away so they wouldn't see his tears.

Norma took a dinner tray up to Danny's room and sat with him while he ate. A video of *The Little Mermaid* was playing on the television screen, and Danny was watching intently, losing himself in a story he'd seen dozens and dozens of times. He probably had over a hundred videos. His favorites were Disney true life adventures and fairy tales.

An elaborate electric-train layout with a village, tunnel, bridge, and farm covered a wooden platform on the far side of the room. A bookcase held family pictures and the collection of seashells Danny had accumulated during trips to Padre Island—but no books. Danny had no need of books. Or games. Even the simplest board or card games were beyond him. He understood that to win tic-tac-toe, he needed three of the same marks in a row, but he had no notion of strategy, no clue that whatever wins he garnered were gifts from his opponent. In his closet, he had wooden building blocks that he still enjoyed on occasion, but they had been kept out of sight for years—since Matt started teasing him about still playing with toys. Also in the closet, residing in a wooden chest, were the tattered stuffed animals from his childhood that Norma suspected he still got out from time to time. But for the last six weeks, he'd done nothing but watch videos. He didn't want to visit Grandma Belle or swim, ride his bike, take a walk. He didn't want to help Manuel in the yard or lick bowls in Maura's kitchen. He never asked anyone to dial phone numbers for him. He didn't want to talk to Frank, Matt, Gretchen, Julia, Nathan, or Mary Ann.

For more than five years, he and Mary Ann talked to each other several times every evening—brief childish conversations about what they had for dinner, if a thunderstorm was scary, what they were watching on television, what they were going to have in their lunch box the next day. Sometimes they'd sing songs together. "Jingle Bells." "Bingo." "Deep in the Heart of Texas." Year after year, they'd done that. Two children in adult-sized bodies. Danny had said on numerous occasions that he and Mary Ann wanted to get married. And always Norma and Perry would explain to him that he and Mary Ann needed parents to help them do things and to keep them from being too lonely. Norma had wondered about sex. But Danny had calmed considerably since his horny adolescent days when he masturbated several times a day and almost drowned Beth in the pool trying to get at her. And Norma knew that two of the Friends people had actually gotten married. Which had shocked her. Like the Singletons, the thought of the simple, innocent Friends people being involved in sexual relationships made her uncomfortable. But intelligence had nothing to do with sex drive. She'd thought that was all it could be with Danny and Mary Ann. They were like two kindergarten children who somehow developed too soon.

Norma picked up the remote and turned off the set. Danny looked at her, scrunching up his forehead.

"You can turn it back on later," Norma said. "I need to talk to you."

"I don't want to talk," he said, reaching for the remote in his mother's hand.

"Later," Norma said firmly, putting the remote on the dresser out of his reach. "Do you know that your friend Mary Ann is very sad because she thinks that you don't love her anymore?"

"I love Beth Williams, and Mary Ann is mad at me."

"Beth may love you, but not like Mary Ann does. Beth loves you more like a teacher loves her students, or like Frank loves the people who come to his church. Or maybe Beth loves you like she would love her little brother if he hadn't been run over by a car. But I think you and Mary Ann love each other like your daddy and I do—like Matt and Gretchen. And Julia and Nathan."

"I love Beth Williams like the Prince loves Snow White," Danny said, pushing the tray away and folding his arms across his chest. "I love her forever 'n' ever 'n' ever 'n' ever 'n' ever 'n' ever. But Beth said I can't love her anymore. She said I'd jus' been dreamin' and she wasn't goin' to come see me at work anymore. Mary Ann stopped coming to work, and everybody said I'm a bad person to make Mary Ann so sad."

Chapter Twenty-four

*I*t wasn't until Angie locked the door behind her and headed for her car that she remembered Frank was coming to dinner. She glanced at her watch. Almost seven. And she'd promised to get home in time to convince Danny to join them.

She often found herself thinking of things she'd forgotten to do during the day—like depositing a check, picking up clothing at the cleaners, an appointment to get her hair cut or her teeth fixed, seeing about the "check engine" light on the dash of her car. But when she walked into her shabby office every morning, nothing else existed except the people who came to her for help—like the young couple who'd come in after they got off work to ask about bankruptcy. After two years of marriage, they were in arrears with payments on their house, car, refrigerator, and big-screen TV, and they had creditors camping on their doorstep. Before them Angie had seen a grandmother who wanted the right to see her grandchildren. Before her, a battered woman who wanted a restraining order against her boyfriend. Angie put in long full days helping people who couldn't afford to pay for solutions to their legal problems. She supposed at some level she was doing penance for her family's wealth with her low-wage, long-hour job. But she'd ceased to worry about why she did it. She just did. It had become who she was. Angie Tarrington, legal aid attorney.

And at night she drove home to a mansion. When she first went to work at the legal aid office, she tried to keep that fact from the people she worked with. But Tarrington was not a common name, and her great-grandfather had been the infamous governor "Preacher" Tarrington, who had ridden with the Ku Klux Klan. She was the sister of the victim in the city's most famous kidnapping case. One of her brothers was the youngest and certainly the most photogenic member of the state legislator. Her father was a federal judge. Her mother was active in civic affairs, sitting on boards, heading drives. Their home had been featured on the annual charity garden tour a number of times.

But when her colleagues figured out who Angie was and where she lived, Angie was surprised at how relieved she felt. Having nothing to hide was better. If they hated her because her family was rich, so be it. But nobody did. And the only male lawyer in the office confessed that his family owned a shipping company in Houston.

Every night when Angie pulled into the driveway and looked up at the house with which she had such a love-hate relationship, she would tell herself that she really must get a place of her own. But Angie didn't want to be bothered with domesticity. She didn't want to be responsible for her own meals and laundry. She didn't want to deal with cobwebs in the corners and bathtub ring. At least, that's what she told herself. Or maybe it was just that she was so consumed with her work, she couldn't imagine taking the time to make other arrangements in her life.

At what age did one become the spinster daughter, she wondered. She hadn't had a date in over a year, and what was worse, she didn't even fret about it. In the years since her one and only engagement to a college sweetheart, she'd had numerous crushes but never really been in love. And she had grown weary of the bad scenes at relationship's end and found herself wondering if it was better not to get involved in the first place. Julia, of all people, claimed that Angie was afraid of commitment. Julia used to toss a man out of her Austin apartment as soon as he put his name on the mailbox.

Now that Frank no longer lived in the garage apartment he—like Matt and Julia—had become a guest in the home of their childhood, his visits generally arranged beforehand. Like the one tonight. He'd called yesterday to make sure his parents would be at home this evening and invited himself to dinner.

Angie was supposed to entice Danny downstairs with the promise of Frank's visit. But Frank had been ignoring Danny. He hadn't invited him to spend the night or asked him to help in his garden since Beth reappeared—over a year ago. At least he hadn't married Beth as they had all feared.

But often Beth's car was parked in front of Frank's house, not that Angie would admit to anyone she drove down Frank's street at odd hours. And Angie had stopped going to Frank's church because she couldn't stand seeing Beth there in the fourth row.

Whenever Angie asked Frank if he and Beth were involved, he clammed up. "You're a fool," Angie would say. "She does bad things to people. She's evil." Angie realized that only she knew how evil.

Everything had been just fine until Beth came back. Angie kept thinking that. Over and over. There could be no good reason for her to resurface in their lives. Only bad ones. Was there something she should be doing? Frank was screwed up. Her parents were at their wits' end over Danny, who was now sullen and reclusive because Beth didn't love him and just sat in his room all the time watching videos. Angie wanted to shake Danny. To tell him to grow up. Beth was a creep. And he was being an idiot.

But then poor Danny was a certified idiot. A pretty woman had singled him out for attention, and he thought she loved him. What did the poor schmuck expect—that she'd marry him and have a retard for a husband? That she'd become *Mrs. Danny Tarrington?*

"Promise Danny that you'll take him to the wax museum if he has dinner with us tonight," her mother had suggested that morning while Angie was having coffee and a piece of toast before rushing out.

"Good grief, Mom! I don't have time for the wax museum. Besides, I took him on his birthday. It's

Frank's turn to take him. And besides, I thought you didn't believe in bribery."

Her mother was wearing a pair of worn jeans—probably old ones of Julia's. From behind she looked like Julia. Slim and athletic. Her face was too old for her body. The worry lines didn't help. "All right—promise that Frank will take him," Norma said, rubbing her forehead, ignoring the bribery remark. "When I took him his breakfast this morning, he put a pillow over his head until I left the room."

"Why don't you get rid of Beth? Have her fired? Give her a big check and send her packing like before?"

"Mr. Bittle said that Beth was very upset about the situation with Danny—that she offered to resign if he'd come back to work," Norma said, standing up straighter as though reminding herself that she was the strong and reasonable mother. "He said that she was just trying to be nice to Danny, that she felt like she had a special relationship with him from before, that she still thought of him like her little brother and was devastated that he'd misunderstood her affection for him."

"Maybe. Maybe not. I don't trust her."

"Oh, come on, Angie," Norma snapped. "Why in the world would she deliberately try to make a mentally challenged man fall in love with her?"

Since her mother had joined the board at Friends, she'd adopted the more politically correct term "mentally challenged." But Angie thought "retarded" was more truthful. It had the same root word as tardy. As in slow. *Very* slow. But eventually Danny would get there. He'd learned not to pick his nose or play with his penis in public. He'd learned table manners and hygiene. He learned to do a job. But now, he had slowed down so much he was going backward. Because of Beth.

"Maybe she's hedging her bets in case Frank doesn't come through. Maybe she got Danny to fall in love with her so she can share in the family money," Angie replied. "And don't bother with looking incredulous. I know it's crossed your mind, too. Beth seems bound and determined to worm her way into this family one way or the other. But she can't marry Danny because you and Daddy would have the marriage annulled. I wrote her a letter explaining that retarded adults who were in a guardianship situation have to have parental consent to get married."

"You wrote her a letter?"

"Yeah. In FYI terms," Angie said, grabbing her briefcase, kissing her mother's cheek. "I didn't specifically mention Danny, but I imagine she got the message. I can't think of any legal means of keeping her away from Frank. I have, however, thought about wringing her neck."

"Try to get home by six," Norma had said. "Seven at the latest."

Remembering her mother's words, Angie glanced at the clock on the dash. Almost seven-thirty. And the traffic was backed up on Central Expressway. A recent study out of Texas A&M ranked Dallas as one of the ten most congested cities in the United States—right up there with L.A. and New York—which didn't surprise the people who lived there. Such a waste of time—traffic. Sometimes she wished she'd moved to Austin with Julia and Nathan. She'd wanted to. There was plenty of room in Grandma Edna and Grandpa Paul's wonderful old house with the big fish still hanging in the entry hall. But Angie couldn't leave her parents with Danny. If she ever got a place of her own, it would be close by. Danny was her responsibility, too.

Angie called on the car phone to say she was running late. Maura answered. "I'll be there soon," Angie said. "Tell Mom, okay?"

"Yes. You need to be here, Angie," Maura said. "Beth Williams came with Frank."

Out of respect to devout Maura, Angie pressed the end button before she uttered a string of oaths.

She wasn't sure what to expect when she got home. But the presence of a police car, with lights flashing, parked in front of the house was shocking. As she pulled in behind it, she realized the living room bay window was shattered.

Angie slammed on the brakes and ran inside.

Her father was talking to two uniformed policemen in the entry hall, one of whom was staring up into the domed, stained-glass skylight high above them. Angie relaxed a bit. No guns were drawn. No dead bodies on the floor.

Perry excused himself to the two policeman and took Angie aside. "Frank and Beth are getting married tomorrow evening. Danny was coming down the stairs and heard Frank make the announcement. The broken window set off the burglar alarm—that's why the police are here."

"Where's everyone else?"

"I told Frank and Beth to leave. Your mother and Maura are out looking for Danny. Matt and Gretchen are on their way over. Manuel is coming to board up the window."

They hunted for hours, in the pool house, the garage, the empty garage apartment, in Clifford and Belle's yard and garage, up and down the streets of the neighborhood, knocking on doors, asking neighbors to check their backyards. At midnight, Julia and Nathan arrived from Austin and went to look at the school grounds and drive through the SMU campus. Finally, they all came straggling back to wait until daylight.

Matt sent Gretchen home and went upstairs to his brother's room. "Where are you, Danny?" he asked the empty room. "Where the hell have you gone off to?" There was a picture in the bookshelf of the two of them before Danny got sick. Two peas in a pod. Matt didn't know which little boy was him and which was his brother.

He stretched out on the bed and closed his eyes. And probably slept for a time. But suddenly his eyes were open, and he knew where his brother was.

The tree house had been built by Matt and four of his friends in a giant mesquite tree about a half mile up the creek bed in a tiny passed-over wilderness. A primitive affair of discarded lumber and added to over the years, the tree house was interchangeably a clubhouse, castle, fort, headquarters for an international spy ring and space station. During their childhood, Matt had taken Danny there only a couple of times when no one else was around, just to show it off. Danny wasn't a member of the club. Matt wouldn't let the other boys make fun of Danny, but he had been embarrassed by him and never wanted Danny to be part of his world away from home.

Danny had been enchanted with the secret place where only kids went and only kids knew about. He was always asking Matt to take him there again. Matt remembered wishing he'd never showed it to him in the first place. Danny could be a real pest.

Back when he and Gretchen were first dating, Matt had told her about the tree house, and she'd insisted they take Danny there for a picnic. Gretchen was perfect with Danny. Maybe that was how he knew she belonged with his family. The rest of his family was all perfect with Danny. Only Matt had never bothered much with Danny skills. When Danny got upset, he left him to the others. When he had cried out in the night, Matt had put his pillow over his head and waited for someone to calm him.

Matt went down the back stairway and carefully let himself out the back door. He didn't need the flashlight in his pocket. A misty first light made everything look ethereal, like a painting.

Danny was in the tree house, curled up like a baby, his thumb in his mouth. His clothes were wet from the morning dew. His skin felt like ice.

Matt took off his jacket and wrapped it around his brother's shoulders. "Ah Jesus, Danny, please don't be sad," he said, pulling Danny's thumb out of his mouth.

"Go 'way," Danny said.

Matt took his brother in his arms. "I don't want you to be sad."

Matt began to cry as he rocked back and forth with his twin in his arms. He kissed his brother's neck and ears and cheeks and wondered if he'd ever kissed Danny before. In his whole life.

Twins. That image had always made Matt uncomfortable. Being part of the same whole. He didn't want that. He didn't want to be connected in such a mystical way to poor old stupid Danny.

He'd never felt guilty about Danny having all the bad luck and he himself all the good. Those were just the breaks, the cut of the cards, the roll of the dice. He hadn't felt grateful or blessed either. Just entitled somehow.

Until he found out that he was sterile. Not perfect. Not entitled. It was the most humbling thing that had ever happened to him. And the most devastating—until Gretchen lost the baby and her uterus. By then he had completely embraced the idea of Gretchen having a baby for the three of them—her and him and Danny. How he wanted that. For so long his grandfather's money had been the driving force of his life, and now he would have gratefully traded every cent of it for that baby.

Now Gretchen was making her pursuit of adoption into a religion. She and Julia. Uncle Danny would hold a baby named for him in his arms. That was a picture Matt wanted to see. Needed to see.

Chapter Twenty-five

"Of course Beth is pregnant," Angie snapped at Julia. "Why else are they having this instant wedding?"

The sisters were in Angie's bedroom, the door open so they could hear Danny when he woke up. They had sedated him after Matt brought him home early that morning. Angie had been in the kitchen making coffee when she heard the back gate open, seen them coming up the hill, arm in arm. And had closed her eyes to thank God or whomever.

"God, it's spooky after all those years that she can just show up, crook her little finger at Frank, and have him come crawling back to her," Julia said, from the window seat. "Surely he doesn't think he's in love with her, but I just can't imagine the Reverend Doctor Frank giving himself over to plain garden-variety lust."

Angie was stretched out on the bed, her hands behind her head. "He probably makes a sacrament out of sex. She probably lets him. Poor Frank. It took him years to get his sexual self back together again in the wake of Beth. He was about to let himself fall in love with a wonderfully suitable woman. Danny was already in love with a wonderfully suitable woman. Now look at the mess they're both in."

"Yeah, but there's something I don't understand. I thought that Beth was . . ." Julia paused, then shrugged, not willing to say the word that was on her tongue.

"If you're referring to Beth's sexual persuasion," Angie said, "maybe she doesn't have one. Maybe sex for her is a way to pull people's strings."

"But why did she mess around with me?" Julia

asked, drawing her knees up and hugging them to her chest. "I was just the number two daughter of the household. Just a kid. She didn't gain a thing out of it."

"I think she would have slept with every member of the family if she could have managed it. Then all of us would either be in love with her or afraid that she would tell or both."

Angie closed her eyes, remembering the night when her misgivings about Beth Williams turned to something else altogether—to revulsion and fear. And such puzzlement. How could the woman who loved and cared with such compassion for a retarded boy engage in an act that could destroy that boy's family?

Angie had awakened in the night and been unable to go back to sleep. She was at the top of the stairs, on her way to the kitchen for a glass of milk, when the door to her parents' room creaked halfway open. A dim light from inside the room backlit the figure peering out into the dark hallway. For an instant, Angie thought her mother must have returned early from Austin. But the female figure was Beth, in her nightgown, her hair disheveled. And behind her, sitting naked on the side of the bed, Angie could see her father.

A sound came from Angie's mouth that made Beth and her father look in her direction. Suddenly the hall light was on, and Angie was running toward her room. The slam of her door sounded like a rifle shot.

Throughout the night, she thought that her father would come to her—to beg forgiveness, plead with her not to say anything to her mother, swear never to do it again. But he didn't come. And Angie realized that he had placed his future with their family in her hands. Beth's future, too. If she told, they would both be sent away. The decision was Angie's.

Her relationship with her father had been different from that moment forward. Even now. In so many subtle ways. He overdid his response to her, was too nice, too solicitous, never casual or dismissive, never playful or silly, too adult. She had ceased to be his little girl and in that one sickening moment had become his conscience. After all this time he realized that she would never tell. But he also knew that he was forever diminished in her eyes. That he had disappointed her and destroyed her faith in him in a way that could never be completely repaired. What he probably didn't realize was that she had painstakingly concentrated her hatred on Beth so she wouldn't hate him. But after all, it had been a seduction on Beth's part. Angie had no doubt that she went to him. Her father's sin was weakness.

And Julia? She'd been little more than a child. An innocent. If at a later age Julia had had a tender love affair with a loving female, she might have slipped comfortably into a life as a lesbian. Or not. But it wouldn't have left her scarred. Beth hadn't made Julia feel loved, only different. Depraved even. Uncertain where she belonged. She and Nathan seemed to have forged a good marriage out of mutual need, but Julia confessed once after too many glasses of wine that no matter what mind games she played with herself, orgasms usually made her think of Beth.

Then there was Frank. Beth sleeping with Frank, making a baby with him—such thoughts brought a nasty taste to Angie's mouth. The taste of hate. And for the first time in her life, Angie wished another human being dead. Soon. Before the baby became any more of a reality.

Julia went to get dressed for the wedding, but Angie didn't move from her bed. Her mother came to remind her that it was almost time to go.

"I'll stay here with Danny."

"That's not necessary. Manuel and Maura will both be here."

"I'm not going, Mom."

"But what should I tell Frank?" Norma asked, sitting on the side of Angie's bed. "You'll be conspicuous by your absence."

"Danny and I *both* will be conspicuous by our absence," Angie pointed out. "Tell Frank that it was a choice between my staying away or strangling the bride."

"Beth will be your brother's wife," Norma said, her voice more weary than stern. "I've arranged a nice family wedding for them at the Melrose with a dinner afterward. We need to welcome Beth into this family and hope for the best."

"Not me, Mom."

"Think of the baby," Norma said softly.

"I'd rather not," Angie said, rolling away from her mother. "The only good outcome for this union that I can think of is for Beth to die in childbirth. And even then, I'd always be watching the kid for signs of the bad seed."

After everyone had left and the house was quiet once again, Angie fixed a sandwich and opened her briefcase. She stared at some paperwork for a time but couldn't make herself concentrate. Frank was making the mistake of his life. Danny was facing an uncertain future. Matt couldn't produce an heir. Her own life was one endless rut. Of the Tarrington offspring only Julia seemed reasonably content. She and Nathan trusted each other. They loved their house, their garden, their animals. They found satisfaction in working with the troubled teens who passed through their lives. They both still swam all those laps every day. And now they wanted babies. Gretchen was giving them courage finally to do that—actually assume total responsibility for the life of another human being.

Angie gave up on work and ended up napping in the easy chair in Danny's room, waiting for him to wake up. Finally about six, she realized he was sitting up in bed, looking at her. "Hi, guy. How are you feeling?"

"Did Frank and Beth have a wedding?"

"I'm afraid so, honey. Beth is your sister-in-law now. Like Gretchen. Can I get you something to eat? You've been asleep for a long time."

He didn't say anything but seemed calm enough, so Angie headed downstairs to warm something for him. She was starting back up the stairs when she heard a loud crash.

She left the tray on a step and ran the rest of the way.

Danny had pushed over the book case. And was punching his fists through the wall. Methodically. Making one hole after another in the wallboard. Like a robot. Not a sound coming from his mouth. Angie watched helplessly, afraid to interfere.

Finally, he hit a stud and crumpled to the floor, cradling his hurt hand with the other, whimpering like a hurt animal.

Angie left a message on the kitchen table and drove him to the hospital. He was moaning now. Loudly.

By the time she reached the hospital, he was losing control, hitting his head against the car window so hard Angie was afraid he was going to break it.

The emergency room physician gave him a shot to calm him, with almost immediate results. "Beth Williams loves *me*," Danny said as he drifted into pain-free limbo.

Surgery would be required to mend his hand, the orthopedic surgeon told Angie—in the morning. They'd keep him knocked out for the night.

By the time Norma and Perry arrived, still in their wedding finery, Danny had been admitted and moved to a private room. Perry arranged for a cot and sent his wife and daughter home.

"We'll have to put him on some kind of heavy duty tranquilizers," Angie told her mother during the drive home. "It's either that or a straightjacket."

"Perhaps. But all these years, we've worked so hard to make him as aware as possible, to push his horizons as far as they would go. Isn't it ironic—Beth taught us how to do that, and I've always been grateful to her. But now because of her, we're losing him. If we put him on drugs, I'm afraid he'll slip into some sort of dim-witted fog and the part of him that makes him Danny will disappear."

Norma fished around in her purse for a tissue and blew her nose. "I still don't understand how all this

happened," she continued, her voice tearful. "He was
doing so well. A happy young man. He liked himself. He
had a girlfriend. He seemed to be handling Beth's return just fine. He actually seemed indifferent to her.
What changed everything?"

Angie didn't bother to answer. Beth herself had
changed everything. She hadn't wanted an indifferent
Danny. Indifference was intolerable. None of them
were indifferent now. She was a member of their family.

Once Danny was home from the hospital, Dr. Burk
prescribed a mild tranquilizer. But it didn't help. He
pushed over the grandfather clock for making a sound
that hurt his head and the china cabinet in the dining
room for no reason at all, breaking every dish of
Norma's grandmother Havelin. Even with his left hand
in a cast, Danny managed to hack down all the yellow
rose bushes. He wouldn't or couldn't say why. The yellow ones had been Beth's favorite, but Danny wouldn't
remember something like that.

With Danny's reactions to his brother's marriage, it
was out of the question for Frank and his new wife to
come to his parents' home for family gatherings. The
week after the wedding, Clifford and Belle gave a reception for Frank and Beth at their home. And the family
gathered there for Clifford's birthday, Easter dinner,
Norma and Perry's anniversary. Danny would stay at
home with Maura or her daughter, sometimes with
Manuel if he seemed to be having an especially bad day,
while his family gathered without him.

Dr. Burk prescribed a stronger medication that
made Danny sleepy and docile. The first time Julia saw
him all doped up, she became hysterical.

Frank opened the door to his church office, promising himself that he would at least go through the
backed up mail on his desk. He looked around for his
letter opener but couldn't find it, so he ripped open
two envelopes. The first envelope contained a letter in-
viting him to become a board member of the local

Planned Parenthood chapter. The second was a survey
of Unitarian ministers in the region about what topics
they wanted covered at the next regional meeting. He'd
trashed both and sat staring at the rest of the mail.

Maybe there was no point in opening it. He no
longer had any desire to attend meetings, pay bills, give
money, address theological questions, join yet another
liberal organization, take part in yet another pro-choice
rally, give another speech on why the nation's forefa-
thers separated church and state. And once he had
been so pleased to assume his role as a voice of reason
in the Dallas–Fort Worth area, one of the handful of
people television news programs contacted if they
wanted a statement from the liberal side on such issues
as prayer in school, Nativity scenes in public parks, abortion rights.

Before Beth reentered his life, his desk had always
been immaculate. And his office. His new house. The
church. The grounds. His whole life was immaculate.
Then one day after church, Beth had led him in here,
closed the door and, without a word, taken off her
clothes. They'd made love on this very desk. He'd been
a virgin. At age thirty-five.

Frank began trembling just thinking about it. The
sight of her body. The feel of her. The smell of her. He
groaned and put his head down in the middle of the
clutter on his desk, scrunching envelopes in his fists.
"Beth," he said into the pile of mail. "Beth." A holy
word or a curse, he wasn't sure which.

When he lifted his head, a young Hispanic man
with a plastic identification badge hanging from his
shirt pocket was watching him from the doorway. "I—
I'm sorry," the young man stammered, holding out a
letter. "Are you Dr. Tarrington?"

"I suppose," Frank said. He signed for the letter,
tossed it in the middle of the pile. And considered not
opening it.

But a messengered letter commanded attention. It
bore no return address. Was that usual? He supposed a

return address wasn't necessary if the letter was going to be hand-delivered to the addressee.

He looked around again for the missing letter opener, then tore open the envelope without it. The one-page letter was from Clayburn Stockton, the president of the congregation. They'd had called a meeting of the executive board yesterday evening, it seemed. And had unanimously voted to ask for Frank's resignation.

"It is with great regret that we take this action," the second of two paragraphs read. "Until recently, you were the most successful pastor in the history of this congregation. The church was experiencing growth and attendance at an all-time high. But recent events have led us to believe you are no longer able to deal with the responsibilities of your position."

Recent events. Like forgetting a wedding. Screwing up a funeral by repeatedly calling the deceased by the wrong name until the man's son stood and corrected him. Climbing into the pulpit unprepared and preaching rambling, stream-of-consciousness sermons that caused parishioners to avoid him in the fellowship hall afterward, glancing at him over their shoulders as they gathered in tight little groups.

Frank tried to decide if he was devastated by his termination. He decided that he would decide later. Without bothering to turn off the lights or lock up the building, he left his office and walked across the yard to his church-owned house. The tulips he and Danny had planted were finished blooming, but the irises were beginning to show themselves. And Belle's oak tree was leafed out. He'd have to leave the bulbs and the tree. His church and house. Move away.

Beth was still asleep. Pregnancy made her lethargic, and she often slept late. He sat in the chair across the room and watched her, as he sometimes did at night, a pillow clutched against his middle to ease the hollow feeling that now resided there. He didn't sleep much anymore. Maybe he had a disease. Maybe he was going crazy—like before, when he was a freshman at Rice and

couldn't study, listen, read, write, eat, think, when his
family had receded into the dim outer reaches of his
consciousness along with his goals, politics, religious
struggle, everything, when Beth was all that mattered. It
had taken him most of his adult life to climb and crawl
and tunnel back from that time. He didn't have the
strength to do it again. This time he was lost.

She slept on her side, which accentuated the curve
of her hip. Her brilliant hair fanned on the pillow behind her. Goddess hair. Her right breast was partially
exposed, the top half of its nipple visible. And he felt
the beginnings of an erection. He would sit here and
watch her until she woke up. Then he would fuck her.
She never said no. Whenever he wanted her, she would
receive him with perfect passivity, allowing him to do
whatever he wanted. He could enter her body wherever
he desired, have orgasms in or on whatever part of her
person he wished—in her hair, between her breasts, in
every orifice. Sex with Beth was what he lived for. He
seldom thought about anything else. Sometimes he entered her with great reverence and tenderness, allowing
the lovemaking to become a spiritual thing. Other
times, he thought of killing her—of taking the pillow
from under her head and suffocating her. Snuffing out
her life. But gently. He didn't want to hurt her. Just be
free of her. So he could think again.

He watched her intently, as though there might be
some meaning in a muscle twitch, a fluttering eyelid, a
sigh. But she made no sound. No movement. He imagined the bed as a stone altar and Beth the chosen one
waiting in perfect repose for the sacrificial knife to
pierce her heart. How pleased the gods would be.

Her eyes opened. But she didn't move. Her face
bore no expression. Frank began pulling off his clothes.
His penis was fully hard now. In great need. Painfully so.
He would die if he didn't have her.

She didn't change her position, so he pulled back
the sheet, rolled her onto her back, pushed her legs
apart and went down on her, burying his face against
her crotch, straining his tongue to go as far as it would

inside of her. She smelled of last night. Tasted of last
night. His own semen fermenting in her warm vagina.
He reached down to take his penis in his hand and
began masturbating. Then suddenly, with frantic urgency he threw himself on top of her, entered her,
shoved himself hard inside of her.

And came immediately. Volts of electricity coursing
through his veins, curling his toes, shriveling his penis
and his soul.

He always wept afterward. He didn't know why.
Maybe because he had gone that far and hadn't seen
the face of God or begun an eternal fall into a bottom-
less pit.

Later, with his head resting against her breasts, he
told Beth about the letter, and she told him it didn't
matter. He had a nice income from the Ledbetter estate. Money and name were what was important. She'd
learned that the hard way.

Chapter Twenty-six

*E*ven with just the four of them, Norma insisted on making Sunday dinner an occasion, with fresh flowers for a centerpiece and everyone suitably attired. Perry would take off his coat and tie but wait until after dinner to put on sweats or golfing attire. And even if Angie didn't go to church, which in recent years was usually the case, she knew better than to come to the table in jeans. She understood that as long as she remained in this house, she was to abide by her mother's rules.

Today Angie was wearing a shapeless brown thing that looked more like a sack than a dress, with her hair in braids, no jewelry other than what looked like a man's watch, and no makeup that Perry could discern. His older daughter was a beautiful woman, but she made people work to see it.

Norma was stylish in a blue suit with white trim around the collar. But so thin and tightly strung. The situation with Danny was taking its toll. Sometimes, in the night, she would creep into her bathroom to cry. Sometimes Perry cried, too, over his inability to help his son. It wasn't supposed to be like this. They'd gone through so much with Danny, and these last years, with him doing so well, had been the payoff. They had been as proud of him as they were of the other children. More. He'd started from so far back and come such a long way.

Thanks to Angie, Danny's hair was carefully parted and combed, and he was neatly dressed in khaki slacks and a navy shirt. Someone had to supervise his getting dressed now, telling him what to put on next, to comb his hair. He had to be reminded to take showers. Shave.

Clip his nails. He still could do those things, but he now spent most of his hours in a drug-induced haze and needed to be prodded.

Danny was eating his food like a robot, showing no excitement over roast beef and mashed potatoes with rich brown gravy, which not too long ago would have evoked a series of "oh boys" and dibs on seconds before he'd even tackled the first plateful. At least he was joining them for meals again.

But dinner had been less of a strain when Danny was still refusing to come downstairs. Now mealtime conversation dealt mostly with the logistics of getting the food served, the salt and pepper passed, perhaps a nominal rehash of the daily news. They were too stifled by Danny's silent, hulking presence to argue about politics or discuss interesting law cases. They carefully avoided any mention of Frank and Beth, although Danny seemed unaware of the conversation around him. Sometimes Perry wondered if he even remembered the cause of his depression.

When Danny was five years old, it was necessary to say his name—often two or three times—to get his attention. Perry remembered having to take Danny's face between his hands and establish eye contact in order to summon what was left of his mind from the dim recesses it kept retreating to. The medication Dr. Burk had finally resorted to made Danny five years old again. But without it, his mood turned black, and he broke things.

After dinner, Perry usually took Danny for a walk or a drive just to get him out of the house. Otherwise, he spent his entire day sleeping or watching videos. They called his medication "feel-better pills," but Perry thought "feel-nothing pills" might be more appropriate. Dr. Burk was hopeful that over time they could reduce the dosage or only use the drug when Danny became agitated. She wouldn't promise, however, that he would ever be the same happy young man he was before Beth broke his heart. All those years ago after the kidnapping, Beth had helped Danny find himself again. How ironic that because of her he was once again lost.

Maura always made a pie for Sunday dessert. Today's pie was apple with raisins and freshly ground cinnamon and served warm with cheddar cheese. But Perry had no appetite for anything scrumptious. He'd have a piece this evening, he promised Maura. Just coffee for now.

Even Maura wasn't herself these days and was talking about retiring. Which added to their sadness. Maura had been with them since Angie was a toddler. But Perry couldn't blame her for wanting to leave. She was getting old, and the Tarrington household wasn't a pleasant place to work anymore.

Because of Beth.

Perry had tried to hate Beth all those years ago—after he woke and found her in his bed. But he could have sent her away. And his relationship with Angie would not have been forever compromised. So in the end, he had hated only himself.

Norma had never allowed the children to say they hated somebody. "You can dislike someone a great deal, but you mustn't hate," she would insist. "Hate makes you ugly and shrinks your heart."

Perry glanced at himself in the mirror over the sideboard. He couldn't decide if older was the same as uglier, and his heart felt heavier rather than smaller. But certainly hate was demeaning. And it took up all the space and left no room for happiness, contentment, peace. He used to hate his father. But he'd gotten over that. Now he hated Beth, and he doubted if he could ever forgive her for what had happened to his family—to his beautiful family.

And last week, when Frank lost his church, even Norma finally admitted that she hated Beth. Of course, she kept trying to talk herself out of it. Beth was part of their family. And the child she carried bound her irrevocably to them for all time. Even if Beth's marriage to Frank didn't survive, they would forever be the grandparents of her child. Maybe Beth had meant no harm in befriending Danny and couldn't have foreseen the disastrous outcome. But at the end of such litanies, Norma always returned to the irrefutable fact that Beth was using Frank. Beth wanted Frank's name and his money. She didn't love Frank. Norma did—and she couldn't stand what was happening to him.

Perry wished Claire Ledbetter were still alive. She would have known how to save Frank and have the courage to do it. He remembered Lucy telling him about how her mother once killed a man with a pitchfork—an escapee from the New Mexico State Reformatory who held them hostage during a snowstorm. Even with Beth pregnant, Claire would rather have had her dead than harming Frank. Perry allowed himself to imagine how Claire might have killed Beth. Push her out of the hayloft. Drown her in a farm pond. Drive her out in the middle of noplace and leave her to freeze in a blizzard. Then he shook his head to clear it of such thoughts. And looked at himself again in the mirror. Maybe he was uglier. Certainly sadder.

The phone rang as he poured himself a second cup of coffee. The call was from Mary Ann Singleton's father. He thought Perry and Norma would want to know that Mary Ann was dead. She'd died early this morning after drinking bug killer.

Perry carefully hung up the phone, put his face in his hands, and moaned. It was too much to bear. Too much.

"This used to be my bedroom," Perry said, looking around the third-floor room with its dormer windows and sloping ceiling that was now filled, along with the other long unused third-floor rooms, with a jumble of furniture and boxes brought over yesterday from the Unitarian parsonage.

"That's what Grandma Belle said. She said you moved up here when you were in high school so you could play your drums without complaints from Clifford. I didn't know you ever played drums."

"Only briefly. In between tennis and poetry. I was trying to find a calling so I wouldn't have to go to law school. How long do you think you and Beth will stay with your grandparents?"

Frank shrugged. "Forever, I guess. Clifford said he'd leave the house to us."

Perry moved a desk chair over by the bench where Frank was sitting, his skinny legs jutting out from his bathrobe, several days' worth of stubble on his chin—at almost five-thirty in the evening. Belle and Beth weren't back from a shopping trip to buy curtains and rugs for the third floor, Beatrice had said. She hadn't seen Frank all day. Frank had been in bed when Perry came upstairs looking for him.

"I'm having a hard time understanding why my father has had this sudden change of heart about your status in the family," Perry said. "Besides leaving you the house, your grandmother tells me that he plans to change his will in favor of your baby if it's a boy, with you and Beth as trustees."

Frank rested his head against the wall and closed his eyes. His eyes were sunken in his head and rimmed by dark shadows. And he was so thin he looked wasted. "It's not so hard to understand about the will when you consider that the baby isn't mine," Frank said, "and Clifford obviously knows it."

Perry replayed his son's words. *Not Frank's baby?* "Are you sure?" he asked.

Frank offered a small shrug. "Beth was already throwing up in the mornings by the time we started having sex."

"And you married her anyway."

Frank began to shiver and picked up a towel from the floor to cover his legs. "Sure," he answered. "I figured I was following in your footsteps—entering into a marriage that shows every promise of being just as disastrous as yours was to my mother and raising a baby that isn't mine."

"Look, son, if you think Beth trapped you into

marriage with another man's child, no one would blame you for getting out."

"Not just any other man, Dad. I'd be willing to wager that Danny is the father of Beth's baby."

"Danny?" Perry stared at Frank. "Danny?" he repeated. "What the hell are you talking about?"

"Why else would Clifford be changing his will?" Frank asked, wrapping his arms around his thin body.

"Because he's old, and it's time to get his affairs in order," Perry offered.

Frank shook his head. "The old man's been on a mission to perpetuate the Tarrington name and his precious seed ever since he nominated Matt as heir apparent. But now Matt and Gretchen can't have children. And Tarrington blood doesn't flow in my veins. Which leaves Danny, who's brain-damaged but genetically sound."

"You can't be serious. Beth had sex with Danny?"

"Why not?" Frank asked. "Remember when Danny was a horny adolescent and couldn't keep his hands off of her, how he would push her down and crawl on top of her? I rather imagine poor Danny was quite easy to seduce. It's a brilliant plan really. I provide the baby with the Tarrington name, and Danny gives it the Tarrington genes. And his majesty King Clifford can die knowing that he will live on through his progeny. The fortune begun by his father and so lovingly nurtured by Clifford's capable hands will continue reasonably intact minus a few million or so for lesser heirs. He didn't think his own son was up to tending all that money, did he, Dad? Matt showed promise but can't have a kid. But with Danny's kid, Clifford gets what he wanted and a bonus in the bargain. He gets Beth. Even if the kid turns out to be a wimp, Beth will be in charge. And Beth is a woman after Clifford's own heart. She believes in doing what needs to be done to accomplish her goals. Clifford admires that. He's decided to mentor her. Last night after dinner, they went into his office and talked business. For hours."

Perry got up and walked to the window, staring out

at the treetops, fully leafed out now, ready to provide shade against the hot summer sun. The back of his own house was barely visible through the foliage. And the roof of the pool house. Norma was just saying this morning that it was time to uncover the pool. Maybe Danny would perk up if he could swim every day.

Danny. Would Beth do that?

Perry remembered the time he'd awakened to find Beth in his bed—building job security, he'd later decided. Or maybe she did it for the money she later extorted from him—for an abortion, she said, which he translated to hush money. He'd given her ten thousand dollars. And expected her to hit him up again in the future. Such power she had over him. When they dismissed her, Perry expected her to tell Norma. She was on the verge of hysteria—seemingly more from the prospect of leaving than from her close call in the swimming pool. She begged them not to send her away. She'd done her best for Danny. He loved her. She'd thought they all loved her and were her family. Their house was her home, the only real home she'd ever had.

"If what you say is true," Perry said, still staring out the window, "why would you be party to such a plan. Why not walk away?"

"I didn't figure it out until after we were married," Frank admitted. "And walking away wouldn't change anything except make Beth a single parent. And in her defense, I honestly believe that she wants a baby. She said that she had a baby once—a little girl named Annie —but she didn't get to keep it. She keeps talking about how much she loves this baby already and how much the baby will love her. She says that only two people have ever really loved her—her brother and Danny."

"You don't love her?" Perry asked.

"No. What I feel for Beth isn't love. Did you love Lucy? You said once that you knew you never should have married her. I knew that I never should have married Beth. Was Lucy like Beth?"

"No," Perry said. He put his hand on Frank's thin shoulder for a minute, then returned to his chair.

"Lucy told me from the very first that I should stay in Texas and marry Norma. I went with her because I was running away from my father and the life he had planned for me—including marrying a fine, upstanding woman like Norma. And Lucy was running away from her mother and West Texas and all that land. Claire thought the land was sacred. Lucy wanted no part of it. Then I wanted to come home. So she ran away from me, too. But I never even considered not keeping you, Frank. I wanted something good to come out of the disaster she and I had made."

"So what do you think?" Frank asked, gesturing at his own unkempt self. "It appears as though the 'something good' is starting to rot."

"How can I help you, Frank?"

Frank shook his head back and forth, tears flowing down his cheeks. "I feel so lost, Dad. I try to think about the baby and plan for it. But it will be *her* baby. What if she won't let it love me?"

Chapter Twenty-seven

"Why in God's name would you do a thing like that?" Angie demanded.

"Because we have to try to get along—for Frank's sake," her mother said. Norma picked up a pitcher of heated milk and poured a generous amount into her coffee.

Angie sighed and sipped her own coffee, without milk, fine strong coffee that her mother ordered directly from a coffee importer. At the legal aid office, the coffee was a weakly brewed store brand. And the view out the window was of a dumpster, not a well-tended rose garden. But at the office, Angie could forget about the misery at home. "How can you want to 'get along' with Beth after what Dad told us last night. She ripped Danny's heart out of his chest and stomped on it. For God's sake, Mom, she seduced him! Used him to get herself pregnant with a baby that would make her rich. And poor dumb Danny thought she loved him! Because of her, he's turned into a zombie, Mary Ann Singleton is dead, and Frank has lost his church and self-respect."

"We don't know anything for sure," Norma said, staring down at the unopened morning paper. "Frank himself admits he's not sure. And I find it difficult to believe that Beth would do such an evil, calculating thing. I'm not sure how she feels about the rest of us, but she's always cared about Danny. You know that."

"You just want the baby," Angie accused. "But that baby will belong to Clifford—bought and paid for by him. He probably put her up to it."

"Clifford won't live forever," Norma said.

"Yeah, and when he's dead, Beth will be the

mother of one rich baby," Angie persisted. "Don't kid yourself, Mom. Beth's not going to let you have anything to do with that kid."

"If the baby does turn out to be Danny's, what would you have me do, Angie? A mentally deficient man can hardly sue for custody. If we pressure Beth, she can always claim that Danny forced her to have sex. It seems to me that all we can do is bide our time, see what happens. And you're right. I do want that baby. I'm going to try and get along with the woman who is carrying it. When Beth asked about using the swimming pool, I told her yes." Norma opened the newspaper and adjusted her reading glasses, signifying an end to the conversation.

"What about Danny?" Angie persisted. "Is it fair to him that we get chummy with Beth?"

"He doesn't need to know."

"Mom! This is Danny's home. The swimming pool we are discussing happens to be in our backyard. And you've been hoping that warm weather and opening the pool will be good for him, get him outside some, get him moving again. Now you want to let Beth use the pool whenever she wants?"

"I'm not sure that anything will get Danny moving again. And quite frankly, your father and I don't know how much longer we should try to keep Danny at home," Norma said, avoiding her daughter's gaze.

Angie sucked in her breath and put a hand to her face as though she'd been slapped. "He'll never get better if you send him away."

"I don't know what to do for him anymore," Norma said with a helpless flutter of her hands.

"Well, you certainly don't let the woman who got him all screwed up in the first place take over his swimming pool!"

"She's coming over this evening," Norma said, ignoring Angie's comment. "I wish you'd join us. I need you."

"Hell no!" Angie said, tossing her napkin on the table and storming from the breakfast room. Jesus

Christ! Her mother talking about sending Danny away! Angie felt like the walls of the house had just collapsed around her. Would she really do that? Her mother and Danny were what made the family special. What made them all good people. Angie had known that someday, when her parents were old, Danny would probably live someplace else—maybe at Friends House. But he'd be able to come home anytime he wanted. And someday the home he came to would be her home, whether here or someplace else. But what her mother was talking about wasn't Friends House. The Friends organization wasn't set up to deal with emotional problems. He'd have to go to someplace with a high fence around it. Like a prison.

Angie called the office to tell them that she'd be late, then flew up the steps two at time.

She tossed her bathrobe on the bed and rummaged around until she found a bathing suit—a rather threadbare bathing suit, but she didn't bother to look further and pulled it on, then grabbed a towel and headed across the hall to Danny's room.

She tapped, then said his name and opened the door. He was still in bed, of course. Sleeping on his back, his mouth open. Angie rumpled his hair then kissed each closed eye, his nose, chin, forehead, cheeks. She picked up a hand and begin kissing it. "Wake up, sweet Danny," she cooed. "We're going swimming. The pool is full of sparkling clean water that's been warmed up just for you. And wait till you see the cool rubber boat I bought for you. You can sleep in the rubber boat if you want. But I want you to get out of this bed right now."

He opened his eyes but didn't move. Angie rummaged around in his bureau until she found a pair of swimming trunks. Then she went back to his bed and pulled the covers back.

"Such a serious face," she said, pulling the corners of his mouth into a smile. "Come on, Danny. I'm going to work late this morning just so you and I can have the first swim of the summer. Let's go get baptized in the pool. Be born again. A new beginning. A new Danny. Let's go get all wet. Please, Danny, please, you'll be my best friend forever if you'll just get out of that bed and come swimming with me."

He pushed her hands away from his face and very slowly, like a mechanical man, one movement at a time, got out of bed and went into the bathroom. Angie could hear him using the toilet, flushing. She realized she was holding her breath. If he came out that door with his trunks on, everything was going to be all right.

The trunks were too big for him. He'd lost weight. Gone soft. And so white. Like someone who'd been living in a cave.

Still wearing her robe and house shoes, Norma came down the hill to watch them. Danny sat for a long time with just his legs in the water, like when he was a little boy, before Beth came and taught him to love the water. Angie paddled around, not daring to splash him or throw taunts. Finally he slipped into the water and began swimming up and back in a clumsy crawl. Angie swam alongside him. Feeling hopeful. Wouldn't it be wonderful if right this minute he was turning the corner and getting ready to come back to them, to be himself again, to go back to Friends. Beth wasn't there anymore. She was the lady-in-waiting over at Clifford and Belle's. Clifford was on top of the world. Belle was wondering if she should move out. Let Clifford dig Beth a pool over there if she wanted to swim.

With silent Danny following, Angie and Norma walked back up the hill to the house. "You've made your point," Norma said. "Swimming could help. But Beth is still coming over here tonight to go swimming. Maybe we can work out a schedule so they can both use the pool."

At the back door, Norma grabbed Angie's hand. "Don't be mad at me, honey. Your father and I won't do anything unless we think it's best for Danny. But we're tired. I think we'd like a little freedom before we're too old to enjoy it—a summer in southern France maybe, a Mediterranean cruise, see the Pyramids. As long as Danny was at Friends, everything was fine. But nothing is fine now."

"But it's not fair," Angie said, repeating herself, knowing that she sounded like a whiny child.

"Few things in life are," Norma said, kissing her daughter's cheek. "Let's see what happens, okay?"

"You're his twin brother. Think of something!" she demanded after her second gin and tonic.

Matt was wearing the usual dark suit, white shirt, necktie. But his hair was a bit longer. And his necktie had a floral design rather than the usual boring stripe, which was borderline risqué attire for a lawyer from an old-line firm like Tarrington's. But he'd been in Austin today, on legislative business.

They hadn't done this for a long time—met for a drink after work. Her fault, not his. She stayed too long at the office. He didn't like waiting around for her. He still hurried home to Gretchen—not because she expected it but because he wanted to. Which Angie found sweet and rather amazing.

"This whole shitty business is killing Mom and Dad," Angie went on. "Killing us all. We used to be the best family ever, and now look at us. I can't stand what's happened to Danny, to the sweetest human being that ever walked the face of the earth. I'd rather see him dead than have him like he is now."

"I wonder if killing Beth would help," Matt said, almost casually, cradling his beer mug in both hands.

Angie looked around to see if anyone might have heard his words. "You really shouldn't say things like that. Someone might take you seriously."

"Just suppose for a minute," he said, leaning forward, lowering his voice. "Would killing Beth help?"

"I'm not sure."

"You've thought of it, too, then?"

"I'm sure we all have in passing—except Clifford. Even Frank. Maybe most of all, Frank. Julia says we should kill Beth and tell God she died. Mom doesn't even tell her not to talk like that. But it all falls into the category of wishful thinking—like when I wish that someone would drop a boulder on Rush Limbaugh's head."

"The problem with Beth goes way beyond Danny," Matt said. "She's ruining this family."

"And stealing all those beautiful millions you thought would be yours," Angie reminded him.

"Do you want *her* to have the money?" Matt demanded. "You want her to destroy Frank? And our family? Think of the hold she'll have over Mom and Dad when that baby is born. They'll have to beg her to take the kid for a walk. I wish she would die. Now. Before there's a baby. I see now how sick all this dynasty crap really is."

"That's a pretty incredible statement coming from the guy who would have sold his soul to get his hands on Grandfather Clifford's fortune."

Matt studied his sister's face for a few seconds, then sagged against the high back of the banquette. "You never were one to mince words. You're right, of course. In a way, I'm no better than Beth. I used Danny, too. Just like Beth did. I used him as a donor for artificial insemination to make my wife pregnant."

"I wondered if that's what happened."

His eyes widened in surprise. "You did? Why?"

"Because it took years for Gretchen to become pregnant, then suddenly she gets pregnant three times in fairly quick succession. But any baby she had would have been more than just an heir. It would have been wanted and loved."

"Yes, but when I asked Mom to arrange things, I can't honestly say that my desire for a baby wasn't at least in part a means to an end. Mom didn't think of it that way, though. She said Danny's baby would be genetically the same as my own. That it would be our baby—Danny's and mine. I wanted that, Angie. More than all the money in the world, I wanted that baby."

"But if Frank is right in his supposition, the baby Beth carries is genetically yours *and* Danny's, too."

"But Beth will be the mother, not Gretchen. If Grandfather Clifford hadn't been so fixated on continuing the Tarrington name, things wouldn't have gone this far. Frank would still have his church. Danny would still be the strongest worker at Friends. Beth would be long gone. And I could convince Grandfather to endow a foundation, with you, Julia, Frank, and me as trustees. His name could live on by the good that came of his money. We could endow a Clifford Tarrington Chair of Criminal Defense at UT. We could build a new law building and call it the Tarrington College of Law. We could start Friends organizations in other cities. Feed every hungry kid in the state of Texas. Do lots of things. Good things."

"But that's not going to happen," Angie said, methodically tearing her napkin in half, then fourths, then eighths.

"No," he agreed. "Not as long as there's Beth. I don't want her to have that baby, Angie. And I don't want her to have our family's money."

"I hate her," Angie said, concentrating on her tearing.

"Maybe if you forgot to give Danny his medicine, he might kill her during one of his rages? Or someone else could kill her and say that Danny did it during one of his rages."

Angie stopped tearing. "Why Danny?"

"Because he's protected?"

Angie stared down at the pile of napkin pieces, contemplating what her brother had just said. "He might be protected from the death penalty," she said, "but he'd still be facing some sort of incarceration."

"I think he's facing some sort of confinement regardless of what happens," Matt pointed out.

Angie regarded the deadly serious look on her brother's face. And felt an involuntary shiver raise the hair on her arms. "Hey, we're just kidding, aren't we?"

"Sure," he said, patting her hand. "Gretchen says to tell you she's met the perfect guy for you."

Angie relaxed. They were back on safer ground. "Even more perfect than her last find?"

"Hey, she didn't know that he communicates with his dead mother until he mentioned it at dinner."

Norma pulled on her suit and scrutinized herself in the full-length mirror. What she saw was a still-attractive woman in spite of passing years.

She swam laps almost every night in the summertime, and in the winter, she went two or three times a week to the pool at a nearby health club. Swimming kept her stomach flat. Tennis made her legs strong. Plastic surgery kept the sags in her face under control. How she looked was still important to her even though she admired women who simply got older and didn't fight the bulges and gray hair, couldn't be bothered with lid tucks and face lifts, didn't mind wearing the same dress to the symphony's opening night three seasons in a row. But these women lost some of their effectiveness as human beings, some of their power. The world took firm, middle-aged women more seriously than it did plump, white-haired ladies. And so much of her life was based on making an impact and getting things done. Like keeping Friends going. The organization would have folded long ago if it hadn't been for her influence, her organizational skills, her determination.

Now, it was her family she was trying to keep from folding. She needed to be strong, to be ready for whatever lay ahead.

She probably shouldn't have said that about sending Danny away this morning. She could practically feel the pedestal that Angie had erected under her crumbling. Angie wasn't ready to face the truth about Danny—or her mother. Angie still wanted to believe that love conquered all and that her mother would live out her life being as selfless as Mother Teresa even though Angie herself would never choose to repeat her mother's life.

And what Norma had said wasn't exactly the truth.
Before Danny's troubles began, she and Perry had
talked about allowing him to live at Friends House. And
the idea of him marrying Mary Ann no longer seemed
as outrageous as it once did—not since that Friends
couple got married last year. Clyde and Sara. That really
impressed Danny. He'd wanted to marry Mary Ann and
for them to live at Friends House with a microwave in
their room.

But now that Mary Ann was dead and Danny was a
management problem, she and Perry never discussed
their options. They were both hoping for a miracle, she
supposed.

Norma was ready for a little freedom in her life, for
more travels with her husband. Because of Danny,
they'd never seen the world. Perry had lived in New
York when he was married to Lucy, but except for skiing
trips to Colorado with Danny along, Norma had never
been outside the state of Texas more than a few days at
a time. She'd never been out of the country. Never seen
Venice or Paris. Never seen her ancestral village in
Wales. Never been someplace else. Never been a for-
eigner. Was she terrible for wanting those things? Was
she terrible for not wanting to deal with a retarded
adult son who no longer seemed to care if she was with
him or not?

Norma sighed. Yes, probably she was. Before, she
could have made other arrangements for Danny and
sent him off to a happy new life with family members
nearby. Now, she wasn't so sure. Maybe Angie was right.
If they sent him away, maybe they would be destroying
any chance of his finding himself again.

Norma checked on Danny in his room, his glazed-
over eyes staring at the television screen. When she
touched his cheek and kissed the top of his head, he
made no response.

"I'll be down by the pool," she told Maura. "Listen
for Danny."

She unlocked the back gate and waited for Beth

inside the pool enclosure. She'd a had a key to the back gate made to give Beth so that she could come and go on her own when Danny wasn't in the pool. Afternoons were probably best.

Norma took a beer from the pool-house refrigerator and sat in her favorite chaise. How much enjoyment this old pool had provided over the years. It had been built as a surprise for her and her brother. They'd come home from camp and there it was in the backyard. Such excitement. They'd run down the hill and jumped in with their clothes on—their parents, too. A nice memory. She and Perry had added the pool house and enclosed the area with a high iron fence. The trees surrounding the enclosure had grown tall, and their leaves made upkeep more difficult. Keeping the area around the pool hosed off and tidy had been Danny's job. Now Manuel and his sons would have to tend to it.

She'd gotten tears in her eyes this morning, watching Danny in his man's body sitting there on the side of the pool, not sure if he dared to get in. Like when he was little boy. Beth had helped him overcome his fear of the water and taught him to swim. She had taught Danny so many things. Most of the time she had spent with this family had been good.

Norma heard the gate squeak open. And stood. She'd either come to terms with Beth or . . .

Or what? At this point, she wasn't sure. But she would find a solution if one was needed.

Norma tried not to stare at Beth's stomach, which was just beginning to swell. Norma wanted to feel joy at Beth's pregnancy, at the grandchild that would be born. Instead, she found herself hoping that the pregnancy was a lie. Or that Beth would miscarry.

For whether this baby was Frank's or Danny's or some man's off the street, it would be Beth's. And Norma wasn't sure she was capable of loving a child of Beth's.

But then she once wished that Lucy Ledbetter

would swim out in the ocean and drown. Or be eaten by a shark. And Norma had loved Lucy's baby for a lifetime.

"Swimming will be good for you," she told Beth. "And the baby."

Chapter Twenty-eight

"*J*ust come with us for a few minutes—to sing happy birthday to Granny Belle," Angie begged.

"She wants you to come to her party," Matt added. "She says it's not fair that she comes to see you, but you haven't crossed over the bridge to her house in a long time. She even has a surprise for you."

"What surprise?" Danny asked, eying the remote control on the table by his chair. Angie had turned off the video. About Alaskan brown bears—Danny's current favorite. He played it over and over. Last week, it was a documentary about a man who sailed a home-made boat around the world.

"A really cool surprise," Matt said. "Something you'll like. But you have to go to the party to get it. Come on, Danny. Julia and Nathan have driven up from Austin. We have presents for Granny Belle."

"Yes," said Angie, shaking her head in agreement. "And Beatrice is frying catfish and baking a big birthday cake. Chocolate, I'll bet. With lots of icing. Granny Belle wants you to put the candles in the cake and help her light them. I've bought some balloons to blow up. And you blow up balloons better than anyone because you're big and strong and can blow harder."

"I don't want to see Beth," Danny said.

"I know, honey," Angie said, exchanging glances with Matt. "But you can't stay away from your own family because of her. We can just pretend like she's not there. I'll tell her not to talk to you. And I'll give you a 'feel better' pill right before you leave."

"I don't want a pill. They make me sleep."

"What about the surprise?" Matt asked. "Don't you want that?"

Danny reached for the remote and restarted his video. The bears were fishing. A mother and two cubs. Angie leaned over the back of his chair and hugged him from behind. "I love you, Danny Tarrington."

She stayed like that for a minute, her arms around his neck. "Touch my hand, Danny. Please."

He did. His hand on hers. It was something.

Matt knelt in front of his brother and hugged him. Danny kept watching the video over Matt's shoulder. Matt sat back on his haunches. "Do you still love us, Danny?" he asked.

But Danny was staring hypnotically at the flickering screen.

Angie wondered if he would ever again hug them back or say he loved them. Did any part of the Danny who had loved his family still live inside this man who spent his waking hours staring at a television screen and having occasional destructive fits that terrorized those who looked after him? And if the Danny they all had loved was no longer, what was their obligation to this unresponsive shell of a person who occupied his room and sat all day in his chair?

But he was better, Angie reminded herself, as she changed into a khaki skirt and white blouse. Now and then he'd ask for a specific food—a bowl of chocolate ice cream, a banana, some pancakes—instead of simply eating whatever was put in front of him. He came downstairs on his own occasionally, to get something out of the refrigerator, to sit and watch Maura fix dinner, or to roam about the yard and house before returning to his room. He wasn't sleeping most of the day, unless they had to give him a second pill. It was the second pill that turned him into a zombie.

But not giving the second pill was like walking a tightrope. Less now, but still they never knew if and when he might suddenly begin beating his head against the wall or start breaking things.

All summer, Angie had taken him swimming first

thing every morning, and Norma had taken him every evening before dinner. Perry took him for either a walk or drive after dinner. Angie took turns with her mother reading to him and tucking him in at night like when he was a little boy. But he didn't look at the pictures in the book or listen to the stories. Didn't care if she kissed him good night. Didn't seem to care about anything except his videos, which he watched impassively with no laughter, no tears, no looking away at the scary moments. He just watched. Dr. Burk called it "lack of affect." The strange part was, his depression or whatever it was, no longer seemed to have much to do with Beth. The mention of her name—or Frank's—evoked little response. There now seemed to be no predictable factor that precipitated Danny's loss of control. He'd get very quiet—almost rigid—then erupt like a volcano. If Beth and Frank moved away tomorrow and Danny never saw either of them again, Angie wondered if it would make any difference in his condition. Some vital part of him seemed to have been permanently altered or erased, with the remainder reconfiguring itself into a creature that was only a partial person.

Beth was noticeably pregnant now, her baby due in less than three months. Danny's baby, too. If Frank's assumption was true—which it probably was. Granny Belle had heard Beth tell Clifford it was Danny's baby. Danny didn't know, of course. Would never know, if she had any say.

Frank had spent the summer on the third floor at Clifford and Belle's. Reading. Staring at the wall. The only reason he ever left the house was to go to the liquor store. He too suffered from lack of affect.

Belle had bought Danny a pair of canaries in a beautiful white wicker cage. She thought it would give him something to watch beside videos. Belle was still convinced that they just hadn't found the right door to open, that if they kept trying they would find the way to Danny's soul. They'd talked about a dog. Another big-hearted mongrel from the pound—like Buddy. But they remembered the time after the kidnapping when

Danny killed the momma cat who'd chosen their pool house to have her kittens. The possibility of two dead canaries didn't seem as grim as a dead or injured dog.

Clifford was giving Norma and Perry a hard time about not institutionalizing Danny, bringing up the subject at every opportunity. "What are you going to do? Wait around until he hurts himself or someone else?" he would ask. Norma would get a pinched look on her face. Perry would say that they were well aware of Danny's problems and change the subject. Angie wondered if Clifford's meddling was all that was keeping her parents from finding a place for Danny. Her mother especially wouldn't want Clifford to think he'd won.

Belle's birthday party was a strain for everyone—except Clifford, who hardly took his eyes off Beth the entire evening, smiling when she smiled, frowning when she frowned. She was tan and radiant in a white maternity pants outfit, her magnificent hair piled loosely on her head. "If he wasn't such an old man, I'd swear he has a thing for her," Julia whispered to her sister.

Angie nodded. Their grandfather was smitten, which made him seem foolish and pathetic—this man who had always ruled by intimidation. But he was so old now, his flesh hanging loosely on his body. The enormous body he'd lived in all his adult life was shrinking. Maybe his mind was, too.

Belle, on the other hand, seemed almost timeless. She took walks, went to an old ladies' exercise class three times a week, still planted flowers and pulled weeds.

Frank hardly said a word the entire evening, and the rest of them tried to pretend that they didn't notice his silence. Belle, Gretchen, and Julia did most of the talking at the dinner table, with a polite comment every now and then from the others. Perry did make a lovely toast for his mother, recalling the gardens they'd planted together, the songs they'd composed, the birds they'd watched, the storybook they'd written when he was seven years old, which she still had, along with every

picture he'd ever drawn. "Talk about always being there
for someone," he said with an affectionate laugh. "I
grew up knowing my mother would do anything for me.
That's the most wonderful gift imaginable." Then he
raised his glass. "I love you, Mom. More than ever."

Then Norma stood. "Imagine having a mother-in-
law who is also my best friend! What a blessing that has
been. I love you, too, darling Belle."

Matt and Gretchen gave Belle a music box that
played "The Yellow Rose of Texas." Julia and Nathan
gave her an assortment of pickles, jams and relishes
they'd made themselves with produce from their garden. Clifford, with Frank's and Beth's names also on the
card, gave his wife a rather stunning gold pin in the
shape of a bell—selected by either his secretary or Beth,
no doubt. Perry and Norma gave her an oil painting of
a field of Texas blue bonnets.

And Angie presented her grandmother with a
handsomely framed certificate stating that the names of
Belle's mother and grandparents had been added to a
memorial honoring immigrants who had entered the
United States through Ellis Island. Belle cried a bit and
said she wanted to go there with Angie and see their
names for herself.

Danny's name wasn't mentioned the whole evening, but Angie knew that everyone was remembering
other birthday celebrations with Danny setting the tone.
Until this last year, a birthday party still required balloons and streamers, secrets and surprises. Danny would
always insist on lighting the candles more than once so
the honoree had more than one opportunity to make
his or her wish come true. Once when they asked Danny
what he'd wished for, he said that he wanted to learn to
read books like Matt. Angie got tears in her eyes remembering. Poor Danny.

The evening ended rather abruptly with Frank
standing and saying good night. They all watched si-
lently as he slowly climbed the stairs, then one by one
began standing themselves, hugging Belle. Julia and Nathan cut a generous slice of cake to take to Danny and

made plans with Matt and Gretchen for an early morning trip to the farmer's market, a Sunday-morning event alongside the railroad tracks in downtown Dallas.

"I'd like to come over and swim later," Beth said. Norma nodded.

They all went out the back way for the walk over the bridge and up the hill. Nathan and Julia were spending the night. Matt and Gretchen had to retrieve their car, which was parked in front of the other house. Belle decided to walk home with them for a nightcap. She locked arms with Angie to navigate the bridge and hill in the darkness. "You'd think it was her pool," they could hear Julia telling her mother. "I don't see how you put up with her, Mom. I can't stand to be around her. I think she's poisoning Frank. He looks ghastly. And she has Clifford wrapped around her little finger. It's disgusting. How does Granny Belle stand it? If I were her, I'd move out."

They said good night to Mark, the youngest of Manuel's sons, who had come to watch Danny. Mark was majoring in botany at UT-Arlington.

Matt carried the bushel of peaches that Julia and Nathan had brought to Gretchen out to the BMW. Gretchen wanted to try her hand at making preserves. She promised everyone a jar and gave good night hugs all around.

By the time Norma noticed that Matt had left his keys on the entry hall table, the BMW was pulling away. Gretchen must be driving.

Julia and Nathan headed up the stairs with Danny's cake. Perry poured himself a brandy and went upstairs with a newspaper under his arm.

Angie and her mother and grandmother took a bottle of wine out to the terrace to enjoy the night air and full moon. The moon was so bright Angie could read the label on the wine bottle. Black Opal. A good name for a mystery, she remembered thinking.

They had had wine with dinner—and after-dinner brandy. Their tongues were already loose.

"I wish she would go away or just die," Norma said. "I can't even recognize our family anymore."

"Just think of the power that baby will give her," Belle said. "She'll be the queen regent. Clifford told me that he wants this baby more than he's ever wanted anything in his life. He already loves it more than he's ever loved anyone or anything—even his own mother. He wants to live until he's a hundred so he'll be able to know him and influence him. Beth has agreed to name him Aaron for Clifford's father. The boy will be a *true* Tarrington, whatever that is. All that name nonsense! A name is what a person makes it. Frankly, I hope the sonogram is a mistake, and the baby is a girl. God, I'd love to see the look on his face."

"Julia and Nathan told me that we can come see them anytime in Austin, but they can't bear to come back here anymore," Angie said with a deep sigh. "I'd like to move to Austin, myself and never come home to witness the sadness, but I'm not sure that would be fair to the rest of you. Frank will either have to break away from Beth or blow his brains out. And Danny. Will he ever be the same? Is the innocent lamb still there, or has she destroyed him altogether? And that poor little Mary Ann Singleton—I find myself thinking of the wedding that will never be—of Mary Ann and Danny as the bride and groom. God, it makes me cry just to think about it. Mary Ann should have joined this family, not Beth. I don't want Beth. Damn her to hell anyway. I'm with you, Mother. I wish she'd just die!"

"She's down there now," Norma said, lowering her voice, looking toward the pool.

"How do you know?" Angie asked. "The lights aren't on."

"I heard the gate squeak when she came in. She's down there. She never turns on the lights. When I start down the hill, I never know if she's there. I don't go at night anymore—to my own pool, because I don't want to be there with her. I wonder how much money we'd have to pay her to have an abortion and go away."

"I've thought of that," Belle said. "I'd give her everything I own just to get her to leave. Everything. And I'd do just about anything, too."

"Let's talk about something else," Angie said. "Something nice. I get sick of Beth dominating our every thought, our every conversation."

"What should we talk about?" Belle asked.

"It's a pretty night," Norma offered.

"Yes," Angie agreed. "Such a mild summer."

They sat there for a time in silence. Finally, Belle stood, and Angie offered to walk her home. But Norma said she would, for Angie to go on to bed.

Manuel began his workday early in the summertime. By five minutes after six he was pushing a wheelbarrow full of gardening tools out of the shed behind the pool house. He usually worked four hours at the Tarringtons and spent the rest of the day operating his landscaping service.

He liked the early morning hours with the dew on the grass and the air cool and clean. And he still took enormous pride in the Tarringtons' yard, which they had entrusted to him almost thirty years ago, allowing him to create the most beautiful yard in all of Dallas without hiring some college graduate with letters after his name to tell him what to plant here and what to plant there. So many times over the years, pictures of the Tarringtons' yard had appeared in newspapers and magazines—and Norma always insisted that it say under the picture the yard had been designed and was maintained by Manuel Rodriguez.

Because of the Tarringtons and their yard, he had his own business. Manuel still took care of their yard personally, with help from his sons only for major tasks. He owed the Tarringtons too much not to. The family had treated him like a human being from the first moment he set foot on their property as part of a crew of Mexicans who took care of yards in the neighborhood. One day Norma walked across the yard to compliment him on what a fine job he'd done with the trimming and pruning.

"Where did you learn about shrubs and trees?" she'd asked.

Manuel told her about helping his grandfather, who'd tended the private garden of the bishop of Guadalajara. Then she asked if he thought there was enough sunlight in front of the house for a rose garden. And she listened while he explained that the front yard was already too cluttered with small beds. Three or four of the native blackjacks needed to be taken out to provide sunlight for two or three spectacular beds with changing displays of seasonal flowers. Hundreds of tulips in the spring. Petunias in the summer. Chrysanthemums in the fall. But not roses. Then she followed him around back and listened while he explained that the perfect place for a rose garden was in front of the terrace. Full sun. Good drainage. For row after row of rosebushes of every color, from the purest whites to the deepest maroon. Climbers on the walls. Norma nodded, seeing his vision. "Do it," she had said. "All of it."

Manuel loved Norma Tarrington as he would love a patron saint. She and Mr. Perry came to his mother's funeral and his children's graduations and weddings—and invited him and his wife to Matt's and Julia's weddings. But not to Frank's, which was a hurry-up wedding to Beth Williams with only family members in attendance.

Before he got to know the Tarringtons, Manuel would have sworn that rich people had fewer troubles than poor people. But the Tarringtons had had more than their share over the years. And now there was trouble again with both Danny and Frank. Maura told him about the crazy things that Danny did—knocking over the grandfather clock and the china cabinet, breaking windows, poking his fist through the wall. And Beatrice, the housekeeper over at the senior Tarringtons, said that Frank just sat around all day in his undershorts and didn't bother to shave.

Today, Manuel planned to fertilize and spray the

roses. But before heading up the hill, he needed to check the chemicals in the pool and empty the skimmer baskets.

He saw the body before he opened the iron gate. Floating facedown.

He stood there, with his hand on the gate, struggling to find some alternative explanation for what he was seeing. Not a person, perhaps. Maybe it was one of those giant blow-up dolls. A joke. Maybe if he closed his eyes, it would go away.

But it didn't.

Slowly, holding his breath, he approached the side of the pool. It was a woman. With long hair. Not Mrs. Tarrington. Not Angie. He used the long-handed leaf basket to pull the body over to the side. His stomach began to heave as he pulled the body, still facedown, onto the deck. There was a neat, bloodless wound in the middle of her back. *Holy Mother of God. A dead body. Don't let it be Julia. Please. Mrs. Tarrington has enough sorrow without that. Please.*

The bloated body no longer looked like a real person, but he realized it was Beth. That hair, when it was dry, would be fiery red.

He sobbed as he ran up the hill. *Holy Mother of God.* Beth Williams. He thought of the baby inside of her and crossed himself as he ran.

He pounded on the door to the kitchen. Then ran around to the front of the house and rang the doorbell. Over and over.

Still pulling on his bathrobe, Perry heard the door to Angie's bedroom open as he hurried down the stairs. Norma was behind him, but she waited at the top of the stairs while he saw what all the commotion was about.

Manuel was on the front porch. Gasping. "Beth's body was in the pool. She's dead."

"You're sure?" Perry asked.

Manuel nodded, his chest heaving. "I pulled her out, but she's dead."

Taking Manuel's arm, Perry guided him to the hall-way bench. Perry's heart was pounding, but he felt oddly detached from the scene he was playing out—as if it wasn't real. He was just an actor.

The others were filing down the stairs, except for Danny. Julia, Nathan, Norma, and Angie gathered around him with stunned looks on their faces while he called the police.

Then he dialed his parents' number. His mother answered the phone.

"Manuel found Beth's body in the pool. She's apparently been murdered."

"How do know it was murder?" Belle asked.

"Manuel said it looked as if she'd been stabbed in the back."

"Dear God! Why couldn't she have just drowned? What about Frank? Should I tell him?"

"Yes, and Dad. The police are on the way. Frank will need to be here."

"You don't think he did it?"

"No. I guess not. But I suppose one of us did."

When he hung up the phone, they all stood there looking at one another. Manuel offered to go down by the gate to direct the police. Perry nodded.

Angie looked over at her mother, who was staring at the table in the entry hall. Angie looked toward the table, which was bare but for its usual vase of fresh flowers.

Chapter Twenty-nine

"I'm not sure how I'm supposed to feel," Norma said to the assembled family. They had gathered around the dining room table at the request of Detective Olson, a tall angular man who had arrived in the second wave of police and taken command.

Clifford had taken Perry's usual seat at the head of the table. Frank was sitting in Norma's place, his head buried in his arms. Angie suppressed an urge to rearrange them, to get everyone in what she thought of as their proper places around the big table. She tried to remember the last time they'd all gathered here. A year ago Thanksgiving, she decided. Beth's death had brought them all together again.

Danny was slouched in the chair beside her, his hands in his bathrobe pockets. Angie reached over and patted his arm. He actually turned and looked at her. "We really should have gotten you dressed," she said. "Do you remember what I told you about why we have to sit here and talk to the policeman?"

"Beth Williams is dead," he said, his voice a monotone.

"Yes. Will you touch my hand, please?"

He did. Angie leaned over and kissed his cheek.

"Somber," Julia made a delayed response to her mother's comment. "I think that's how we all feel. And perhaps a bit guilty for all those times we wished her ill."

" 'Wished her *ill*?' My, how genteel," Matt said. "I believe the sentiments most of us expressed toward Beth were a little stronger than that. But you're probably right about the guilt. It's strange to have someone you *wished* dead actually *be* dead. But regardless of any feelings of remorse, please do not share them with Detective Olson. None of us is required to answer any of his questions. If you're unsure, don't say anything. Volunteer nothing. And it would be nice if someone could manage a few tears." Matt looked across the table at his grandmother. Belle shook her head. No tears.

"What about Danny?" Norma asked, frowning. "They won't ask him any questions, will they? They know about Danny, don't they?"

Perry reached for his wife's hand. "Yes, I told them about Danny. But it won't do any good. They have to find out things for themselves."

"I suppose it's going to come out that no one liked her," Matt said. "But let's not dwell on it, okay?"

"I liked her," Clifford said from the head of the table. His hands were resting on his belly, his chin on his chest. "She had more spunk than the lot of you put together."

Frank lifted his head from the table, using a hand to shade his bloodshot eyes from the sunlight streaming through the front window. A thread of drool was hanging from the corner of his mouth. "She stole my soul. What happens to it now that she's dead? Is my soul dead, too?"

Gretchen leaned over and put an arm around him. "Your soul is a bit battered, but I'm sure it's still there someplace."

"And I suspect it's also pretty soused," Nathan added. "It's time to get off the booze, old man. Julia and I want you to come to Austin when this is all over. Try a little clean living."

"No, I'm going to Lubbock," Frank said, carefully leaning his head against the back of the chair. "That's the first thought I had when Belle told me what had happened. *I'll go live in Lubbock.* And become my Uncle Luke, growing cotton, watching the seasons go by, buying a new Cadillac every year. You can see all the way to the horizon from Grandma Claire's porch. There's something symbolic in that. Clear vision. No clutter. No distractions. And maybe someday, years from now, I'll think about the weather and boll weevils the first thing when I wake up in the morning instead of Beth.''

"You don't still love her?" Angie asked.

"Love. Hate. Something," he said with a shrug.

Angie heard the back door open, voices in the kitchen. "Just remember, at this point, we all are suspects," Perry warned. "Olson will be auditioning us for his short list."

Detective Olson came striding into the room, an unlit pipe in his mouth. He nodded in Perry's direction. "Judge Tarrington, sorry about all this."

Olson took the last empty seat at the table—next to Danny. A younger detective named Crowell stood off to one side. Perry related the events of the previous evening up until the time he went upstairs. Angie told them how she and her mother and grandmother had had a drink together on the terrace. They'd heard Beth in the pool about eleven o'clock.

Frank remembered Beth telling him she was coming over to swim. No, he didn't know what time it was. And he was unaware that she never came back.

"My wife and I have different rooms," Frank said. "She doesn't like the smell of Scotch."

"So no one actually saw her after the birthday party," Olson said, looking around the table for confirmation. "What does this mean? That the lady stabbed herself in the back? That either the maid or the gardener did it? Or that she met a mysterious lover at her in-laws' pool, and he did it? Or I suppose it could mean that someone is lying."

Olson took a slow perusal around the table. "I'm not seeing a whole lot of grief. No red eyes, with the exception of Frank here. No tears. No sniffles. No Kleenex clutched in hands. I take it that the lady was not the most beloved member of this family." He looked around the table again.

"There were problems," Clifford acknowledged.

"Such as?"

"I don't believe any of us are ready to discuss that at this point," Matt answered.

"I see," Olson said, taking his pipe from his mouth and staring into the empty bowl. "I used to smoke this thing. Gave me mouth ulcers," Then he looked at Perry. "What about the victim's family? Parents. Siblings. Have they been notified?"

"As far as we know, she has no living relatives," Perry said.

"The maid tells me that the lady used to work for the family—after the kidnapping."

"Yes, when Danny was a youngster," Perry said, indicating Danny. "Beth helped us take care of him."

"I remember that kidnapping," Olson said. "I was in the police academy when it happened. Really something. You ever find out who did it?"

"No," Perry said.

Olson looked toward Frank. "I understand that your wife was pregnant. How far along?"

"I don't know," Frank said with an airy wave of his hand.

Gretchen grabbed his hand and held it. "About six and a half months," she told Olson.

"Mrs. Tarrington," Olson said, directing his question to Norma, "this would have been your first grandchild, I believe."

"Yes. That's right."

"This must be very upsetting for you?"

"Yes. Of course, it is. But I think at this point we're all feeling rather numb. It's such a shock."

Olson took another look around the table. "Which two of you live in Austin."

"We do," Nathan said, putting his arm around Julia's shoulders.

"Sorry, but I'm going to have to ask you to stay put for a while. Until I get a direction on this thing, no one is to leave town. Now, what do you want me to do about the ladies and gentlemen of the media who have gathered outside your front gate? Will anyone be making a statement?"

"No," Perry said. "No statement."

"We'd like to look around inside both houses, if that's all right with everyone," Olson said as he pushed himself back from the table.

"No, we'd rather you didn't do that," Matt said.

Olson shrugged. Again, he nodded in Perry's direction and left them, Detective Crowell on his heels.

Silence fell over the table as they stared blankly at its center. "Jesus," Nathan muttered. "He thinks one of us killed her."

"Well, he's probably right," Julia said.

"On that cheerful note, I think I'll play nursemaid to Frank," Angie announced.

"I'll see to Danny," Norma said.

Angie took Frank upstairs to her room and got him a drink of water from the bathroom. "Drink," she insisted. "You're dehydrated."

"Among other things," Frank quipped, but he accepted the glass and took several sips.

"Are you sad?" she asked.

"Right now the pain behind my eyeballs supersedes all other sensations. But I think what I will eventually feel is like a death-row inmate who's strapped in the chair when the call from the governor finally comes through with a full pardon. But that doesn't mean I'll stop thinking about her. I've been thinking about her for half my life. And I'll probably be sorry about the baby. But maybe some people should never be born."

Angie didn't ask what he thought had happened to Beth. By unspoken agreement, they all were avoiding that question.

"If this was a nightmare, I wish I'd hurry and wake up," Angie said, sitting beside Frank on the bed. "Or that someone would yell 'cut,' and we could roll the film back. Just erase it. None of it had really happened. Beth isn't dead. The police aren't here. No one is going to be arrested."

"I'm going to be sick," Frank announced, heading for the bathroom.

The sounds of retching came from the bathroom as he threw up the water she'd made him drink. Angie remembered the time she'd gotten on a bus and gone all the way to Lubbock to bring Frank home. She'd felt like such a good sister as she proved that love conquered all.

Maybe Frank would have been better off staying in Lubbock. Or would Beth have gone out there and fetched him back?

Olson hunkered down on the side of the pool as the last few gallons of water were drained away. He could already see the butcher knife. Probably no hope of fingerprints.

And the decking around the pool had been hosed clean, the hose neatly put away. A real tidy murderer.

The hair-and-lint trap probably wouldn't help either. The entire family swam in the pool.

He had no doubt the knife would match the set in the kitchen, one slot in its wooden block empty—which would seem to limit the suspects to someone who had access to the house. Family members. The housekeeper and her daughter. The gardener.

One of the crime team investigators made his way down the steep incline to the drain and retrieved the knife along with two other items.

Olson met him at the steps. "A medal of some sort and a button," the man said, opening his plastic-gloved hand for his partner to see.

Olson leaned forward. A plain white plastic button about three-quarters of an inch across, with a piece of cloth still attached. And a track medal. For Special Olympics. "Isn't that for retarded kids?" Olson asked.

The investigator shrugged.

"Turn it over," Olson instructed.

He leaned forward. Then reached in his pocket for his reading glasses.

The button would get him a search warrant. If he was lucky, there was a garment in that house missing a button.

Justin stood when Angie Tarrington and her brother entered the waiting room.

"Justin Garrett," he said, offering his hand to Angie.

"I'm from the firm. Your grandfather sent me to represent your brother at the interrogation."

"This is Danny," Angie said.

Danny had already sat down and didn't bother to look up when Angie said his name. Justin tried not to stare at Danny. Matt Tarrington's twin brother. Danny was heavier than Matt. He looked like Matt and he didn't.

"They insisted he come down here to be interviewed," Angie was explaining. "I guess that means he's officially a suspect."

"Yes, ma'am. Your grandfather explained about"— Justin looked over at Danny, who was staring at the scarred tabletop—"about his mental deficiency," he continued, his voice lowered. It seemed strange talking in the third person about someone in the same room. He drew Angie to the corner of the room and lowered his voice. "He doesn't seem very responsive."

"Danny's been having problems since our brother Frank married the woman who was killed," Angie explained. "She used to take care of him—kind of our own Mary Poppins—until Danny got the hots for her."

Justin nodded. "Your grandfather said that the victim was pregnant with . . ." He nodded in Danny's direction.

"Right. At least that's what she told Grandfather Clifford. Danny doesn't understand any of this. All he knows is that Frank married Beth, and Beth was going to have a baby."

"How do you think he'll respond to police interrogation?" Justin asked.

"Danny's not talking much these days. I doubt if you'll have any trouble keeping him from saying anything incriminating. He wasn't always like this, you know. I want you to understand that Danny is a very special part of our family. We love him a lot."

"Yes, ma'am."

"Do you have to say that?" Angie's brow creased with displeasure.

"I beg your pardon."

" 'Ma'am.' I hate it. Where are you from anyway?"

"Here originally. But I moved to Memphis when I was ten."

"It shows," Angie sat down next to Danny, who was slouched down in his chair, staring at his hands. "So how did you get to be a hotshot criminal defense lawyer at Tarrington Law Associates?" she asked Justin.

"Actually, all I've done so far is some property work and a couple of probates," he said, taking a seat by Angie. "I don't think they've figured out what to do with me yet. I didn't make law review and had to take the bar twice. But my uncle was a partner. Harold Hardesty. As a matter of fact, you and I have met before. At a firm barbecue in my aunt and uncle's backyard. You wore braces then."

"You're new?" Angie asked incredulously. "Fresh out of law school?"

"Well, not exactly. I worked in a bank for a year while I was waiting to retake the bar."

"And my grandfather sent you down here to represent my brother?"

"I was kind of surprised myself. But it's all pretty routine," Justin said. "Mr. Clifford said the case will never go to trial."

"Oh? I wonder where he got his crystal ball."

Detective Crowell stuck his head in the door. They were ready for Danny. Angie stayed behind while a neophyte attorney took her brother to be interrogated.

* * *

Detective Olson was waiting in the interrogation room. He and Crowell both had clipboards. Justin directed Danny to a seat.

"This interrogation is being recorded. Would you please state your name for the record," Olson instructed Danny.

Danny just looked at him. Justin realized he didn't understand Olson's request. "Tell him what your name is," Justin said.

"Danny Tarrington," Danny said obediently. "I can write my name."

"Danny Tarrington, you have the right to remain silent. Anything you say may be used against you. You may have a lawyer present. If you cannot afford a lawyer, the court will appoint one. Is this man here your attorney?"

Danny looked in Justin's direction. And said nothing.

"The family has engaged me to represent Mr. Tarrington," Justin said. "You do realize that Mr. Tarrington is mentally impaired and not capable of understanding the Miranda."

"Hey, Danny," Olson said, "you don't have to say anything if you don't want to. Do you understand that?"

Danny nodded.

Detective Olson held up a medal on a chain, and Danny reached for it. "That's mine."

"Hold on," Olson said, drawing the medal out of Danny's reach. "You can't have it back. This is evidence."

"It's mine," Danny repeated.

"Not anymore," Olson said. "When was the last time you saw Beth Williams?"

"I don't see Beth," Danny said, covering his eyes. "She said she loved me but she's a liar-liar-pants-on-fire."

The two detectives gave each other a can-you-believe-this look.

Justin wondered if Danny had a clue about what

was going on. He seemed like such a simple soul, incapable of deep thought or feelings. Could he have gotten angry enough to kill his brother's wife? And methodically clean up after the crime?

It would seem so. Not only was his medal at the bottom of the pool but a button missing from the pajama top he'd worn to bed the night before. The button had been torn off, a piece of the cloth still attached.

Chapter Thirty

Angie sat with Danny until she was sure the pill had taken effect, watching his eyes glaze over while he watched beetles burying a dead rat on the television screen. What was the appeal of all these nature documentaries, she wondered. Perhaps it was the narrators, who all had soothing, reasonable voices. They never got excited, even when the lion was about to eat the antelope. There were no heroes, no villains, just life and death. Danny seldom watched fairy tales anymore. Maybe he'd given up on Snow White and Cinderella when he didn't get to live happily ever after in a room at Friends House with Princess Beth or plain old Mary Ann. "The simpleminded aren't so simple, are they, Danny?" she said, smoothing back his hair. "I wish I could get inside that head of yours and look around, maybe blast away some of the roadblocks."

He'd done well today, even at the police station. Not a hint of trouble. And he'd actually seemed a bit more responsive. She wondered if Beth's death would bring any sort of absolution to his torment or if his problems had become chronic.

Angie put on a fresh blouse and combed her hair. And wondered if she even had the energy to walk down the stairs and over to her grandparents'. The day had been too long, its events too disturbing. She wished she could take one of Danny's pills and drug out for a while. Her entire body ached with fatigue. But she dreaded going to bed, dreaded the images that might be waiting for her when she closed her eyes.

Norma told Maura to call if Danny came downstairs. Maura was baking cinnamon rolls. The wonderful yeasty aroma seemed so homey and normal.

Maura locked the door behind them. After all, there was a murderer on the loose. She was certain the murderer was one of the gypsies she'd seen on the news. Bands of them were going about Dallas pretending to be roofers, swimming pool refurbishers, cement finishers, and running off with people's down payment without doing the work.

They set off down the hill. Norma and Perry. Matt and Gretchen. Julia and Nathan. Angie brought up the rear as they made their way to the family conference Clifford had called. Walking downhill made Angie's legs hurt. And each step set a wave of pain through her head. Yes, she was definitely going to take one of Danny's pills. Abandon ship for a while.

As they passed the dark pool enclosure, she deliberately averted her eyes. She'd never be able to go swimming there again, she realized. Maybe they should just fill it in. Or move away.

As soon as they arrived at her grandparents' house, Clifford sent Angie upstairs to get Frank. "You tell him that if he has any concern for the family whose name he bears he'd damned well better get his worthless ass off that bed and get down here."

Briefly, she thought about telling him to send someone else. But climbing the stairs seemed like less trouble than standing up to her grandfather.

The third floor was dark. She turned on the light in the hall. And in Frank's room.

From the bed, Frank groaned and shaded his eyes from the offending glare. He looked like shit—unshaven, matted hair, ashen skin. An opened bottle of Dewars was beside the bed. "You have to come downstairs," she said. "We need to plan."

He rolled his head back and forth then reached for the bottle, but Angie grabbed it. "We're in this together, Frank. The whole family. It's time to close ranks." She took his feet and swung them toward the edge of the bed. His toenails were so long they curved over the end of his toes.

He let out another groan when he lifted his head from the pillow. Slowly he managed to get to a sitting position. She gathered a set of clean clothes for him, pulled him to his feet, led him into the bathroom, and started the shower. "You smell," she said and left him.

He emerged some fifteen minutes later and leaned heavily on her arm as they went downstairs. Somehow Angie found the strength for both of them. "No more drinking tonight," she told him. "Tomorrow I'll help you move back home. No reason for you to stay around here putting up with abuse from Clifford."

"What a jolly household that will be," Frank said. "A retard, a fallen clergy, and a bleeding-heart spinster lawyer all living with their weary, puzzled parents, who did everything right but still got stuck with the likes of us. We can all sit around wondering who's going to get arrested for slaying the wicked witch."

Angie poured Frank a cup of coffee and sat on the sofa beside him. Then the room grew silent, the only sound the ticking of the mantel clock. All eyes turned toward Clifford in his oversize wing chair—his belly resting on his lap, one hand resting on top of his cane. A potentate on his throne. But a diminished one. Clifford looked like he'd aged ten years since yesterday.

Angie had never liked her grandfather. Now she wondered if she hated this brilliant, probably corrupt old man who had so dominated their lives. Whether in the boardroom, courtroom, or with his own family, power was the lifeblood of a man like Clifford. He'd spent God knows how many hours trying to figure out ways to outwit the rule against perpetuities so his money could be doled out according to his wishes for generations to come. Except thus far, the only known members of the next generation were dead fetuses—Beth's and Gretchen's. Danny's progeny.

"Rather than sit around waiting for the law enforcement officers of the city to decide the fate of this family, I propose we deal with this situation ourselves," he began.

"As I suspect you all know by now, the DNA tests will show that the father of the baby Beth was carrying is not Frank. They will show that she could have been impregnated by either Danny or Matt."

"Not Matt," Gretchen interrupted.

Clifford glared at her, but Gretchen refused to wither. "I don't want anyone to think that he'd been fooling around with Beth," she said.

Clifford cleared his throat to signify he would begin again. "Until Matt can offer proof that he couldn't have been responsible for the pregnancy, the police will put the three Tarrington brothers, natural and adopted, on their suspect list. The victim had cheated on her husband with one of her husband's brothers."

Gretchen started to protest further, but Matt offered a slight shake of his head and took her hand.

"This is a case where motive, opportunity, and circumstantial evidence will weigh heavy since forensic evidence will be limited," Clifford went on. "Water—especially heavily chlorinated water—is not a friend of the forensic investigator, and bodies that have been immersed in water are difficult to deal with. Exact time of death is impossible to establish. Blood is washed away. And semen. And to complicate things still further in this particular case, the murderer apparently hosed off the deck."

"Which is hardly the behavior one would expect from a retarded person," Julia interjected, anticipating the direction her grandfather was heading.

"Ah, but it was one of Danny's jobs before he became infatuated with Beth and decided to become a nonparticipant in this family," Clifford said. "I think it makes perfect sense that he would clean any blood off the deck. In fact, it's hard to imagine a normal person taking the time to do such a thing when he might be discovered any minute." He looked over his reading glasses at Julia, to make sure he had squelched her objection.

"As for the murder weapon, Maura told the police that she was sure the knife found on the bottom of the pool had been in the kitchen yesterday morning—she used it to cut up fruit for lunch. Anyone in this room could have taken the knife at any time during the afternoon or evening. And the gardener's son. But he was apparently home with his family by the time Beth was murdered."

Clifford looked around the room to make sure everyone was with him so far. Satisfied, he continued, "Apparently Beth had sex with Danny in order to bear a child who would be an heir to Tarrington money. And she married Frank to give the baby the Tarrington name. These actions have incurred a great deal of wrath among some members of the family. I'm sure the topic of 'what to do about Beth' has been bantered around a great deal.

"And I must point out that if Danny's not guilty of killing Beth, some other member of this family probably is. Including Gretchen and Matt. I have it on good authority that a neighbor told the police he saw a light blue BMW pulling in the driveway sometime after eleven."

Matt sat up very straight. "I came back to get my keys. I needed them to get into my briefcase."

"Maybe so. The neighbor couldn't say if a man or a woman was driving the car. And the rest of us never left these two houses. So instead of trying to think of reasons why Danny didn't do it, let's think about the problem carefully, rationally, and without sentimentality. Danny's well-documented decline began when Beth returned last summer. He became obsessed with her and had to stop working because of her, a situation the people at his workplace can certainly corroborate. And they will surely tell the police about the young woman who killed herself because Danny was in love with Beth. When Beth married Frank, Danny began having jealous rages. He's a large, strong, retarded young man who can be dangerous when upset. The household help and his physician can testify to that. Medication is a partial solution, but yesterday evening, I understand that he refused to take the medication. Is that right, Angie?''

Angie nodded. He had refused.

"Unfortunately other members of this family were also known to have problems with Beth, and perhaps one of us is the actual killer," Clifford went on. "But in Danny, we have a man who either destroys things or hypnotically watches television—hardly a functioning family member. Surely by now, Norma and Perry have considered placing him in an institution—if not immediately, then in the very near future. Should Danny be charged in this case, I believe that he's too retarded to assist counsel in his own defense and to understand the nature of the proceedings that he is facing and could not, therefore, stand trial for a capital crime. Consequently, he is not eligible for the death penalty and, as a result, is the ideal defendant in this case."

Angie glanced at Matt, remembering the conversation they'd had exploring the same line of reasoning. Matt was listening intently. All of them were—as Clifford offered them a way out of a dilemma.

Clifford carefully itemized the case against Danny. He had been wearing his medal when he ate an early dinner in the kitchen with Maura.

Then he'd gone up to his room to watch videos while the others went over to Belle's birthday party. When Angie tried to get him to take a pill and join the family, he refused because Beth would be there.

Julia and Nathan told the police that they couldn't remember if Danny had on the medal when they went upstairs to take him a piece of cake, but Clifford believed that, if they put their mind to it, they would remember that Danny was indeed wearing the medal. "Danny *always* wore his medal. His mother expected him to—it had his name, address, and phone number on the back in case he got lost. I think that any one of us would notice if he wasn't wearing it."

Because of the animosity Danny had felt toward Beth since she married his brother, Clifford continued, she wasn't allowed to swim when Danny might be using the pool. But he knew that Beth sometimes came to swim late at night—after he and his mother had their swim. But yesterday evening, he hadn't had his usual swim because Norma was at Belle's birthday party. Yet, his medal was found on the bottom of the pool and could only have gotten there after Julia and Nathan saw him.

And a button that was torn from the pajamas that he'd been wearing was also found on the bottom of the pool.

"Think about this long and hard," Clifford told the assembled family. "I don't know that Danny actually killed Beth, although it would seem that he was at the pool last night and certainly had the opportunity. But I do know that of all the members of this family, he's the only one who's destined to spend the rest of his life in an institution. He's the only member of this family who has a built-in protection from being punished to the fullest extent of the law no matter how cold-blooded or premeditated the murder appears to be or how far an ambitious prosecutor would like to take it. The worst that could happen to him would be a long prison term during which he would go to work every day doing some task about as mindless as lifting boxes of brooms and sanding broom handles. Ideally, we could arrange for him to be institutionalized in a private sanatorium—like the one in Virginia where the Hinckley family has maintained their son after he tried to assassinate Ronald Reagan. Danny's family would probably be allowed unsupervised visits with him—picnics on the lawn—that sort of thing. Perhaps some psychologist could eventually be persuaded to say that Danny was no longer a threat, provided he receives his daily dose of whatever, and he could be relocated if the family so desired. But probably by then, wherever he was initially sent would have become home to him and the kindly thing would be to leave him there."

Clifford paused again, taking a sip of brandy, preparing his audience for his conclusion. "In short," he said, "Danny is the only one of us who doesn't have anything to lose if he's convicted of this crime."

"He didn't kill anyone," Norma said. "I'll have no part of this."

"And if Danny didn't kill her, who did?" Clifford demanded of his daughter-in-law.

"I don't know. But the hose was left in an untidy heap. Danny always wound it in a perfect figure eight after he hosed the decking. Manuel taught him to do that, so the hose wouldn't get tangled."

"When did you view the murder scene, Norma?" Clifford wanted to know. "The police have it roped off."

"I didn't. Manuel told me about the hose."

"I'm surprised that he noticed. From what Perry said, the man was hysterical."

"He noticed the hose before he saw the body," Norma said.

"Well, I doubt if the way the hose was wound will determine guilt or innocence, but let's suppose that you are right, and Danny didn't kill her," Clifford said. "Then tell me, Norma, which member of this family do you want charged in his place?"

She sagged against the back of the sofa and shook her head. She had no answer for that question.

"They probably won't set bail in a capital case," Angie pointed out. "He could be in jail for months before there's a trial."

"There mustn't be a trial," Clifford said. "The police already think he did it. Because of his retardation, it's an obvious plea-bargain situation—a lesser sentence in exchange for a confession. And then we pick up the pieces. Do damage control. Present ourselves as a well-meaning family who tried to do right by a mentally retarded young man and maintain him throughout his life in the family home. But it backfired. Brought about a family tragedy. A daughter-in-law and an unborn first grandchild were murdered. Which brings me to the funeral. I've arranged for a tasteful funeral for Beth day after tomorrow. I want every one of you there, including Frank. Is that clear?''

Then Clifford sighed and looked around the room. ''I wanted that baby. It was a boy, you know. She'd had a sonogram. She showed it to me. A little boy. Beth's little boy.''

And then they all witnessed a most extraordinary sight. Clifford put his huge, hamlike hands to his face and wept.

Chapter Thirty-one

"Sara Hutchinson, KDAL News. I'd like to speak to Judge Tarrington."

"How in the hell are you people getting this number?" Angie demanded.

"Is the judge in?"

"He's not speaking to the media."

"Are you a member of the family?"

Angie hung up and went to sit with the others as they waited for the late news. The media had been waiting when Perry and Matt arrived at the police station with Danny—"swooped in like vultures," Matt said. After the episode at the house earlier in the evening with the two detectives trying to handcuff him, Danny had huddled on the floor of the backseat and refused to get out of the car. With his brother and his father trying to convince him that he had to get out, two waiting policemen intervened and a scuffle resulted—with cameras rolling. Two other policemen joined in the fray. It had taken four of them to subdue him, handcuff him, and drag him inside.

The doors to the armoire where the living room television resided were open, the set on but muted, as the final minutes of *Dateline* were played out. Jane Pauley was frowning at the answer of the distinguished-looking elderly gentleman she was interviewing. A familiar face. Angie knew she could come up with the man's name if she tried.

"Why are we doing this?" Julia asked from the sofa. "It's just going to make us feel worse to see them dragging Danny into the jail. I already know that it was terrible. Do we really need to know how terrible?"

Her observation recorded, Julia slumped against her husband, and Nathan's arm slid protectively around her shoulders. They'd become even more joined at the hip than usual these last few days.

"We need to watch in order to feed our collective guilt," Matt said. He had aged noticeably in the months since Danny's reverse metamorphosis. Their mother had been right about Matt after all. Humility had indeed lain dormant in his soul.

"What do you mean?" Gretchen asked her husband. "What do we have to feel guilty about?" Even Gretchen looked worn down, exhausted.

"He means that we've sacrificed Danny on the altar of family, and the least we can do is witness the carnage," Frank said from a side chair he had pulled over by the bay window, separating himself from the rest. He would be leaving them soon, Angie realized, going to Lubbock where he would become the son of Lucy Ledbetter, grandson of Claire, to ease the pain that being a Tarrington had brought him.

"But the police were going to arrest him anyway. The evidence points to him," Gretchen pointed out.

"Yeah, but we augmented the process," Matt said. "We did not gather around to protect one of our own. We all could have sworn that he was locked in his room all night, that he took two pills and was totally drugged up, couldn't even have gotten down the stairs without falling. I could have said that I slept in his room and know for a fact that he didn't get out of bed the whole night. We all could have insisted that Maura was wrong, that he lost his medal days ago, that he didn't wear it all the time. And that he sometimes wore the pajama top down to the pool at night, over his bathing suit. The button must have gotten ripped off last week when he and I were horsing around by the pool. We could have said that he worshiped the ground that Beth walked on and would never have lifted a finger to hurt her."

"Yes," Belle agreed. "Our poor Danny. First that horrible woman destroys him, and now we're doing it to him all over again. And I for one don't think he killed her, no matter what they found at the bottom of the pool."

Norma moved over to the arm of Belle's chair and put an arm around her mother-in-law's shoulders. "I don't feel right about this either," she said. "I'd rather go to jail myself than send Danny."

"No, it has to be Danny," Clifford said. He was sitting in the handsome oversize colonial arm chair that Norma had placed in her living room years ago for her father-in-law. Clifford looked pale, not well at all.

"I asked Danny if he went down to the pool while Beth was there," Perry said. "But he wouldn't answer. He acted like he didn't hear me and just kept watching the television screen. Angie said he did the same with her. It seems to me we have to at least find out if he really was there so we know what we're up against. What if the court declares he's death eligible? What if we can't plea bargain out of this mess? Good grief, Dad, as many times as you've whipped Cord Davis's butt in court, I doubt if our esteemed DA is going to be granting this family any favors."

Clifford sighed. "We've already been through all this, son," he said, not unkindly. "How could a judge declare that Danny is capable of cooperating in his own defense? Or that he understands the nature of the proceedings? His defense is innate. The law is limited in what they can exact from the mentally impaired."

Angie picked up the remote control from the coffee table. It was time.

Danny was the lead story. The son of a prominent Dallas family arrested for the murder last week of his pregnant sister-in-law. Angie felt physically ill as she watched the scene outside the police station. Perhaps it would have been kinder to take Danny out back and shoot him than subject him to what lay ahead.

Back at the news desk, the anchorwoman began a history of the Tarrington family, starting with Danny Tarrington's great-grandfather, Governor "Preacher" Tarrington. The front page of the *Dallas Morning News* for the day after Danny's kidnapping flashed on the screen, with a picture of the twin brothers covering much of the top half of the page. Next there was a picture of the entire family at a Special Olympics meet with Danny in track clothes. The family home. Footage of Perry being sworn in as U.S. district court judge. Norma cutting the ribbon for a teen center in Oak Cliff. Matt on the floor of the state legislature speaking in favor of legislation to make deadbeat dads accountable. Frank in a clerical collar—the same picture the paper had used in a story announcing his appointment as pastor of the Channing congregation. No pictures of Beth. There wouldn't be any, Angie realized. Not even a wedding picture. She wasn't really family. Her background was a mystery.

District Attorney Cord Davis himself was at the station to be interviewed by the anchorwoman. He planned to charge Daniel Tarrington with two counts of first-degree murder.

Angie moaned. *Two* counts. Could he do that? Beth was a living, breathing human, but the baby had never taken a breath.

Cord continued, saying that he realized the accused man was mentally deficient. But Mr. Tarrington knew he wasn't supposed to go around killing people. He knew that his brother's wife was pregnant, that the baby in her womb would never be born if he killed its mother.

The anchorwoman asked what bearing the prominence of the Tarrington family would have on the case. Cord Davis assured her that Danny Tarrington would receive exactly the same treatment as any other person accused of a brutal multiple murder. The interview concluded with Davis reflecting on Beth Williams Tarrington's last horrible minutes, with possibly mortal wounds, sinking to the bottom of the swimming pool, knowing that her baby would die with her.''

"What's he talking about?" Julia demanded.

The anchorwoman also wanted to know. "You mean she did not die of her wounds?"

"The autopsy showed that the actual cause of death

was drowning," Davis was saying. "She was still alive when the murderer threw her into the pool."

Angie was sitting there motionless, with the unused remote in her lap, so Matt got up and turned off the set. "Two counts of first-degree murder," he said, shaking his head. "He's trying to make this a capital case."

"Who says he's not politically ambitious," Perry said. "With that one move, he made himself the darling of the religious right."

Angie clenched her fists. "I'd like to—" She started to say that she'd like to kill the district attorney but realized she couldn't. Never again could any member of this family use the word *kill* lightly. "I'd like to cut off his balls," she said, not caring that her mother and Belle were in the room. "Danny is *retarded*, for God's sake! And is probably trying to beat his brains out against a cell wall. Would they let me go down there and give Danny a pill? Or Dr. Burk? Christ, what a mess! What a fucking mess! What the hell is going to happen to us? To Danny?" She was sobbing now. Losing control. She could feel Julia's arms come around her, feel herself being led toward the stairs. Already she knew she'd take another one of Danny's pills.

All through law school, Justin Garrett had known that he would join the prestigious Tarrington law firm, where his uncle Harold had been a senior partner until his death two years ago. Justin's father had been killed in Vietnam before he was born, and his mother had never coped well with widowhood, motherhood, or life in general. When his mother was hospitalized for depression, alcoholism, suicide attempts, or various other ailments that garnered her an amazing collection of prescription drugs for the top of her bureau, Justin lived with his aunt and uncle, who had already raised their four children. And he all but lived with them even when his mother was at home in their apartment behind the Preston Road Target store.

Aunt Faith was his mother's sister, and they looked

very much alike, which had always seemed strange to
Justin because they were completely different. Faith
loved to tell jokes and laughed a lot. He couldn't remember his mother ever telling a joke or even laughing. When he was ten, he and his mother moved to
Memphis to live with his grandmother.

Justin couldn't understand why Granny Nelson
never insisted that his mother help with the cooking,
cleaning, laundry, shopping, gardening. But she didn't.
His mother spent her time reading magazines, watching
television, eating candy bars, and drinking a two-liter
bottle of Diet Coke every day. Granny Nelson didn't
complain about her daughter or make excuses. She said
it was worth all the trouble to have Justin live with her.
Justin felt guilty when she said that. He'd far rather live
with his aunt and uncle in Dallas and looked forward to
the two months every summer that he spent with them,
playing golf and tennis with Aunt Faith and her daughters, hunting and fishing with his uncle Harold and his
sons and sons-in-law, sometimes going with all or part of
the family to Harold and Faith's cabin in Colorado or to
their beach house on Padre Island.

When Harold died two years ago, Aunt Faith
grieved sincerely for six months, then set about finding
a second husband who was rich enough not to be a
fortune hunter and young enough to still get it up. She
hadn't found a man that met both criteria but was en-
joying the search.

Harold had paid for Justin's education and paved
the way for his nephew's entry into the Tarrington law
firm, where he was all but guaranteed a six-figure income by his second year with the firm. The firm was his
ticket to the good life and the world's finest golf
courses. Justin was determined to handle Danny Tarrington's case with the dispatch requested by Mr. Clifford Tarrington.

The family members were all present at the arraignment. When Danny entered the courtroom, he
barely glanced their way. He didn't answer when the
judge asked if he understood the charges against him.

Justin entered a "not guilty" plea as instructed in order to give him a stronger position in the subsequent plea bargaining. And he asked for bail, pointing out the Tarringtons' position in the community. But in fact, Mr. Clifford had told him to go through the motions of asking for bail but not to push for it. Normally a young assistant DA would be handling the arraignment, but Cord Davis didn't want to miss an opportunity for publicity and was there in person to ask that the request for bail be denied based on the probability that the defendant might commit further violent acts. The judge concurred.

According to Clifford's instructions, when it was time to negotiate a plea bargain, Justin was to point out the special circumstance of Danny's retardation. In exchange for a guilty plea, Clifford wanted permission for the family to institutionalize Danny in a private facility. A boy like Danny couldn't handle prison. "Remind them of John Hinckley," Clifford had told Justin, giving him an *ABA Journal* article to read on the Hinckley case.

Justin feared it was not going to be that simple. Hinckley was insane, not retarded. And judging from Cord Davis's statements to the press, the DA wasn't interested in plea bargaining. He had every intention of going for the death penalty. Under Cord Davis, the Dallas County District Attorney's office had probably sent more convicted murderers to death row than any other office in the state of Texas. They tried for murder-one indictments on cases that other district attorneys would have sought a lesser charge. Davis had pointed out in a CNN interview that all the people on death row were mentally deficient or else they wouldn't have committed murder. Murder wasn't something that nice, normal people did. Cord said he was sure a family as fine and upstanding as the Tarringtons had taught Danny that it wasn't all right to kill people.

Chapter Thirty-two

Justin Garrett went to Clifford's office to report that the grand jury had just indicted Danny, which came as no surprise given the evidence against him. He'd been bound over for trial, and a hearing had been set in three weeks to determine death eligibility.

"I've been reading about the law and retardation," Justin said. "The outcome of this hearing is not cut-and-dried."

"The boy is dumb as a post," Clifford said across the expanse of his desk. "He doesn't read. He can't tell time. He doesn't know his own telephone number. If you tell him something is going to happen next month, he doesn't have a clue what you're talking about. The law says the accused in a capital crime has to understand the charges against him and to be capable of assisting in his own defense. Danny has no concept of crime and punishment. And the idea of him assisting anyone with anything more difficult than carrying a heavy box is ludicrous."

"That's only your opinion, sir. The court may rule otherwise."

"That's up to you, Garrett. You find the experts who will say the right things at that hearing. You convince the judge that Danny doesn't know shit. You hear me, Garrett? *He doesn't know shit!* Then get this thing over with. Make a deal. Manslaughter. Murder two. Aggravated assault. I don't give a damn so long as his parents can tuck him away in some nice safe place, otherwise the whole family will come apart and start saying he didn't do it after all."

"Did he?" Justin asked.

"Hell, yes," Clifford said and slammed his fist on the desk for emphasis. "Now, go buy some experts. Pay what you have to. Get good ones with white hair and tidy little beards who've written books and testified before Congress. Cord Davis is going to find esteemed scholars and physicians who will say that Danny is really some sort of latent genius who could make an atomic bomb in his closet if he felt like it and if he's turned loose he'll go out and kill every pregnant woman he can get his hands on. You just make sure your expert witnesses are more esteemed than his and can make it sound like the boy couldn't even wipe his own bottom without two people helping him."

Justin's experts were esteemed, legitimate, and impressive. As were the prosecution's. When both sides were finished presenting, the elderly judge cleared his throat and offered his own logic on the issue before him.

"I find it interesting that two groups of supposedly learned people can be in such total disagreement on what they would have you believe is a measurable human condition. They want us to believe that they can calculate whether or not someone is too retarded to know what he's doing and realize he shouldn't be doing it and could very well be held accountable for having done it. These experts would like us to believe they are putting forth well-documented, totally accurate evidence to support their point of view." The judge paused to take a sip of water and peer over the top of his glasses, apparently making sure he had everyone's attention.

"For the most part, the consensus seems to be that Mr. Tarrington here is not profoundly retarded," he continued, pointing in Danny's direction. "And he's probably not severely retarded. This makes Mr. Tarrington fall in that big gray area called moderately. Now we've got our low moderates and our middle moderates and our high moderates. We've got all sorts of different testing instruments, all sorts of different theories on how to test. We know that test scores vary depending on

the person administering the test and the test itself. We
know that test scores can be influenced by other factors,
like the subject being frightened or drugged or sick or
exhausted. So what do we do? How do we decide? By
which set of experts used the biggest words, have the
most letters after their names, written the most articles
for scholarly journals?''

Once again, the judge peered over the top of his
glasses, then leaned back in his high-backed chair and
put his fingertips together.

''The murder of Beth Williams Tarrington was premeditated in that the murderer selected a weapon and
carried it to the pool where the victim was swimming.
The crime was committed under the cover of darkness,
which indicated the murderer had some sense that he
shouldn't be doing it and didn't want people to know
about it. And the murderer destroyed evidence, which
meant he didn't want to get blamed.

''Now, the person who in truth committed that
crime is smart enough to understand the charges
against him, participate in his defense, and be eligible
to stand trial for a capital crime. Maybe Mr. Tarrington
will be found innocent. But if he is found guilty of this
crime—if a jury decides he's the one who did it—that in
itself would indicate he must be smart enough to be
held accountable.''

Justin couldn't believe his ears. The judge had just
made a joke out of the entire issue and thrown Danny
to the wolves. He looked over at Cord, who looked
equally astonished but was wearing a wide grin.

Then he looked back at Angie, who was burying
her face in her hands.

''You've got to talk to me, Danny. If you don't talk,
I can't help you. And I want to be your friend and help
you. So what do you say, pal? Will you talk to me?''

Danny stared at the scarred tabletop, saying nothing.

''Did you kill Beth?'' Justin asked. ''Just say 'yes' or

'no.' Or nod your head. I need for you to tell me. It will be our secret.''

Danny kept staring at his hands.

Justin wanted to shake his client. Hard. And tell him that goddamnit, that judge had decreed he was capable of participating in his own defense so he jolly well better get busy and do it or he could be a retarded dead man.

"Do you want to go home?" Justin asked.

Danny actually gave a small nod.

The question may have been a cruel one since Danny might very well never go home. But Justin was at his wits' end, and that small nod was the first response he had gotten from his client.

"Did you kill Beth?" he asked.

Danny turned his hands over and stared at the palms.

"Are you protecting someone?" Justin asked, then decided to rephrase the question. "Did you see someone kill Beth and don't want to tell on them, you know, be a tattletale? Or were you watching out your window and saw someone come back up the hill from the pool?"

Using both hands, Danny pinched his lips together very tightly. He wasn't talking.

"You really think he's protecting someone?" Angie asked.

"Why else would he refuse to talk?" Justin demanded. He was excited. His client might be innocent. And in need of a defense.

"He used to be absolutely incapable of keeping secrets," Angie said. "It was like he had to tell someone or he would burst. But he's different now. He hasn't been saying much of anything since Beth got him all screwed up."

Angie had dressed up for their dinner at the Crescent. She was wearing a form-fitting black dress and actually had on makeup. Justin wanted to tell her how

beautiful she looked, how much he had looked forward
to having dinner with her, and while he wanted to discuss her brother's case, he also wanted to spend the
evening with her—a date, not a conference. But he
never knew quite what to say to Angie when she was in
her usual jeans and a blazer, and he certainly had no
idea how to proceed with this more sophisticated Angie.

"Your grandfather doesn't really care if he did it or
not," Justin said. "In his eyes, Danny is expendable.
Right?"

"It's not that simple," Angie said, twirling the swiz-
zle stick around in her gin and tonic. "My grandfather
wants to believe that Danny did it. Even if Danny has to
stand trial, Clifford doesn't think that Danny will be
held as accountable for the crime as a person of normal
intelligence would be, and he thinks it will do less damage to the family if Danny is deemed to be the guilty
party."

"A body floating around in a swimming pool for
eight or ten hours doesn't provide much forensic evidence," Justin said. "I may not be able to prove that
Danny didn't do it, but the DA will have a tough time
proving that he did. If Danny didn't kill her, and I can
prove it, some member of your family could be in a hell
of a lot of trouble."

Angie looked away for a minute, composing herself. "We thought that Danny would be safe," she said.
"We thought that we could find a nice, kindly private
institution with enough security to satisfy the court and
relocate Danny there for a few years. Then maybe when
things had settled down, bring him home or at least
someplace close to home. But the damned DA wants a
circus with media attention, no special perks for the
rich, the right-to-life people waving banners. They care
more about the fetal death than that of the living,
breathing woman. None of us thought Danny would be
declared death eligible. Hell, when he was five years old,
he scored forty-two on an IQ test! The irony of it is that
Beth was so damned good for him. She brought him

along. Forced him to use his mind. To think. To make the most of what he had left.''

"So, this was a family decision to let Danny take the fall?''

"Sort of,'' Angie admitted. "But it's backfired. Cord wants the death penalty.''

"So, what will it be now?'' Justin wanted to know.

"Can't we prove that Danny didn't do it without implicating the person who did?''

Justin wanted to tell her hell no, that the best defense was always implicating others. But she was so hopeful as she leaned across the table, her hand on his arm. God, she was even wearing perfume. "Maybe,'' he said. "I'd like to help your brother, but I'll need you to pull his strings. He won't talk to me. You have to convince him to keep me on as counsel when your grandfather tries to take me off the case.''

Angie hesitated. "I don't want Danny sent to prison,'' she said, tears welling in her eyes. "Or worse. *Jesus.* My little brother. You can't imagine how much we all love him. He was so sweet. So loving. When he laughed, we all laughed. When he cried, we all cried. He made our family better.''

"So, we're agreed,'' Justin said. "We investigate. Try to find out if Danny really killed your sister-in-law?''

"No. We investigate to find a way to get Danny off. I don't give a damn about who did or did not kill Beth. I just want to protect my family. And don't call her my sister-in-law. Gretchen is my sister-in-law. Beth wasn't one of us.''

Justin knew that he should walk out the door. The Tarrington family was nothing but trouble. There would be no good outcome in this case. A mysterious stranger did not kill Beth Williams Tarrington. Setting Danny free could mean locking up another member of the family.

Maybe even Angie herself.

And he wouldn't like that at all. With her no-nonsense ponytail and jeans, it had taken him a while to realize it, but Angie Tarrington was a very appealing

woman. He found himself thinking about her at odd
moments. Every time he saw her, he noticed something
else about her to admire. Her clear skin. Her wonderfully full mouth. Her dark shining hair. And she was
smart. Damned smart.

When Justin informed Clifford that he was planning to launch his own investigation of Beth's murder,
Clifford slammed his massive fist on the desk and informed him that he'd do no such thing. "You're fired
from this case," Clifford roared.

Justin could imagine the people up and down the
hallway listening, wondering who the poor slob was getting crucified by Clifford. "That's up to Danny," Justin
said, amazed at his own calmness in the line of fire.
"The law says your grandson is intelligent enough to
stand trial. That means he's also smart enough to say
who he wants for defense counsel."

"If you proceed with this investigation, you're history at this law firm and in this city! In this state!" Clifford yelled at him.

Justin wondered if he was doing something he'd
regret for the rest of his life. Only an idiot would throw
away a position at the Tarrington firm. He was all but
guaranteed a full partnership down the line, if he didn't
cross horns with Clifford.

But Justin was discovering that he had more ethics
than he had heretofore assumed. He was actually getting up out of his chair, walking out on the old man.
Clifford was still yelling. About who in the hell did Justin think he was. How ungrateful could a man be. He
was a disgrace to his aunt and uncle. To the University
of Texas College of Law.

Clifford calmed himself with a cigar. And longed
for a shot of whiskey. But didn't feel up to walking
across the room to get it.

He yelled into the intercom for Mrs. Richter to get

his granddaughter on the phone—at the legal aid office.

As soon as he had Angie on the line, he started yelling at her. "You get rid of Justin Garrett, you hear me, girl. I don't want him going near Danny. He's off the case. Fired!"

"Firing Justin would have to be Danny's decision," she told her grandfather.

"That's a bunch of nonsense, and you know it. Danny will do whatever you or his parents tell him. And I'm telling you that I want Garrett off this case. I don't want an *investigation*. For our purposes, Danny killed her, which I happen to believe is what actually happened. And we don't need to know if it isn't."

"We thought everything was going to be tidy and simple," Angie said. "We'd plead Danny guilty in exchange for institutionalizing him, with the family picking up the tab—an acceptable outcome that's not going to happen. Have you turned on the television lately? The media are making it out to be the Dallas murder of the year—like a pregnant woman has never been murdered before in the history of the world. And everyone is pointing out that if Danny were black and poor, no one would care what his IQ was, that death row is full of retarded murderers who might be dumb but know it's wrong to kill pregnant ladies."

"All right, if Danny didn't do it, then Frank is the number-two person on the suspect list," Clifford reminded her. "Shall we just go ahead and turn him in? Then the media would really have another heyday. *Minister Kills Pregnant Wife.*"

"They're going to have a heyday anyway when DNA evidence is introduced that proves Minister Frank wasn't the man who impregnated his wife, that one of the minister's brothers was responsible for that. But I don't want Frank or anyone else arrested. I just want to muddy the waters enough that a jury can't convict Danny beyond a reasonable doubt but everyone still thinks he did it. Or maybe we can show that Beth tormented him and drove him to it—like the Menendez case. Dig up dirt on the victim. Put Beth on trial.''

"I don't want an investigation, and Justin Garrett is fired,'' Clifford said, slamming down the phone and yelling for Mrs. Richter to fetch him a glass of whiskey.

Danny's case had indeed become a media bonanza, with newspapers and television stations searching through archives for any picture, any piece of information, to enhance their coverage. Last night there was footage on the evening news of Danny and Matt in their Cub Scout uniforms marching in a Christmas parade. How in the hell had they dug that up? Two little boys, for God's sake! Had someone filed that away all those years ago in hopes those two Cub Scouts would someday be involved in a famous murder case?

The same newscast showed the antiabortion forces in front of the courthouse staging a demonstration in support of the DA. "God bless Cord Davis,'' one of the placards said. Another called for "Death to Murderers.''

The case had spawned a round of debates on the local talk shows. Was the fetus that died with its mother in the Tarrington swimming pool a fully franchised human being or just an organized group of cells that had only the potential to become a human being? Clifford ordinarily would have dismissed the entire issue as nonsense. There were too many people in the world the way it was. But in this case, Clifford agreed with Cord and the right-to-lifers. Whoever killed Beth's baby had been a murderer. That baby was precious. It wouldn't have been just some other poor kid. Some black or Hispanic to clutter up the streets and steal radios out of cars. That baby had been his hope for the future. His immortality.

He'd lived his entire life being his father's son. What was life about if not continuance? Family used to matter. Family was who a man was. People used to understand that.

Chapter Thirty-three

"What about letters of recommendation?" Justin asked. "Surely they wouldn't have hired her off the street."

"I doubt if there were any letters of recommendation," Angie admitted. "Beth was a college student. Clifford had suggested she apply for the job. As I recall, she'd come to his office soliciting contributions for Special Olympics. She was majoring in special education at UT-Arlington and had some experience working with low-mental kids. He knew Mom and Dad were looking for someone, and I guess he thought she seemed right for the job."

"The formidable Mrs. Richter obviously wasn't guarding his office back then," Justin observed.

"Mrs. Richter has been Clifford's private secretary ever since I can remember. But Beth was a pretty little coed with masses of gorgeous red hair and a disarming smile. Knowing Beth, I'm not surprised that she managed to talk her way into my grandfather's office. And I'm sure he gave her a donation. Even Grandfather Clifford is susceptible to attractive young women."

A frown was creasing Justin's otherwise smooth brow. With his conservative dark suit and expensive shoes, he looked decidedly out of place among the clutter in Angie's legal aid office with its mix-matched furniture, dingy walls and view of a back alley. He had tried not to stare at the pile after pile of folders, papers, books, and journals stacked on Angie's desk and on every other available surface. The stacks in themselves were rather tidy, but the overall effect was of disarray. Angie thought about the contrast between her office

and those at the paneled and pristine Tarrington Law
Associates, with its small army of paralegals, secretaries,
clerks, and even a librarian to keep visible clutter to a
minimum.

Angie could already imagine the kidding she'd take
from her colleagues over the pretty lawyer boy from the
uptown law firm.

Except Justin had evoked her grandfather's wrath
and probably was history at the firm. Her dad admitted
that it wasn't Justin's fault that Danny's situation turned
out to be more precarious than they anticipated and
that Justin had Danny's best interests at heart. But in
truth, both her father and Matt were also pissed at Justin. The family was in charge of Danny's case. Not Justin.

"What about the college?" he asked. "Did your
parents get a copy of her transcript?"

"Look, Justin, Beth showed my parents a picture of
her dead Down's syndrome brother. She'd helped care
for him and had really been crazy about him, and it
showed whenever she talked about him. Mom and Dad
were impressed, charmed, bewitched, reassured, whatever. And she would be living and working right under
their noses. Anyway, they hired her on the spot. I know
that must seem strange to you now, but Beth was remarkable, and she seemed like the answer to their
prayers." Angie paused, remembering when her parents had them all come into the living room to meet
Beth, remembering the sunlight on Beth's hair and the
way she smiled as if she already loved them. She knelt in
front of Danny and told him she had always wanted a
friend named Danny. "It's the sweetest name in the
world," she'd said. No, Angie couldn't fault her parents
for their hasty decision to hire Beth. She would have
done the same.

"All any of us wanted was for Danny to get back to
where he was before the kidnapping," Angie continued. "But Beth was able to reach inside of him and find
things that none of us dreamed were there. She never
could teach him how to read or add or tell time, but she

got him to sing again after months of silence. She overcame his fear of the water and taught him how to swim. She taught him to take care of himself and look past his nose and dance and play. In many ways, she was magical. She was also cunning and corrupt, but I didn't know that until later. In the beginning she was Danny's fairy godmother, and we all loved her.''

Angie handed Justin the picture of Danny with his Special Olympics medal that she kept on her desk. ''Beth was Danny's coach. She taught him about training and pushing himself to the limit and trying again and again. Because of Beth, he got to be a champion in his limited little world, and what a glorious day that was! Daddy bought Beth a car, and Danny gave her the keys at the celebration dinner that night. A brand-new red Volkswagen convertible. We collected Maura from the kitchen, and all went racing out to the garage to dance around the car. Mom bought Danny a gold chain so he could wear his medal always, and anytime he felt bad, he was supposed to touch it and remember that he was a champion. Isn't it ironic—that same medal is now the cornerstone of the case against him.''

Justin handed Danny's picture back to her. ''But what makes you say that she was corrupt?''

''I don't doubt that she loved Danny. He took the place of the brother she'd lost. But she didn't love the rest of us. Back then, she did hurtful, confusing things to my family that left permanent scars. Then she came back and did it again. She was a fortune hunter. She used us.''

''We all use people,'' Justin said. ''My aunt and uncle made it possible for me to have a good education and get a good job. But I really loved and respected them.''

Angie shrugged. ''I have good reason not to love and respect Beth. And I don't think that digging around in her past is going to change the basics of this case.''

''Maybe you're right,'' Justin admitted. ''But if we

knew more about Beth, we might be able to figure out who killed her."

Angie shook her head. "You still don't have it straight. We're supposed to be searching for a way to get Danny off without incriminating anyone else."

"Look, if we find out something, we can always decide what to do with that information. We already know about Danny. But we don't know much about the woman he was supposed to have murdered. Where did she go after she left your family? Where did she work? Who were her friends? Had she ever been married? Why in the hell did she resurface after so many years? Frank married her yet claims he doesn't know anything about her life. That seems if not suspicious at least strange."

"I suppose. But where would we begin?"

"Maybe we could talk about it over dinner," he said hopefully.

Angie laughed. "And where would you suggest that a man straight from the pages of *Gentlemen's Quarterly* dine with a woman in Birkenstocks and faded blue jeans?"

Justin stood up and removed his coat and tie, rolled up his sleeves. "Will this do?" he asked.

They went to the nearest T.G.I. Friday's. After they ordered, Angie told him how sorry she was about his job. "Maybe when this is all over, you can make things right with my grandfather."

Justin took a swallow of beer and wiped the foam from his upper lip. "You know, all I've ever wanted was to get a good job, make a lot of money, and play as many of the world's great golf courses as could be managed in one lifetime. I'd never really thought much about ethics except as an abstraction. But when it came down to doing what your grandfather wanted or doing what was right for my client, I didn't even hesitate. So except for wondering how I'm going to support myself, I actually feel pretty damned good. Of course, my aunt has called me twice from Switzerland to tell me that lawyers have to pick and choose their cases to be suc-

cessful and that I'd better unpick Danny Tarrington in a
big hurry."

"Your aunt is right. I can afford to be the world's
most ethical lawyer because I don't have to pay my own
way. Of course, we could find a corner for you down at
legal aid, but you couldn't afford the green fees on all
those golf courses."

"Let's just play this thing out and worry about my
golf game later, okay?" he said, putting his hand on her
arm. A tentative gesture. And he had that hopeful look
on his face again. It was enough to give a grown woman
pause.

They began with the registrar's office at UT-Arlington. A number of Beth Williamses and Elizabeth Williamses had attended, but none had been enrolled at
the school the year Beth began working for the Tarrington family. There was a Beth Ann Williams who'd
graduated from high school in Fort Worth and received
a degree in education, but her first enrollment at UTA
hadn't been until the following year.

"She can't be the right one," Angie insisted. "Our
Beth had lived with an aunt in Mineral Wells. And Frank
picked up Beth and her possessions in front of one of
the UTA dormitories and brought her to our house."

"Do you think she could have been attending under a maiden name?" the clerk asked.

"At this point, I don't know what to think," Angie
admitted.

Over lunch at a Mexican restaurant near the college, Justin had gone to the library and called up the
newspaper coverage of Danny's kidnapping. He quizzed
Angie about the police investigation of the case and
wanted to know about Clifford and Belle's longtime
chauffeur who had resigned shortly before Danny was
taken.

"But what could that have to do with Beth's murder?" Angie wanted to know, dipping a tortilla chip in a

dish of salsa. "The kidnapping happened before she came to live with us."

"Probably nothing," Justin said. "But the case was never solved. And the kidnapping led to the hiring of a caretaker for Danny, who happened to be our very mysterious Beth Williams. Do you remember the chauffeur?"

"Sure. His name was Roy Gunnison. He had a ponytail and tattoos all over his arms and the back of his hands—flowers and animals all swirled together. He used to give Frank and me each a dollar for helping him polish the cars. It was the first money I ever earned. I know the police wanted to question him. But he'd apparently left town before the kidnapping."

"I'd still like to know more about him," Justin insisted. "He's the only possible lead I can think of."

After lunch, Justin suggested they ask Belle about the chauffeur. "Or would she be going against her husband's wishes by talking to me?" he asked.

"My grandmother pretty much manages her own life," Angie said. "If she thinks it might help Danny, she'll talk to you."

Belle had just returned from her exercise class and apologized for her attire.

"Don't worry. You look adorable in sweats," Angie said with a kiss. "This is Justin Garrett."

"So you're the young man that almost gave my husband a coronary," Belle said extending her hand. "Come join me for my afternoon sherry. After I've exercised, I always feel like I've earned it."

Belle led them to the living room and poured three glasses. Angie had to smile at Justin's struggle not to make a face after his first tentative sip.

"You're certainly a handsome young man," Belle told Justin. "Are you and Angie involved?"

"Behave yourself, Granny," Angie warned. "He needs to ask you about Roy Gunnison."

"The chauffeur? My goodness, I haven't thought of him in years," Belle said.

"It may not be important," Justin said. "It's just a hunch I have."

"I didn't like the man much, but maybe it was just the tattoos. He was always polite. I usually drove myself anyway, so I didn't have much to do with him. Clifford had gotten too fat to fit comfortably behind the wheel of a car. Roy was the first chauffeur he hired way back when, and he worked here for years. I think Clifford used him sometimes to intimidate people. Of course, I wasn't supposed to know that. I remember thinking when he quit that he must have gone too far with his 'intimidating' and needed to leave town. Clifford seemed to accept his leaving and said something about giving him a grubstake."

Belle sipped her sherry and recalled how the police had asked to be notified when Roy sent for the possessions he'd left with the cook. But as far as she knew he'd never contacted Beatrice or Clifford.

Belle suggested they talk to Beatrice. Roy had spent a lot of time in the kitchen, and she might remember something more.

"Well, he was a nice enough fellow," Beatrice said as she rolled out dough for an apple pie. An old-fashioned crockery bowl was filled with sliced apples already covered with sugar and cinnamon. "He'd help me carry the groceries in, even peel potatoes and crank the ice-cream freezer. I think he had relatives around here someplace—a sister and her family."

"Do you think that Roy might have had something to do with kidnapping the Tarrington's grandson?" Justin asked.

"I couldn't say," Beatrice said, the flesh on her meaty arms jiggling as she moved the rolling pin back and forth. "The police came around asking questions 'cause Roy'd done time. But taking a kid is a long shot away from stealing a car."

"Did my grandfather know he had a record?" Angie asked.

"Mr. Clifford knew," Beatrice said as she expertly folded the dough in half and placed it in a pie plate.

"Roy was mighty beholden to your grandpa for giving him a job when no one else would. He used to say he'd do anything for Mr. Clifford. He looked respectable enough in his uniform as long as he wore gloves to cover up the tattoos. Now why do you suppose a man would get his body all marked up like that? Never did understand that. Maybe a secret tattoo to show off in the bedroom, but not all that other stuff."

They followed Beatrice up a set of narrow steps to the attic, and she showed them a box of Roy's possessions. "He never sent for any of it. There was some other stuff—clothes, books, a television, records, but after a few years when I hadn't heard hide nor hair from him, I gave most of it to my church for a rummage sale," she said. "All that's left is the personal stuff—in case he ever did come back or his sister showed up."

She left them to look through the dusty box. There wasn't much—a couple of army medals, a high-school yearbook, postcards, a cigar box of photographs, an old Bible, and a framed picture of a 1940s family on the front steps of a frame house.

Two photographs were stuck inside the Bible. Both pictures had been taken on the steps to the upstairs garage apartment.

Angie recognized the man in the pictures as Roy. In one photograph, he was with a woman she didn't know. Then she looked at the other picture. Roy Gunnison had his arm draped around the shoulders of a young Beth Williams.

Angie felt the small hairs on the back of her neck rise. And carried the picture to a window to be sure. Justin came to stand behind her and look over her shoulder.

"I don't understand," she said, staring at Beth's face. "She didn't come to live with us until four or five months after Danny's kidnapping. But here's a picture of her taken before the kidnapping, and she's sitting by my grandparents' garage, right across the creek from our house."

Justin took the picture and looked at it. "Are you sure it's her?"

"Maybe we should just put this stuff back and get out of here," Angie said, looking over her shoulder as though she expected to see Roy standing there. Or Beth's ghost.

But she sat on an old steamer trunk with Justin and looked through the lone yearbook—a 1952 edition from Handley High School in Fort Worth. Roy Gunnison had been a senior. A Lorraine Gunnison had been a sophomore that same year.

"I think Lorraine is the woman in this other picture," Justin said excitedly.

Angie wasn't sure. It could have been.

"The Beth Ann Williams you said couldn't have been your Beth Williams listed her mother's name as Lorraine Williams with a Fort Worth address."

"Are you sure?" Angie asked.

"Absolutely. She'd listed her father as deceased."

"Beth was a lie," Angie said. "From the very beginning, she was a lie."

Chapter Thirty-four

When the knock sounded at her door, Lorraine assumed it was her friend Goldie from three trailers down. She pulled the walker close to her chair and hoisted herself to her feet. Goldie always brought doughnuts and the morning newspaper. They'd eat doughnuts, drink a pot of coffee, and work the crossword puzzle in the newspaper while watching morning television, such as it was. Real television didn't start until the afternoon with *As the World Turns*.

But instead of Goldie, there were two young people standing at her door. A man in a suit. A woman in worn jeans, a wrinkled jacket, and cowboy boots.

"Are you Lorraine Williams?" the man asked.

"Who's asking?" Lorraine demanded. The only strangers who ever came to her door were bill collectors and magazine hucksters.

"I'm Justin Garrett, and this is Angie Tarrington."

Lorraine stared at the young woman. *Tarrington?* She and her walker took a half step back from the door.

"We'd like to ask you a few questions about your daughter," Justin was saying in a rush, obviously worried that she was going to shut the door in their faces. Lorraine wondered if he had a gun in a holster under his arm, like Roy used to wear when he drove for Clifford Tarrington. Rich people had enemies, he'd say, like it was the most normal thing in the world for a chauffeur to have a gun.

"You have the wrong person," Lorraine said, closing the door. Locking it. Fastening the security chain.

Then she heard Angie Tarrington's voice coming through the open window by the door. "The picture on your television set—Beth had one just like it on her dresser when she lived with us. Please Mrs. Williams, we mean you no harm.''

Aware of the listening ears and spying eyes of her neighbors, Lorraine opened the door the three or so inches the chain would allow. The man and woman huddled close to the opening. ''Let the dead lie,'' she told them in a hushed voice.

''Then you know that your daughter is dead?'' the man asked, his voice also lowered, apparently understanding her concern. ''How did you find out?''

''I read it in the newspaper. Saw it on television. It would be hard not to know.''

''I don't remember seeing you at the funeral,'' Angie said.

''Beth wouldn't have wanted me to come,'' Lorraine said. ''It was a Tarrington funeral. That's what she always wanted—to be a Tarrington. I used to tell her to be careful what she wished for. Are you really a Tarrington?'' Lorraine asked Angie.

''Yes, ma'am,'' the young woman said.

''Then why are you dressed like that?'' Lorraine asked.

''I'm the misfit of the family. Why don't you want to talk to us? Are you afraid of something?''

''Yes. I'm afraid of the past. I didn't think that any of you knew I existed.''

''We didn't until today. Beth told us she was an orphan. But we found pictures of you and Beth with your brother. The three of you were standing on the steps to the apartment over my grandparents' garage.''

''Do you know who killed her?'' the man whispered. A handsome blond man in an expensive suit.

''No, but I knew Beth should have stayed away from the Tarringtons,'' Lorraine said, her voice matching his. ''I begged her not to work for them all those years ago. And then, when she decided to go back, I told her she'd come to no good end.''

Angie glanced over her shoulder at the nearest

trailer. "Couldn't we please come inside where it's more private?"

Lorraine regarded Angie Tarrington through the small opening. "You didn't like Beth," she said, her tone accusing.

"Beth did some things to members of my family that I found very upsetting. But she was good to my brother. I had mixed feelings about her."

Lorraine nodded. Yes, that's how she felt about Beth. Mixed feelings. Mother love and resentment all jumbled up together. Lorraine reached up and unfastened the chain, then backed away with her walker so they could come into her tiny living room. And felt a wave of humiliation at the shabbiness.

Angie stepped inside and picked up the framed photograph from the television. "So she really did have a Down's syndrome brother. Was his name Willy?"

Lorraine nodded. "His real name was Wilburn, but we called him Willy."

"That was about the only truthful thing Beth ever told us about herself," Angie said, replacing the picture. "She said that Danny made her think of Willy. We'd like to know about Beth, Mrs. Williams. I promise that we mean you no harm. And if you could see your way clear to help us, I'll be glad to pay you for your time."

Pay her?

Lorraine thought of the unpaid bill for the new hot water tank she'd had to buy three months ago when the old one burst. And she thought of the chair she'd seen advertised on television. It tilted forward and kind of lifted people up on their feet.

Then she sighed. A mother shouldn't profit from her daughter's death.

Beth had brought it on herself, though. Lorraine warned her that she was playing with fire, that people like the Tarringtons didn't want some hireling they'd fired years ago to show up on their doorstep.

One of those special chairs would be a godsend. It was getting harder and harder for her to get up out of a chair, and she worried so about what would happen to her when she simply couldn't do it anymore.

"What did you say your name was?" she asked the young man.

"Justin Garrett."

"Why do you want to know about my daughter?"

"I'm an attorney representing Danny Tarrington. Miss Tarrington and I don't believe that he killed your daughter."

"How much?" she asked.

She'd had only one doughnut with Goldie and hurried her out the door. "I'll tell you about it later," Lorraine promised. But probably she wouldn't.

In less than an hour, Angie Tarrington and Justin Garrett were back with a cashier's check for five thousand dollars.

Lordy, she didn't want to do this. Go back. She had learned a long time ago that it's best to live in the present with the *TV Guide* mapping her days and weeks—a life she now shared with Goldie, who was almost ten years older than Lorraine but not crippled. They kept each other from loneliness.

And they didn't inflict too many memories on each other—just enough to establish how they had gotten to this point in life. Goldie had been jilted at the altar and spent her life as a schoolteacher—second grade. She'd had three lovers along the way. An abortion. Cared for her mother and older sister until they died. Her drink of choice was Scotch.

Neither one of them kept journals. That was one of the things Goldie had asked Lorraine the first night they got together—to watch Princess Di marry Prince Charles. When Lorraine said no, Goldie had smiled. "Me neither. If I can't remember it without writing it down, it must have been pretty boring anyway."

In the top of her closet, Lorraine had photograph albums filled with pictures of her parents, Roy, her two children growing up. But she never took the albums down and looked through them. Not for years. She had her favorite picture of Willy there on top of the television. On the bookcase was a picture of Beth at thirteen in her track clothes holding a trophy. Pictures of Ward and her parents were on the shelf by her bed. That was all the homage she paid to the past. More was too painful. Maybe on her deathbed, she'd look at those albums and get ready just in case there was a hereafter and families were reunited for an eternity. But probably not even then.

The present was safer. Strange how agreeing to take a painful journey into the past would allow her to buy a tilting chair, a better television for her and Goldie to enjoy, and maybe one of those easy-to-use VCRs so they wouldn't miss a single soap opera or episode of *Dateline* or *48 Hours* and therefore have a more pleasurable present.

Beth was four years old when Lorraine married Ward Williams, a retired army sergeant, she told the two lawyers sitting side by side on her sagging sofa—one of them a Tarrington. So hard to believe.

She really should have asked for ten thousand dollars. Or twenty—the amount that Beth never got for kidnapping Danny Tarrington. But what's done was done. And five thousand was certainly going to come in handy.

Chapter Thirty-five

She'd met Ward waiting in line to see one of the *Godfather* movies. A girlfriend had stood her up, and she'd surprised herself by going alone, leaving Beth with a neighbor. The man standing in front of her thought she was pretty. She could see it in his face, which made her smile more and feel like flirting for the first time in she couldn't remember when. Ward was kind of old but nice looking. They sat together, and he walked her home. They stopped to fetch Beth at the neighbors, and he carried her next door to Lorraine's wrapped up in his sport coat.

Ward was twenty years older than Lorraine and diabetic. His erections were short-lived, but he told her she was beautiful and treated her well. And he had a military pension.

Lorraine was weary of struggling to pay the bills. In three years, Beth's father had sent a grand total of $150 in child support. The last letter she'd sent telling him how much money he owed had come back marked "addressee unknown." She taught girls' physical education at a Christian academy where she didn't have to have a degree. After car payments and child care, there was barely enough to make it though the month.

She didn't exactly want to marry Ward, but it seemed like a better idea than not marrying him. She was tired of secondhand clothes and worn-out shoes. She needed to have her teeth fixed.

Ward lived in a trailer, which Beth hated, especially when the wind blew. She said she didn't like living in a box and wanted a house like other people. Or go back to their tiny apartment made out of a garage. Lorraine didn't much care for the trailer either, but it was paid for, and the trailer park had lots of trees and a small playground.

When she realized she was pregnant, Lorraine was shocked. She'd hardly bothered with birth control, but their sex life was so minimal, it hardly seemed necessary. On the infrequent occasions she and Ward had sex, she'd had to all but stuff his flaccid penis inside of her. How could a man like that be potent enough to father a child?

Willy didn't look a lot different from the other babies in the nursery. But after the doctor explained about Down's syndrome and what they could expect from their child in the years to come, Lorraine looked down at her baby's ugly little face and wished that he would die so she'd never have to take him home from the hospital. She cried as they wheeled her down the hall to the exit and her aging husband waiting in his aging Dodge, their defective baby in her arms.

The first time Beth saw her baby brother, she kissed his little mouth and told him that she would love him forever and ever, and he would love her forever and ever, and they would be the best friends in the whole wide world. She insisted on holding him on her lap and sang him nursery songs. She even pulled up her shirt and pinched her flat little chest, trying to make breasts so she could feed him, too.

Lorraine thought Beth's fascination with the new baby would be short-lived, but it wasn't. They explained to her that Willy would always look kind of funny and never be very smart. He wouldn't be able to read and write like other children. He would never be able to look after himself. "That's okay. I'll take care of him," Beth said.

And she did. Beth taught her mother and stepfather to love Willy. In fact, their feelings for Willy went beyond love. They came to adore him. He became the center of their world. Down's syndrome had robbed him of intelligence and left sweet innocence in its stead.

For ten or eleven years, they were happy—the four

of them. Beth ran track, and some of their best times
were spent at track meets all over the state. Ward looked
after Willy while Lorraine was at work and took great
comfort in the company of his affectionate boy with the
strange little face.

Beth did well in school and had lots of friends in
spite of living in a trailer park. Lorraine thought it was
because of the hair she'd inherited from her long-gone
birth father. Beth stood out. She was more than just a
pretty girl—she was a pretty girl with masses of glorious
red hair. And was elected yearbook queen when she was
only a freshman.

Then the good times ended. Lorraine developed
arthritis. She could no longer teach PE and took a low-
paying job at a suburban police department as a dis-
patcher. And Ward's diabetes caused circulation problems in his legs and feet, making him wheelchair bound
and in constant pain.

Ward's savings were used up by the time he finally
died of kidney failure. With her husband gone, Lorraine had no one to look after Willy during the day. She
quit her job, and they lived off of her government
widow's pension and what Beth could make working
after school.

One day, Beth promised Willy she'd walk him
across the highway so he could buy a candy bar at the
convenience store. She told him to wait for her outside
on the stoop. But she starting talking to a friend on the
phone and forgot about him until they heard the sirens.

Beth threw down the phone and went running out
the door. Bystanders tried to hold her back, but she
managed to break away and throw herself on Willy's
body in the middle of the highway. Screaming. God,
how she screamed and screamed and screamed. She hit
and kicked at the people who tried to pull her away
from Willy, even bit a man on the hand. Finally one of
the paramedics who came in the ambulance gave her a
shot.

Lorraine thought Beth was going to go crazy. She
didn't sleep. Barely ate enough to stay alive. Stopped

wearing makeup. Wore the same old jeans and sweat-shirt every day. Refused to go to school. Lorraine took her twice a week to a state mental health counseling center, but she didn't want to be healed. She wanted to suffer for her sin. If she'd been with Willy like she was supposed to be, he would still be alive.

But she was young. The grief and the staying home all the time got boring. Beth gradually began to come out of it. To go back to school. Fix herself up a bit. Get back some of her old spunk.

Even though Beth still talked about winning a track scholarship to college and majoring in special educa-tion, her times fell off and she didn't seem to have the heart for running anymore, for pushing herself to the limit. Maybe it was because Willy wasn't there in the stands anymore, cheering for her, telling everyone that his big sister was the fastest girl in the world. Or maybe it was because Beth realized that she'd already achieved her personal best, already run her fastest race. Whatever the reason, no college program took an interest in her.

Beth was afraid that she was going to end up wait-ing tables all her life and sank back into depression. Lorraine worried about her but also worried about her-self. She was poor and crippled but wanted to enjoy what life she had with her books and television and neighbors. She could feel Beth pulling her down. There was no enjoyment with Beth around.

Then Lorraine's brother Roy told Beth how she could make a lot of money—enough to go to college. He claimed that the man he worked for was going to pay a lot of money to have his retarded grandson se-creted away and taken to a special home up north. The boy's parents thought they should keep him at him at home, but he was a real burden. The mother was de-pressed all the time and neglected her other children. And Mr. Tarrington was afraid his son wasn't going to run for reelection to the state legislature because of his family situation.

"The boy isn't like Willy," Roy explained. "He was okay when he was born, but he had a fever that fried his

brain. And now he's not much more than a vegetable.
For a kid like that, what difference does it make who
feeds him and keeps him clean? One caretaker is as
good as another."

A kid like that wouldn't cause any trouble, he insisted. It would be like taking a puppy dog. And he
wouldn't be smart enough to give any clues—like in the
movies when the victim had been blindfolded but could
still tell the cops about railroad crossings and how many
right turns and left turns and the house had been on a
hill. But Roy needed Beth's help to take the kid.

At first, Lorraine and Beth were horrified at such
an idea. Of course, Beth would have no part in it. Kidnapping was a serious crime. They could all end up in
prison. Even waiting tables was better than going to jail.

But Lorraine and Beth listened while Roy explained the plan he had devised. For her part, he would
give Beth twenty thousand dollars in cash. She would be
able to live in a dormitory, have nice clothes, be a real
college girl.

Lorraine and Beth argued all the way home. Lorraine didn't want Beth to have anything to do with the
scheme. "But what if this is my only chance to get
enough money to do something with my life?" Beth
demanded.

For days they argued, with Lorraine insisting that
Beth would end up in jail, and that Clifford Tarrington
was playing God, that the whole thing probably was a
publicity stunt to get media attention for his politician
son with no consideration for what it would do to the
little boy and his parents. But Beth wanted out of the
trailer park, out of her waitress uniform. And the boy
hardly knew his own mother from the housekeeper.
"Then why does she love him so much?" Lorraine
asked. "Why has she refused to give him up?"

But Beth was reaching for the golden ring, the only
one that was likely ever to come her way. Finally, Lorraine gave up. Nothing she could say was going to
change Beth's mind. And after all, it wasn't a kidnapping for ransom. Roy would just be taking the boy up

north to a place that Mr. Garrison had arranged for—a place where the boy would be well taken care of. His mother's heart would be broken, but there would also be relief for her. A lifelong burden would have been lifted from her shoulders. She could live a normal life as the mother of normal children. Lorraine knew all about such feelings. Grief and relief, all mixed together.

They met Roy at a restaurant in Arlington. He gave Beth a brunette wig and some business cards that said she was the education reporter for the *Dallas Morning News*. Roy explained that he'd go to the school himself, but with his tattoos and ponytail, he didn't look the part. He practiced with Beth about how she should act and what she should say. And told her she had to be smart. Look for the right opportunity. That she could go back another day if the opportunity wasn't right the first time.

The next day, Lorraine insisted Beth pad herself to look less slender and wear a navy suit that made her look dowdy and not quite so young. And she darkened Beth's eyebrows to match the wig. Beth was to dispose of the suit afterward. And the wig.

After Beth took the boy, she drove him to a deserted farmhouse near the town of Forney and waited for Roy to come. She sang songs to calm the boy and rubbed his back like she used to do for Willy. Danny Tarrington wasn't a vegetable. He cried for his mother. For his family. For his dog.

"You lied to me," Beth told Roy. "That boy may be more retarded than Willy was, but he knows more than you said he did."

"I was just tellin' you what the boss said to me— that the kid is a basket case." And he picked up the frightened, crying child and put him in the backseat of his car. Beth covered Danny with a blanket and tucked the teddy bear she'd bought for him in beside him.

"Where's my money?" Beth asked.

"Later," Roy said.

"No, damn it. You said you'd have the money for

me when you picked up the boy. Twenty thousand dollars.''

But he slammed the door and drove away, with Beth running after the car screaming. Finally, she fell to the ground exhausted. There would be no money. And what was going to happen to that poor little boy?

Two days later, the lead story on the evening news was that Norma and Perry Tarrington had paid a huge ransom to get their retarded son back. Roy had lied about everything. He'd cooked up the whole story to get Beth to help him. He wasn't helping Clifford Tarrington solve a family problem—he was extorting money from the boy's heartsick parents.

''But what's he done with Danny?'' Beth kept asking. Lorraine had no answer. Surely Roy wouldn't kill the child. But he might abandon him by the side of the road.

As the days ticked by, the faces of news anchors became more and more somber when they reported on the kidnapping. Hope was dwindling for the boy's safe return.

One evening, a pert news anchor reported on a possible suspect in the Tarrington murder case. The police were looking for a former employee of Danny Tarrington's grandparents—a chauffeur named Roy Paul Gunnison. Roy's senior yearbook picture from Handley High School started appearing on the screen alongside Danny's.

Which made Lorraine's blood run cold. Her picture was in that same yearbook. She knew that the police would eventually discover Roy had a sister living in the Fort Worth area. Would they also find out that he had a niece about the same size as the woman who took Danny Tarrington from his school?

Two days later, while Beth was at work, a pair of Dallas detectives came to Lorraine's door. No, Lorraine didn't know where her brother was. She hadn't seen him in months—or spoken with him on the phone. No, she didn't know anything about Clifford Tarrington's grandson other than what she read in the newspaper.

Lorraine felt them scrutinizing her, noting that she was too short, wide, and old to have been the woman who took Danny Tarrington from his school.

They didn't ask about a daughter.

She found out later from her neighbors that the police had asked around, showing them the yearbook picture of Roy. A couple of neighbors remembered him from the funerals—Ward's and Willy's—but they hadn't seen him since. And if he'd come around, they would have seen him. There were no secrets in trailer parks.

When Beth heard the boy had been found, she was overjoyed. Exuberant. Couldn't stop crying and laughing and hugging her mother. Finally, to calm herself, she went to the high-school track and ran and ran until she was so exhausted she could hardly walk home. For days, she was on a real high. Danny Tarrington had been found. She was redeemed.

But she couldn't stop thinking about Danny and his family. She put a newspaper picture of Danny in a frame. She went to Dallas and drove by the Tarrington's very impressive home. A real mansion. She went to the library and researched the family. She poured over newspaper stories, beginning in Preacher Tarrington's era. She read about Clifford's glory days with the Providence Steamrollers, his mother's death, newsworthy law cases he'd been involved with over the years. She read the announcement of Norma and Perry's engagement. And then the story of their wedding two years later. She read about Norma's father's retirement from First Bank of Texas, Perry's campaign and subsequent election to the state legislature. And she read the stories in recent papers about the kidnapping and about the happy family reunited at last. There were four other children—Frank, Angela, Julia, and Danny's twin brother, Matthew. Frank, the oldest son, was only a few years younger than Beth. Angie drove by their house again and imagined what it would be like to live there.

She volunteered to coach Special Olympics just so she'd have an entree into their life. She had some notion about recruiting Danny, being his coach, his pal.

One day, she put on a kelly green dress and presented herself at the office of Tarrington Law Associates. Mr. Perry Tarrington wasn't in, so Beth talked her way into Clifford's office and asked for a contribution to Special Olympics. Clifford was gruff at first and told her his secretary would write out a check for $100. But she asked him if he'd ever participated in sports. And he talked on a bit about football in the old days. Beth said she'd love to see his scrapbook. What wonderful memories he must have. Did his mother ever see him play? He told her her hair was magnificent. She blushed a bit and said she was happy that his grandson was safely back home with his family—what a horrible ordeal for the family. Had Danny ever participated in sports? "I'd love to coach him," she said.

"Danny needs more than a coach," Clifford said. "He needs a nursemaid. His parents are so worried about another kidnapping that they're keeping him home from school."

He explained that Danny belonged in an institution. But if he had a full-time caretaker, his daughter-in-law would be a better candidate's wife, his son would be more willing to devote himself to a political career.

Beth's heart took a leap. *Danny Tarrington's nursemaid.* She could live in that house. She'd get to know the Tarringtons, be a part of their family. She'd make them all love her. Not just Danny. All of them.

Beth told Clifford about Willy, about how she had taken care of him. Talking about Willy always brought tears to her eyes. She made up a story about majoring in special education at UT-Arlington and explained how she was looking for work so she could stay in school at least part time.

Clifford picked up the phone to call his daughter-in-law. "You take a picture of your brother when you go talk to them," he told her.

"It was so easy," she told her mother that evening. "I'm going to talk to Danny's parents tomorrow. I know I'll get the job. I'm the right person for that boy."

"But what if he remembers you?" Lorraine demanded, appalled at the whole insane idea. Beth must have some sort of secret desire for self-destruction.

But Beth wasn't worried. She'd worn a dark wig when she took Danny. Six months had gone by since the kidnapping. And after all, the boy was only seven years old and seriously retarded.

Beth was already smitten with the idea of Danny. It would be like having Willy again. Maybe she had found a way out of the trailer park after all.

She wore a simple white blouse and navy skirt to her interview with Norma and Perry Tarrington. She told them about her brother Willy with tears in her eyes. About her dream to be a special-education teacher. About how she had prayed for Danny's safe return.

When she saw Danny, it was love at first sight.

"I wanted to hug him and kiss him like I used to do with Willy," she told her mother. "Remember how Willy would put his arms around my neck and say, 'I need hugs and kisses.'"

For the first year or two, Lorraine was certain that the Tarringtons would discover Beth was Roy Gunnison's niece and realize she was the women who had stolen Danny from his school. Beth would be arrested, sent to jail. Lorraine herself would face charges as an accomplice.

But Beth made up a story about growing up in a foster home so that no one would connect her to Roy. They didn't know she had a mother living in Fort Worth. Beth called her mother occasionally, visited the trailer park less and less. And when she came, she stayed only a short time before announcing she really had to get on home. "Home" for Beth had become the Tarrington's gracious house in Dallas.

Lorraine used to wonder if the sole purpose of her daughter's visits and phone calls was to talk about Danny. She'd tell how she'd taught him numbers and how to write his first name. How the family treated him like a pet instead of a child. How sweet he was. How he wanted her to sleep with him at night. *Danny. Danny. Danny.* She said that no one had ever loved her like

Danny loved her. Even Willy. Danny loved her more than he loved his own mother. Beth seemed to think that Lorraine should live vicariously through her daughter's experiences with Danny and her life at the Tarringtons'. But Lorraine knew that Beth's good fortune was temporary. She was an employee. Not family.

Beth didn't want to hear it. She was absolutely smitten with the Tarrington family. She wanted to learn from them, be like them, enter their world. She fell in love with their house, their clothes, their cars, their manners, their style. The longer she lived in the Tarringtons' house, the less Beth came home. Every time she came back here to the trailer park, she hated her old life even more.

For a while, Beth even claimed that she was going to marry Frank and become a Tarrington herself. She would be rich and live in a big house. She would be *someone*.

Then suddenly, Danny was no longer a little boy. He was a horny adolescent who seemed incapable of controlling his sexual urges. When he assaulted Beth in the swimming pool, the Tarringtons terminated her employment. Beth came back home terribly depressed. Hysterical even. Like after Willy was killed. She had allowed herself to believe that she would be with the Tarringtons forever. She should have run off with Frank and married him when she had the chance.

She called Clifford and asked him to intercede on her behalf. Danny needed her. He was just going through a difficult period. He'd calm down. She'd help him.

But Clifford was using the incident to convince Norma and Perry that Danny needed to be institutionalized. He offered to help Beth find a job with another family. But she didn't want another family. She wasn't just a nursemaid. That house had been her home.

She tried to arrange a meeting with Julia to plead her case, but Julia said she thought it best that they not see each other again.

Once again, Lorraine helped her daughter put herself back together again. But this time, she found herself resenting the turmoil that Beth brought to her carefully regimented life. Beth and her despair filled up the small house trailer.

Finally Lorraine called around and found an opening for a special education teacher at a grade school in Grand Prairie. At first Beth resisted. She was too upset, not ready to find work. But from the minute she walked into the classroom, she was in her element. Instead of Willy or Danny, she had seven retarded children to dote on and love and be loved in return.

The following year, she even got married. Lorraine liked her son-in-law. Bruce. He fixed things for her around the trailer and brought her bottles of really fine bourbon. Bruce was older, like Ward had been. A pharmacist. Beth didn't love him, but he had a good income, and she wanted to have a baby. Within a couple of months, she was pregnant.

But because Beth's brother had been a Down's syndrome child, Bruce insisted that she have an amniocentesis and a sonogram. He didn't want children who weren't normal.

Beth's baby wasn't Down's syndrome, but it did have a serious heart defect and would not live more than a few days once it was born without a heart transplant. Beth begged Bruce to let her have the baby anyway. Even if the baby only lived a few days, she wanted to hold her. A little girl. She wanted to name her Annie. But Bruce said that he'd leave her if she didn't have the abortion. It wasn't like they couldn't have other children.

She had the abortion but ended up hating Bruce. She moved back home to the trailer park. And worked hard being a good special-education teacher. But she grieved about baby Annie. At least with Willy, there was a grave in a cemetery. Annie didn't even have a marker in a cemetery. Nothing. But she would have been spared the tragedy of Annie if the Tarringtons hadn't let her go. Her sadness was their fault.

"Beth never got over losing that baby, and she

never got over your family," Lorraine told Angie at the end of her tale. "A couple of years ago, she all but convinced herself that your grandfather Clifford was her father. Which was ridiculous. I'd never laid eyes on the man. Never heard of him until Roy went to work for him when Beth was a little girl.

"Then she lost her teaching job—for taking a couple of children home with her without telling their parents. She said that she had forgotten to call them. The parents called the police. Beth was arrested. A real mess.

"Sometimes she was like that—forgetful, vague. Once she looked at me and asked what time her daddy would get home. When I reminded her that daddy was dead, she said, 'Oh, yeah. I forgot,' and started crying. Then one day, out of the clear blue, she was talking about Danny again. And the Tarringtons. One minute she'd be saying how she missed them. The next she'd be saying that they owed her. It was time for her to go back and collect her due. I told her the Tarringtons didn't want to see her, that Danny had forgotten all about her. But she had that look on her face. She'd left me and gone someplace else in her head, someplace she'd rather be than with me. Losing her job put her over the edge. She needed to have people around her who loved her completely. Like Willy and Danny."

"Did you ever hear from your brother again?" Beth asked.

"Two months after the kidnapping, there was a letter with a Billings postmark. There was two thousand dollars cash inside. No message. I guess we were lucky to get that. After all this time, I don't expect to ever see him again."

Chapter Thirty-six

Clifford slumped in the backseat of his limousine and closed his eyes. More and more, he ended every day this way—exhausted, with no energy left to join cronies at the club as he'd done for so many years. He did well to get himself home, fed, and propped up in bed with a channel changer in his hand.

He thought about pouring a brandy for a little quick energy. But his stomach was feeling raw—probably the beginnings of an ulcer. No wonder, with that upstart Justin Garrett out there poking around, trying to prove that Danny didn't do it. God knows what he might turn up—like the fact that Beth was Roy Gunnison's niece. Beth didn't know that Clifford knew that, didn't know that he had known all along about Roy's sister and niece in Fort Worth and had eventually figured out that the niece was the woman who'd taken Danny from school all those years ago. That had been Clifford's ace in the hole. If Beth gave him trouble, he would tip off the police—anonymously, of course. Beth would be arrested, sent to jail. Matt and Gretchen could raise the baby. God how he wished he'd done that—had Beth put in jail for the rest of her life. But there would have been such a scandal. The very woman who had given the family such grief by kidnapping one son had come back and married his older brother. The whole paternity issue would probably have surfaced. And Clifford would have hated to lose Beth. He was captivated by her. Maybe even in love with her—the bittersweet love of a very old man who could do nothing about it except feast his eyes, soak up her presence, share his wealth with her.

Clifford reached for the brandy decanter, his stomach be damned. He poured a finger in a crystal glass. Maybe if he took tiny sips, it wouldn't bother him too much.

He relished the feel of the warm liquid on his tongue, sliding down his throat. It was enough to make a man believe in God. He closed his eyes, leaned against the seat, and went back to his musing.

When Roy quit his job, Clifford assumed he was in some sort of trouble. Gambling debts perhaps. He all but knew Roy was involved the minute he learned Danny had been taken. But Clifford said nothing to the police about his suspicions—after all, Roy had done some things for him that he'd never want to come under scrutiny. And he secretly hoped that Danny would never be returned. He didn't wish Danny dead, but maybe Roy would decide to keep him as a companion up there in Montana where he had always said he would go someday if he ever had enough money to buy himself a spread. And Danny was a sweet little thing. Rather like a pet. Clifford would miss him.

When Beth showed up at his office under the guise of soliciting for Special Olympics and saying how she had prayed for Danny and would love to be his coach, Clifford knew right away the girl was up to something. But he rather enjoyed playing out the little scene with her. She asked him about his sporting career and said she would love to see his football mementos. She knew who his father was and said what a shame about the lynching. Governor Tarrington had been between a rock and hard place on that one. And Beth mentioned her dead brother, who'd been retarded. Clifford was fascinated by her hair, her smile, her moxie, the way she lifted her chin when she spoke. He surprised himself by calling Norma and arranging an interview for Beth. He was just trying to find out what she was up to, he told himself.

It wasn't until later, after Clifford had done a little checking and found out that her mother's maiden name was Gunnison that he figured out who she was—

and realized he'd been right about Roy and the kidnapping. His niece must have been the young woman who took the boy from his school. And her visit to him would not have been coincidental. But what the hell was she up to? Did she want to take Danny a second time? Had Roy cheated her out of her share of the ransom money? Was she feeling guilty and wanting somehow to make amends?

Intrigued, Clifford became a Beth watcher. He witnessed with amazement the way she managed to ingratiate herself with the family and make them all fall in love with her. Especially Frank. For a time, she thought she would marry Frank but came to have doubts when she learned his true status in the family. She stayed on, however, even after Frank left. She really cared for Danny, it seemed. And had genuinely loved her dead brother. Beth was a consummate liar, mixing just enough truth with her fabrications to make her totally believable.

After the swimming pool incident and Beth was sent away, Clifford went less often to Perry and Norma's house. It wasn't the same without Beth.

When Beth resurfaced in his life, Clifford found her even more enchanting than before, more beautiful, more wily, more of a kindred spirit. He had been glad that she would become the mother of his heir rather than Gretchen, who was certainly beautiful but not daring like Beth. Not exciting.

But he was too old for exciting. Too old for anything. For the first time he considered the possibility that he wouldn't make it to his eighty-ninth birthday. And even if he made it to his ninetieth, there would be no picture of him with his great-grandson on his lap, helping him blow out the candles, no continuance of the name he'd spent his life restoring to its former luster. The bitterest of pills. Maybe that was why he was so tired. He'd taken his father's fortune and multiplied it more than a dozen times over. And would have been willing to use every dime of it to buy Matt's way into the governor's mansion. Matt understood about money and power but wasn't sure he wanted the responsibility that went with it. Too bad Matt hadn't married Beth. The two of them could have raised this baby, their future guaranteed. But now, the money was losing its meaning even for Clifford. He'd end up leaving the bulk of his fortune to the University of Texas. Or start a charitable foundation. Except there was no charity he really cared about.

A few sips of the brandy was all he could manage. Tomorrow, he'd have Mrs. Richter make a doctor's appointment—with someone new who'd give him a shot of something potent or prescribe the right combination of vitamins and leave off all the preaching about taking it easy, not drinking or smoking. And losing weight, of course. Hell, doctors had been preaching at him to lose weight since he was thirty years old, telling him he was in mortal danger. He'd outlived most of them.

He didn't drink nearly as much as he used to because hangovers had become more severe. And he smoked only one cigar after dinner because more than one caused his heart to race. And he had lost weight but not from trying. His flesh hung on his body like that of an old walrus. No, eating wasn't his problem. Eating made him feel better, not worse. And he had long theorized that his weight was a genetic thing and therefore tolerated by his body. If he'd been a skinny little thing and then gotten heavy, it would tax his system. But he'd always had the constitution of a horse. Until lately.

Maybe he should put in shorter days at the office. Resign from all those boards.

And do what?

Stay at home with his wife? Clifford chortled out loud at the thought.

Ah, if only Miss Mae were still alive. God, how he missed his evenings with her. At least three or four times a week, they'd have dinner in her private dining room, brandy in her bedroom. He hadn't been able to mount her for years, but she always took care of him.

Sometimes he wondered if he'd loved Mae. It never occurred to him to think in such terms while she was alive. Hell, she was just a well-paid whore. The only woman he'd ever really loved was his mother.

Now, however, he wondered if what he'd felt for Mae wasn't some sort of love. He used to think of things he wanted to tell her during the day—like he had started doing with Beth. He liked to buy Mae presents and see her face light up when she opened them. He looked forward to being with her, missed her when he went too long between visits.

He wished he'd said something to her before she breathed her last—at least told her that he was going to miss her. That she was very important to him. *Something*.

Clifford pulled a handful of tissues from a holder and blew his nose. Damn her anyway for dying. Ten years ago. She'd only been sixty-two. It just proved his theory. She'd been a skinny little thing who'd gotten too heavy. Her heart couldn't take it.

And then Beth got herself murdered. Matt had changed.

He tossed the tissues on the floor and grabbed some more. God, he was acting like a sentimental old fool. He blew again, dabbed at his eyes. And realized that the driver had turned into the cemetery. Clifford had forgotten it was Wednesday. He always came on Wednesday evening. He hadn't missed a Wednesday night with Mae in more than forty years.

He'd had a bench placed in front of Mae's grave so he could sit down when he visited her. But he hadn't been foresighted enough to have her buried close to a drive, and getting to the bench required a bit of walking.

The ground was soft from an early morning rain, making his cane ineffective and his feet bog down with every step. And it was cold. He should have put on his overcoat. The cold air was making his chest hurt, breathing difficult.

He hadn't gone more than twenty feet before he realized he wasn't going to make it. He dropped his cane and placed his right hand on the nearest tombstone to steady himself, his left hand over the pain in his shoulder.

He tried to remember the driver's name. Not Cate. Cate had been the last one—the nigger. This man was a big, blond Swede. Jenson.

"Jenson," he called out as best he could. "I need you here."

Jenson came running, took one look at his employer, then returned to the car and drove it over several graves to reach him, scraping the side of the limo on a tombstone.

With Jenson's help, Clifford managed to get back into the limo. He was gasping for air, drenched with sweat, and crying out with the pain in his arm and chest. Knives. He was being stabbed with knives. And fear.

Please, he prayed. He didn't want to die. Not yet. He hadn't taken care of his money yet.

He'd give a million dollars to the church if he just didn't die. Two million. Ten.

Clifford never did lose consciousness. He felt the car careening through the city, heard the horn blaring for what seemed like hours, the pain going on and on and on. He heard the men who met the car with a stretcher wondering how in the hell they were going to get him out of the car and onto it? Other men came.

Clifford tried to help them by crawling out of the limo, but he couldn't. There was too much pain.

Men came around to the other side, got in beside him, and pushed. Others outside the vehicle pulled on his feet. People were gawking.

Finally he was in an examining room. Still alive. The worst was over. Surely. They'd fix him up. He tried to talk, tell them who he was. Not just a nobody off the street. But then the driver would have told them. Jenson.

He could hear someone in the hall whispering about the whale with a coronary. And suddenly a woman was there, introducing herself. Giving orders to the people around her. Dr. Lopez was her name. Clifford tried to tell them his own doctor's name. But his tongue was too big for his mouth.

"You're an amazing old cuss, Clifford," Brent Dexter told him as he checked the chart at the end of Clifford's bed. "By all odds, you should have died ten years ago—maybe twenty. But I can promise that you won't live out the year if you don't change your ways."

"Just tell me what I need to do," Clifford said.

Dr. Dexter chuckled. "Well, I never thought I'd live to hear such words coming out of your foul old mouth, Clifford Tarrington. For now, all you can do is rest. You're stabilized. The initial danger is over. We'll talk about some serious lifestyle changes when you're up to it. You're a very old man, Clifford. You need naps and bland food."

Like a dutiful wife, Belle sat with him through the day and night. The others came and went, but she stayed, doing needlework, watching television with him. He was grateful—even thought about thanking her. But he didn't.

Occasionally they'd hear a monitor in the CCU go off. People scurrying around. Family members weeping.

Would anyone weep for him if he died?

In a biography of his father published by the University of Texas Press, there had been a photograph of that nigger boy, hanging dead from a tree, his swollen tongue protruding from his mouth. Clifford had slammed the book shut and thrown it in the trash bin, but the image stayed in his head. The boy was skinny and barefooted, dressed in tattered overalls. He'd probably crapped in his pants. Cried for his mother. Called out to Jesus. Experienced the worst kind of fear imaginable.

The coloreds came from all over the county to have a big funeral for him. The sheriff told them not to, but they did anyway. Hundreds and hundreds of them, mostly on foot. Too many of them for the sheriff to scare away. Clifford could imagine how Clem Washington's mother must have wept and carried on when they buried him. She probably threw herself on the raw earth after they'd filled in the grave. His whole family would have been there. Lots of weeping and carrying on.

But why in the hell was he thinking about Clem Washington? That had been more than seventy years ago.

From his hospital bed, with tubes in his arms and nose, electrodes on his chest, monitors overhead, the wife he'd never loved sitting at his side, Clifford found himself needing to talk, to try and make some sense of his life. He rambled on and on—about his father not getting to serve a second term. About his days on the gridiron being the only time in his life when everything went according to plan. In spite of vast wealth and great power, nothing had worked out the way he wanted. The Tarrington line was going to die with Matt. None of his progeny would ever be governor of Texas. Ever be truly important. Wield power. What was a man without power? The family was falling apart, and not one of them would even miss him when he's gone—after he's devoted his life to taking care of them.

"Well, that's not exactly so," Belle interrupted, peering at him over the top of her reading glasses. "You tried to run their lives, to make them do what you wanted them to do."

"Matt's the best of the lot," Clifford said, ignoring Belle's remarks.

"Matt has turned out to be a fairly decent young man in spite of your interference," Belle acknowledged. "You dangled the prospect of immense wealth in front of him all those years. Then when he and Gretchen couldn't have children, he had to figure out what was really important. And it wasn't money. And when you're gone, he'll forget all about politics. He doesn't want it more than anything. He'd rather play golf with his wife. The best thing Matt ever did was marry Gretchen. And when their adoption comes through, some precious little bastard child will carry on the Tarrington name. Isn't that just too rich for words?

"Julia's a sweet child, too," Belle went on. "But she had to get as far away from being a Tarrington as she could."

Clifford snorted, which hurt his chest. "That girl is totally worthless."

"She and her husband have carved out a life for themselves. They garden. And swim. Have their causes. They're adopting, too. Finally. They've been saying they were going to for years. But I think it's taken them this long to trust each other and their marriage enough to really do it. I'm proud of them. Angie, too, devoting her life to helping the poor. And Frank. With Beth gone, he'll find his way back.

"Then there's Danny," Belle went on, words absolutely pouring out, more words than Clifford had ever heard from her. He closed his eyes, wanting her to stop. He and Belle didn't live on the same planet.

"I often wondered if you didn't put Roy Gunnison up to kidnapping that boy. I wouldn't put it past you. And even if you didn't, when the police started asking around, you assured them that you'd trust Roy Gunnison with your life, that he was a fine Christian man. You didn't want them to look for Roy just in case he had taken Danny. You wanted that boy to stay gone. You wanted to break his parents' hearts so that your stupid ambition could be served."

Clifford open his eyes and stared at her. "What the hell are you talking about?" he said, trying to sound gruff. But that made his chest hurt, too. Don't get upset, he told himself. She's just a stupid old woman.

"And now you're at it again, using Danny as a human sacrifice," Belle was saying. Her voice was calm but there was such purpose in her eyes. "I can't let you do that, Clifford. I've decided that I'll confess to killing Beth, so they'll let Danny out of jail."

Finally she stopped, her arms folded across her meager bosom, waiting for him to say something. A silly-looking woman. No bigger than a child. A wrinkled child.

"Did you kill her?" Clifford asked, his voice no more than a croak.

"What difference does it make?" she said with a shrug. "Someone in the family did. Of course, if you'd go ahead and die, I wouldn't have to confess. I could say that you killed her. I'll say that you confessed to me on your deathbed."

"You almost sound like you mean it."

"Oh, I do. A dying declaration. I looked it up in one of your law books—Rule 803 of the Evidence Code. It's an exception to the hearsay rule. And I'd make such a good witness. A little old lady who's a paragon of virtue. I give to the poor and go to church every Sunday to pray for the sins of my sometimes corrupt husband."

He wanted to grab her. To hurt her. To break her tiny little arms. But he was impaled on this bed by a maze of tubes. And so weak. God, he was weak. "I saved you from being an old maid, and you never had one ounce of affection for me."

"Ours was never more than a marriage of convenience. But out of it came Perry—and our grandchildren, none of whom you deserved. Yes, I do mean it, Clifford. I want you to die. If there's a hereafter, maybe you can spend it with Mae Masters. I certainly don't want you with me."

At the mention of Mae, Clifford felt himself losing control, words of rage pouring out of him in spite of the pain they brought—about what an insipid, bloodless little person Belle was, how he loved a whore more than he loved her, how she wasn't half the woman that Mae Masters was.

"I'll bet you never had an orgasm in your entire life," he screamed. "You screwed just to get pregnant, and then you'd had enough."

"At least I never pretended," Belle said. "Can you say the same about Mae?"

He was still screaming at her as she picked up her

purse and walked down the hall. She smiled and nodded at the staring nurses.

As she stepped into the elevator, she heard an alarm sound. Running feet. Someone yelling, "Code blue!" Maybe it was Clifford, she thought as she pressed the button for the first floor.

Chapter Thirty-seven

*I*n the night, Brent Dexter called. Clifford had taken a turn for the worse and was near the end.

"We've said our good-byes," Belle told him. "Call Perry. He can do the death watch."

Belle got out of bed and opened the window. She took a deep breath of the cold night air. Her skin prickled with chill bumps. Her nightgown fluttered about her. She was alive. She didn't even feel old.

She was to be a widow. Finally.

She'd thought about leaving Clifford from the very first, but while her parents were still alive she wouldn't have dared. Which seemed silly now, but that's how it was back then. It took so long for a woman to grow up. And then she was already old and running out of options.

So often she'd think, how much longer can the man live? He should have died years ago. Everyone said that he was going to drop dead. Soon. More than one doctor all but promised.

Even as a bride, she hoped that Clifford would die every time his huge body shuddered in orgasm. But once she shut him out of her bedroom, he didn't bother her anymore, and for that she was very grateful. But probably, she should have thanked Miss Mae Masters. Belle wondered if Mae really loved Clifford—or even cared about him. Maybe there was another side of Clifford that Belle never saw. A sad thought that they had failed each other that completely.

Of course, she did owe Clifford something. He did save her from being the spinster daughter who lived out her life taking care of aging parents.

She had found her joy in Perry and Norma and
their children. The grandchildren gave her life and
love. Especially Danny. His love was the purest. She
hated Beth for the way she changed everything. And
she hated Clifford for serving Danny up like a sacrificial
lamb.

She wished that she could have Clifford buried by
Mae and be done with him. Belle certainly wasn't going
to be put to rest with him under one of those joint
tombstones. She needed to make sure she had a stone
of her very own.

The moon was enormous. The stars very bright.
Belle took another deep breath. Was he dead yet?
Would he be thinking about Mae when he breathed his
last? She hoped so. It would make his passing easier.

She went downstairs for a glass of sherry and carried it back upstairs to her room. Should she stay on in
this house now? Belle wondered. She liked being just
across the bridge from her family but had always hated
this old mausoleum with all the Tarrington furniture,
Tarrington mementos, Tarrington art. Maybe she'd
have Gretchen help her redo it. Tear down the drapes.
Get rid of all the furniture. Every stick. Paint the walls
white. Fill the rooms with white wicker and ferns and
flowers and light. Put a fish pond out back for Danny.
They could feed the fish every night and give them
names and watch them swim around so peacefully.

She missed Danny so. He'd been such an important part of her life—the touching part. She went to see
him at the jail twice a week, but she couldn't hold his
hand. He just sat there on the other side of the glass,
saying nothing, not even picking up the phone. Angie
said he was like that most of the time now. But if the
glass weren't there, Belle could hold his hand. He
needed people to touch him and remind him who he
was.

The little Danny that Belle loved was still in that big
man's body. Somewhere. He just had to be. And the
thought of holding his hand again made tears come to
her eyes.

*   *   *

The next morning, Belle put on a navy linen suit and navy-and-white spectator pumps and drove herself to the police station. She asked to see Detective Olson. He was an awful man, but she thought it best to see someone who would understand who she was and know something about the case.

Olson had just heard about Clifford's death and offered Belle his condolences. He was very polite but obviously puzzled by her freshly widowed presence in his office.

She accepted his offer of coffee. And took a few sips of what tasted like yesterday's brew before stating her business.

"My husband murdered Beth Williams," she said, carefully placing her cup on the corner of the desk. "Or should I say Beth Tarrington. I never did get used to thinking of her as part of the family. She had caused a lot of trouble, you know."

Olson's eyes narrowed a bit. "Clifford Tarrington murdered Beth Williams Tarrington?"

"I believe that's what I just said," Belle said, wondering if he was following procedure or being condescending.

"Did you see him kill her?"

"No. He told me. Just hours before he died."

"He *told* you?" Olson repeated.

"Yes, he told me."

"It's not in writing? With his signature?"

"No. He couldn't even sit up, much less write out a confession. He said that, if he died, a dying declaration to his wife would be admissible. He felt bad about Danny and wanted to leave things right for the boy. He didn't confess sooner because he thought Danny wouldn't have to stand trial—because he's so retarded, you know. But nothing turned out the way Clifford thought. The DA wants a full-blown trial and the death penalty. Which is ridiculous. That sweet boy. He wouldn't ever kill anyone."

"But your husband did?" Olson asked.

Belle sighed, not concealing her exasperation. "Yes. He killed her. Clifford killed her."

"And he confessed before he died?"

"Well, he certainly didn't confess after he died. Don't you need to get a stenographer in here to take this down—so I can sign something?"

"Not yet," Olson said, tipping back his chair, putting his hands behind his head. "Did your husband by any chance share his motive for brutally murdering the young woman who was carrying his great-grandchild, which from what we've been able to learn was very important to him? I understand he planned to leave a lot of money to the kid."

"Beth was blackmailing him. If he didn't give her full control of the baby's money, she was going to abort it and tell everyone that he was responsible for kidnapping Danny back when he was a little boy."

"I beg your pardon." The front legs of Olson's chair hit the floor with a thunk.

"Clifford arranged Danny's kidnapping. Surely you know about the kidnapping. The whole story was in the papers again after Danny was arrested."

"Yes, I'm aware he was kidnapped when he was a little boy. But why would Mr. Tarrington want his own grandson kidnapped? And what did the murder victim have to do with it?"

"Beth must have been the one who took Danny from his school. Clifford's chauffeur Roy Gunnison was somehow involved in it. Clifford probably thought that if he got rid of Danny, our son Perry would concentrate more on a political career. He didn't want to run for the state senate because of Danny. And the other children. But Danny took a lot of time and love. Perry and Norma were wonderful parents."

"I see," he said, his voice a careful neutral. "Is there anything else?"

"Yes, but why aren't you writing any of this down?"

"Mrs. Tarrington, your husband was a very heavy, elderly man, who had difficulty walking across a room. As I recall the murder scene, he would have had to walk

down the hill behind your house and up part of another
to reach the pool. And what about getting the knife
from the kitchen? I find it hard to believe, first of all,
that he was able to walk that far and that a very athletic
woman would just stand there and let a slow-moving,
knife-toting man the size of a buffalo get close enough
to stab her. Now, I appreciate the fact that you want to
have your grandson freed, but the case against him is
substantial—and there is a penalty for perjury. I want
you to keep this in mind before you tell anyone else this
story about your husband's deathbed confession."

Damn, she thought on the way home. He thought
she was a dotty old fool. And he was right.

She probably should have left out the part about
Clifford arranging Danny's kidnapping. She didn't
know that for sure, and it did seem far-fetched.

And Clifford probably couldn't have walked over to
the pool. And back. Anyone who'd ever seen Clifford
would wonder about that. And she'd forgotten about
the knife.

Then she remembered the golf cart.

For a number of years, he'd driven a golf cart
across the bridge and parked it by Norma and Perry's
terrace. But then even that got to be too much trouble,
and he started being driven from front door to front
door. There was less walking and fewer stairs that way.

The golf cart was still there in the corner of the
garage. The battery charger was rusty and covered with
dirt. But she plugged it in and watched the needle move
on the gauge. It was possible. He could have driven the
cart. She wiped the dust from the seat. Added air to the
tires with a portable air tank. And left it charging
through the night. The next morning, before she got
ready for the funeral she drove the cart back and forth
across the back of the garage. It worked just fine.

Belle had decided there would be no parade of
mourners by an open casket. Everything else about the
funeral she left to Perry. She really didn't care about

the special music. The Scripture reading. The sermon and eulogy. She didn't even listen. She thought instead about Danny coming home.

She would go to the animal shelter to look at puppies. She wanted two, so she and Danny could watch them play. Tomorrow evening, she'd invite Angie and Justin to dinner so they could plan. She'd give Beatrice the day off and cook dinner herself.

Such a quiet funeral. No sniffing or nose blowing echoing through the sanctuary with the oversize casket in front of the altar.

If she had been a different sort of woman, could she have brought out better things in Clifford? She never even tried. And for that she felt sorrow.

She made clam chowder, corn bread, and a fruit salad. A simple meal—the way people should eat. She told Beatrice she could have all the steaks and roasts in the freezer. And the freezer, too, for that matter.

Over coffee, Belle explained about her trip to the police station to Angie and Justin.

"That detective didn't believe me, but Clifford really did kill Beth," Belle insisted. "At first I thought he was confessing just to clear Danny—sort of a noble parting gesture on his part. And the detective is right. It would have been hard for him to get down our hill and up to the swimming pool. But now I've figured out how he did it. He drove the old golf cart over. Remember, Angie, how he used it all the time, until he started demanding door-to-door service. The cart has just been sitting there for years. I checked it this morning. It's been charged up. He could have driven it across the bridge and waited for Beth by the pool."

Belle took a breath. And looked hopefully from one young handsome face to the other.

"What about the knife?" Angie asked.

"He must have gone over there earlier in the day to get it."

"Why wouldn't he have just waited for her on your

side of the creek?" Justin asked, pouring himself a second cup of coffee. "She'd have to come back across the bridge after her swim."

"He wanted her killed by the pool so he could blame it on Danny. You heard what he said the next day. He thought Danny would never stand trial—the perfect scapegoat."

"How did Danny's medal end up on the bottom of the pool?" Justin asked.

"Clifford explained about that. He heard Danny coming and hid in the pool house. Danny had a towel around his neck and apparently had been planning to swim. When he saw Beth's body in the water, he just stood there and stared for a long time. Then he took the medal from his neck and threw it in the pool. I guess it was his way of signifying closure. A final gesture. She'd given him a lot but caused him so much grief. Then he hosed the blood off the decking."

Angie and Justin looked at each other. Belle held her breath.

"And the button from Danny's pajama top?" Justin asked.

"Well, like Matt said, he could have worn it down there another time, and the button might have accidentally gotten torn off. The button could have been there for days."

"Mrs. Tarrington," Justin said, "Angie explained to me about how fanatical your husband was about family, how much he wanted for the Tarrington bloodline to continue. But I find it hard to believe that he would have killed the only hope he had for that to happen."

"Yes. What would his motive have been?" Angie asked with a frown.

"If he didn't change his will, Beth was going to tell Norma and Perry that Clifford had planned Danny's kidnapping."

"Did Grandfather Clifford tell you that?" Angie asked incredulously.

"Oh, yes. Roy Gunnison, the chauffeur was involved."

"I thought Grandfather had already changed his will," Angie said.

"No. He decided that he'd wait until the baby was born. Make sure it was normal. Have a paternity test and make sure Beth wasn't putting one over on him. And he wanted to name Matt as trustee. Not Beth. She was furious. He had promised her. She wanted a will signed and witnessed. She wanted guarantees.

"When Clifford refused, Beth told him he had a week to think it over before she told Norma and Perry the truth about the kidnapping. Clifford didn't like loose cannons rolling around. And Beth was crazy, you know. Worse than Clifford. They both wanted to control people. She'd even told him that she'd have an abortion if he didn't do as she said. I think he realized that he'd created a monster—that she'd use the baby to control him and his precious money."

"I don't know, Granny," Angie said, shaking her head. "Clifford and Beth looked pretty cozy to me—not like they were arguing about wills and blackmail."

Justin was nodding. "It isn't going to fly," he said. "Clifford Tarrington was about as agile as a beached whale. All Beth had to do was duck."

"But she didn't know he was about to kill her," Angie pointed out. "Her guard could have been down."

Justin shook his head. "That isn't the way it happened, and you know it."

"But my grandfather is already dead, which makes him the perfect murderer," Angie said. "You don't have to prove he did it. Just muddy the waters."

The next time Belle talked to the police, Justin and Angie were with her. Olson listened politely and went out to the garage to look at the golf cart. He would certainly inform the DA, he said, and thanked her for the information.

"He still didn't buy it," Belle said, dejected.

"Do you know any reporters?" Angie asked Justin.

The next day the picture of a twelve-year-old Danny clutching his Special Olympics medal was again on the front page of the *Dallas Morning News* alongside a mug shot of Clifford. The headline said, "DA Rejects Deathbed Confession." The accompanying story was an interview with Belle, who had no doubt that her husband killed their grandson's pregnant wife.

Chapter Thirty-eight

*A*ngie was in her usual place behind Justin and Danny, the family seated on either side of her. Even Frank. Fanned out behind them were Maura and her daughter, Rosie. Manuel, his wife, and two of their sons. Colleagues from the legal aid office. Justin's aunt and cousins. Assorted members of the Tarrington law firm. All assembled for the final day of the trial. For the summations.

She looked over at the jurors, who would soon be in charge of Danny's fate. Seven men and five women who had endured the five weeks of the trial, a formidable number of witnesses, more media attention than any case had garnered in years. The average age of the jurors was forty-seven. Two were Hispanic. One black. Three had college degrees. Only one juror—a retired carpenter—had dozed off with any regularity.

Angie glanced at the prosecution table where Cord Davis was conferring with his assistants. Such an impressive-looking man with his steel-gray hair, athletic body, impeccable grooming down to his manicured fingernails. Along with their placards bearing pictures of aborted fetuses, the antiabortion activists who came every day to demonstrate in front of the courthouse carried pictures of Cord Davis. The district attorney recognized that a fetus could be murdered and was therefore a human being. Along with the pro-life posters were several in support of capital punishment. On both counts, Cord Davis was a hero.

Danny actually turned around and looked at them. Angie offered a little wave. Julia blew him a kiss. Norma nodded her head and smiled. Angie glanced at the jury box to see if anyone noticed. Danny was human. His family loved him.

The bailiff heralded the entrance of the judge, and everyone stood. And suddenly the final day had begun. Angie's stomach gave a jump. All that coffee she'd consumed since early morning felt as if it were eating a hole —but she'd been too nervous to eat, too nervous to sleep. She searched her purse for a roll of Tums or package of restaurant crackers but turned up only a piece of unwrapped peppermint covered with gray fuzz. She picked off the fuzz and sucked on it gratefully.

Cord Davis began by thanking the ladies and gentlemen of the jury for their diligent attention for these past five weeks. He put both hands on the railing in front of the jury box and made eye contact with each one in turn as he spoke. They had endured long weeks of tedious testimony. They were doing an important service for their state. They were good citizens.

Then he stood up tall and backed away a few feet so he could regard them as a group. "Never in all my twenty-five years of practicing law have I participated in a more disturbing trial," he said.

"The defense would have you believe that Danny Tarrington doesn't have to play by the same set of rules as the rest of us, that he should have special consideration because he's not very bright—even though it has been shown that Daniel Tarrington does know right from wrong. Even his own mother admitted that he knew killing people wasn't right. Daniel Tarrington falls within the death-eligible limit set by state statute. He is smart enough to understand the charges against him and to cooperate in his own defense whether he chooses to do so or not. He is smart enough to plan a murder, secure a weapon, and destroy all physical evidence following the commission of the crime.

"Other people of Daniel Tarrington's same intelligence level have been convicted and even paid the ultimate price for the crime of murder," Cord continued. "Why should this man be an exception? Because his family is rich? Because his father is a respected judge?

Because his brother is a state representative? Because his great-grandfather was governor? Because his family loves him? Because he was kidnapped when he was a little boy? Because his family supports Special Olympics?''

Once again Cord drew very close to the jury box. Put his hands on the railing. Wrinkled his brow. "I'll warrant that the Tarringtons are an interesting, powerful family. But does that exempt one of their own from being found guilty of first-degree murder? I don't think so. And I doubt if any of you do either.''

Then he let go of the railing, walked across the room, back again, staring at the floor, his hands behind his back. A man pondering his next words.

"He makes me gag,'' Julia whispered. Angie nodded. So contrived. But the jury looked impressed. Several of the women were leaning forward slightly, waiting expectantly for the next words from the handsome district attorney.

"Now let us look at the facts in the case against Daniel Tarrington,'' Cord said, his voice more brusque and businesslike.

"We know that Beth Williams Tarrington was involved with the murder victim. She was carrying a baby that DNA testing shows only he or his twin brother Matt could have fathered, and medical records were introduced showing that Matthew Tarrington was incapable of fathering a child.

"We know from the testimony of those who supervised and worked with Daniel Tarrington at his workplace that he was infatuated with Beth and came to consider her as his girlfriend. That he dropped his previous girlfriend, Mary Ann Singleton, because of his involvement with Beth, and that Mary Ann subsequently committed suicide because Daniel Tarrington was in love with Beth Williams Tarrington.''

Julia leaned close. "Why does he keep calling him 'Daniel'?'' she whispered. "No one calls him that.''

Angie didn't bother to answer. Julia was commenting more than asking. The name "Danny'' was a sweet word. "Daniel" sounded more formidable, biblical even.

Cord continued his litany of damning facts. "We know that Daniel Tarrington had convinced himself that Beth was in love with him, but she threw him over for his own brother. His devastation was complete when Beth married Frank. He refused to go to family gatherings when either Frank or Beth would be in attendance. His behavior changed. He was angry much of the time, to the point of violence. Don't be misled by his placid behavior in this courtroom, ladies and gentlemen. You heard testimony from the man who repaired the walls of Daniel's room after he put his fist through them more than thirty times.

"Now you might be asking yourself if it wasn't a bit irrational for a retarded man to think a woman of Beth's beauty and intelligence could be in love with him. But remember, she had been involved with him sexually—and apparently she had initiated the sex in an effort to become pregnant by him. Daniel isn't the first man who set his sights too high when it comes to a woman. Commoners have been falling in love with princesses since the world began. Schoolboys with teachers. Moviegoers with film goddesses. Daniel put too much credence in what Beth obviously intended as a simple seduction. When she married his brother, Daniel was filled with white-hot fury. Beth was *his* woman. And now she was the wife of his own brother, living with his brother, having sex with his brother. He raged. He destroyed things. Then the rage seemingly burned itself out. But it was smoldering inside of him, eating him. If he couldn't have Beth, no one would, most especially not his brother.

"The defense has attempted to put the victim on trial, portraying Beth Williams Tarrington as a corrupt woman who used Danny to further her own dream of controlling the Tarrington fortune. And that may very well be, but did that give Daniel Tarrington the right to take her life and that of the baby boy she carried? And he knew she was pregnant. That was obvious to see. His mother told us she didn't believe he knew it was his own baby that Beth carried, but she herself had told him that Beth was going to have a baby. Maybe he thought it was Frank's baby. Maybe he wanted to kill it as much as he wanted to kill its mother.

"Daniel Tarrington certainly had the opportunity to kill Beth. The window to his room overlooked the pool. True, Beth did not turn on the pool lights, but the moon was very bright. And the night was very still. Through the open window of his bedroom, he could have heard the back gate open when Beth entered the backyard. All he had to do was get the knife from the kitchen and walk down the hill.

"I ask you, ladies and gentlemen of the jury, how else did Daniel Tarrington's medal and the button from his pajamas end up on the bottom of the pool if Beth didn't pull the medal from his neck and rip off the button while fighting for her life and that of her unborn child? But the strength of a small pregnant woman is no match for that of the defendant. And he had a knife with a seven-inch blade. Daniel Tarrington stabbed her and threw her into the pool. Imagine the terror of her final moments. Horribly wounded, drowning, unable to save herself and her son."

Cord paused, allowing the picture he had just painted to sink in. One of the women in the jury box was shaking her head. So terrible.

"The defense would ask us to believe that Daniel came upon the scene later, after someone else had thrown her body into the pool, and that he threw the medal in the pool as some sort of final gesture. But if Daniel is not the murderer, as the defense claims, why didn't he then pull the body out of the pool? Why didn't he make some attempt to find out if she was still alive—unless he truly was the murderer and had no intention of saving her?

"As for the defense's inventive theory that Clifford Tarrington was the murderer, that this elderly, obese man drove a golf cart to the swimming pool because he wasn't able to walk that far and killed the active young woman who was carrying his great-grandchild so she wouldn't blackmail him for kidnapping his own grandson more than twenty years ago is preposterous, to say the least. By defense's own admission, there is no proof whatsoever that Clifford Tarrington had any role in that kidnapping. And there is no clue to connect him to the murder other than a supposed dying declaration given to his wife, who according to the testimony of two CCU nurses did not have a very pleasant final visit with her husband and left with him yelling insults at her, not making tearful confessions.

"The evening of the murder, Danny had not attended his grandmother's birthday party because of Beth. He was sitting there alone in his room all evening while his family celebrated without him. His girlfriend of several years was dead—because of Beth. He no longer went to work and experienced the sense of self-worth that working gave him—because of Beth. He had been used and cast aside. And Beth got to go to family parties when he couldn't.

"You heard testimony from Manuel Rodriguez, the Tarringtons' gardener of many years, who admitted that Daniel almost drowned Beth Tarrington while she was working for the family. Daniel also killed a mother cat because she scratched his hand. Stomped the cat to death. And he beat up Mr. Rodriguez's son, breaking the boy's nose and collarbone. Daniel Tarrington was not the sweet, innocent person defense would have us believe."

Cord was back at the railing, pointing across the courtroom at Danny. "Ask yourselves, ladies and gentlemen, would you be comfortable turning this man loose so he could get angry at some other woman and kill her? Do you want that responsibility?"

Then he turned to face them again, to drive his final point home. He paused. There was not a sound in the courtroom, not even a cough or shuffling foot. He leaned close. "No jury member wants to find a defendant guilty of murder in the first degree. You probably came here hoping that the defense would prove his case and you could set the accused free, see him joyfully reunited with a family who obviously cares about and loves him. But if you believe that Daniel Tarrington did indeed commit the brutal murders of which he is accused, you have no choice but to find him guilty. I would ask that during your deliberations, you remember the victims, Beth Williams Tarrington and her unborn child. Think of the horrible circumstances of their deaths. Their *murders*. If Beth had been your wife or daughter or sister or friend, what would you want the jury's verdict to be?''

Angie uttered a ''shit'' under her breath.

''Ditto,'' Julia said beside her.

Cord thanked the jury for their attention and took his seat, his face the very picture of thoughtfulness and humility.

Justin stood, put a reassuring hand on Danny's shoulder, and began speaking from the defense table. His voice was quavering with nervousness. Angie held her breath.

''Congratulations, ladies and gentlemen, for bearing with us through this very complex trial. I'm sure there will be books written about it. Most likely none of us will ever again meet a family like the Tarringtons or ever again hear of a case even remotely like this one.''

Justin began walking toward the jury box. ''And now that it's over, I have a confession to make.'' His voice was stronger now.

He stopped in front of the jurors. Angie willed him not to put his hands on the railing, not to seem like he was imitating Cord.

Still a few feet back, Justin made his confession. ''I don't know who killed Beth Williams Tarrington.'' Then he paused.

Julia squeezed Angie's hand. He had certainly gotten the jurors' attention. They were all staring at him. And the judge. Cord Davis. Every eye in the courtroom.

''I believe that some member of the Tarrington family probably committed this crime,'' Justin said, ''but I don't know which one. I *think* it was Clifford Tarrington, but Mr. Davis is right. I can't prove it. Just like I can't prove that Danny Tarrington didn't kill his brother's wife. But has the prosecution proved beyond a reasonable doubt that it was Danny who did kill her?

"I've asked Danny numerous times if he murdered Beth, but he doesn't answer me. In spite of a judge's ruling that he is capable of aiding in his own defense, Danny hasn't told me one thing about what happened that night. He's all but nonverbal these days. His sister Angie can get him to talk sometimes, to tell her if he wants a Coke, if he has a stomachache or a headache. He asks her why he isn't allowed to have a television in his 'room' so he can watch videos. But he won't talk to Angie about Beth either. He won't say if he went down to the swimming pool the night of her murder. When you asked him if he knows who killed Beth, he holds his lips together with his fingers.

"As the prosecution pointed out, Danny does know right from wrong. I also think he also knows about loyalty. I think Danny knows who killed Beth. Or thinks he knows. And he's not talking. He's afraid to talk. If he starts answering questions, he might give his secret away. Danny has never been very good at keeping secrets. He's been teased about that a great deal over the years. So, to be on the safe side, he's simply stopped talking.

"Do I know for sure that's what is going on in Danny's head? No, I don't know anything about this case for sure. You've watched Danny during this trial. You've seen him doze off. Write his name over and over on page after page of paper tablets. Chew on his fingernails. Stare out the window. Try to catch dust motes floating in a shaft of sunlight. But according to a previous court ruling, he is capable of understanding the nature of the proceedings in this courtroom. I think all he understands is that he must not be a tattletale—that something bad will happen to someone he loves if he tells what he knows. I think that Danny is protecting someone in his family—a brother or sister, his mother or father, his grandparents, his sister-in-law or brother-in-law, maybe even a loyal housekeeper or longtime gardener.

"It would appear that Beth was not a nice person. Or maybe she was just a very confused person. But for whatever reason, she had all but destroyed Danny and his brother Frank. The baby she carried, not Clifford's wife or son or grandchildren, stood to inherit Clifford Tarrington's fortune. Everyone in the family knew that Clifford planned to make Beth's baby—the one she contrived to bear—heir to his vast fortune. What a blow that must have been to Matt Tarrington and his wife, Gretchen, who had thought they stood to inherit one of the largest fortunes in the state of Texas. And the rest of the family didn't want an outsider, a woman they hated, to control the family fortune. Make no mistake about it, the Tarringtons hated Beth. Seethed with hatred. Talked about it all the time. Even openly wished her dead.

"Beyond a reasonable doubt. That's what you have to believe in order to find Danny guilty—that beyond a reasonable doubt, he killed his former teacher, friend, and lover, Beth Williams Tarrington—that no other member of this family killed her. No reasonable doubt can exist in your minds even though you heard from Angie Tarrington about the family conference in which Clifford Tarrington convinced them that Danny would not stand trial for a capital offense because of his retardation, and that Danny probably was going to live out the rest of his life in an institution anyway because he had become such a management problem. Clifford Tarrington said that Danny was the only family member with 'nothing to lose' should he be found guilty of Beth's death, therefore they should all stand back and let him be accused, arrested, and eventually sent away, hopefully to an institution of the family's choosing.

"You've heard the testimony of Beth Williams Tarrington's mother, Lorraine Williams, linking her brother, Roy Gunnison, and her daughter, Beth, to Danny's kidnapping. Gunnison had been Clifford's chauffeur for more than ten years. You know that Clifford was the one who got Beth a job taking care of Danny after he was returned to his parents. Several family members have testified to the unusual relationship between Clifford and Beth. Did she know something that could ruin his credibility with his family, perhaps even send him to prison?

"If you think there is a reasonable possibility that one of the other family members could have killed Beth, you must vote for acquittal. That is your sworn duty. His grandmother told you that her husband, Clifford Tarrington, had wanted to sacrifice Danny on the altar of family. Let us not here in this courtroom be responsible for sacrificing him on the altar of very arbitrary and capricious laws that allow an individual as mentally deficient as Danny Tarrington to be put on trial for first-degree murder.

"Thank you very much, and God be with you in your deliberations."

Angie let out her breath and grabbed her sister's hand. Tears of pride ran down her face. He'd done well.

But so had Cord Davis.

They waited in Matt's law office throughout the rest of the day. And the next day. Norma found it impossible to sit for very long. She walked up and down the halls.

That evening, they ate in the kitchen. Maura had left a ham and potato salad. While Perry and Gretchen cleaned up the kitchen, Julia, Nathan, and Gretchen went for a swim. Matt and his mother carried their coffee out on the terrace.

"It's not going well, is it?" Norma asked.

"It's hard to say," Matt said.

Even in the soft twilight, Matt could see the strain in his mother's face, hear it in her voice. She was so thin, she hardly looked like herself, not like the pretty mother he'd always been so proud of.

"I agreed to this scheme only because I thought

Danny would never stand trial," she said. "I should have stopped it before it got this far."

"If the trial ends badly, we'll deal with it, Mom."

"How? We've already done a horrible thing to him by letting it go this far."

"Are you that sure he didn't kill her? Just because a garden hose wasn't put away right?"

"Yes, I'm sure. And I'm wondering if the person who really killed Beth will let this farce continue if he's found guilty. What happens if they sentence him to death?"

Matt knelt in front of his mother's chair. "I didn't kill Beth, Mom."

Norma was very still for a minute, like a statue. Then she reached for her son.

The morning of the third day, the jury informed the judge they were deadlocked. Judge Bowie ordered to them to continue deliberations.

The fourth day, Bowie called everyone back to the courtroom. Angie held on to Julia's hand for dear life. She couldn't breathe, couldn't bear the wait as the jury filed into the box.

"Have you reached a verdict?" the judge asked.

The foreman, a high-school football coach, stood. "No, your honor. We have not been able to reach a verdict."

"Please tell me the vote, without indicating the leaning of the jury."

"Seven to five."

"And you are quite certain that should you return to your deliberations, there is no hope that a consensus can be achieved?"

"Yes, your honor."

A moment of stunned silence descended over the courtroom. Judge Bowie thanked the jurors and dismissed them.

"What happens now?" Julia whispered as the jurors

filed out of the box and Danny was removed from the courtroom.

"I hope they'll plea bargain," Angie said, which is what they had wanted in the first place. All this agony to get back to square one.

Jim Bowie was in his shirtsleeves, a cigar firmly planted between the fringe of his salt-and-pepper mustache and the bush of his very white beard. Hanging behind him was an impressive oil painting of a buckskin-clad James Bowie, the judge's forefather who died at the Alamo. He leaned back in his chair and put his hands behind his head while Cord Davis and Justin filed into the room and took their seats in front of his enormous and very cluttered desk.

"Well, gentlemen, have you worked this thing out?" Bowie asked.

"Guilty of manslaughter and remanded to the custody of his family provided he is maintained in a secured environment," Justin said.

Bowie turned to Davis. "Mister District Attorney?"

Davis nodded, accepting Justin's offer of closure. And face-saving. No way was he going to try the case again. And the guilty plea indicated, at least for the record, that he had not put the wrong man on trial. By accepting, he would be declaring the case closed. The state would look no further for the murderer of Beth Tarrington.

Bowie couldn't help but take a degree of satisfaction in the humbling of the pompous district attorney. The case had not been the career-building opportunity Davis thought it would be. The tremendous publicity surrounding the trial had raised questions about his handling of the case. He had not proven that the Tarrington boy was guilty, and the public knew it.

"Very well," Bowie said, and sent for a court reporter and the defendant to make the decision official.

Danny looked rumpled and confused. Justin stood and guided him to a chair. The court reporter set his machine on a small table by the judge's desk and pulled up a chair.

Bowie repeated the agreed-upon plea and both lawyers concurred for the record.

"I'd like to request that Danny be let out on bail while the family is making arrangements," Justin said.

Bowie agreed. He would sign a court minute to that effect. Bail would be set at $300,000. Formal sentencing was set in two weeks. The family could take him home.

When Angie saw Justin's face, she started to cry. It was over.

Later, when Justin and Danny appeared at the front entrance to the jail, the family rushed forward. The women were crying, the men trying not to. News cameras and microphones were being thrust in their faces.

What were their plans?
Where would Danny be sent?
Was he really guilty?

The crush of people brought a panicky look to Danny's face. Perry grabbed his arm and hurried him into the waiting limousine—Clifford's limousine, which Belle had not yet sold. Clifford's estate was in limbo. He had indeed changed his will, leaving the bulk of his estate to an unborn child and nullifying all previous wills.

As they pulled away from the curb, Norma took her son's face between her hands and kissed his mouth. "We're taking you home now, darling? Are you glad?"

Danny nodded. "I can watch videos."

Chapter Thirty-nine

Angie was sitting on a bar stool drinking wine, watching him prepare dinner—just as Justin had imagined so many times. But in the scenes he conjured up, Angie was always radiant, never melancholy as she was tonight.

This was supposed to be a celebration. The ordeal had ended. He had "muddied the waters" and achieved a good outcome for her brother and her family. No one else would be accused of the murder. Her parents could place Danny in an institution of their choice.

"It's over, but I wonder if Danny's going to be a zombie for the rest of his life," Angie admitted as she watched him toss a salad.

"Maybe not," Justin said. "Now that he's out of jail, maybe he'll find himself again."

He opened a second bottle of wine to serve with dinner—a really good pinot noir that he'd saved for weeks in anticipation of this night.

The table was aglow with candlelight. The wine was perfect. His spaghetti with clam sauce was damned good. Angie drank the wine but didn't eat much.

They lingered a while over coffee and carried their plates to the kitchen. And kissed. Long and deep. She'd been thinking about it, too. He could tell.

For a long time, they kissed in the kitchen. When his hands began to roam up and down her body, she welcomed his touch. And initiated the move to the living room sofa.

"I want to make love with you," he said, rubbing

his hand up and down her back, delighting in the feel of her.

"Why?" Angie asked.

Justin laughed. "Because I just do. I've wanted to for a long time. But you've been strung tighter than a top. I think I've done a remarkably fine job of not pushing this thing."

"I'm older than you."

"True. But you look as though you have a few good years left, maybe even time to have a kid or two."

"You really want me? Blue jeans and all?"

"Well, actually, I'd prefer you without the blue jeans."

Her frown said she wasn't interested in humor. "What I mean is where would it lead? I don't just fall in bed anymore. Not for a long time. I've been hurt and done some hurting. It always seems to end with pain."

"Not this time," he said, kissing her neck.

She scooted away from him. "I'm not going to change, Justin. I'll never be my mother or your aunt. I'll never be a proper lady in the big house. I don't golf. I just practice law."

"I know. You'll screw up my life."

Angie felt a smile forcing its way onto her face. "I suppose you could play golf with Matt and Gretchen," she allowed.

"Fine," he said, touching her lips with his fingertips. "May I take off your clothes? I'd really like to be naked with you."

"Kiss me some more first," she said.

He obliged—with deep, wonderful kisses that made her reservations melt away. When he pulled her to her feet and propelled her into the bedroom, she offered no resistance.

She wanted to want him more than anything, wanted the release that only good lovemaking can bring. She fell short of that goal, however, but just being with him was lovely—its own reward. And in time she would adjust to the sadness.

In the afterglow, she told him what a brilliant attorney he was. "With Clifford gone, I'm sure you'll have no trouble going back to the firm."

"We'll see," Justin said.

He was on his back, not holding her when he asked the question she knew he'd get to eventually but wished he wouldn't, especially not tonight when she wanted so desperately to believe they were right for each and might indeed have a future together.

"Who killed Beth?" he asked.

"My grandfather Clifford."

"Let me rephrase the question. Who *really* killed Beth?"

"If my grandfather didn't kill her, I wouldn't want anyone to know who did," she said, putting distance between their bodies, pulling up the sheet to cover her nakedness. "I'd want to protect my family, wouldn't I?"

"I think I've earned the right to know," he said. Firmly. He wasn't going to be put off.

Granny Belle had warned Angie that she might have to face this moment. And had told her what she must tell Justin.

But first, Angie got dressed. She needed to be wearing clothes when she talked about murder. And there would be no more lovemaking this night. The spell was broken.

They returned to the sofa, to more wine. She didn't turn on the lamp, knowing it would be easier to talk with just the light from the open patio door. She sat facing him, her arm resting on the sofa back—and began the story at the point when she, her mother and Granny Belle took a bottle of wine out on the terrace.

The moon was brilliant. A soft breeze carried the scent of Manuel's roses. But there was no pleasure in the night or the wine. All they could think about and talk about was Beth and the grief she had brought them.

They grieved for Danny and Frank and Mary Ann Singleton. They grieved for the family they once had been and would never be again. They dreaded a future with Beth always there, the mother of their own flesh and blood.

And admitted as they had before, that in spite of the baby, they wished Beth would leave. Disappear. Die. *Something* that would remove her from their lives.

Norma heard the gate open. They knew Beth was down there. Sounds of splashing seemed exaggerated in the night air. They tried to keep talking but all they could do was listen—to Beth in the family pool. Finally Norma told Angie to go on to bed, that she'd walk Belle home.

Angie went to bed but knew she wouldn't sleep. How venomous they had all sounded, so full of hate. The words floated around in her head. Her entire perception of who they were and what they stood for was destroyed.

Her mother and Belle would have walked by the pool enclosure. Was Beth still there? Did they stop or just walk by? Neither woman was capable of a violent act, yet for no reason that she would have been able to articulate, Angie pulled on a pair of shorts and a T-shirt and walked down the hill.

Beth was beside the pool, curled on her side in a pool of blood—with a knife in her back and a croquet mallet on the deck beside her. It was a scene from a movie come starkly and hideously to life. Angie even smelled the blood.

Her stomach heaved, and she took several deep breaths to calm herself. But she didn't scream. The thought of calling the police never crossed her mind. Instead she pulled out the knife, rinsed off the blood in the pool, then carefully wiped it clean with her shirttail and tossed it in the water—then tried to think what evidence they might have left behind.

She rolled Beth's body into the pool in hopes of destroying any forensic evidence and, for the same reason, hosed off the deck.

"I suppose I should have felt for a pulse before I rolled her into the pool," she told Justin when she reached the end of her tale. "It crossed my mind, but maybe I didn't want her still to be alive to tell what happened. So, you see, *I* killed Beth Williams.''

She watched his profile as he stared across the dimly lit room. ''What about Danny's medal?'' he asked. ''And the button. How did they get in the pool?''

''I don't know.''

''Now wait a minute,'' he said, turning on the lamp, facing her. ''I'm trying to buy this story about two very genteel ladies from old Dallas families stabbing almost to death a pregnant woman who carries their progeny, and then the daughter/granddaughter of these two, who happens to be a very bright woman and an attorney to boot, doesn't bother to see if the pregnant woman is dead before she rolls her unconscious body into the swimming pool and destroys the evidence. But I cannot buy the medal and button miraculously getting into the swimming pool.''

''Maybe Danny was there,'' Angie suggested. ''Maybe he heard the gate squeak and came down the hill to be with her. After all, the pool house is probably where she had sex with him. Or maybe he was there with Mom and Granny Belle. Or maybe Mom and Granny Belle didn't stop at the pool at all. Mom walked Granny across the bridge and came home, and Grandfather Clifford came later and really did kill Beth after all. And Danny threw the medal in the pool like Granny said. Maybe Danny ripped off his pajama top, planning to go in and save Beth, but changed his mind. I don't know. I don't want to know. I came down that hill with such foreboding. And my first impulse when I saw Beth was that my mother and grandmother had killed her, and I needed to clean up the mess.''

''Did you ask them if they killed her?'' he asked.

''No. No one in the family ever discussed how it happened. We all assumed that someone in the family did it, but no one wanted to know who.''

''Then tell me what you *think* happened,'' he said, rubbing the frown lines in his forehead.

''I think they offered Beth money if she'd leave and never come back. Granny had said earlier she would

give everything she owned to get rid of Beth. Both Mom
and Granny are wealthy women in their own right. Not
like Grandfather Clifford, of course, but between them,
they could have come up with a very impressive figure.
Beth probably laughed at them, and they went back to
the house for a weapon and ended up with a butcher
knife—not to kill her, but just to scare her, to show that
they meant business. But Beth came at them with the
croquet mallet, and whoever had the knife stabbed
her.''

"But neither your mother or Belle told you this is
what happened?" Justin asked.

"No."

"And how do you feel about it?"

"Looking back, I didn't hate Beth as much as I
thought. She was pitiful, really. And maybe with a baby
and some friendship, we might have turned into a family again. But maybe she was too sick for that. A part of
me is horrified and repulsed by what happened. And
another part of me is rather proud of two fearless
women fighting for their young.''

"And obviously, you want them to get away with
it?''

"Yeah, I do. They shouldn't have killed her. But
maybe I would have done it myself if things had gone
on much longer. Or Dad, Matt, Frank, Julia. Even
Gretchen or Nathan. As it is, we're all guilty of letting it
happen. We should have come to some better solution
than murder. Granny has gotten pretty blasé about
death because she's old. But Mom suffers. I see it in her
eyes. And I know she thinks about that baby.''

They sat there side by side, saying nothing. When
she rose to leave, he pulled her back. "This is the end of
the discussion, I take it," he said.

Angie nodded. "I have nothing else to say. Except
it's late, and I need to go home."

"And tomorrow night?"

"What about it?"

"Will you need to go home tomorrow night?"

"No. Tomorrow night, I'll need to stay."

She managed the drive home dry-eyed but began to cry the minute she closed her bedroom door behind her. She was truly in love for the first time in her life. Her parents and brother were asleep in this same house. And she had never felt so alone. She was alone with her secret except for Granny Belle, who was old and would die long before Angie did.

Granny Belle had told Angie that no, Angie absolutely should never tell Justin. "That's your punishment, child. Except for me, and I'm old and will die soon, you must bear alone the knowledge of what you've done. You've told me. That's all the confessing that you can allow yourself."

"But doesn't Justin deserve to know what really happened—especially if we get married?"

Belle took Angie's hands in her own. "You listen to me, child. You have a chance for a good life with a decent man who loves you. Don't test that love . . . maybe on your deathbed, but not now. Not while you're still young and need his love and trust. You listen to me, and *I'll* tell you what to tell Justin when the time comes."

Angie had done as her grandmother said. The story she told Justin was Granny Belle's lie. Not her own.

Norma had already walked Belle home and gone upstairs to bed. Angie was the one who had taken the knife from the kitchen to scare Beth, to show her that she meant business when she offered Beth money and told her she had to go away. Lots of money. Her mother and grandmother would contribute. A small fortune. "We don't want you here," Angie told her. "You cause too much pain. I'll kill you if you don't go away and leave us alone."

"Don't be silly," Beth said as she towel-dried her hair. "You're just like Frank—too ethical ever to do anything like that."

"Does Frank want to kill you?"

"He put his hands around my neck once, like he

was going to choke me. But he couldn't do it. Now he thinks about killing himself.''

Beth's maternity bathing suit had a little skirt that made it look juvenile. Standing there in her bare feet, she looked like a little pregnant girl.

"Don't you care for Frank at all?" Angie asked.

"I care for him a great deal. I let him have sex whenever he wants. I try to make him laugh. But he makes me angry. All he'd have to do is relax and let me take care of everything. But he broods all the time. And when he drinks, he quotes the Bible like some crazy man on a street corner. He's decided that he believes in hell after all. And he'll welcome the flames when they come. I can't listen to him anymore. It would probably be better for the baby not to have him around.''

Then Beth saw the knife in Angie's hand. Flat against her leg. Not pointed at Beth. Just there. Angie would never forget the look of such infinite sadness on Beth's face. Then she backed away, ran into the pool house. When she came out, she was brandishing a croquet mallet. "Get away from me," she said. "All I wanted was for your family to love me. But you hate me. Even Danny and Frank. Only Clifford doesn't hate me.''

Angie was amazed at the anguish in Beth's voice. But was it real? With Beth, it was impossible to know what was real and what was deceit.

"Yes, we all hate you." Angie turned to leave, to take the knife back up to the kitchen. It was stupid to have brought it.

"Don't you turn your back on me like I don't count," Beth said.

Angie looked back in time to see Beth coming at her, the mallet raised. Angie sidestepped. Beth tripped on the edge of the decking and stumbled past her.

Angie hadn't realized she was going to stab her until she felt the knife plunging through flesh, scraping against bone.

A gasp came from Beth as her body hit the deck. Then a moan.

Angie knelt and pulled the knife out of Beth's

body—to undo what had just happened. And stared in horror as blood gushed out of the wound.

Beth had been stabbed.

By the knife in Angie's hand.

Angie dropped the knife. And mashed her hands against the wound to make the blood stop. But Beth groaned and rolled away from her. To the very edge of the pool. "Get away from me," she said. And scooted closer to the edge.

"I'll go for help," Angie said, waves of panic rising in her. And hysteria. Fear. *What had she done?* "I'll call nine-one-one. I'm sorry, Beth. Oh God, I'm so sorry."

Angie grabbed her arm to pull her away from the edge. But Beth gasped. And her body began to convulse.

Angie leaped to her feet and ran toward the gate. She'd call for help. Paramedics would come in an ambulance and save her.

But before Angie reached the gate, she heard a splash. And walked back to the pool.

She watched Beth's submerged body for signs of life. For a long time she watched.

Only later did she wonder if Beth might still have been alive, if she could have been saved. But as Angie stood motionless beside the pool, transfixed by the sight of the body in the water, her only thought was that it was over. Finally over.

And a feeling of calmness settled over her like a soft blanket. Her family could begin to heal.

Had she meant to kill Beth or had it just happened? She had thought about killing her. Even wondered if she would have the courage. Wondered what it would feel like. But she had no memory of actually planning to use the knife as she carried it down the hill. Hadn't she planned only to frighten Beth?

But premeditated or not, the deed was done.

She went to the shallow end of the pool and waded into the water to rinse off the blood. She took off her nightshirt and left it soaking while she hosed off the deck. She couldn't even remember why she'd done it.

Maybe it was to destroy evidence. Maybe it was because she couldn't stand the mess.

She wrung out her shirt and used it to pick up the croquet mallet and return it to the pool house. Then she put on the wet nightshirt and trudged up the hill to the house.

In her room, she shed the wet shirt, put on a bathrobe, and crossed the hall to Danny's room, where she removed the Special Olympics medal from around her sleeping brother's neck. And kissed his forehead. "I'm sorry," she whispered.

And then, as an afterthought, she jerked the button off of his pajama top. The material was soft and worn from many washings, and the button came off easily. His eyes opened. She kissed him again. "Good night, darling. Sweet dreams."

She went back down to the pool and threw the medal and button into the water, thereby implicating her own brother in the killing—just as she and Matt had talked about doing. But their discussion had been hypothetical, a way of easing their frustration because Beth was evil and Danny and Frank were good. And Mary Ann Singleton was dead.

Several weeks after Beth's death, Angie went to the library to look at a picture of a six-month fetus, a tiny little thing who'd never had a thought. It wasn't the fetus Angie grieved for, though. It was Beth. A living, thinking person who had died.

She wondered if the word *murderer* would ever stop bouncing around in her head, repeating itself as it hit against the sides of her brain. That's what she was now. She would have to live with that knowledge for the rest of her life. Would have to remember how it felt when the knife went in, when she stabbed another human being. Killing Beth was supposed to have saved the family. But the family was forever altered. The family home was for sale. Danny would be sent away soon.

He was like he was after the kidnapping. Withdrawn. He never sang songs or laughed. He was no longer one of them.

And this time, there was no Beth to make him right again.

Just his sister Angie.

She didn't know where Danny would be sent. But wherever it was, she would go see him often—maybe even move nearby like her parents were talking about doing. She would sing the songs Beth taught him. Run with him. Swim with him. She would find the way to his heart if it took her the rest of her life.

And she would follow her Granny Belle's advice. She would not test Justin's love.

Maybe she would tell him on her deathbed. Maybe not. Perhaps she would speak only of love. Thank him for the good life she hoped they would have together, for the children she hoped they would share, for defending Danny and giving him and her family a second chance.

ABOUT THE AUTHOR

While growing up in a military family, JUDITH HENRY WALL developed a lifelong passion for travel to distant places but continues to derive much inspiration for her writing closer to home. She lives in Norman, Oklahoma, where she raised her three children and works at the University of Oklahoma as a research writer and editor of the alumni quarterly. She is also the author of *Mother Love, Love and Duty, Handsome Women,* and *Blood Sisters,* and is presently at work on a new novel.